Your favourite authors love to curl up with
Cathy Bramley's feel-good fiction . . .

'Comforting, funny, warm and wise. The perfect
cocktail of emotions, hopes and dreams'
Veronica Henry

'Filled with warmth and laughter'
Carole Matthews

'Full of Cathy's wonderful warmth, wisdom and wit'
Alex Brown

'Warm, cosy and deliciously romantic'
Holly Martin

'A ray of sunshine'
Phillipa Ashley

'A real treat. No one does friendship better than Cathy'
Karen Swan

'A wonderful story of family, sisterhood and finding
yourself'
Emily Stone

'The perfect romantic tale'
Ali McNamara

'A heartwarming tale of self-discovery'
Woman & Home

Cathy Bramley is a *Sunday Times* bestselling author whose uplifting novels have sold over two million copies worldwide. These include *A Patchwork Family*, *My Kind of Happy*, *The Merry Christmas Project*, *Merrily Ever After* and *The Summer That Changed Us* which was nominated for the Pageturner of the Year Award at the British Book Awards.

Before becoming a full-time writer, Cathy ran a PR and Marketing Agency working with a variety of clients across a plethora of industries from shoes to stately homes, food to fabric, Ninja Turtles to Mary Berry! Her experience in helping businesses to prosper often finds its way into her stories; many of her female characters have an entrepreneurial streak.

She has a BA (Hons) in European Business, a love of languages and a passion for travel shared by her two adventurous daughters. She counts seeing her novels translated for foreign territories as one of her greatest achievements, alongside her beloved family.

Cathy loves to hear from readers and seeing pictures of her books from around the globe. You can get in touch on Facebook @CathyBramleyAuthor, on Twitter @CathyBramley or on Instagram @CathyBramley. For all the latest book news, exclusive content and competitions, visit Cathy's website and sign up to her newsletter at www.cathybramley.co.uk.

Cathy Bramley

The
Sunrise
Sisterhood

ORION

An Orion paperback

First published in Great Britain in 2023 by Orion Fiction
an imprint of The Orion Publishing Group Ltd
Carmelite House, 50 Victoria Embankment
London EC4Y 0DZ

An Hachette UK company

1 3 5 7 9 10 8 6 4 2

A CIP catalogue record for this book is
available from the British Library.

ISBN (Mass Market Paperback) 978 1 3987 0143 4
ISBN (eBook) 978 1 3987 0144 1

Typeset by Born Group
Printed and bound in Great Britain by Clays Ltd, Elcograf S.p.A.

MIX
Paper from
responsible sources
FSC® C104740

www.orionbooks.co.uk

For Tony
1964-2023
my best friend,
my incredibly brave husband.
What fun we have had.
How lucky I am to have been loved by you.
CT x

Chapter One

Skye

I checked the front pocket of my rucksack for my passport. It was there. Just as it had been the last five times I'd looked. The taxi I'd booked to take me to the airport on the other side of Kampala was due any minute. My throat was tight with the anxiety which had been building over the last forty-eight hours.

Was I doing the right thing? I thought I was. But it didn't stop the niggling voice in my head telling me I was running away. Back to the place I'd run *from*.

I'd initially come to Africa to travel, to do some volunteering, to escape from a life that had felt pointless, and from my parents, specifically my father, who made me feel as if nothing I did was ever good enough. Within days of arriving here at the Hope Foundation charity project in Uganda, I felt sure I'd found the place I was supposed to be. Here I felt valued; I had a role to play and, for the first time, my life had purpose.

Before long, the emotional baggage I'd brought with me became irrelevant in a country where life felt raw and vivid – bigger than anything I'd experienced. The red dirt roads, chaotic traffic and crowded towns were islands in a vast ocean of green plains inhabited by animals I'd only seen in zoos. Scorching dry heat was counterbalanced by torrential rain, and, despite the poverty, I'd encountered friendship, community and pure happiness. Uganda was a country of contrasts and, for a young woman who wasn't quite sure who she wanted to be, it was the perfect place to be while she figured it out.

Five years on and apparently I still hadn't figured it out.

My case was sitting in the doorway, stuffed with as many mementoes from my time here as I could fit in it. Even so, I was leaving a lot behind. I cast one last look around the house and walked outside onto the porch, where I could avoid seeing all Jesse's pairs of flip-flops piled up by the door, and the knick-knacks we'd accumulated over the years to make this tin-roofed house feel like a home: the wood carvings, wall hangings and the children's art I'd been given and couldn't bring myself to throw out.

I kept my eyes on the entrance to the camp, willing the taxi to hurry up. My palms were clammy and my stomach was fluttery with nerves.

My plans to return home to the UK had been made so quickly that I kept expecting to wake up and find it was a dream. That what had happened at the party two nights ago wasn't real and that any minute now everything would be back to normal.

But then I'd catch Jesse's eye and my stomach would plummet all over again. My carefully curated, simple life managing the volunteers who came here to work at the Hope Foundation was over.

My friends, Aster and Dembe, crossed the yard separating our houses and came to join me on the porch. Dembe had her new baby, Kemi, swaddled close to her body, tied in a scarf as usual.

'You're really leaving?' Aster asked as she sat beside me. 'I don't believe it.'

'I'm really leaving.' As I squeezed her hand between both of mine, I felt a lump form in my throat, and it hit me just how much I'd be giving up if I didn't return.

Officially, Aster was our cook. She'd been preparing meals for the volunteers since before I arrived. But she was so much more than that; she was the maternal figure the volunteers turned to when they were missing home or when they were feeling under the weather. She had twelve grandchildren of her own, but counted everyone at the Hope Foundation as her family too.

'Don't worry, Aster. She will come back, her heart is in Uganda. This is her home now.' Dembe held my gaze, as if challenging me to argue with her.

'It does feel like home and I've been very happy here,' I admitted. 'Happier than I've been anywhere.' I leaned forward to peek at the baby's face. 'One last cuddle?' I said, holding my arms out.

'One last cuddle for *today*,' Dembe corrected me, unknotting the scarf.

I cradled Kemi to me, her little body totally relaxed in my arms, her knees tucked up towards her chest.

When I'd first arrived five years ago, Dembe was newly married. Now she had three children, all of whom I'd held in my arms, just like this. Motherhood hadn't stopped her working for long; she and her husband were in charge of transporting our volunteers on trips, airport runs, medical emergencies . . . you name it.

Aster frowned. 'It's not right that you are leaving without a celebration. The community will be disappointed they were not able to thank you for all you have done for us.'

'And the schoolchildren haven't said goodbye, performed their songs and dances for you,' Dembe added.

The children loved to put on a show for the volunteers to thank them for whatever they had achieved: sports coaching, English classes, music lessons. It was always a highlight of any stay here for the volunteers.

'There's no time, I need to go,' I replied. 'When I come back, we can have a party then.'

'I don't understand. Why so quickly?' Dembe asked, folding her arms. She and Aster shared a look. 'Is it because of the boss?'

'Jesse can be . . .' Aster paused, choosing her words carefully. 'A bit bossy?'

I lowered my head and kissed Kemi's soft dark hair so that they couldn't read my expression. 'This isn't about Jesse.'

A white lie, and only told because I didn't want to make anyone out to be the bad guy. This was about me.

My friends gazed back at me, uncomprehending, worried. I had to tell them something.

'It's . . .' I cleared my throat. 'My family needs me.'

Now that was a lie. But I knew it was something they would accept easily. Here in this small community where I'd been welcomed so warmly, family was at the heart of everything. Generations lived under one roof, grandparents looked after grandchildren, sisters were each other's best friends. When someone was taken to hospital, one family would step in to care for another. A life made up of big hearts and small kindnesses. Maybe it wasn't just Uganda where this happened. Maybe it was common in the UK too. But not in my family. Months would go by without even a phone call between us. A shiver ran down the length of my spine at the thought of what I was going back to, going *home* to. But I had to go, I had no choice.

'Someone is ill?' Dembe asked, eyes wide with worry.

I shook my head. 'It's complicated.'

An understatement where my family was concerned.

'You are a good girl,' said Aster. 'You go to your family, but don't forget about us.'

'Never,' I promised easily. 'As if I could.'

My taxi pulled into the yard, sending a cloud of dust into the air. At the sound of the car, other friends and their families appeared, their faces solemn. Babies in arms, children too young to be in school, aunts, uncles and grandparents. People I'd come to care about; leaving them was so difficult and, for a split second, I wavered, my head doing battle with my heart.

Aster picked up my suitcase while I handed Kemi back to her mum.

'Where is Jesse?' Dembe cast her eyes around, worriedly.

'We said goodbye this morning,' I replied quietly. 'Neither of us wanted a fuss.'

Jesse had offered to drive me to the airport, but I couldn't bear the thought of a journey spent in silence, or perhaps, even worse, being told that I didn't need to leave, that I was doing the wrong thing. Instead, we'd hugged each other for a long time and promised to take care of ourselves until we saw each other again.

'Write to us,' Aster's husband said, loading my suitcase into the car.

'I will.'

'Please bring me a Manchester United shirt when you come back,' asked Apolo, the school cleaner. Technically he should have been in school now, but I was glad he'd come to see me off.

'Just come back,' said Aster, nudging Apolo out of the way so she could put her arms around me.

Half a dozen children formed a circle around us, holding on to the back of my skirt as they always did when they couldn't catch hold of my hand.

'God bless your family,' said Dembe, grabbing my face and kissing my cheeks as I tried to peel myself away from my dear friends.

Finally, I climbed into the taxi and I took one last look at the place I'd called home for five years, drinking in every detail, committing it all to memory.

Just in case I never returned.

Chapter Two

Liz

From her table on the upper deck of the Kings Arms, Liz gave the wine list a cursory glance before turning her attention to the scene in front of her. Salcombe was beautiful all year round, but now, in mid-July, with the water sparkling in the sunshine, it was paradise. Down on ground level, holidaymakers milled around, eating ice cream, browsing the shops and taking selfies. A flotilla of tiny boats sailed by, little ducklings all in a line hugging the coastline. Kids on paddleboards, the ferry doing its loop from here to East Portlemouth and back and sleek yachts moored at the quay, masts tinkling as they bobbed on the gentle waves. Across the estuary, crescents of golden beaches were dotted with figures. Liz could just make out coloured rectangles of beach towels and children charging into the waves, then running back to the safety of parents' arms. Life in all its summer glory.

She was fortunate to live here, she knew that, but lonely. Oh so lonely.

'Liz?' called a surprised voice from below, jolting her from her thoughts.

She looked down to see Viv waving to her and waved back in trepidation. Viv Carroway was a business contact who Liz had got to know well over the years. She ran a

7

successful holiday lettings agency and was always rushed off her feet managing the expectations of homeowners and holidaymakers. She was brilliant at her job, which meant that her properties were full almost all year round. Viv's company had put a lot of work Liz's way at one time. But not anymore.

'It is you!' Viv cried and promptly ran up the steps to join her.

Liz stood to greet her and then wished she hadn't. Her linen tunic dress had creased into pleats, and, oh no, was that a sweat patch under one boob? Some women could wear linen and look effortlessly cool and bohemian. Liz looked like she'd slept in her clothes. Viv, by contrast, was in heeled sandals and a hot-pink tailored shift dress which looked sensational against her tan.

'How lovely to see you out and about again!' Viv kissed her cheeks; Liz was assailed by her perfume. Viv didn't know the meaning of the word subtle. 'And not before time. How *are* you?' She cocked her head to one side waiting for Liz to answer.

Liz felt her eyes begin to burn.

'I'm well,' she said, nodding as much to convince herself as Viv. 'Getting there, you know.'

'Excellent news!' the other woman beamed at her. 'I can't tell you how many clients are desperate for your services. Just say the word and I'll get those bookings flowing again.'

'I don't think so,' Liz stammered. 'But thank you.'

She wished Viv would go away and leave her in peace. She felt bad enough as it was about her lack of motivation without Viv flaunting her energy and drive in front of her.

Viv studied her for a moment as if she was about to pass comment, but her phone buzzed inside her bag, distracting her. 'Listen, I'd better dash. I'm meeting a new client. But let's catch up soon, yes? I'll be in touch.'

'Sure.' Liz sank back onto her chair, already planning to fob her off when she called.

As soon as Viv was out of sight, a waiter appeared. Liz did a double take; it was none other than Viv's handsome son, Noah.

'Hey, Liz, sorry about the delay coming to take your order,' he said with a grin. 'I wanted to make sure the coast was clear, if you know what I mean. What can I get you to drink?'

'A glass of sparkling water please.' She smiled at him. 'I take it you're referring to your mum?'

She'd known Noah since he was a little boy obsessed with dangling his crabbing line over the quay with bacon as bait. Now he was all grown up, with beach-tangled hair and a suntanned face.

He laughed. 'Got it in one. She takes every opportunity to comment on me waiting tables, when I could be suited and booted and earning more money working for her.'

'And you're not interested?' She could see why Viv would want him; he'd be a great asset.

Noah wrinkled his nose. 'I'm proud of what she's done, but I want to go my own way, start my own business one day. Like she did, and you.'

Liz looked down at her hands; she hadn't done it on her own though, unlike Viv.

'Haven't seen you in here in for a while,' Noah continued. 'Special occasion?'

'Sort of.' She glanced away before meeting his eye again, buying herself a moment to take control of her voice. 'It would have been my friend Jen's birthday today.'

The second birthday since her death. Time had both flown and dragged, if that was possible. Liz had read the books,

9

listened to the podcasts, heard the platitudes; she knew time was supposedly a great healer. But the pain of losing Jen seemed as sharp now as it had on the day she'd died.

Noah's face fell. 'Ah, I'm sorry, I didn't know. I'll go and get you that water.'

'Actually,' Liz blurted out with a sudden change of heart. 'Make it a bottle of Sauvignon Blanc instead.'

He smiled with sympathy while he tapped her order into a handheld device. 'Sounds like it's a glass-of-wine kinda day.'

'Definitely,' she agreed.

Liz had started the morning with a brief phone call to Clare, Jen's daughter, who, as usual, was racing to get the baby fed and dressed and out of the door for work and nursery. They'd only spoken for a minute or so, but it was long enough for Liz to let her know she was thinking about her on what she knew would be a tough day, and for her to connect with someone who had loved Jen too.

Her plan had been to catch the ferry and walk to the Gara Rock hotel, Jen's favourite place, to toast her best friend with a glass of champagne. But Jen's ex-husband, Mike, had phoned this morning and invited her for an impromptu lunch. It had been so thoughtful of him and she'd accepted without hesitation.

'Hey, did Mum tell you she's dating again?' Noah said, collecting the wine list from the table.

Liz raised her eyebrows in surprise. Viv must only have been divorced a matter of months after kicking her husband out for cheating on her last year.

'Good for her. Anyone special?' The sun was getting stronger, and she shaded her eyes as she looked up at Noah.

He grinned. 'She's got a few on the go. I don't think she's too fussed about getting tied down again. She's got a better social life than me, these days. Now I'm working full time here, I hardly get to see my girlfriend.'

'Who's the lucky girl?'

'Jade. Manager of the coffee shop the other end of Fore Street?'

'I know the one.' Liz nodded, although not being much of a coffee drinker herself, she'd never been in. Jen had been a coffee fiend, as was Clare, so she always kept the good stuff in. Had a proper machine and everything.

'I'll go and get that wine,' said Noah.

As Liz watched him walk away, her thoughts wandered back to Viv. Holidaymakers and people with second homes liked to be cooked for and Viv had put a lot of work their way.

After Jen died, Liz hadn't been in a fit state to cater for herself, let alone anyone else, and she'd let Viv down repeatedly. She'd felt guilty, but incapable of doing anything about it. Eighteen months on, Liz was still barely working, and certainly not enough to cover the business's bills. The only catering jobs she would even consider were small ones for people she knew, in kitchens she'd cooked in before. Viv had been disappointed by Liz's reluctance to come back to work and a bit bewildered too. No doubt she would take Liz's lunch out as a sign that things were getting back to normal. As if that was ever going to happen.

A dart of sadness pierced Liz's heart.

Liz and Jen, Jen and Liz. Inseparable since the age of eighteen. They'd been known as The Gourmet Girls at university because of their infamous supper clubs, to which every student in their circle wanted to be invited. When they'd reunited a decade and a half ago to set up in business together in Salcombe, the name had morphed into The Seaside Gourmet Girls.

It had been the best decision Liz had ever made. Dinner parties, anniversary celebrations, even elaborate beach picnics – Jen's *joie de vivre* and 'nothing is too much trouble' attitude coupled with Liz's knack of conjuring up the perfect menu for any occasion had been a winning combination. The Seaside Gourmet Girls had become the 'go-to' catering company in the area. Few friendships would have endured a lifetime of so many ups and downs, but theirs had. With Jen gone, Liz's world would never be the same again.

Deep down, Liz knew that life was a gift which could be taken away at any moment and it was high time she started living again – she owed that to Jen. Knowing it was one thing, *doing* it was another entirely. For a start, The Seaside Gourmet *Girl* didn't have quite the same ring to it. And she was sixty-bloody-two, for heaven's sake; it had been fun to call themselves girls when there were two of them. Girl – singular – was just . . . odd.

Her mouth felt dry; she was ready for a drink to settle her nerves, help her relax. Where was that wine? And where was Mike, come to that? Not that she'd expected him to be on time. He'd always been one to underestimate how long things took, like driving from his house in Exeter to Salcombe on a Friday in tourist season. But at least he'd remembered it was Jen's birthday and, for that alone, he would be forgiven.

By the time Mike arrived, Liz was on her second glass and feeling pleasantly buzzy. Her arms were tingling from being in the sun and she hoped her face hadn't gone too red.

She heard him talking to the staff in a loud, confident tone and turned to watch him run up the steps to join her. She wasn't the only one; women shot him sneaky glances when their husbands weren't looking and she noticed more than one man sit up straighter, pulling in his stomach as Mike passed by. Tall, silver-haired and impeccably dressed in a crisp navy shirt and chinos and a cross-body bag, very trendy. He'd got broader over the years, but there wasn't an ounce of fat on him. She wouldn't have been surprised if he'd been out for an early-morning run before breakfast. He'd always had more energy than anyone else she knew. Mike Marriott, object of a hundred and one crushes and as handsome now as he'd been at university when she and Jen had first met him.

Liz quickly dabbed her upper lip with her napkin to remove any perspiration.

'Not bad.' She looked from Mike to her watch. 'Only ten minutes late.'

'Sorry, sorry, parking was a bloody nightmare.' He took off his bag and set it down on the table before kissing her cheek. 'Have you got an elderflower pressé or something?' This comment directed to Noah, who'd followed Mike to the table.

'You'll have a glass of wine, surely?' Liz tapped the side of the ice bucket.

Mike shook his head. 'Better not. Got a packed day, need to keep a clear head.'

Liz swallowed her disappointment; it would have been nice to have a drinking partner for once, she would have felt less . . . conspicuous.

'Coming up,' Noah said. 'I'll give you a few minutes to look at the menu.'

'No need.' Mike took a seat. 'I already know what I want. Liz, how about you?'

'It's got to be the fish and chips.' She'd been too caught up in her memories to look at the menu. But the Kings

Arms did the best fish and chips; she couldn't go wrong with that.

'Sea bass fillets with salad, for me, please,' said Mike. 'Dressing served on the side.'

Liz cringed inwardly. Salad and a soft drink. Now she looked like a boozer *and* a greedy pig.

'Actually,' she blurted out, 'that sounds delicious. I'll have the same. Thanks.'

When Noah left, Mike reached for her hand across the table and gave it a squeeze.

'You look well, Liz, really great.'

'No I don't, I feel a hundred years old. But thanks for being kind.' Liz felt herself redden under his scrutiny and picked up her glass to hide behind. 'You, on the other hand, really do look great.'

'You've got to watch what you eat at our age.' Mike patted his lean stomach. 'I'm all low carbs and no eating after six if I can. I feel great for it.'

'You've changed.' Liz shook her head fondly. 'I remember you at uni ordering takeaway pizza at night and polishing off the leftovers for breakfast.'

He held her gaze. 'Of course I've changed. Life moves on, our goals shift, and the people we love come and go.'

Liz didn't feel as if she'd changed. She still loved the ones she'd always loved. Her eyes tingled, a warning sign that tears weren't far away.

She swallowed a large mouthful of wine. 'Thanks for suggesting lunch; I'd planned on spending the day on my own, thinking about how Jen and I would have celebrated her birthday. It means a lot to me that you were thinking of her too.'

Liz's stomach lurched as she registered his blank expression. He had no idea what day it was. How could he have forgotten? She was so disappointed that she could almost taste it. If that was the case, why were they both here? What was this lunch all about?

Mike recovered quickly, his brown eyes soft with sympathy. 'Of course. Today must be hard for you. For all of us. Dear Jen.'

His fake sincerity infuriated her. At that moment, Noah appeared with Mike's drink, giving Liz a chance to compose herself.

'Come off it,' she said, draining her glass once Noah had gone. 'You forgot about it. It's written all over your face. But now I've reminded you, please do the decent thing and call your daughter. Clare needs your support: she's looking after Ivy on her own, trying to hold down a big job. She'll be missing her mum terribly today.'

Clare was Jen's only daughter, but Mike also had Skye, who was younger by five years. Liz was godmother to both. Mike hadn't been a great father to either of them as far as she was concerned.

'I know all that,' Mike said tetchily. 'But I also know Clare; she'll be fine, she can cope with anything, that girl. Top-up?'

Liz didn't reply. She looked at him, marvelling at how dense he could be. No one who had lost their mother suddenly and became a mother herself while still in the grip of grief could possibly be *fine*. Surely, he must realise that.

Mike lifted the bottle out of the ice bucket and looked pointedly at the amount of wine already gone. 'Good grief, Liz, I was only ten minutes late.'

She flushed. 'Whoops. It's fatal when the waiter tops up your glass; it's impossible to keep track of these things.'

'Luckily, our food is here,' said Mike, sitting back as Noah set their plates down for them. 'Would you like some bread to soak up the wine? Can't have you going back to work tipsy, can we?'

'I am not tipsy!' Liz was mortified. Noah took the hint and slipped silently away. 'And even if I was, it wouldn't matter. I'm not working for the rest of the day.'

'Really? On a Friday?' Mike flicked his napkin and settled it on his lap. 'I thought you'd be rushed off your feet now holiday season has started. The bookings must be pouring in.'

'Not exactly.' Liz's chest tightened.

She contemplated confiding in him. It would be a relief to get it all out in the open, tell him how she felt. About how running the business without Jen held no appeal, so she'd let it slide. How she was torn between walking away from it and feeling duty-bound to stick at it, for Jen's sake. About how small her life had become; how lonely she was without Jen brightening up her days.

Mike tipped the smallest amount of dressing over his salad and eyed her beadily. 'Come on, old thing, spit it out.'

'Do you ever think about retiring?' she said. 'Because I do. I'm getting too old for hustling. Negotiating prices. Working unsociable hours. Schlepping to other people's inadequately equipped kitchens to whip up some culinary wonder. Catering – quite literally – to a customer's every whim. I'm not sure I want to go on.'

'Good grief, Liz.' Mike glanced at the nearby tables as if checking they hadn't been overheard. He leaned forward, lowering his voice. 'No way. Retirement is for old folk, and we're not in that bracket. You and I are in our prime. Anyway, what would you do all day?'

'Plenty of things.' She shrugged, not wanting to admit that some days she could barely be bothered to get dressed and leave the house.

Since Jen had died and Liz had pressed pause on the business, she'd realised just how much her life had revolved around work. She hadn't felt up to filling that gap much in recent months, but as soon as she did, she was going to make herself a priority. A partner was number one on the list. If Viv could do it, so could she. She missed being needed, and she missed being someone else's significant other. Liz had a lot of love to give, always had, it was getting the right person to notice her, that was the issue.

'This fish is melt-in-the-mouth, try it,' said Mike, adding casually, 'besides, I couldn't afford to retire if I wanted to. Not right now. Bit of a cash-flow situation, to be honest.'

'Oh Mike, I'm sorry.' She removed a bone from her fish and set it on one side. 'I assumed business was booming.'

He dismissed her concern with a shake of his head. 'The company is fine. I've got a great new assistant, Harriet, who's keeping me on my toes. It's my personal finances that are taking a bit of a hit.' He paused and stared at his plate. 'The thing is, Liz, I need you to repay me that loan I gave you and Jen to set up the catering business.'

She blinked at him, horrified. That twenty thousand had been a *loan*? Adrenaline shot through her; Jen had never told her that. She racked her brains to try to recall the details. 'There's no paperwork about it being a loan.'

Mike winced. 'I know. It was all a bit "back of the envelope" and, if I'm being honest, I wanted the money to fly under the radar, so Frankie didn't find out at the time.'

'Ah.' Liz sniffed. Frankie, Mike's second wife. The stunning redhead ten years his junior. The one he'd cheated with behind Jen's back. This was ringing a bell now.

'Jen promised the two of you would pay me back after fifteen years,' said Mike.

Which was this year. Liz gulped her wine, no longer caring if he thought she was knocking it back too quickly.

'I would have asked before now,' he continued softly, 'but with Jen's passing, I haven't wanted to bring the subject up. But, I'm afraid, I'm going to have to call in my debt. I've got some unavoidable expenses coming up and I need cash to pay for them. Shall we say beginning of September?'

Liz felt panic surge in her chest. 'It's only six weeks until September. I'm not sure I can do it.'

'A catering business in prosperous Salcombe?' He eyed her sceptically. 'Come off it, you must be sitting on a gold mine.'

'I'm really not.' She'd woken up feeling awful, now she felt even worse.

'If you say so.' Mike winked, as if he was humouring her. He forked up the last of his salad leaves and wiped his mouth on the napkin. 'In other news, I've got a new project in the offing. Harriet suggested we take them out for lunch. But I thought I'd book my favourite caterers to do lunch for the big meeting. If you can fit us in of course?'

'I'm sorry, but no I can't.' Liz picked up her glass, but somehow it was empty, and she set it down again. 'I can't run The Seaside Gourmet Girls without Jen. I don't have it in me.'

'Of course you do.' He stared at her, bemused. 'You could run it standing on your head.'

'I couldn't, *I can't*,' she retorted fiercely. 'The business worked because we had complementary skills. Jen was the "seal the deal" girl, the one with the big, sunny smile to smooth over any client wobbles. I was the back-room girl, the slicer and dicer, and happy to be so.'

'Who also has a big, sunny smile,' Mike countered. 'Not to mention you're a talented cook and a brilliant business brain. *Of course* it's different without Jen, but you can do it, I have every faith. Really.'

She held his gaze. He'd always managed to make her feel good about herself, that the world was hers for the taking.

Except the one thing that had mattered most to her, that was.

Liz shook her head, annoyed with her mind for going there.

'Our website is full of pictures of Jen, she even recorded the greeting on the answer phone, which I can't bring myself to delete. Jen runs through every strand of the business, always has, right from day one. I can't do it without her, and even if I could, I'm not sure I want to.' She blinked hard to keep her tears at bay. 'My only option is to cease trading.'

'You can't do that. At least not until you've paid me,' Mike spluttered, before clearing his throat. 'I need that money back, Liz.'

Her heart thumped; he was serious about this. Where was she going to get that sort of money from in such a short space of time? Even the thought of getting the business back up and running made her feel exhausted.

'I can't do it by myself,' she murmured, looking up at him.

'Which leads me nicely into why I asked you to meet me for lunch.' A satisfied smile spread across Mike's face.

'You mean as well as it being Jen's birthday, *and* asking me for money?' Liz gave him a stern look.

He shrugged sheepishly.

'Out with it then.' A combination of wine and sunshine and the emotional load of the day had given her a headache. She'd had enough of Mike's relentless energy; she was ready to go home.

'It's Skye,' said Mike, his face softening.

Liz frowned, wondering where Mike was going with this. Skye had arrived back in the UK unexpectedly a couple of weeks ago after working for a charity in Africa for the last five years.

'Since she came back from Uganda, she seems a bit lost,' he continued.

'I'm sorry to hear that, poor love. I must give her a ring.' Liz registered a flash of guilt for not getting in touch with her god-daughter before now. 'Is she back for good?'

Mike held his palms out. 'I'm not sure that even she knows the answer to that one. She's been very evasive whenever I've tried to talk to her. But you know what she's like; she's never really managed to stick at anything.'

'That's not very fair,' Liz retorted. 'She stuck at this job for a long time.'

'Hardly a career, was it?' he growled. 'And now she's no further forward in her life than she was when she left home. Not like Clare. Jen did such a good job with Clare.'

'She was a great mum,' Liz agreed. She felt a pang remembering the last conversation she'd had with her. Jen had been marvelling at how well Clare was doing and how much she was looking forward to a spa day with her.

'Frankie and I were never as good at parenting as she was,' Mike admitted. 'I've contacted Frankie to see if Skye could stay with her for a while. But she said she hasn't got the room or the time.'

'I see.' Liz just about managed not to roll her eyes. Mike had cheated on Jen with Frankie, so, unsurprisingly, Liz had never thought very highly of the woman, but not having time for her own daughter? Unbelievable.

'I think what Skye needs is to spend time with you,' said Mike. 'You'd be such a good influence on her.'

'Me?' She hadn't been expecting that. 'Do you really think that, or does Nilla not want Skye back living at home?'

Nilla was Mike's third wife. Each one younger than the last. The man was a walking cliché.

'Nothing of the sort.' There was a sudden flush to Mike's face, and he took a long sip from his glass before answering. 'Nilla's in Copenhagen spending some time with her mother, who hasn't been too well. That's why I thought of you. I'm sure you could help Skye to winkle out what she wants to do next with her life.'

Liz gave a snort. 'I'm not even sure what I want to do with my *own* life.'

Mike laid a hand on her arm, his fingers cool on her warm skin. She felt a trickle of sweat run down her back. Thank goodness she'd decided against her silky dress, it would have been clinging to her skin by now.

'Then maybe you'll be good for each other. And you've just admitted that you can't run the business alone; Skye would fit the bill nicely.'

Liz was nonplussed. 'So you want me to give her a job as well as some life coaching? But she's living with you in Exeter, that's an awful commute in summer, as you well know.'

Mike gave an awkward laugh. 'I was hoping that as you've got goodness knows how many spare rooms in that huge house of yours she could live with you. It would be company for you you'd be doing me a great favour. I'm so busy right now and I can't give her the attention she needs.'

'Attention?' Liz scoffed. 'She's not a child, she's almost thirty. Anyway, it's just not practical for Skye to live and work with me. Firstly, I'll be honest, I can't afford it. There's not enough profit in the business to pay someone a regular wage.'

'Hmm.' Mike chewed the inside of his cheek, frowning. 'OK. I'll pay Skye's wages. But it must be just between you and me. She's very proud and wouldn't accept the job if she knew I was funding it.'

'I thought you said you had cash-flow problems?' she reminded him.

He waved a hand. 'I'll pay her out of my business. Creative accounting. Leave it to me.'

Liz pulled a piece of bread off the slice on her plate, playing for time. He really seemed keen on this. And it would be lovely to reconnect with Skye. It had been years since they'd spent any decent length of time together. But there was one big spanner in the works.

'Clare and Ivy are coming to stay with me tomorrow, I'm sure I told you that. Clare has been looking forward to it for weeks and I'm not sure how she'll take it if I spring it on her that Skye will be there too.'

The two half-sisters weren't close. Inevitably, when Skye had arrived on the scene, five-year-old Clare had resented the new baby who had replaced her in her father's affections; this had set the tone for their relationship.

'I hadn't forgotten at all. This is a perfect opportunity for them to get to know each other properly. Spending time with you, someone who loves them both, on neutral territory, will help them to bond.' He sat back and folded his arms, pleased with himself. 'Trust me, Liz. I'm right about this.'

Liz nodded thoughtfully. If Jen had still been alive, the territory would have been far from neutral. But now . . .? 'I'm not sure Clare will see it that way.'

'I'll give Clare a ring about it, leave that with me,' Mike assured her. 'I think you're underestimating her; Clare will be grateful for another pair of hands with the baby.'

'Hmm,' said Liz, mulling it over. Clare was, at her core, a kind and loving woman; maybe without Jen, Clare might find it easier to let her half-sister in without fear of being disloyal to her mum. Perhaps Mike was right, perhaps this could be the making of them. Both women might benefit from having a sister in their lives. 'It would be nice to see them get on,' she admitted.

'It sounds like The Seaside Gourmet Girls might be welcoming in a new generation of the family?' Mike looked at her hopefully. 'Come on, Liz, what do you say?'

She bit her lip. Could she throw herself back into the business again?

'Think of the money,' he urged. 'You'd be able to pay me back before I could say solicitor's letter.'

'You wouldn't!' she gasped. 'Would you?'

He grinned and then patted her hand. 'Only joking. I'm sure it won't come to that.'

Liz wasn't daft, and she wasn't fooled by that smile. Mike Marriott had a ruthless streak running through him a mile wide. If he wanted the money back, he'd make sure he got it. It didn't look like she had much choice.

'I'll take Skye on for six weeks,' Liz found herself saying before she could change her mind. 'Just until the end of August. I'll repay the loan I didn't realise I even had and then I'll decide whether to close the business or not.'

'That's fantastic,' said Mike. He grabbed her hand and pressed an exuberant kiss to it. 'You're doing the right thing.'

'Let's hope so,' she muttered, wondering how on earth she'd just got herself talked into upending her entire summer.

'Shall I tell Skye the good news, or will you?' he asked.

'I will,' Liz replied firmly. 'It needs to come from me. Give me a couple of hours to get my head around it and I'll phone her later.'

She'd have to clear a bedroom for her and conjure up some work if the need for a member of staff was to have any chance of looking genuine. Her first port of call would be Viv. At least she'd be happy to hear The Seaside Gourmet Girls were back in business. Hopefully, she'd help her get some orders on the books.

Liz felt a wobble of nerves; was she doing the right thing? Would Clare really be OK with it? The two of them had made plans, things they were going to do this summer, places they were going to take the baby. The dynamic would be completely different with Skye there. Plus, now, of course, Liz would need to be working as much as possible.

'And you promise you'll let Clare know?' she reiterated. 'Because for this to work, both girls need to be on board.'

'Sure.' Mike chuckled. 'Look at you. Your eyes are sparkling, I can virtually see the cogs in your brain making plans already. Retire? You? Not a chance.'

He was up to his usual tricks: making her feel like she could do anything. Just like he had when they were on the same project team at uni.

She shook her head, bemused. 'You old charmer.'

He reached for her other hand. Anyone looking over would think they were a couple. His face lit up with a smile that spoke straight to her heart. The years fell away and in front of her was the boy with the infectious laugh, the intoxicating energy she remembered being entranced by when she was eighteen.

The searing heat of his gaze made her heart pound, and she leaned in closer.

Everything had changed in those intervening years. Well, almost everything, she thought, willing her heart to stop racing. There was one thing that hadn't changed at all. Not one bit. But that was her secret, no one else needed to know.

Chapter Three

Liz

I first noticed Mike Marriott at the cheese and wine party for the Business course during Freshers' Week. I remember being so nervous. It seemed so grown-up and such a sharp contrast to being at school. I'd gone from running around Salcombe in denim cut-offs and flip-flops to *this* in the space of a few short days. I could hardly believe this was my life now. A student in Bath, wearing proper shoes at a proper party.

Mike was talking to the head of Business. Looking back now, the man was probably in his forties, but at the time, I'd considered anyone over the age of twenty-nine ancient.

Mike looked completely at ease with the older adults. He was so confident that I assumed he was a member of staff. He was also gorgeous: dark-haired, brown-eyed and suntanned. He commanded everyone's attention. One of the female lecturers fancied him, I could tell.

Most of us had only gone to the event because of the promise of free booze and to see who we'd be studying alongside for the next three years. I didn't meet anyone else there who gave a toss about chatting to the staff. No one except Mike.

25

I later learned that this was a strategy of his: identify the most powerful people in the room and align yourself with them. That sounded a pompous thing to say, but I did get it. He had goals in life, he'd read that to be successful, you had to seek out the company of those who'd already made it. Learn from them and follow their lead.

Mike seemed so unattainable that night, that after I'd clocked him and thought 'phwoar', I stopped thinking about him. Instead, I hovered around the edges of the room and nibbled cheese like the country mouse at the town mouse's party and sipped dry white wine wishing there was some lemonade I could slosh into it to sweeten it. I'd got used to the taste over the years; the drier, the better these days.

When lectures started properly the following week, I was gobsmacked to see Mike sitting with the rest of us students and that was when my crush really began.

Of course, me being me, I did absolutely nothing about it. There were over one hundred people on my course. We were divided into smaller groups for seminars and tutorial groups, but, in the first and second year, I was never in his group for anything but the big all-course lectures.

For two years, I watched him from afar. He had girl-friends. Lots of them. One of his exes told me that he was boring, that he was here to work not play. I was definitely here to play, although I respected his commitment. But in my final year my patience was rewarded: Mike and I were assigned the same group for the marketing team project.

For a month and a half, I got to spend three glorious hours a week with him. He was clever and enthusiastic and somehow managed to galvanise the group into action. He inspired me to produce the best work I'd done during my university career, and the two of us gravitated together, putting in extra time to polish our presentation.

I was so happy. Even my best friend Jen, who I shared a flat with, couldn't understand what was going on with me, why I was so upbeat all of a sudden. I had never told another soul about my secret adoration of Mike. Not even Jen. I couldn't bear anyone to know how hard I'd fallen for someone who was so out of my league. I didn't want to hear their amusement, or their pity.

Also, if I was honest, I kept him secret from Jen because telling her about the absolute god that was Mike Marriott would have been too dangerous. Where I was shy, a home-bird, too scared to put myself out there in case anyone laughed, Jen was completely the opposite. If Jen fancied someone, they'd know about it in around thirty seconds. I had had a crush on Mike for coming up to thirty *months* and he still didn't have a clue.

Outside of classes, I had become something of a cook. Jen wasn't bothered about cooking back then, but she did love a party. She loved organising and adding the final touches, like decorations and table setting and mix tapes. So dinner parties became our thing and because most students couldn't be bothered to cook from fresh, we were very popular.

I couldn't remember who started calling us The Gourmet Girls, but we liked it and it stuck, and by my final year, dinner at ours was the hot ticket. So much so that it was costing us a fortune in food shopping. I told Mike about the dilemma, bashfully explaining that our dinner parties had got a bit out of control. It was his suggestion that we should start charging people and make some money out of it. He'd read an article about supper clubs being all the rage in London. Jen thought it was a brilliant idea and so we set the date for the first one.

Meanwhile, back in the marketing module, Mike and I and the other two (whose names I can't even remember) gave our presentation to the rest of the course. It was an absolute triumph and the lecturer asked if he could use it as a template for best practice for future students. A week later, our grades came through – we were awarded a first for the project. Mike and I jumped up and down, clinging on to each other with excitement. I remember squealing and the next moment, he picked me up, spun me around and kissed me.

Mike Marriott kissed *me*.

On the mouth.

It lasted maybe half a second, but it changed my life.

Until then, I'd resigned myself to being eternally in the friend zone. But that kiss gave me wings. The memory of his lips against mine added flames to the gentle heat of my feelings towards him. For days afterwards, I could think of nothing else. Perhaps, I thought, maybe, I wondered, could he feel the same? I mused . . .

I became consumed with the ticking clock of that last term. In a matter of weeks, my three years at university would be over and we'd be scattered all around the country as the next phase of our lives began. If I was going to tell Mike how I felt about him, it needed to be soon. The worst that could happen was that he'd turn me down, I reasoned. But imagine if he didn't. Imagine if I ended my time at the University of Bath as Mike Marriott's girlfriend. Now wouldn't that be something?

The next time I bumped into him, he asked me how plans for our supper club were going.

'The first one is next Saturday. Come along,' I said without giving myself time to think it through or wimp out. 'There's a space left.'

There wasn't, we were sold out and Jen would probably kill me, but I didn't care.

When Mike pressed the five pounds ticket price into my hand, I could barely believe it. He wanted to come to my flat. He didn't know anyone else who'd be there except me. It was a sign.

I almost told Jen several times between then and the big night. But I was worried she'd make a fuss and make it too obvious about my crush on him when he turned up. Plus, she'd never have stopped going on about what I was going to wear; she'd have made me even more on edge than I already was.

The night finally came around. I was making mini goat's cheese tartlets for starters and had attempted chicken Kievs for the first time. Dessert was Eton mess, chosen because I could assemble it at the last minute.

'How do I look?' I asked Jen, peeling off my apron five minutes before our guests were due to arrive.

Jen stood back, head tilted, and appraised my appearance.

'Gorgeous,' she nodded her approval. 'Voluptuous and cute all at the same time. Is that a new top?'

'Yes, I thought I'd better make an effort tonight.'

She poured us both a glass of wine. 'Intriguing. Is there someone you've got your eye on?'

I swigged the wine, praying I could pass off my pink cheeks as a result of slaving over a hot oven for the last hour.

'No, but this could be the start of something exciting,' I said. 'The first of many.'

'To The Gourmet Girls!' she said with a grin.

We tapped our glasses together and knocked back our wine. The doorbell rang and our supper club had officially begun.

The first half an hour whizzed by in a blur of chatter and chinking of bottles. Everyone had come and our tiny ground-floor flat was bursting at the seams. Luckily, we had access to an outside yard and most of our guests headed outdoors for some fresh air. I managed a quick hello to Mike, but then had to race off to sort out a red wine spillage. Jen handled all the pre-dinner stuff while I headed back to the kitchen and my checklist. The pastry tartlets were due in the oven and, for the next twenty minutes, I didn't dare leave their side. I kept popping my head out, hoping to catch Mike's eye and invite him over for a chat, but he was working his way around the room, chatting to everyone.

'Take your seats, please, folks!' I heard Jen yell at eight o'clock sharp.

I smiled with pride to myself, as I took the tartlets out of the oven. What a team we made, I thought.

Seconds later, Jen skittered into the kitchen like a whirl-wind, shutting the door behind her.

'Liz!' she hissed, gripping my arm.

'Get off, you idiot,' I laughed. 'That one nearly hit the deck.'

'Leave it,' she said urgently, 'and look at me. I've got something to ask you. Something important.'

I looked at her properly, taking in her dilated pupils and the high colour to her cheeks.

'OK,' I laughed, 'out with it.'

'Why didn't you tell me?' she half-squealed. 'About Mike? You dark horse!'

Anticipation swirled through me. I pressed a hand to my heart, aware of it thudding against my ribs. Was it possible he felt the same as I did?

'I . . . well, I didn't want to,' I stuttered. 'I didn't know what to say, I mean, what has he said?'

She gripped my shaking hands. 'Just tell me, do you like him?'

'Yes!' I cried. 'He's . . . oh God, he is gorgeous, and clever and so sophisticated. When I'm with him, I—'

'Thank goodness,' she whispered, blowing out a breath. 'I hoped you'd approve.'

I stared at her. 'Approve? What do mean?'

'He's asked me out.' She jumped up and down on the spot, still holding my hands. Just as Mike and I had done after we got our grades for that presentation. 'I spotted him straight away and made a beeline for him. We hit it off immediately.'

'Wow,' I said weakly, my throat suddenly constricted. 'That's . . . just wow.'

'I know.' She hugged me. A tight, brief hug filled with excitement. 'And I know this is ridiculous, but I've got a funny feeling about him.'

'It's not ridiculous,' I said flatly. Because I'd had that same funny feeling since Freshers' Week. 'He's a nice guy.'

'Yay! I'm so pleased you like him because I've already told him yes,' she gushed and kissed my cheek roughly. 'So glad you invited him. You absolute star.'

'Yeah, you owe me one.' I mustered up a smile and handed her the tray of starters. 'Take these in please.'

As she bounced back out of the kitchen, I blinked back tears of frustration and poured myself a massive glass of wine. The joy had gone out of the evening, and I couldn't wait for it to be over. I'd missed my chance. I'd never told him how I felt and now I never could.

Mark Twain had said that twenty years from now you'd be more disappointed by the things you hadn't done than the things you had. But, in my case, it was forty years and still counting.

Chapter Four

Clare

'Good luck with your final year and thanks for the flowers!' Clare smiled at Phoebe, the twenty-two-year-old trainee teacher who'd dashed in with a bunch of roses for her on the last day of term.

'You're welcome! One day I want to be sitting in the head teacher's chair, just like you – you're my inspiration,' the girl replied with a wave from the doorway of Clare's office.

Heaven help her, thought Clare, watching her leave. She wasn't sure she'd done much worthy of inspiration. Since coming back from maternity leave at Easter, she'd clung on by her fingernails, muddling through, putting on a good show for parents, staff and kids while gradually sinking under the weight of her responsibilities.

She turned her attention back to the stack of paperwork on her desk. She was going to need the six-week school holiday to recover from clearing her inbox for the summer. Still, at least being busy had kept her mind off the date.

Mum's birthday.

Clare's throat thickened instantly. Mum's second birthday since her death; even thinking about her brought Clare up short. If she'd still been alive, they'd have had a lovely evening together, just the three of them. An alternative universe fluttered briefly into her mind of a picnic on the beach and blowing out candles on a birthday cake until the voice of her deputy head teacher, Andrea, drifted through her open door and cut into her thoughts.

'Yes, darling, I'll be leaving soon. It's six-fifteen now, so I guess if I—'

'You are kidding me!' Clare gasped. A gasp filled with horror, from deep at the base of her lungs. *Six-fifteen?* How, *how* could it possibly be that late?

She leapt to her feet so fast that her chair tipped over.

'Oh my God!' she yelled at the top of her voice.

'What's happened?' Andrea careered into Clare's office, wide-eyed.

'Ivy.' Her mouth was so dry, she had to peel her tongue from the roof of her mouth to speak. 'I forgot to collect her from nursery. I should have left ages ago. How the hell did I do that?'

Her baby girl. The most precious thing in the whole world and she'd been so wrapped up in work that pick-up time had slipped her mind. Clare was all Ivy had. She couldn't let her down, she just couldn't.

This was her worst nightmare.

'Because you're busy, because you never cut yourself any slack,' said Andrea, already unplugging Clare's laptop from the wall and shoving it in its case. 'And you forget that you're just like the rest of us – human.'

Clare's panicked gaze flicked over her surroundings, at the remaining jobs, the secret pile of detritus under the desk, where she'd been shoving things she didn't know what to do with . . . fear had paralysed her; she couldn't move.

'Leave all that. Just go!' Andrea shook Clare's arm, jolting her back into action.

'Right. Yes. I'd better phone the nursery first.' She grabbed her handbag from under her desk and riffled through it to find her mobile. The screen showed two missed calls from them. 'Shit.'

They'd be trying to close up for the weekend. All the other little ones would be gone. Just her baby left all alone with one solitary, resentful member of staff. What sort of mother did that?

'I'll call Little Acorns for you,' Andrea said, steering Clare to the door and handing her the zipped-up laptop bag and the bunch of roses. 'And let them know you're on your way.'

All the senior team knew which nursery Clare sent Ivy to during the school day. She'd made sure of it. Just in case anything happened to her. Because if, for some reason, Clare wasn't there to pick her up, there was no one else.

'They close at six,' Clare swallowed a sob. 'I'm not going to be there for ages yet and with Friday traffic—'

'But you will get there,' said Andrea calmly, closing Clare's office door behind them. 'And Ivy will be fine. Take some deep breaths, drive safely and I'll see you in September.'

'OK. Yes. Thanks.' Tears pricked at Clare's eyes.

It was always the way when someone did something kind. Especially now that it happened so rarely.

'Hurry!' Andrea flapped her away, scrolling through her own phone for the number.

So Clare did.

It was an excruciating forty minutes before Clare pulled into the Little Acorns car park. Her hands were sweaty on the steering wheel, and she felt sick with guilt. This wasn't her first offence; she'd been one or two minutes late before when she'd got embroiled in a meeting or been stuck in traffic. But forgetting about Ivy completely – this was a new low.

She yanked the keys from the ignition and raced to the security gate on shaky legs. She fumbled with the code, and it took her two attempts to gain access. She closed the gate firmly behind her, even though there were apparently no other children left to escape.

The nursery manager, Anya, was waiting in the front garden with Ivy in her arms. Clare felt a wave of relief; she got on well with Anya, she was a young mum herself and no stranger to the demands of juggling a career with childcare.

'I'm so, so sorry,' Clare exclaimed, scurrying towards them.

Anya smiled and handed Ivy over. 'Here's Mummy, look.'

For a moment, Clare didn't speak. The relief of having her baby safely back in her arms was overwhelming. The soft fuzz of her hair, the scent of her peachy skin. She rested her cheek on the crown of Ivy's head and felt the tension ebb away. 'My precious girl.'

Ivy clapped her hands, evidently none the worse for being the last kid in the nursery.

'Is that applause for me,' Clare said, rocking her from side to side. 'Are you clapping because I'm finally here?'

'We were getting a bit anxious.' Anya took Ivy's little rucksack, containing spare clothes, sun hat and sunscreen, off her own shoulder and handed it to Clare.

'I can't apologise enough, it's been one of those days.' Clare heard the tremble in her own voice as she stroked the tiny curls at the nape of Ivy's neck. 'It won't happen again.'

'I understand. But we have strict rules about lateness, which we have to adhere to. Imagine if all the parents did it.' Anya's voice was firm, but she softened the impact by tickling Ivy's tummy, making the little girl squeal.

They wouldn't though, would they, Clare thought despondently, because they were probably all better parents than her, with proper backup for emergencies. Not some lone operator juggling all the balls like she was.

'Of course,' she agreed. 'There's a late collection fee, I know, and I'm happy to pay it. No question.'

'It'll be added to the next invoice . . .' Anya paused, '. . . along with the other late collection fees this month.'

'Fine, fine,' said Clare, hiding her embarrassment by peering into Ivy's bag to check everything was there. 'We'll be off now, let you close up. Thanks again.'

'Um, I think you might have something on your trousers?' Anya waved a finger vaguely at Clare's crotch area.

She looked down at the brown blob on her white linen trousers and groaned. More last-minute laundry. Melted chocolate. 'I missed lunch so I ate a Magnum ice cream at my desk. Must have dropped some.'

Anya gave her a reproving look. 'We had fish pie and peas for lunch today, didn't we, Ivy?'

'Very healthy,' said Clare, feeling judged. 'Tomorrow we're off to Salcombe to stay with my godmother for a while. She's an amazing cook, so we'll be eating lots of wonderful home-cooked meals.'

Ivy started to arch her back, wanting to be put down. She wasn't walking on her own yet, but loved holding on to Clare's fingers and staggering around their flat.

Anya put her hand on Clare's arm and nudged her gently down the path towards the car park. 'I'd love a godmother to look after me for a change, that sounds fantastic.'

'It will be,' she agreed.

Although if anyone needed looking after, Clare had a feeling it was Liz. She'd sounded very down this morning. Admittedly, today was a sad day for both of them. But even during their last conversation, Clare had come off the phone feeling worried about her. It had only been seven thirty in the evening and Liz had sounded dazed and confused, as if she'd just woken. So out of character.

'She's the nearest thing that Ivy has to a grandmother,' she continued. 'And it'll be Ivy's first proper holiday.'

'And talking of family members,' Anya opened the gate for her and together they walked to Clare's car. 'Little Acorns strongly recommends that you provide us with an alternative contact number, for when you aren't available.'

Clare frowned. 'But you've already got my work number and mobile and my landline, not that I'm ever there when Ivy is at nursery.'

'Another *person*,' Anya clarified. 'Not another number for you. Someone who can take responsibility for Ivy when you can't. Even Superwoman needs help occasionally,' she teased.

'Not me,' Clare replied. 'I don't *need* help.'

'Accepting help isn't a sign of weakness, it's the opposite. Let someone else take the pressure off you,' said Anya kindly.

'I'm not under any pressure,' Clare replied briskly. She opened the rear door and slid Ivy into her car seat.

The nursery manager maintained eye contact long enough to let Clare know that she wasn't fooled for one second. 'A relative? Ivy's father perhaps?'

Clare felt her hackles rise. That was what Mum had done and look where that had got her. She and Ivy were managing just fine on their own, thanks very much. And as for relatives, it was slim pickings on that front.

'I'm not relying on anyone else, Anya. And certainly not a man. Not for anything,' she said, keeping her voice even as she did up Ivy's straps.

Anya gave her an apologetic look. 'We're going to have to insist, I'm afraid. Procedures are there to safeguard the children in our care. We had a situation last year when a parent died suddenly. I'm not suggesting for a moment—'

'Oh my God.' Clare's lungs felt as tight as if someone had put iron bars around her ribs. If anything happened to her, where would that leave Ivy?

'Sorry.' Anya withered under the intensity of Clare's horrified stare.

'I'll find someone,' she promised. 'When we come back in September, I'll have another number to give you.'

Anya breathed a sigh of relief, said her goodbyes to Ivy and set off back inside.

There were tears in Clare's eyes as she drove home. She'd been wrong earlier when she'd said that being late to collect Ivy was her biggest nightmare, because this – the fear of leaving her daughter orphaned and alone in the world – was far, far worse.

Chapter Five

Skye

'It's buzzing, isn't it?' Skye linked arms with her dad, forcing him to lower his phone.

The Night Market at Exeter's Quayside was clearly a very popular event. Skye's senses were alight with the sights, smells and sounds as they followed the crowd towards the marquees that formed a square beside the quay.

Mike gave an impressed whistle. 'Sure is. What a great place; they've made a nice job of it. I'm glad you suggested coming, it was an excellent idea. Gives us chance for a chat, too.'

'Thanks.' She felt her heart swell.

She'd always craved her dad's attention. Mike was a hard man to impress and so far in her twenty-nine years, she hadn't managed it often. Her half-sister Clare, on the other hand, seemed to get it effortlessly.

'Work hard like Clare and you'll go to university too.'

'Failed again? Hard luck. Not everyone passes on their first attempt, like Clare.'

'I remember teaching Clare to ride a bike, she got the hang of it in no time . . .'

And so on.

Not that Skye had anything against Clare. Credit where it was due, Clare was bloody amazing. She'd climbed the ladder to a successful adulthood without a single misstep. Whereas Skye was still flailing around at the bottom, trying to get her foot on the first rung. And Clare was a mother now, with a baby Skye hadn't even met yet, she thought with a twinge of guilt. But no doubt Clare was a wonderful mum; she'd have taken to motherhood like a duck to water. Interesting that she was a solo parent, mind you. Although, knowing her, it would have been a carefully calculated move. She'd probably decided that she'd do a better job of raising a child alone than letting anyone else have a say.

Skye mentally chided herself. She'd only been back in the UK for two weeks and already the old feelings of inferiority were creeping back.

'Let's walk down to the far end by the water's edge,' she said, focusing on the present. 'Something smells delicious, and I want to know what it is.'

'Sure,' said Mike, glancing quickly at his phone before falling into step with her.

Exeter was gorgeous in the summer. She'd forgotten how much she loved being close to the sea, where blue dominated the colour palette. Dusk was Skye's favourite time of day, the harsh heat from the sun had mellowed into a pleasant warmth and the sky was painted an ombré of violet, pink and palest blue. A soft breeze ruffled the bunting strung across many of the stalls, and tiny swifts, their bodies black silhouettes against the sky, wheeled and squealed overhead.

Skye had never noticed this before, but here in Devon the night crept in gently, like a lullaby, easing you from day to night. So different to Uganda, where night fell swiftly, like a curtain plunging the world into darkness. She felt a sharp pang of longing for her old life, for the children she'd left behind at the little ramshackle school, and for the many friends she'd made over the years.

She brushed the thought away. She was home now, for the foreseeable future at least. And while Nilla, her stepmother, was away and Dad was on his own, she was going to make herself useful. He wasn't as young as he used to be and, deep down, although he'd never admit it, she knew he'd appreciate having someone around to organise him. The house had been a tip when she arrived; he'd blamed it on work, saying that he spent all his time in the office down the bottom of the garden. He needed her, she thought, and she felt a bit guilty about this, but it was a bonus that Nilla wasn't there. It made a pleasant change to have him all to herself.

Well, almost to herself; there was his assistant – a smart twenty-something high-flier called Harriet who worked very long hours and popped into the house now and again.

If Skye was going to be staying for a while, she needed to work too. No one was going to say that she lived off Daddy's money. She shuddered at the thought. Hence tonight's excursion to the street-food market.

As luck would have it, one of the food companies here tonight was advertising a temporary position. Applicants were supposed to send in a letter and CV. But if she could have an informal chat with the manager while she was here, she might be able to bypass the interview process altogether. This was where her dad might come in useful. Skye wasn't the most outgoing of people, but Mike was great at breaking the ice.

And so far, so good.

A guy stepped forward offering them samples of turmeric-coloured dhal. Mike declined but Skye accepted a small pot. She ate some and closed her eyes with pleasure.

'Mmm. That is so good. I love how vibrant this place is, I mean look at the colour of this.'

'You fit right in then,' Mike grinned, flicking his eyes to her batik print dress.

Skye laughed nervously, unsure whether this was a good thing or not. Perhaps she stood out too much? 'Standing out' was usually something she avoided.

She'd had several dresses made while she was in Uganda. All you had to do was walk into a fabric shop, where there were always one or two women labouring away on sewing machines. You picked out your chosen print, pointed to one of the mannequins displaying wrap skirts, or halterneck dresses, or kaftans and, as quick as a flash, one of the ladies would whip out a tape measure, jot down your measurements and tell you to come back in a day or so for your new garment.

'Sunshine colours, Dad,' she said, deciding to take it as a compliment. 'I like to dress myself happy.'

'I still remember your black phase.' He shook his head fondly. 'I'm pleased you're over that.'

Skye remembered that phase too. She'd thought it made her look serious. But looking back at old pictures of herself, she saw that black washed her out and made her features almost invisible. Ironically, that was how she'd felt for much of her childhood.

She finished the last morsel of dhal and dropped the empty pot in the nearest bin.

'Wow, look at that!' She pointed to the biggest paella pan she'd ever seen. Through the steam, they watched as the vendor scooped the vendor portions of saffron-coloured rice, plump prawns and green beans for eager customers.

'There's a vegan stall there,' said Mike, pointing to the next pop-up marquee. 'Let's try it. I'm reducing my meat consumption these days – good for my digestion.'

'Good plan,' Skye replied diplomatically.

She remembered one of her birthday meals out when Mike had ordered a steak to be served blue. Clare had come along too and rolled her eyes at the prices, before telling everyone that for her last birthday she'd had three friends for a sleepover and they'd made pizza, and that all this excess was gross. Skye had felt sick looking at Mike's plate swimming in blood and had thought that Clare's evening had sounded far nicer.

'Well, that can't be vegan,' Mike said, peering into a sizzling dish.

'It's pulled jackfruit.' A man wearing an apron with the slogan 'Vegan for Life' on the front put some into a pot for him. 'One hundred per cent vegan, I assure you. Try it.'

Mike tasted it and Skye and Vegan Man waited for the verdict.

Mike shook his head in wonder 'If you hadn't have told me, I'd have thought that was chicken. That's really tasty.'

'Yes, another convert!' Vegan Man hi-fived her.

'Good, isn't it?' said Skye, pleased, as they walked on. 'Jackfruits everywhere in Uganda. You should see them growing on the tree. Huge! Bigger than watermelons. The fruit out there is incredible. Mangoes, pineapples, bananas – they all grow wild and you can just pick them straight off the tree. So delicious.'

'Sounds it.'

'I wish . . .' she began, but Mike had turned away and was looking at something else. 'Never mind.'

I wish you had visited me, Dad. Just once.

She'd have loved to have shown him around, introduce him to the village ladies, who she just knew would have giggled and probably run away at the sight of this handsome British man with the twinkly eyes and charming smile.

43

But he hadn't come and now it might be too late. Mum had been over once, but she'd struggled with the heat and washing her hair under a hosepipe. wasn't what she was used to. It hadn't helped that her mum had fainted in the night and hit her head on the wooden bedstead either. The visit hadn't been repeated.

'This has been great, Skye.' Mike glanced at the time on his phone. 'I'm glad you brought me. I think we've seen everything now, so shall we head off? I fancy nipping to the gym for half an hour if we get back in time.'

Her stomach flipped, aware that her time slot was nearly up.

'Not yet.' She put her arm around his waist while they walked, to ensure he stayed close. 'There's a stall selling preserves and pickles that we haven't seen yet. They've got a job vacancy . . . I thought I might apply for it.'

He looked at her with bemusement. 'So you're planning on staying here then, not returning to Uganda? That little interlude is over, is it?'

'That little interlude was five years of my life, Dad,' she retorted, disappointed with him. 'I've got some extended leave from the Hope Foundation, that's all. And while I'm here, I don't want to rely on your charity. So I'm going to get a job for the summer. Dad! Are you listening?'

He'd taken his phone out again and was tapping at the screen. He quickly closed it down but not before she'd read the message.

'Hmm? Sorry, sweetheart. Just answering an email.'

'On Friday night? Can't it wait?'

He laughed under his breath. 'It's still morning in LA. My guy over there can't wait until Monday for an answer just because I'm swanning around a food market eating vegan chicken.'

'For goodness' sake, Dad! The subject of the email was "Fancy a game of golf tomorrow?" So unless your guy is already at the airport or you're telling porkies.'

Mike laughed and threw his arm around his daughter's shoulder. 'OK, you got me, it wasn't LA. Let's go and look at the jam you wanted to show me.'

'Would you like to taste our locally made cider, sir?' A girl stepped in front of them holding out a tray of taster glasses.

'Now you're talking,' Mike said with a grin.

Skye took one too and tapped hers against her dad's. 'Cheers.'

'Now that is delicious.' Mike groaned with pleasure, making the girl blush. 'That fizz on the tongue and a hit of sweetness. Tell me, what sort of apples are in it? Local, I presume?'

Skye just about managed not to roll her eyes; she'd forgotten just what a flirt he could be. It had been so embarrassing when she was younger. Her mum used to laugh it off, saying that he wasn't even aware he was doing it.

Skye's phone began to ring and she smiled with surprise when her godmother's name flashed up.

'Call me Mikey,' she heard her dad say to the girl.

'Ugh,' she muttered under her breath before answering the call. 'Hi, Liz, how are you? Hold on, I'll just move somewhere quieter.'

'Fine, sweetheart, just fine,' came Liz's voice down the line as Skye leaned on the railings overlooking the water.

'I was going to come and see you soon,' Skye began. 'But I've been worried about Dad being on his own while Nilla's away.' She glanced back over to the cider stall. Mike had attracted another woman to his little harem now. 'He's fine though.'

Liz harrumphed. 'Your father's always fine, he's got skin thicker than a month-old bowl of custard.'

Skye grinned. Liz always did have a way of cutting her dad down to size. 'True.'

'Now,' said Liz, 'I know you've probably got a million and one things on, but I wondered if you'd consider coming to work for me for a few weeks?'

Skye made a noise somewhere between a choke and a laugh. She hadn't expected that. 'Me?'

Liz laughed. 'Yes, darling, you.'

'What sort of work?'

'Bookings for The Seaside Gourmet Girls have been pouring in and I can't cope on my own.'

'But I thought . . . since Jen . . .' Skye stuttered. The last time she'd facetimed Liz from Uganda, her godmother had confessed that she'd lost interest in the business. She'd seemed in quite a state and if it hadn't been so early in the day, UK time, Skye might have suspected she'd been drinking.

'I've had my arm twisted to give it another go.' Liz explained. 'Besides, I'm too young to retire and I can't really do anything else. So what do you say? I need someone I can trust to help me out, and you were my first thought.'

Her first thought. Skye could have wept, 'I'm flattered and I am looking for a job for the summer. But it must be about fifty miles from Salcombe to here. It took Dad a couple of hours to get back this afternoon.'

'You'd stay with me, of course. I'm rattling around here on my own.' There was a pause. 'Most of the time.'

'Is this anything to do with Dad?' Skye was suspicious; this seemed almost too good to be true.

'Sort of, but in a good way. I happened to mention how busy I was. He suggested you would be perfect for the job.'

46

'Did he?' Skye stole a glance at her father. The girl was scribbling something down on a piece of paper. She handed it to Mike and he touched her arm, while whispering something in her ear.

Really, Dad? She was practically a child. Skye turned away so she couldn't see him making a fool of himself.

Of course, her dad didn't need her here. He'd be fine on his own; he was more than capable of entertaining himself while Nilla was gone.

Maybe she'd be better off away from Exeter. She was almost thirty, for heaven's sake, far too old to be hanging around the family home like a bad smell. And it sounded like Liz genuinely needed her. Plus, she'd be working with someone she knew rather than strangers, which would be far more enjoyable.

'So what do you think?' Liz prompted. 'Will you come?'

'When do you need me?' Skye asked, suddenly sure this was the right thing to do.

'Is tomorrow too soon?' said Liz. 'I've agreed to do a dinner party on Monday and it'll be my first one for . . . since Jen died . . . I haven't agreed the menu and I'm going to have to ferret out all the equipment and . . .'

Skye's heart went out to her godmother as she continued the list of jobs she had to do; she sounded completely overwhelmed. 'I'll be there tomorrow,' she promised. 'We can work it all out together.'

Liz sighed, 'You're a lifesaver.'

'Not at all.' Skye smiled. In fact, she had a feeling it might be the other way around.

They ended the call and Skye turned back to see her dad approaching, eyebrows raised and his thumb up as if checking she was OK.

He said you'd be perfect for the job.

OK, it was hardly the most complicated job in the world, but who cared. She smiled and stuck her own thumb up in reply. This had worked out brilliantly.

Chapter Six

Clare

Clare waited under the porch with Ivy in her arms, glad of the shade to protect her daughter's delicate skin from the sun. It was Saturday afternoon and she'd made a pitstop at her dad's house on the way to Salcombe.

She was in dire need of the loo and Ivy had just woken up, hot and clammy from the two-hour car journey. From the smell of her, she was ready for a clean nappy too. Clare predicted that she had about two minutes before Ivy started to complain vociferously about the situation.

She deliberately hadn't called ahead in case her dad had fobbed her off and said he was busy. She'd pretty much given up trying to call him for a chat. He was invariably tied up when she rang and would terminate the call as quickly as possible, which left her feeling rejected. She'd been delighted when he'd actually called *her* recently, until he confessed that he'd called her by accident because her name was stored alphabetically next to 'cleaner' in his phone.

Hence she'd decided to drop in unannounced. Although, of course, it might backfire if no one was at home. At this point, she'd be happy for anyone to answer the door.

'This is Grandad's house, Ivy, remember?' she murmured, kissing her daughter's warm cheek. 'Posh, isn't it?'

Mike and Nilla's residence in Exeter was a far cry from the tiny, terraced house Mike had co-owned with Jen. It had been sold once her parents divorced and Jen had rented a succession of houses ever since. Mike, however, had ploughed his money into bricks and mortar and had successfully ascended the property ladder. This one was a handsome Victorian house with an in-and-out driveway and a separate servants' annexe, which now functioned as Mike's office.

Clare had never fully understood what her dad did. Something to do with finding investors for businesses which needed funding, and getting a fee for doing so. A financial matchmaker basically. Whatever he did, he seemed to be good at it.

She knew someone was in because the sound of Smokey Robinson was drifting out from one of the open first-floor windows. That had to be her dad.

She had a sudden flashback to being jammed into the back of Dad's old Triumph Spitfire, which Mum used to joke was held together with rust, her parents up front with the top down and wind in their hair, singing 'I Second That Emotion' at the tops of their voices. A happy memory, she thought, smiling. How she wished those days had gone on forever.

As soon as the music stopped, Clare quickly rapped on the door as loudly as she could and then finished with a double ring on the doorbell before the next song began.

It was another minute before the door opened and there was Mike, wearing an unbuttoned linen shirt and a short towel wrapped around his hips. His hair was wet and he was smiling, teeth bright white against tanned skin.

'Sorry, I was . . . Oh, Clare!' He looked furtively over her shoulder and down the drive as if checking there was no one else there. 'And the baby. How lovely!'

The baby. For goodness' sake, was it too much to ask for him to use her name?

She stepped forward and kissed his cheek.

'Surprise!' She did her best not to take the lacklustre welcome to heart. 'We thought we'd pop in on the way down to Salcombe.'

'Salcombe.' Mike's face slackened and he rubbed a hand through his wet hair. Clare thought she heard him swear under his breath. 'Ah, yes, I'd forgotten.'

'Say hello to Grandad, Ivy!' said Clare.

But Ivy had gone shy and buried her head into her mum's shoulder.

'Hello, Ivy, nice to see you,' said Mike, with forced jollity, taking the little girl's hand and waggling it.

Clare managed not to roll her eyes. 'She's your grand-daughter, Dad, not a client.'

'I'm aware of that.' He frowned. 'But I'm not about to start talking like an imbecile to her just because she's small.'

'Fair enough.' She couldn't abide that either; all that coochy-coo stuff. 'But I draw the line at shaking her hand.'

'Point taken. And sorry I kept you waiting, there's no one else in and I was in the shower.' He gestured down at the towel.

She shrugged. 'It's fine, I was enjoying the music. It reminded me of Mum. She loved Smokey Robinson, didn't she?'

He looked at her blankly. 'Can't remember.'

'You must do,' she insisted. 'That's why we played "You Are Forever" at her funeral.'

'Possibly,' he said vaguely.

She suppressed a sigh. Getting her dad to talk about her mum since her death was impossible. Clare understood that he and her mum had divorced twenty-something years ago, but surely he could go through the motions of bereavement, if only for her benefit? It did Clare good to speak about her mum.

'Are you coming in, or . . .?' He raised an enquiring eyebrow and Clare had a suspicion that he hoped the answer was 'or'.

'We are,' she said, brightly. 'I need to get Ivy's changing bag from the car first. Will you hold her?'

'Absolutely.' He held his hands out. 'Come to Mike.'

She gave him a look. '*Grandad*, you mean.'

'Of course I do.' He took hold of Ivy and she stared at him solemnly, her blue-green eyes wide and her little mouth pursed.

Clare dashed back to the car, smiling to herself. So far, so good. Getting her dad to hold Ivy was all part of her plan to get them to bond. Ivy was his first grandchild, that had to make her special in his eyes. And Ivy was adorable, even the stoniest heart would fall in love with her.

She retrieved the bag, slammed the car door and looked back to the porch. Mike was holding Ivy at arm's-length, his nose screwed up in disgust.

'Bloody hell, she absolutely reeks.'

'Welcome to Ivy's world,' Clare said with a snort. 'All part of being a grandad, I'm afraid. And watch your language. I don't want her first word to be rude.'

He grunted and handed her back. 'Come in, make yourself at home, while I go and get dressed.'

Clare headed straight to the downstairs bathroom, sorted herself and Ivy out, and then waited for him in the sunlit kitchen. Everywhere was spotless; he'd obviously managed to get hold of the cleaner eventually after calling her by mistake.

'Right.' He reappeared in shorts, his shirt partially buttoned up, and clapped his hands together. 'Hot drink or cold? I'm going to have kombucha. Good for the gut.'

Dad and his fads. She couldn't help admiring his quest for eternal youth, remembering his morning wheatgrass shot phase and the aloe vera one before that.

'Normal tea, a splash of milk please.' She tipped out a few toys to keep Ivy occupied while he made it.

'How's life at school?' He dropped a teabag into a mug and filled it from his fancy boiling-water tap. 'Enjoying being top dog?'

'Oh yes,' she said, unable to keep a note of pride out of her voice. 'Youngest head teacher the school has ever had.'

'I knew you'd thrive. A lot of people would have found it tough, being a single parent and holding down a big job. But not you. Never needed anyone's help, have you?'

'Nope.' Just as well, really, she thought darkly, seeing as Mum had passed away and he'd been of very little use since walking out on them both. Determined not to ruin the mood, she changed the subject. 'So where is everyone?'

'Nilla is in Copenhagen with her mother.' He stirred her tea and removed the bag before pouring himself a glass of kombucha from the fridge. 'And Skye is . . . um . . . not here right now.'

He placed a mug in front of her and she blew on it, desperate for a sip. 'Shame. I was hoping to introduce her to Ivy. Oh well, I'm sure I'll see her soon.'

Mike choked on his kombucha. 'Quite possibly.'

Before he could sit down, Ivy scooted closer to him and held her hands out to him. 'Uh-uh!'

'Oh look! She wants a cuddle with her grandad.' Clare's heart gave a lurch. How could he fail to be moved by that?

'Being a grandad makes me feel ancient,' he grumbled. 'It makes me think of my own dad.'

'For heaven's sake. It's time you stopped being in denial about it, your granddaughter is almost one!' she said, irritably. 'It was hard for me getting used to being a mother, especially without Mum around to help. She would have been completely head over heels in love with Ivy. But she's gone. So Ivy needs you to step up; *we* need you. You're the only family we've got.'

'Sorry.' Mike said sheepishly. He picked up Ivy and jiggled her up and down. 'I'm just not used to babies.'

And who's fault is that? Clare stopped herself from saying. She could count the occasions he'd made the effort to visit on one hand.

She checked the time, wondering whether to stay for another hour or so and feed Ivy here or get on the road now and feed her once they got to Salcombe.

Mike must have spotted the gesture because he handed Ivy straight over to her. 'Well, no doubt you're keen to get on with your journey. Don't let me hold you up.'

'You're not holding us up,' she said flatly. 'But we'll get out of your way as soon as I've drunk my tea.'

She waited for him to contradict her, but he took another swig of his kombucha and nodded. 'Good idea.'

'Fine,' she muttered and gulped down her tea as quickly as she could.

Clare packed Ivy's toys away while Mike rinsed her mug in the sink. She planned on taking the full nappy sack with her, but with a sudden burst of defiance, she quickly stuffed it in the kitchen bin. That'd teach him to say his darling granddaughter reeked.

'Let me take a photo of the two of you together,' said Clare, once they were back outside on the front porch.

'Yes, do, I didn't have any pictures of me with my grandparents,' he said. 'They were dead before I came along. At least, Ivy will have one of me to look back on when I'm gone.'

Clare snorted. 'You're not going anywhere. You're in great shape.'

Mike puffed out his chest, looking pleased. 'Do you think?'

'For a grandad,' she added with a smirk. 'And, to be honest, I thought *you* might like to have the photo, to show Ivy off to your friends, rather than the other way round.'

Mike blinked. 'I meant that as well.'

'Course you did.' She flashed him a knowing look, but he was too busy adjusting his hair and checking that his collar was smooth.

She took a selection of pictures and showed him. He made her delete a couple of them because his eyes were half closed, but once he'd found one that he was happy with, she sent it to him. As she went to put the phone back in her bag, a text flashed up on the screen from Liz.

Hello, gorgeous girl! What's your ETA? There's a cream tea with your name on it waiting for you. We can't wait to see you, we're going to have a wonderful summer, I promise! Xxx

Now that was a proper welcome. Clare grinned: good old Liz. She was suddenly desperate to leave her dad's house and be with Liz, with whom she had a far less complicated relationship. The reference to 'we' was a bit weird though. But she pushed it to the back of her mind, she'd be there soon enough.

'Message from Liz.' She held up the phone for Mike to read it. He pushed her hand further away to focus on the small text. 'She's got company by the look of it.'

'Really?' Mike gave a dry cough. 'Lovely. Off you pop then.'

'All right! Keep your wig on.' Clare opened the passenger door and dropped her bags on the seat.

'I've got very thick hair,' he said indignantly, his hand flying to his head. 'I'm . . .'

He didn't finish the sentence because a small delivery van with the logo of a cider brand plastered all over it pulled into the drive at speed and came to a halt alongside Clare's car. The driver's door opened, and a girl sprang out wearing denim shorts and a T-shirt with the cider logo on it.

'Delivery for Mikey!' she sang.

'*Mikey?*' Clare snorted. 'You're kidding me?'

Mike ignored her and sucked in his stomach. 'Hey, great to see you again. I've been looking forward to getting my hands on some more of this cider.'

Clare gave him a sideways look. So that was who he'd been expecting when she arrived. Judging by the way he was preening his hair, he looked more interested in the driver than the cider. He was probably even older than the girl's father. *Men.*

'Right,' she said, in disgust. 'We're off.'

'Yes, yes. Good idea. See you again soon.' Mike attempted to kiss her cheek, but Clare bent down to strap Ivy into the car seat and dodged him.

'Say goodbye to *Grandad*, Ivy,' said Clare, loudly.

'No way!' The girl's eyes widened as Mike's narrowed. 'You don't look old enough to be a grandad.'

Mike set his shoulders back. 'Kind of you to say. I don't feel it either.'

Clare growled under her breath. *Judas.*

'Ooh, am I in your way?' the girl said sweetly, glancing at where she'd abandoned her van.

'Not at all,' said Clare, plastering on a smile as she got into the car.

She looked over her shoulder as she reversed past the van and spotted Mike with his hand on the small of the younger woman's back. *But I am clearly in yours.*

Chapter Seven

Liz

Liz was having major regrets, she'd made a terrible mistake; having Clare and Skye here together had disaster written all over it.

As time ticked on, she was getting more and more hot and sweaty about Clare's imminent arrival. She would have had a glass of wine to take the edge off, but it was still early, and if she had one, she'd want another. She drank some cold water instead and shuddered as it hit her stomach.

The oven timer buzzed and she rushed to take the scones out. They looked perfect: evenly risen and golden brown on top. At least she'd got something right.

She was kicking herself for not telling Clare personally about Skye. It was Liz's house, after all; she was the one who'd invited Clare to spend the summer here. Come to Salcombe as soon as you can, she'd said. It'll be just you, me and Ivy, she'd said.

But now it wouldn't be just the three of them and Liz hadn't let Clare know. Because Mike had said he would do it and she'd been happy to leave that particular nettle for him to grasp. Why had she given him such an important task? He had all the tact of Donald Trump. She was a coward, that was why. A total coward.

Liz transferred the scones to a cooling rack, burning her fingers but too distracted to find a spatula.

And then there was Skye, whom she'd been lying to ever since she'd arrived at Clemency House this morning with a travel-worn rucksack and a big happy smile.

'Clare will be thrilled to have you here,' Liz had declared. 'She's been looking after a baby on her own for almost a year – believe me, she'll be glad of an extra pair of hands.'

What had possessed her to say all that? She had no one to blame for this deception but herself. And Mike, of course. Causing havoc in her life again.

'They smell amazing.' Skye's voice startled her; she wasn't used to having another person in the house. 'You're making my stomach rumble.'

Skye had spent the last hour at the dining table on her laptop learning about the business. She was trawling through The Seaside Gourmet Girls' website, clicking on every picture, reading past menus and jotting notes on a pad. With her blonde hair tied up in a coloured scarf, her deep suntan and bare feet tucked underneath her, she looked like she'd walked straight off a beach in Bali. She could be nineteen, thought Liz fondly, not twenty-nine.

'It's our little tradition,' Liz replied. 'Jen and I always had a cream tea ready for Clare when she arrived. I didn't know whether to do it or not, now that her mum's not here. But in the end I thought it would be worse if I didn't.'

'I'm sure she'll appreciate it. It's nice that you've got your special things,' Skye said with a touch of wistfulness.

Liz could have bitten her tongue off for being so insensitive. She and Skye had no special things. Skye hadn't even visited her here very often. More cowardly behaviour on her part, Liz acknowledged.

Even though Jen had been happy for Liz to be Skye's godmother, it felt a bit like rubbing Mike's infidelity in Jen's face by inviting Skye to stay with her in Salcombe. Even more so once Jen had moved down here from Bath and they had started up in business together. Clare had spent all her holidays here and had helped them out in the summer when she was a student. It had always been Clare's place rather than Skye's.

And although Liz had stayed friends with Mike when he'd married for a second and then a third time, she'd never been friendly with the new wives. All of which added up to Liz having a far stronger bond with her first god-daughter.

Still, Liz had the next few weeks to make it up to her; she'd show Skye that she was every bit as welcome at Clemency House as Clare was.

Liz opened the fridge to take out the butter, it would be soft for spreading on the scones. Her eye fell on the bottle of wine which she'd opened last night. She almost salivated at the sight of it. A cold, crisp mouthful of Pinot Grigio would be just the thing to steady her nerves. She checked to see that Skye was still facing the other way and unscrewed the lid. Just as she took a swig, the business mobile began to buzz. Liz choked as the wine went down the wrong way and almost dropped the bottle in her haste to get it back into the fridge.

Skye leapt to her feet, picked up the phone from the kitchen island and thumped Liz on the back. 'You OK?'

Liz nodded. 'You answer it,' she said with a croaky voice.

Since she'd charged up the business phone yesterday, calls had been coming through steadily all day.

Hard to believe that only twenty-four hours had gone by since she'd been in touch with Viv to say she was open for bookings. Viv had been delighted to be able to offer Liz's services again and had even given her a booking for Monday for a last-minute dinner party.

Viv had also promised that an email would be going out to all her holiday renters immediately, signposting them to The Seaside Gourmet Girls. Fast-forward to this afternoon and the diary was already filling up.

'And on a personal note,' Viv had added before ringing off, 'it's good to have you back. Jen would be proud.'

Which had had Liz's eyes brimming with tears.

'OK, here goes.' Skye cleared her throat before accepting the call. 'The Seaside Gourmet Girls, can I help you?'

Liz listened with half an ear, while Skye gave a hesitant rundown of the services they offered. Skye was a sweet girl and so thrilled at the prospect of working for her over the summer that Liz wished she'd thought to offer her the job herself, instead of entering into a clandestine arrangement with Mike.

Not that there had even been a job before Mike had dropped his bombshell, of course.

'Hold the line please,' said Skye politely, before putting her hand over the phone to muffle it. 'Liz, are we taking bookings for Christmas?'

'Heaven forbid,' Liz blurted out.

'So is that a no?' Skye looked at her unsurely.

Yesterday, Liz hadn't even been sure she wanted to carry on with the business this summer, let alone through the winter. She wasn't ready to think that far ahead.

'I'm planning on taking some time off over Christmas. So the answer is no, not at the moment.'

'Got it,' said Skye. 'Hello? Unfortunately we . . .'

Liz walked through the open sliding glass doors and onto the terrace, leaving Skye to finish the call.

Twenty thousand pounds by September.

Not turnover, profit. To be taken out of the business bank account and handed over to Mike. Liz felt sick every time she thought about it. She sat down at one of the wrought-iron chairs, but instead of looking out over Salcombe and across the water as she usually did, she gazed up at her beautiful home, passed down to her from her parents after her mum died.

Clemency House was arranged over a whopping four storeys, set into a sharp slope and sandwiched between two streets. From the front, it was nothing remarkable: a pretty, if modest, residence comprising a ground and first floor. But at the rear, the view of the property was quite different. Terraced gardens, balconies, a *Juliet* balcony and, finally, tucked under the eaves and taking up the whole of the top floor was the master suite. It was a spectacular home and Liz had had to pinch herself to believe her good fortune on many an occasion.

It was far too big for one, of course, and she lived almost entirely on this floor where the kitchen was, but it was her family home, and full of happy memories. She couldn't imagine living anywhere else.

She could take out a small mortgage, she supposed, to pay Mike off. But at sixty-two Liz would rather not be in debt to anyone if she could help it.

And besides, there was professional pride at stake. The Seaside Gourmet Girls had been a good little business. Mike's money had gone towards investing in good-quality equipment, renting a lock-up to store it in and buying a van which Liz still had. They'd never considered that Mike would want to be repaid.

Jen's theory had been that it was guilt money. She had supported Mike throughout their marriage while he was building his business and not earning a bean. Since the divorce, Mike had gone on to make heaps of money. As far as Jen was concerned, Mike investing in The Seaside Gourmet Girls was his way of making amends.

But Jen had been wrong.

'Sorry,' Skye whispered from the doorway, phone in one hand and diary in the other. 'It's another enquiry and I can't answer her questions. Can we do a dinner party for six and can we cater for vegans?'

'Yes and yes,' Liz confirmed. 'There are sample menus on the website.' She pulled a face, remembering how out of date they were. 'Actually, ignore them, say that prices start at twenty-five pounds per person.'

Skye repeated the information to the customer and waited, crossing her fingers, while whoever was on the other end of the phone presumably weighed up the cost. This was the bit Liz didn't like. It was all she could do not to jump in and drop the price. Jen had been great at it. She'd hold her nerve, add in some little detail that would have the customer eating out of her hand and paying a large deposit then and there.

Skye ended the call, looking deflated. 'I thought that was going to be my first booking, but the woman said she'll think about it.'

'You did well,' said Liz. 'And if the price puts them off, then so be it; if we can't make a profit, it's not worth taking on the job.'

'A vegan dinner party.' Skye whistled, as she took a seat next to her. 'If it wasn't for cheese, I could go vegan.'

Liz chuckled. 'If it wasn't for alcohol, I could go teetotal. Not going to happen, is it?'

They looked at each other and laughed and Liz felt a flush of happiness. This house had been so quiet and joyless for so long. Maybe that was about to change. She hoped so.

A movement down on the narrow street far below caught her eye. She stood and leaned against the glass balcony for a better view. 'That's Clare's car! They're here!'

Liz waved just as Clare noticed them and waved back and Liz's heart lifted. Looking at Clare was like looking at a young Jen. The women were so similar: flashy-eyed and fiercely self-sufficient, although motherhood had smoothed off the rough edges from both of them.

'Let's run down and help her unload,' said Liz, heading for the steps.

Skye hung back. 'Should I wait here, let you say hello by yourself?'

Liz appreciated the gesture but shook her head. 'Let's both go. She'll be dying to introduce you to your niece.'

'Half-niece,' Skye said under her breath, sounding unconvinced.

Liz reached the bottom of the steps as her eldest god-daughter climbed out of her car and stretched.

'Hello, darling!' Liz wrapped her arms around the young woman who she loved as much as if she'd given birth to her herself. 'Welcome back! It is so lovely to see you.'

'You too.' Clare returned Liz's hug and they held each other tight for a moment, before Clare peeled away and opened the rear door. 'I've missed you, Liz. I've been telling Ivy all about the lovely things we're going to do, just the three of us. Bored her rigid, as you can see.'

Liz leaned round Clare to see little Ivy sleeping soundly; her heart squeezed. 'The little angel, she has grown so much.'

Jen would have whipped her granddaughter out of that car seat and cuddled her immediately. Liz'd just have to love Ivy enough for both of them.

Clare grinned proudly. 'I know. And that's just since Easter. I have to warn you, she's very vocal these days.'

Liz laughed. 'I can't imagine where she gets that from.'

'Oi!' Clare pretended to look insulted as she looped her handbag over her shoulder. 'Her grandmother, obviously. Although I was looking at a photo of her and—'

She stopped mid-sentence and stared, as Skye came into view, hanging back on the bottom step.

'Hey, Clare!' said Skye, giving her half-sister a shy wave.

'Skye?' Clare smiled stiffly. 'I wasn't expecting to see you!'

Liz stifled a groan. 'Didn't your dad phone and tell you Skye would be here?'

'Nope.' Clare looked from Liz to Skye and back again. 'But there again, neither did you.'

Liz felt her face flood with heat. 'He wanted to be the one to tell you.'

Clare gave a harsh laugh. 'Well, he must have changed his mind because I've just come from his house, he never said a word. Just said that Skye was out.'

'Out of sight, out of mind probably,' said Skye.

'Nonsense,' said Liz, noting her flat tone. 'He'd never forget you – *either* of you.'

'If it's any consolation,' said Clare, 'I got the impression I wasn't welcome.'

'That can't be true,' said Skye. 'He talks about you all the time. You can do no wrong in his eyes.'

'Except exist,' Clare scoffed.

Oh Mike, thought Liz, disappointed. He'd promised. Two wonderful daughters and he managed to make them both feel bad about themselves.

'Anyway.' Skye gave a weak smile. 'It doesn't matter now. It's great to see you and I can't wait to meet Ivy.'

'You won't have long to wait,' said Liz, as Ivy opened her eyes and let out a loud wail.

Clare bent down to lift the baby out of her car seat.

'OK, darling, we're here. Sh-sh-sh.' She kissed the top of Ivy's head and, with the baby in her arms, she walked towards Skye. 'It's been a long time.'

Liz held her breath as she watched the half-sisters hug.

'Hello, little one.' The tension on Skye's face dissolved as Ivy touched Skye's armful of bracelets. She wiggled her arm, making them jingle, and Ivy's face softened into a shy smile. 'She's beautiful.'

'She is,' Clare agreed. 'Ivy meet Skye.'

Liz exhaled with relief. So far, so good.

'Uh-uh,' Ivy babbled, holding both arms out to Skye.

'Oh, look!' Skye beamed. 'She wants to come to me. May I?'

'I'll carry her up the stairs, if you don't mind,' said Clare, tightening her grip on the little girl. 'Maybe you could get her high chair from the boot? And her changing bag next to her car seat?'

'Oh. Sure.' Skye looked deflated. 'No problem.'

'Probably not a bad idea, in that long skirt,' said Liz, quick to excuse Clare's blunt rebuttal. 'You might trip over. I'll bring one of the other bags.'

'These steps are lethal,' Clare added, pulling a suitcase out of the boot. 'You wait until it's dark.'

'I have been here before, you know,' Skye said lightly. 'And let me take that one, it looks heavy.'

'I can manage,' said Clare. 'I'm used to it. We live in a top-floor flat, and I had to load the car up by myself.'

'But you're not by yourself here,' Liz intervened, taking the case off her. 'So let me.'

Between them, they managed to get most of Clare and Ivy's luggage into the house in one trip. The rest could wait, Clare told them. She lowered the baby onto the tiled floor, and everyone laughed as she crawled straight to the toy box in the corner and pulled herself up to delve inside it.

'She remembers where the toys are!' Liz exclaimed. 'She's made herself at home already.'

'It always feels like home to me,' said Clare, giving her another hug.

'Well,' Liz swallowed the lump in her throat, 'that's the nicest thing anyone's said to me for a long time.' Out of the corner of her eye, she saw Skye hovering awkwardly, so she released Clare and bustled over to the kitchen. 'Now, who's for tea and scones?'

'Me,' said Skye, steering Liz to an armchair. 'But let me do it, you've been on your feet since I arrived.'

'Me too, please. I had to gulp down the drink Dad made me, he was so desperate for us to go,' Clare said. 'I'll just pop some things upstairs in my room first.'

'Actually, darling,' Liz replied, feeling at a disadvantage now that she was sitting down. The atmosphere was so fragile; she hoped everyone would relax soon. 'I've put Skye in your usual room. You and Ivy are at the back away from the road noise. I thought it might be quieter for you.'

Clare looked confused. 'She's staying the night?'

'But if it's a problem, I don't mind swapping rooms,' Skye added.

'No need,' Clare shrugged. 'This is a first, Skye. We've never been at Liz's at the same time as each other. And I must admit I'd like to hear about Uganda and your mysterious return.'

'Not that mysterious,' Skye laughed uneasily. 'And I'm here longer than a night.'

'Skye is staying for six weeks,' Liz said breezily. 'So I've got both my god-daughters for the summer. Aren't I lucky?'

'Gosh!' Clare's eyes widened.

'But don't worry, I won't be in the way of your holiday, I'm here to work,' Skye assured her.

'You've got a job? Amazing. Doing what?' Clare asked.

'Um . . .' Skye looked to Liz for help. 'A bit of everything, I think – admin, waitressing, food prep, isn't that right?'

'Exactly,' said Liz, bouncing to her feet as the kettle came to the boil. 'To help me get through silly season.'

Oh lord, thought Liz, as Clare froze and the smile slipped from her face. Liz hadn't seen her like this since she'd found out that Mike and Frankie had bought Skye a brand-new car for her eighteenth birthday, while she'd inherited Jen's ancient Volvo which stank of fish.

'Skye is going to join The Seaside Gourmet Girls?' Clare said in a low voice. 'You've replaced *Mum* with *Skye*?'

'No, darling,' Liz exclaimed, horrified. 'It's not like that.'

'It bloody well sounds like it.' Clare folded her arms.

'The summer has suddenly become very busy and I can't manage by myself. I needed someone who I could trust and Skye needed a job.'

'You could have asked me! I've worked for you and Mum before, remember? I know what I'm doing. I'd have been a much better choice.'

'No offence taken,' Skye mumbled, turning her back on the conversation to make the tea.

Liz groaned; this wasn't going at all well. 'You're not here to work, you're on holiday. With a baby. Ivy can't be anywhere near clients' kitchens. It would invalidate our insurance.'

Crikey, that was a thought. Did she even have valid professional indemnity insurance anymore? Another job for the list. Liz was feeling more flustered by the second.

'You didn't even mention you needed help,' said Clare, sadly. 'Or that you were really busy. I had no idea.'

Liz's throat tightened. She'd needed help for a long time, not necessarily with the business, but with life in general. She'd been too ashamed to admit how badly she was coping, when everyone around her had their own issues to deal with.

'I'm sorry,' she said wearily. 'It's all come to a head recently.'

'Maybe I should leave,' said Skye. 'I don't want to cause any trouble.'

'Please stay,' Liz pleaded. 'I can't run the business by myself and even if I could, I don't want to. If you leave now, I'll have to cancel the bookings we've taken, and I can't afford to do that.'

'It's fine,' said Clare with a sigh. 'Ivy and I will go. Skye is obviously needed and we'll just be in the way. The last thing you need is more guests.'

'Nobody needs to leave.' Liz rubbed a hand across her forehead. This was not quite the bonding experience she had envisaged. Bloody Mike. Why had she trusted him with such a sensitive job?

Because he'd reeled her in, that's why. Because no matter how many times he let her down, she still fell for his charms. How many things would she let him ruin before she finally gave up on him?

She was a bloody fool.

'OK, how about this as a suggestion. I'll work for you as agreed,' said Skye, 'but I'll move out and rent somewhere close by. Then Clare can have her *own* room.'

'You're not being paid enough to live anywhere else. That's not part of the deal,' Liz cried. 'And you're welcome *here*.'

'Why isn't she being paid enough?' Clare frowned. 'I thought you were super busy?'

Skye scowled at her half-sister. 'What has it got to do with you how much my wages are? We all know I was never going to be earning as much as *clever Clare*.'

'SHUT UP.' Liz slammed her hand down on the kitchen island, making everyone jump. 'Stop arguing! What about what I want? Anyone thought about that? Just for once will someone stop to consider me? I've been stuck in the middle of this family for years and I'm sick of it.'

A moment of silence followed; even Ivy stopped banging a wooden hammer into the skirting board. Liz burst into tears.

'What's going on? Tell me,' Clare said softly, moving closer to her. 'I don't think I've ever heard you yell that loud. Let me help.'

'Tell *us*,' Skye corrected. 'And then we can *both* help.'

Clare let out a faint sigh at her half-sister's comment.

Liz mopped her tears with the sleeve of her cardigan. 'It's your dad. He gave us some money when we started the business. But now he wants it back and I haven't got it.'

'Dad?' both women exclaimed.

'I didn't know he'd lent you money.' Clare looked put out.

Me neither, thought Liz, but she was reluctant to tell the girls the details. It was between her and Mike.

'We needed help at the time, and borrowing from Mike was the quickest and cheapest way to get us up and running.' She said. 'Now he needs the cash for something and I've got six weeks to find twenty thousand pounds.'

'I can't believe he'd do such a thing,' Clare whispered, pressing a hand to her mouth.

'I had no idea he was short of cash.' Skye looked bewildered.

'He told me in confidence,' Liz said, realising her mistake. 'You mustn't let on that you know.'

'OK.' Clare inhaled a deep breath. 'How much money have you got right now?'

Liz's stomach flipped; time to face the music. 'The business bank account is at its overdraft limit, but if we ignore that, zero pounds.'

'Oh *dear*.' Skye winced. 'That is bad.'

'To put it mildly,' Clare snorted. 'Does Dad know you can't pay it back?'

'He knows he's set me a challenge, but he sees this as the kick-start I need to get my mojo back.' She blew out a breath, thinking that her mojo had probably gone for good.

'And you don't want to fail him,' Clare murmured almost under her breath. 'That sounds familiar.'

'Surely if you explained the situation, Dad would back off,' Skye said. 'He isn't a monster.'

'Maybe not,' Liz replied, remembering his off-the-cuff comment about solicitors. 'But I do owe him, and he generally gets what he wants.'

'Yep, that's Dad all right,' Clare quipped.

Liz felt like such a fool. 'The awful thing is that I haven't catered for any party greater than four since Jen died.'

'You could do it in your sleep,' Clare assured her. 'You're a brilliant cook.'

'And I'm a quick learner,' Skye put in.

Liz looked at them with a rush of gratitude; they were so full of faith. More tears slid down her face. She let the girls lead her back to the chair.

'I've let Jen down terribly,' she groaned. 'I don't think we're even insured anymore. She'd be appalled if she could see how I've let things slide without her.'

'Nah,' said Clare, 'she was never bothered about money. But she'd be sad that you've let it get you down.'

'We can smash this, you know,' said Skye, crouching beside her. 'If Clare doesn't mind working on her holiday, between the three of us – four counting Ivy – I have every faith we can do it.'

As if on cue, Ivy crawled over to join them, still holding the wooden hammer, and hoisted herself up using Liz's legs.

'Hello, darling.' Liz gave Ivy a watery smile and took her soft, pudgy hand in hers. 'I've been quite lonely, so having all of you here at Clemency House is wonderful for me. But this enforced proximity for you two—'

'We'll work it out,' said Clare, interrupting her. She picked up Ivy and sniffed her nappy before setting her in Liz's lap. 'And you were right about keeping Ivy away from the clients' kitchens, very sensible. But I can do other stuff – take bookings, do the invoices, go food shopping even.'

'Are you sure?' Liz said doubtfully, turning Ivy round to face her. 'This is supposed to be your holiday, after all.'

Clare thought about it for a moment. 'It'll make me feel close to Mum and that'll make me happy.'

'That's settled then,' said Skye. 'Dad will have that money back in his bank account before you can say—'

'Good grief, is that the time? Must be off,' Clare mimicked Mike's jovial tone perfectly, making them all laugh. She handed Ivy a cardboard book and ruffled her hair. 'Right. I think I'll take charge of the teapot, Skye, or it'll be time for bed.'

'Sorry.' Skye got up from her position on the floor. 'I'll do the scones.'

'Thank you,' said Liz, feeling close to tears again. 'Thank you both.'

'Don't thank me just yet,' Skye confided in a whisper.

'I've never worked in the catering industry before; I'm probably going to be terrible.'

This is what she needed, thought Liz, watching the young women find their way around her kitchen, while in her lap, Ivy babbled to herself, as if reading a story. Life. People to love and look after. And people to care about her.

The Seaside Gourmet Girls might only have one summer left, but she had to make this work. She just had to.

Chapter Eight

Skye

The shrill call of seagulls pulled Skye from sleep the following morning. Despite a very comfortable bed and pillows as soft as clouds, she hadn't slept well. It had been difficult to fully switch off after the events of yesterday and, when she'd finally dropped off to sleep, Ivy had cried out and she'd woken up again with a start. Still, at least she hadn't had to get up and see to her, unlike Clare.

Skye reached for her phone to check the time. Six a.m. Kampala was two hours ahead; everyone would be up and getting on with the day. Jesse would probably be on a weekend trip with the volunteers, ensuring the young people who worked at the Hope Foundation got to see as much of the country as possible while the school was closed for the weekend.

Her stomach fluttered with homesickness, and she scrolled through her phone until she found their conversation thread and typed a new message.

Morning! Just woken up and was thinking about you. Hope all is going well without me? X

She bit her lip, waiting for a reply. She was breaking their agreement by getting in touch. She'd left Uganda because she needed time and space away, to work out what she wanted from the next however many years of her life without someone pushing her for an answer. Fine in theory, but after being together twenty-four/seven, living under the same roof and working side by side for the charity, having no contact was much harder than she'd envisaged.

Jesse is typing appeared on her screen and her heart thumped in anticipation.

> I thought we said no messages!? Not that I'm complaining. All good here, just the usual dramas: a couple of upset stomachs and a lost passport! Dembe says hello and that your Ugandan family misses you. We all miss you. Especially me, J xx

Skye heaved a sigh of relief at Jesse's easy-going response and smiled to herself. Most of the volunteers were aged eighteen to twenty-two and regardless of how many warnings they got about the dangers of too much sun, or getting carried away with alcohol, there were always casualties. She sent her love, finished with two kisses and switched off her phone. They were fine without her, of course they were, and in the meantime, she had her own family to deal with.

She rolled out of bed and tiptoed quietly downstairs to the kitchen. There wasn't a peep from anyone else and she didn't want to disturb them. She was greeted by the smell of last night's fish and chips from the empty takeaway cartons stacked by the bin. Opening the sliding glass doors, she stepped out into the fresh air. The decking was cold under her bare feet, the chairs were covered in dew and too wet to sit on. Instead, she leaned on the steel handrail and gazed down at the pale grey rooftops of Salcombe and the water beyond.

What an unexpected turn of events, she mused, closing her eyes briefly and tilting her face to the early-morning sun. She'd gone from living and working with Jesse to living and working with her godmother in the space of just a few weeks. And now she faced the prospect of spending more time with her prickly half-sister than she'd ever done in her life.

Skye got it: Clare had been expecting her and Ivy to be the sole focus of Liz's attention. She was a new single mum who was bound to be still grieving for her own mother; she was probably desperate not only for a holiday, but for some maternal comfort. Skye was prepared to cut her some slack for all of that. But Clare was like a tiger around Ivy; every time Skye went near her, Clare found a reason to whisk her away. She'd offered to help at bath time, but by the look of indignation Clare had given her, anyone would have thought she'd suggested putting the baby on the barbecue. And her face when Liz had said she'd been given a different bedroom to usual – Clare had some serious resentment issues going on.

Once Ivy had gone to bed, things hadn't improved much. After takeaway fish and chips – another first-day tradition to which Skye had been introduced – they'd sat outside watching the sun go down. Liz had opened a bottle of cava and relaxed once she had a drink in her hand. Clare not so much; she was paranoid that the baby monitor wasn't picking up Ivy's movements on the floor above and kept running up and down the stairs to check on her. Skye had offered to go for her a couple of times, but Clare wasn't having any of it, so she'd stopped asking.

Liz's drinking was a surprise. Skye had even seen her swig straight from a wine bottle yesterday afternoon when she'd thought no one was watching. And there were two empty cava bottles next to the sink this morning. She knew for a fact that Clare had only had one glass because she was still breastfeeding and Skye wasn't a big drinker. Liz must have drunk the rest. Not a good sign.

Then there was the issue of Dad demanding money off Liz. Something felt odd about that. Surely if he was strapped for cash, he could raise it in a way that didn't put his oldest friend under pressure?

Anyway, the long and short of it was that being in Salcombe for the summer didn't feel quite the opportunity it had done when Liz had offered her the job on Friday night.

It was beautiful here, but . . . Skye sighed, watching a yacht glide through the water, leaving ripples in its wake . . . Should she stay, help Liz as promised, or go home and leave Clare to enjoy the holiday she'd expected? If she left now, she could be back in Exeter in just over an hour. She could apply for that job at the Night Market she'd seen instead to earn some money for the summer and then she could . . . what? Do what exactly?

She was almost thirty years old. Wasn't life supposed to be sorted by now? At some point, she was going to have to stop running away and make a choice.

A sudden gust of chilly air sent her back inside; she shut the sliding doors, flopped into a chair and tucked her feet beneath her.

Growing up with two warring parents might have had something to do with her habit of running. She'd left home at eighteen to do Media Studies at university. That hadn't been her first choice, but with her poor A-level results, she was just grateful for an offer. *You should have applied yourself harder*, Dad had said, *like Clare, she had her pick of universities*. (Clare had got straight As, natch.) Skye had

77

finally dropped out of university, after trying two different courses. Dad had all but laughed and said that he'd expected as much, which had made her feel even more of a failure.

She imagined his face if she turned up at his house this morning. 'Back again?' he'd smirk. 'That didn't last long.'

Well, not this time. She wasn't going to leave. She might be feeling as welcome as steak at a vegan barbecue, and she might be absolutely terrible as an upmarket caterer's assistant, but she wasn't going to give up. It was time to show Mike what she was made of. If he wanted his money out of the business by the end of summer, she'd make it happen.

Skye pushed herself off the chair with a burst of determination. She intended to get straight on with it. And she knew just where to start.

She ran upstairs, washed and dressed as quietly as she could and, once back down in the kitchen, picked up the keys to the lock-up and the business phone and slipped out of the house.

It was still early, but Salcombe was coming to life: shutters opening on shopfronts, the buttery smell of fresh pastries wafting out of bakeries, and vans trying to complete their deliveries before the tourists clogged the streets.

Skye stood at the crossroads and looked left and right, trying to decide which road to take. If that wasn't an accurate metaphor her life, then nothing was. She felt the pull of the water and headed towards the quay.

She stood for a second gazing down at the water. The estuary was completely smooth and the sound of two boys messing about in a little dinghy in the distance was as clear as a bell. Maybe she'd take a trip to the beach later. Liz was doing afternoon tea for clients and would be out for a few hours; she could make herself scarce too and give Clare and Ivy some space.

As she turned to walk away, a figure caught her eye. A woman in a bikini was sitting on a towel at the end of the jetty, dark curly hair tied up in a ponytail, her posture faultless. Skye could only see her from the back, but she was struck by the lean muscles across her shoulders and down her spine. She was in lotus position, hands resting on her knees, thumbs to forefingers as if she was meditating. There was noise all around: people preparing their boats for a day on the water; seagulls; the rumble of cars; the roar of a speedboat in the distance, but this woman seemed oblivious to it all.

Skye slid onto a bench absently, impressed with the woman's ability to focus, not to mention how self-confident she must be to sit there in a bikini.

In one fluid movement, the woman stood up and brought her hands to prayer position. Skye willed her to turn round so she could see her face, but instead she stretched her arms up and, with the neatest of splashes, she dived into the water. A second or two later, the woman's dark head, sleek with water, re-emerged and she was gasping from the shock of the cold water, but laughing too. She dived once again, appeared a few metres away and then floated on her back like a starfish.

Skye couldn't drag her eyes away; there was something so joyful about the way the woman gave herself up to the water, completely in the moment. Then she turned and swam back to the jetty and hauled herself out of the water.

'Lovely morning!' the woman shouted over to her as she picked up her towel and dried her arms and face.

'Hey,' Skye replied, embarrassed to have been caught spying on her. 'That was impressive.'

The woman smiled and wrapped her towel around her. 'What – the dive or getting into cold water?'

'Both.' Skye returned her smile. 'I'm not sure I'd be brave enough.'

'Of course you would be! The only limits you have are the ones you give yourself. You just need to have some self-belief.' She slipped on her flip-flops, scooped up a tote bag and walked down the jetty towards Skye. 'Anyway, I do this all year round – the water is practically tropical now compared with February.'

'I do love the water,' Skye admitted. 'I grew up near the sea. And it does look tempting.'

The woman was even more beautiful close up. Similar in age to Skye, her wet skin tanned and goosebumpy, deep brown eyes with laughter lines at each side and a wide infectious smile.

'Then you must try it some time – it's such a good way to start the day. Boosts dopamine levels and gives you an endorphin surge. It makes you feel alive.' She closed her eyes, filled her lungs with a deep breath and let out the air. 'I feel incredible now.'

'You're certainly selling it to me,' Skye laughed shyly. 'Although I usually start my day with coffee.'

'That works too,' the woman replied, sitting beside her. 'I can recommend the coffee from the café on Fore Street. I'm Marta by the way.'

'Skye.' She tucked her hair behind her ears, envious of Marta's ability to chat so comfortably with a stranger. 'Thanks for the suggestion.'

'Nice to meet you, Skye,' Marta said, producing a dress out of her bag and pulling it over her head. 'Maybe next time I see you will be at the end of the jetty in your bikini?'

'Maybe,' Skye replied. 'Either that or in the queue for coffee.'

Marta laughed, getting to her feet. 'Go well, Skye, enjoy your day.'

'You too.'

Skye couldn't resist turning her head to watch as Marta walked away purposefully, still rubbing her wet hair. As she reached the corner of the street, Marta turned back to look at her and both women laughed at being caught out by the other.

She was cool, thought Skye, happy that their paths had crossed this morning. She stood up to leave and, for a moment, she was so wrapped up in their conversation that she completely forgot where she was supposed to be going. Oh, yes, Liz's lock-up. But maybe first coffee.

The door of the coffee shop on Fore Street was open and the smell was amazing.

The girl behind the counter smiled as Skye entered the café. 'What can I get you?'

'Just a black coffee please.' Skye had been a latte lover at one time, but she'd quickly discovered that drinking it without milk was far easier in a hot country.

She sipped the coffee and sighed with joy. It was good, nutty and rich, and by the time she'd reached Island Street and found the little building belonging to Liz, she had finished it. Skye dropped the empty cup into a recycling bin and, after wrestling with a rusty padlock, pushed her way into Liz's lock-up. It was dark inside and smelled musty. She propped the door open with a heavy cardboard box to let in some fresh air and flicked the light switch. As a row of fluorescent strip lights buzzed into life, Skye scanned the room.

'Wow,' she murmured. 'This is a lot of kit.'

It was an Aladdin's cave for keen cooks. On one side, two huge appliances – a fridge and a freezer – hummed industriously next to a stainless-steel worktop which had a double sink and drainer set into it.

Opposite, covering the entire wall, were rows of metal racking, stacked high with all manner of equipment. Skye saw wicker picnic hampers, champagne buckets, serving platters of all shapes and sizes and crates and crates of dishes, glasses and cutlery. Tablecloths, napkins, towels, vases . . . She shook her head, remembering the sparse contents of her kitchen cupboards in Kampala.

Everything was going to need a good spring clean before it was fit to be used. And that she could manage.

There was a water heater above the sink, and after running the tap for a couple of minutes, hot water began to trickle through. She found an upbeat playlist on Spotify, located cleaning materials and got to work.

Two hours later, Skye was in desperate need of a wash herself, but the lock-up was looking a million times better than it had when she'd arrived. She stepped back out into the fresh air for a breather and heard a faint ringing from her pocket. She pulled out the business phone and answered it.

'The Seaside Gourmet Girls, Skye speaking.'

'Hello? This is Ele. Are you the person I spoke to about the vegan menu?' asked the woman from yesterday.

'Yes, hi.' Skye tucked damp tendrils of hair behind her ear.

'It's my friend's birthday and she loves Indonesian food. Rather than a buffet, could you do a tasting banquet?'

'I'm sure we could,' she replied, hoping she was right.

'And I guess that will be more expensive?'

'Um . . . yes?' She was out of her depth here. By rights, she should keep quiet and say that she'd get back to her to confirm. But the thought of landing her first solo deal was too tempting. 'It would be thirty-five pounds per head. Plus another six if you wanted a dessert course.'

'Oh!' Ele sounded surprised. 'Right.'

Skye winced – she'd blown it. Maybe that was too much for dessert. Damn.

'I thought you were going to say much more than that.'

'Did you? That's good then.' Now Skye was worried she'd gone in too cheap. Perhaps she should have waited and checked with Liz.

'How much would you charge for a birthday cake? Vegan obviously.'

Skye had just washed several gorgeous cake stands, so she assumed making cakes was part of their repertoire. 'Fifty-five pounds, including a cake stand to serve it from.'

'It's a deal. I'm not confident enough to make a cake without eggs.'

'Cool. Remind me of the day you were thinking of?'

Ele named a date a couple of weeks away; Skye hoped it didn't clash with anything else.

'Just one more thing,' the client added. 'There will be twenty of us now, not six. It's turned into a full-blown birthday party. Is that still OK?'

Skye told her that it was, although the price she'd given her for the cake had been based on six. She recommended a six-layered rainbow cake (thank goodness for her Pinterest obsession) which they could make for seventy-five pounds. At which point the customer squealed with excitement and confirmed the booking.

Skye was buzzing as she tried to work out the maths. It was a lot, she knew that much. Where was Clare when she needed her? *My eldest is brilliant at maths*, Mike had told her maths teacher at parents' evening once.

'I'll send you an invoice within the next ten minutes,' she said, making a note of Ele's details in her phone. 'And we'll need a deposit to secure the booking.'

Skye could hardly contain her excitement as she finished up and clicked the padlock into place. At this rate, making twenty thousand pounds was going to be a breeze. She'd start by researching Indonesian food, then find a recipe for a vegan birthday cake . . .

All thoughts of slinking back to Exeter were now banished; she couldn't wait to tell Liz the good news. Her dad was right to have recommended her for this job, she was clearly going to be absolutely brilliant at it. She smiled to herself as she set off at a pace to get back to Clemency House; it seemed like she was already taking Marta's advice and having a little more belief in herself. And it felt good. Very good indeed.

Chapter Nine

Liz

'May I help carry anything through?' Patrick Delmarge asked from the kitchen doorway.

'The tea tray is ready,' Liz replied, running her eye over it to check she'd remembered the tongs for the sugar cubes which Patrick's mother preferred. 'If you wouldn't mind taking that, I'll bring the sandwiches.'

'Right you are,' said Patrick, lifting up the heavy tray with ease.

Liz picked up the Royal Albert cake stand, which she'd filled with crustless sandwiches and garnished with peppery watercress, and followed him through to the living room.

Patrick was her favourite sort of client. Even though this was his house, he let her take over the kitchen completely and never once got in her way. Some clients, by contrast, were forever coming and going and getting under her feet, which made her edgy and clumsy.

Two old ladies, as delicate as tiny birds, were sitting in armchairs at the curved picture window, which from its elevated position looked out over the estuary and across the water to Salcombe Harbour. They were identical twins with fine snowy hair, hazel eyes and sharp noses, but it was easy to tell them apart because Agatha wore a full face of make-up and Camilla 'couldn't bear the stuff'.

'Oh hurrah!' Agatha declared, clapping her hands together. 'Teatime.'

Patrick put his tray down first and made space among the piles of books for Liz to set down the sandwiches. His mother, Camilla, laid down her copy of the parish news-letter and changed one pair of glasses for another.

'What wonders have you brought us this week, Elizabeth?' Camilla asked.

Liz had given up reminding Camilla and her sister that she preferred the shortened version of her name. It had been Elizabeth and Jennifer from the very first time that the Delmarge family had ordered afternoon tea three years ago.

'Crab and chilli mayonnaise,' she said, pointing to the top tier.

'Local crab?' Camilla asked.

Liz smiled. 'Yes, Camilla. From Victor.'

He sold the best seafood in Salcombe – a secret locals kept to themselves.

'Ooh lovely, you are spoiling us. Patrick, isn't Elizabeth spoiling us today?' Agatha said, poking her nephew's leg as he took his seat between the two ladies.

'She always spoils you, Auntie. We're very lucky to have her.' He caught Liz's eye as he said it.

'I'm lucky to have you,' she replied, feeling herself blush.

Catering for the Delmarge family was the only regular job she'd continued with after Jen died. Patrick's beautiful Edwardian home in East Portlemouth with its commanding views across Salcombe was a joy to visit, so much so that it was easy to forget that she was being paid to be here. Octogenarians, Agatha and Camilla lived in a residential home together, but Patrick fetched them out every Sunday after they'd had their lunch. Afternoon tea from The Seaside

Gourmet Girls was their monthly treat; both ladies were very fond of their food.

'We've also got beef and horseradish, ham and mustard,' Liz continued, indicating the second tier.

'English mustard?' Camilla interrupted. 'None of that Dijon business?'

Liz bit back a smile. The sandwiches and the questions were always the same. 'Yes, English mustard and plenty of it.'

The twins had spent some of their formative years in India and consequently had acquired palates which demanded strong flavours. Pepper, garlic, chilli . . . Liz had learned that the only thing off the menu was bland, boring flavours.

She poured them both a cup of Earl Grey and pushed the bowl of sugar cubes towards Camilla, who promptly dropped three into hers.

'That's very kind, dear – isn't she kind, Patrick?' Camilla said.

'Very,' Patrick supplied.

'I'm just doing my job,' Liz replied with a laugh.

Agatha blinked spidery eyelashes at her. 'I think of you as family now.'

Liz touched Agatha's hand. The skin was soft and spotted with age. 'I feel the same about you.'

Spending time with the Delmarges was the closest Liz came to family get-togethers. Or had been, until the girls had arrived yesterday.

'Do you like Patrick's shirt?' Camilla asked.

'Oh, Mother.' Patrick shook his head in mock despair.

'I do. It suits him.' If Liz were to describe Patrick's wardrobe, it would be 'crumpled comfort'. His linen shirt, for example, looked like it might have been expensive. He wore it with the sleeves rolled up and untucked over a pair of trousers which looked as if they'd never given the ironing board a moment's trouble.

'We made him change before you came. He was wearing some awful peach thing,' Agatha confided.

Camilla slurped her tea and nodded. 'Washed him out. The French navy makes his eyes sparkle, don't you think, Elizabeth?'

'Very flattering,' Liz agreed. Patrick did have lovely eyes, she'd noticed them the first time they'd met. A deep inky blue, the colour of a summer night sky.

'Have a sandwich, Mum, and stop embarrassing me,' said Patrick.

'I'm just showing you off, darling. Mother's prerogative.' Camilla selected three tiny triangles and bit into a crab one.

Agatha added a splash of milk to her cup. 'I'm surprised you're not married, Elizabeth dear, really I am.'

Liz said nothing, she slid the cake stand towards her and handed her a plate and napkin. Once everyone had been served, she could retreat to the kitchen and then the two ladies would leave poor Patrick in peace. He was a widower and seemingly happy to stay that way, but that didn't stop the twins trying to match-make.

'Don't pry, Aggie, it's not polite. Elizabeth doesn't have to tell us anything about her private life unless she wants to?' Camilla raised an eyebrow hopefully.

'Mum,' Patrick warned. 'Liz, I apologise for my nosy relatives. They're incorrigible.'

'Spoilsport.' Agatha pouted, making her coral lips pucker. 'This is what counts for excitement when you get to Camilla's age: living vicariously through others.'

Agatha was fond of reminding her sister that she was the eldest. Although the age difference was the few minutes, it had taken the neighbour to realise their mother wasn't carrying one but two babies and to resume her position at the business end. A story which Liz had heard several times, each retelling more gruesome than the last.

'Rude, but sadly true,' Camilla admitted. 'Eddie Sprigg had a new mobility scooter delivered last week. The furore created by that, honestly, you'd have thought it was a Rolls-Royce.'

'It beeps when it goes backwards,' Agatha whispered, clearly impressed. 'Quite a machine, I can tell you.'

'Oh shush, Aggie' said Camilla crossly. 'You're changing the subject. Elizabeth was telling us about her private life.'

'No she was not,' Patrick corrected her.

'I should be getting the coffee and cakes ready,' said Liz. 'I'll be right back.'

'Sit down, dear, you're giving me a crick in my neck, looking up at you.' Agatha patted the empty chair.

'Yes, we insist,' Camilla agreed. 'Please, just this once.'

There were always four chairs set up for afternoon tea. Liz usually managed to make excuses not to join them, but today it appeared resistance was futile.

Liz sat. Camilla and Agatha exchanged gleeful looks.

'So. You mentioned an ex-husband?' Camilla prompted.

'How's the crab, Mum?' Patrick said, in an attempt to distract her.

'Delicious. Are you courting, Elizabeth?' she continued.

Patrick stood up. 'Liz, I'm going to fetch you a cup and saucer. No arguments.'

He was such a nice man, Liz thought, watching him leave the room. He carried perhaps a tiny bit more weight than Mike, but it suited him. Today, his nose was peeling, and the tips of his ears were a little sunburned. A complete contrast to Mike, whose year-round tan was suspiciously even. The men couldn't be more different:

Mike was in denial about his age, Patrick was completely at ease with his.

Agatha's cup clattered in its saucer, jolting Liz back to the conversation.

'I'm footloose and fancy-free,' she replied, remembering the question.

'That's why you've got such lovely skin. Not a wrinkle,' said Camilla wisely, folding watercress between her fingers and popping it into her mouth.

'The benefits of being plump,' said Liz, 'I've got natural padding.'

'Rubbish,' said the sisters together.

'That must be why your face looks like a whoopie cushion minus the whoop, Camilla,' Agatha tittered. 'Because you had three husbands.'

Three husbands? Liz marvelled. She hadn't even managed to hang on to one.

Camilla harrumphed. 'All the best things come in threes. Like the three bears, or the three wise men. Or perhaps the three stooges in my case.' She muttered this last bit as Patrick reappeared with a cup for Liz. 'Did you divorce, Elizabeth?'

'Or are you widowed maybe, like Patrick?' Agatha bit the corner off a sandwich and chewed. 'Patrick has been on his own for eight years, you know. Rattling around in this big old house.'

A house which still had framed photographs of him and his wife in every room, Liz noted. He'd clearly loved his wife dearly and Liz felt a bit sorry for him that his mother and aunt badgered him so much to replace her.

'I think you might have mentioned that once or twice, Auntie,' said her nephew wryly. He piled some sandwiches onto a plate and began to eat. Not a man who cared about eating too many carbs, Liz noted. Good for him.

'We divorced,' she said, pouring herself some tea from the pot. 'It was very sad, but it was for the best. Seventeen years ago now.'

Jonathan had remarried. His new wife had already had two children with a previous partner and Jonathan had thrown himself into family life. The last Liz heard, he was now a very happy grandfather.

'Cheat on you, did he?' Camilla pursed her lips.

Agatha gave a disgusted huff. 'Can't bear cheats.'

Liz felt uncomfortable. She could lie and put all the blame on Jonathan, but she was rubbish at lying, except the one big deception she'd been carrying since university.

'It wasn't him, it was me.'

Patrick choked and banged his chest. 'Horseradish,' he gasped, turning puce.

'Oh my!' Camilla clutched her throat.

Agatha gave a delighted gasp. 'Was it a torrid love affair and you just couldn't help yourself?'

'Good Lord, Auntie!' Patrick croaked.

'I wasn't unfaithful,' Liz was quick to clarify, 'but I . . . It sounds so silly when I say it out loud, but I didn't love my husband the way he loved me.'

'Was he a cross-dresser?' Agatha laid a hand on her knee, her eyes bright with curiosity. She turned to Camilla. 'Remember Priscilla Wheatcroft's husband?'

Camilla nodded. 'Wore French knickers under his police uniform.'

'And this was 1959,' Agatha added gravely.

'Nothing like that,' said Liz. 'Jonathan was completely innocent.'

But he wasn't Mike, and he could hardly be blamed for that. She thought back to Friday lunchtime and how her heart had hammered when Mike had wrapped his hand over hers. He still had the same effect on her now as he'd had when they'd met. The admission bubbled up and out of her mouth before she had chance to stop it.

'The trouble was – or *is* – that I've been in love with someone else for forty years. My husband got fed up with being second best.'

Her cheeks flamed. She'd never told a single soul that before. No one. Not even her best friend – *especially* not her best friend. She had no idea why she'd just done it. Her hand trembled as she replaced her cup in the saucer.

'Actually, can we forget I said that, I'd rather not—'

'Forty years?' Camilla cut across her. 'Darling, let that one go. If he was interested, he'd have let you know by now.'

'You're right, I know,' Liz agreed. She had come to that conclusion many years ago. But what could she do? The heart wants what the heart wants.

Opposite her, Patrick was sitting perfectly still, his expression unreadable.

'Poppycock.' Agatha dropped a crust onto her plate. 'Men are useless at saying what they want. I know for a fact that Ivan Davis was sweet on me, and he never said a word. I turned down being Bill Malone's bridge partner for Ivan, just in case he asked me. Then Ivan died, but by then Bill had buddied up with Margo, so I missed my chance.'

'I rest my case,' said Camilla smugly. 'You waited too long for your ship to come in, during which time your other potential ship sailed.'

'I'll get the cakes if everyone's finished with the sandwiches?' Liz suggested, determined to change the subject.

'If he hasn't appreciated how wonderful you are by now, he's an idiot and doesn't deserve you,' said Camilla, dabbing the edges of her mouth with a napkin.

'If you want my advice . . .' Agatha began.

'I don't think she asked for it, Auntie,' Patrick said firmly.

Agatha ignored him. 'You'll forget about him. Put him out of your mind. Ask yourself, do you want to spend the next forty years waiting for him to throw you a bone?'

'Three years of unrequited love is enough, let alone forty,' Camilla said, giving her son a sideways look.

Patrick exhaled. 'I should think Liz has endured quite enough interrogation for today.'

Liz smiled at him gratefully. 'In answer to your question, Agatha, I know I shouldn't waste my time waiting for him. But it's complicated; our lives are entwined. I couldn't escape if I wanted to.'

There was a moment of silence while the Delmarge family absorbed this new piece of information. Liz had an awful feeling that she'd just overshared.

'If you'll please excuse me, I shall go and make the coffee.' She was on her feet and on her way back to the kitchen before anyone had a chance to argue.

She rushed to the sink and ran her wrists under cold water to cool her blood. What was going on with her today? Why on earth had she let her guard down like that? The Delmarges might feel like family, but they were clients.

She blew out a calming breath and forced herself back into business mode.

Right. Coffee. She flicked on the kettle and set about preparing the cakes to take in next. The ladies preferred tea with their sandwiches and coffee with cakes.

Liz was spooning clotted cream into a small bowl when Patrick appeared with the teapot and their empty cups on the tray.

'Please forgive the inquisition back then. Mum and Auntie Aggie shouldn't have pried.' Patrick put down the tray gently and hovered by the kitchen table, sweeping crumbs up into his hand. 'I hope we haven't put you off us entirely?'

'Not at all!' She met his gaze. 'It's me who should be apologising. It's hardly very professional behaviour, raking up one's love life in front of clients.'

'Only under duress.' He grinned at her. 'I do appreciate you coming, I hope you know that. It's the highlight of the month. For them, I mean. They love getting out of the home for a few hours and your food is all they talk about for days.'

'It's my pleasure, catering for an afternoon tea is a piece of cake, pardon the pun.' Liz unpacked the tub of scones, the carrot cake and lemon drizzle cake from her basket and began to arrange them on a tall glass cake stand.

Clare and Liz had made the cakes together this morning while Ivy was having a nap. It had been lovely having company in the kitchen again. And then Skye had arrived brimming with excitement about her new booking.

All of a sudden, what had felt impossible only twenty-four hours before somehow seemed possible. Skye had offered to come with her to the Delmarges, but Liz had declined. It would do Clare and Skye both good, she thought, to spend some time together and have a chance to catch up with each other's lives.

'I'm glad,' said Patrick, pulling Liz back into the moment. 'Because I think about you struggling across on the ferry, weighed down with all those tins of cakes and whatnot, and feel terribly guilty about it.'

'There's no need,' Liz reassured him. 'I'm a lot stronger than I look.'

'I don't doubt it,' said Patrick. He cleared his throat. 'Anyway, I wanted to you let you know how grateful I am. Mum and Auntie are always talking about me taking them for lunch in Salcombe, but the thought of trying to park and then get them both into somewhere: Auntie in her wheelchair and Mum with her walking frame – I wouldn't even attempt it on my own.' He shook his head at the idea. 'You wouldn't believe how long it takes to get them in the car to come here from the care home – and that's with one of the staff helping us.'

'Gosh, yes, I imagine it would.' He had the patience of a saint, Liz thought, doing the bidding of two old ladies every Sunday when surely there must be other things he'd like to do occasionally. 'Perhaps I—' She stopped abruptly and closed her mouth.

It was on the tip of her tongue to offer to go with him, to help with the logistics, before realising that she was doing it again: forgetting her place. Of course he wouldn't want her gatecrashing his family Sunday.

'Yes?' he prompted.

Liz set the cafetière on the tray. 'Perhaps I could ask you to take in the cake stand?'

'Oh.' He blinked. 'Sure.'

While Patrick poured the coffee, Liz served Camilla and Agatha with a slice of both cakes and a scone each. How they maintained their petite frames was a mystery to her, she mused, watching them tuck in with gusto.

'Do you have anything exciting coming up this week, ladies?' Liz asked, before they could ask her anything else.

'No,' said Agatha with an affected sigh. 'It's a dreary existence. Pass the jam, dear.'

Liz handed her the dish of strawberry preserve which she ordered specially from Fortnum & Mason for them.

'Unless you count the monthly visit from the chiropodist,' Camilla shuddered. 'Which we don't. What about you, Elizabeth?'

'Rushed off my feet,' said Liz. 'We've taken on a lot of bookings and it looks as if I'm in for a busy summer.'

The job here was almost over. All she had to do was clear the kitchen, stack the dishwasher and pack her cake tins back in her basket. She smiled to herself, already looking forward to getting back home and spending the evening with the girls.

Patrick looked surprised. 'I was rather under the impression that you were taking on less business these days, not more?'

So was she. Right up until Mike had asked her for his money back.

She smiled brightly, determined not to air any more dirty laundry in front of the Delmarges. 'I changed my mind. I'm going to carry on for the summer and rethink in the autumn.'

'I'm going to pretend I didn't hear that,' Agatha sniffed. 'Or I shall get indigestion.'

Camilla patted Liz's hand. 'You are good, giving up your Sunday to serve us afternoon tea, especially when you're obviously in high demand.'

Liz squeezed Camilla's fingers. 'Not at all. I very much enjoy coming here. Your son has a beautiful home, and besides, I like looking over the water at Salcombe. There's a completely different view from this side of the estuary. I can see this house from my bedroom; I bet you can see mine from yours, Patrick.'

Agatha clasped a hand to her chest and sighed dreamily. 'Do you hear that, Patrick? Elizabeth loves it here.'

'I did hear, Auntie,' he replied solemnly. 'Because I'm right here. Thank you, Liz.'

'Take her upstairs, dear,' Camilla suggested. 'Show her the view from the front bedroom.'

Agatha and Camilla looked mischievously at them both. Patrick raked a hand through his hair. 'Liz, do you—'

'Another time perhaps,' said Liz, doing her utmost not to blush again.

Agatha's shoulders sagged. 'Dash it.'

'I keep saying to him, he'll be retiring soon.' Camilla leaned towards Liz. 'What is he going to do all day in this big house, on his own?'

'Five bedrooms, Elizabeth, *five*,' Agatha said in a hushed whisper.

'I have five too,' Liz replied. 'It is completely impractical for one person, but I love it.'

Camilla raised her eyebrows. 'Both single, both rattling around in big houses.'

'You two have so much in common,' Agatha sighed dreamily.

Patrick dropped his head into his hand and groaned. 'For goodness' sake, the pair of you! Liz, I apologise again. I feel like one of the Bennet sisters in *Pride and Prejudice*.'

That made her laugh. 'I appreciate your concern for me, but I'm not rattling around. In fact, I've got a houseful.'

She told them about her god-daughters and baby Ivy and how already there were little handprints all over her glass balcony, but that she didn't mind in the slightest.

'How lovely,' Camilla sighed wistfully. 'The young are so invigorating.'

'Perhaps you could do afternoon tea for us at your house next time?' Agatha's eyes were bright.

'Well, I—' Liz looked at Patrick for help. She didn't entertain at home. At least not for clients. The last time she and Jen had done anything like that it had been at university, when everyone had had to bring their own cutlery because their student kitchen was so poorly equipped.

'Excellent idea.' Camilla nodded as if to seal the deal. 'Patrick will drive us. No problem.'

The ferry crossing only took ten minutes. But the journey by land took about forty because of the circuitous route via Kingsbridge to cross the estuary. 'Oh yes, got nothing else to do.' Patrick winked at Liz.

'That's settled then.' Camilla and her sister exchanged smug looks.

'Now, hold on,' Patrick shifted uneasily in his seat. 'We couldn't impose. Especially as Liz has house guests.'

Why not, thought Liz, the ladies would get the change of scenery they craved and Patrick would have help getting them in and out of the car. It might be fun, and she was sure Skye and Clare wouldn't mind. 'You'd be most welcome. I think it's a lovely idea.'

'Really?' Patrick looked delighted. 'If you're sure?'

She nodded. 'I'm sure.'

'Fantastic,' he beamed at her, his blue eyes crinkling at the corners. 'We'd pay you of course.'

'And we'd get to see a baby – imagine that, Camilla!' said Agatha, reaching for her sister's hand.

'Heaven.' Camilla dabbed at her eyes with a handkerchief.

The pleasure on the old ladies' faces melted Liz's heart. They settled on a date and she left them to finish their cakes in peace and retreated to the kitchen.

Half an hour later, she was ready to leave. She said goodbye to the twins and accepted Patrick's offer of walking her down the hill to the ferry.

They strolled side by side companionably for a few minutes, Patrick insisting on carrying the wicker basket.

'Thank you,' he said as they drew close to the ferry landing, where a handful of people and a couple of dogs were already queuing. 'It has been absolutely wonderful as always.'

'You're most welcome.' Liz nodded towards the approaching ferry. 'And we've arrived in perfect time too.'

She gestured to take the basket from him, but he held on to it, causing her fingers to close over his.

'Liz.' His tone made her glance at up at him. 'I don't often say this, but my mother was right. Forty years does seem a long time to be in love with someone who doesn't feel the same way.'

Liz looked away and chewed her lip, wishing she'd never opened her big mouth. 'I'm a complete fool. Yes, I'm aware of that.'

'No, not at all!' he replied kindly. 'I didn't mean to insult you. But may I say something? As a friend?'

Liz relented. He was a lovely gentle man. 'You may.'

He was quiet for a second, as if selecting exactly the right words. 'I just want to say that there might be someone else out there for you. To go on this next part of life's adventure with you. Don't give up on love, that's all I'm saying.'

She nodded slowly, thinking of Viv and how she had launched herself back into the world of dating. 'You're right. I know you're right. It's just hard to know how to start.'

'Tell me about it,' he replied with a grin. 'It's been eight years since I lost Rachel and I'm gradually coming round to the idea of someone new, but it has been so long since I last asked a lady out on a date, I wouldn't know where to start.'

The ferry had arrived, and a handful of people were disembarking. She and Patrick stood aside to let them pass before he handed her the basket.

'So you don't believe in soulmates then?' Liza asked. 'That there's only ever "the one"?'

'I suppose I don't,' he said, looking surprised at himself. 'Because that would mean accepting that we're all only capable of being loved unconditionally by one person. Which is terrible odds, don't you agree?'

She smiled. 'If you put it like that, it does seem a bit harsh. Perhaps we should do what your aunt suggests and start dating.'

Patrick rubbed a hand through his hair. 'Crikey.'

Liz blushed, realising he'd misunderstood her. 'I didn't mean each other! I mean throw ourselves into the dating arena. Don't look so worried, it might be fun. We could both give it a go and compare notes.'

'Oh, I see.' He gave her a crooked smile. 'Although I suppose—'

'Are you getting on?' the ferryman called.

'Yes! Hold on!' Liz waved at him and turned back to Patrick. 'It's all websites and apps these days. The girls will know how to do me a profile. What do you think?'

He looked down at his shoes. 'I think I'm terrified.'

The ferryman handed her into the boat, and Liz settled on the bench at the bow.

'Me too,' she said, wincing. 'But let's do it anyway.'

Patrick was still on the jetty, waving to her. 'I'm not sure websites are for me, I think I'd rather ask a real—'

The engine started up with a roar and she missed the end of his sentence, but it sounded as if he already had someone in mind. Good for him, Liz thought, waving back. Patrick Delmarge was quite a catch; once he dipped his toe into the dating pool, he wouldn't be on his own for long.

Agatha and Camilla were right, of course. Mike Marriott was an idiot who didn't deserve her, and it was about time she put him out of her mind and focused on finding someone who did. Online dating. What on earth would Jen have had to say about that? Liz laughed softly under her breath, imagining how Jen would have probably whooped with delight. About bloody time, she'd have cried. And Jen, she acknowledged as the ferry carried her back to Salcombe, was usually right.

Chapter Ten

Clare

Clare heaved a happy sigh as the first glimpse of North Sands beach came into view through overhanging branches of the trees edging the path.

'Look at that, Ivy.' She stopped for a second, catching her breath, and bent down over the buggy to straighten Ivy's sun hat. 'That's Mummy's favourite beach in the whole world.'

Ivy clapped enthusiastically and Clare began to move again, eager to feel the sand between her toes.

It was busy down there, but she'd known it would be. The sand was soft, the water sparklingly clean, there was parking and refreshments and nice clean loos – what more could you want? The tide was out and the beach was stretched to its golden fullest. Groups of all sizes and ages were gathered in clumps, playing ball games, tucking into cool boxes, kids splashing in the shallow water. Good wholesome family fun.

And that was what they were, she and Ivy, a family, she thought, looking down at her daughter fondly; a little one, but a family, nonetheless.

She'd travelled all over the place in her time; a major perk of teacher life was the long holidays. She'd topped up her tan on beaches in the Caribbean, the Med and even Southeast Asia. But the golden sand of this beach held a special place in her heart. So many happy hours had been spent with Mum here. This was where she'd taught her to swim and had whole days pottering with her bucket and fishing net, collecting shells to make words on the sand, and having stone-skimming competitions. It was even where, one dark, drizzly January day with the wind scrubbing harshly at their faces, Clare and Liz had come to scatter her mum's ashes. It would always be their place.

Ivy smacked her hands on the front of her buggy and babbled excitedly, and Clare felt a sudden lightness in her heart. This was what she'd come for, to see her little girl's face full of joy and excitement. The world had turned again, time to make new memories, with her own child.

'Oh wow! I'd forgotten how gorgeous this beach is.' Skye caught them up and tucked her phone in the pocket of her denim shorts.

Skye had taken copious pictures of the scenery en route. All right for some, with her tiny tote bag slung over her shoulder, prancing along like a dressage horse. Clare felt like one of those poor donkeys on the Greek islands, consigned to dragging heavy loads up the steep cobbled streets all day long. Her bum was already aching from pushing the buggy up and down all the hills. Not that she was complaining – well, not much, anyway – she was used to pushing Ivy everywhere.

'Mind you, I've only been a few times,' Skye continued. 'Thanks for letting me tag along.'

'No worries,' Clare replied, prickling a bit. Like she had a choice. 'Come on, let's find a space on the sand.'

They carried on down the hill, passing the beach café and the car park, and headed towards the steps down onto the sand.

Clare was slightly irritated that Skye was with them. She'd tried to sneak out of Clemency House without her noticing, but as she'd unlocked the front door and manoeuvred the buggy over the threshold, Skye had appeared from her bedroom also ready to leave. Both had had the same idea, it transpired, to go for a walk along the coastal path to the beach.

'I can take a different route, if you'd rather be on your own?' Skye had offered.

She'd been so pleasant about it that Clare would have had to have been a monster to take her up on it.

'No, no, of course not,' she'd replied, embarrassed that Skye felt the need to suggest it. 'We're going to be spending the next few weeks together. We might as well try to get on.'

And so here they were.

Clare had nothing against Skye per se – other than the small matter of the years her younger half-sister had had preferential treatment over her, the nice holidays Dad and Frankie had taken her on, the new cars she'd been given, the parties, birthday presents, oh yes, and the fundamental matter of their father deciding to be a hands-on dad to Skye and a hands-off dad to her. None of these things were Skye's fault, Clare was perfectly aware of that, but even so, it still rankled.

Also, this was her and Ivy's first trip to the beach this summer. She wanted it to be just the two of them. A paddle in the sea, a dig in the sand with the bucket and spade Liz had bought them, maybe Ivy's first taste of Salcombe Dairy ice cream . . . And now she'd have to share it with Skye.

'Mmm, smell that fresh sea air.' Skye inhaled and exhaled steadily. 'I love being by the sea. There's something about listening to waves lapping the shore that soothes the soul, isn't there?'

'Definitely,' said Clare. 'Although, strictly speaking, this is an estuary; in fact, it's not even that, it's a ria. A riverbed thingy.'

'I love it. Whatever it is.' Skye shrugged easily. 'Shall we go over there?' She pointed to an empty patch of sand on the right of the beach.

Clare shook her head. 'I want to stick to the left, it's nearer the loos. And not too close to the water.'

'Yes, boss,' Skye pretended to salute and, jumping down onto the sand, turned to lift the bottom of the buggy. 'Here, let me help.'

'I can manage,' Clare insisted, panting as she dragged the buggy backwards across the sand. It was weighed down with beach paraphernalia, as well as the usual changing bag, snack bag and Ivy of course. She gritted her teeth at the obvious lie as Ivy let out a yell, no doubt unhappy with being tipped backwards and bumped across the beach.

Why not say yes please? Why not just accept the help? Life would be so much easier if she did.

Because I can't, she growled to herself. Because being independent at all costs had become a badge of honour and she had to wear it at all times, even when it dug into her.

Finally she came to a stop. 'Here will do, we're by the rocks, so we can store our bags on them to stop everything getting sandy.'

Ivy kicked her legs impatiently and plucked at her straps.

Clare unrolled the beach blanket at speed, spread it on the sand, unclipped Ivy from the buggy and plonked her in the middle of it. 'There! Isn't that nice!'

'It's certainly huge,' Skye remarked, looking at the blanket. 'I'm not sure you'll need extra storage on the rocks.'

'It's all right for you with your tiny bag and tiny towel,' said Clare, finding four large pebbles to weigh down each corner of the blanket. 'Some of us are less carefree.'

Skye shook out her own towel and spread it on the sand, next to Clare's football-pitch-sized one. 'Who says I'm carefree?'

Clare looked at her, trying to decipher her tone, and wondered what had brought her back to the UK. Last night, Liz had asked her about Uganda and Skye had been effusive in her praise of the place and the people, but wouldn't be drawn on what had happened to prompt her return.

'I've had hardly any time off in five years,' Skye had said vaguely. 'I was overdue a break.'

'So you'll be going back?' Clare had asked.

'My job is being kept open for me,' was all she'd say on the matter before getting up and clearing the table.

'Well, aren't you?' Clare prompted now.

Skye sat down cross-legged and gazed out towards the water. 'Does anyone get to twenty-nine completely without baggage?'

'Does that mean you've left someone broken-hearted in Uganda?' Clare quizzed her.

'No, I—'

Ivy chose that moment to crawl onto the sand and shovel a handful of it into her mouth.

'Ack,' she spluttered, her little face screwed up in disgust. 'Ack.'

'You're not meant to eat it!' Clare laughed.

Skye gave her a sidelong look. 'Aren't you going to stop her?'

Clare started assembling the beach tent she'd brought along for extra shade and shrugged. 'Course not. Eating sand is like a rite of passage. And if I did stop her, she'd only do it again.'

Skye raised her eyebrows. 'Wow.'

'What does that mean?' Clare said, defensively.

Skye grinned. 'Just that I thought you'd be a helicopter mum, fussing over her. You've surprised me, that's all.'

'Oh,' Clare said, mollified. 'I'm trying to teach her to be independent.'

'There's no finer role model than you for that,' said Skye, with a twinkle in her eye. She picked up her phone. 'Mind if I take a photo of her?'

'Go for it,' said Clare, secretly pleased, both with the idea of being a role model and the offer of photos.

The downside of being a single parent, working full time with no family close by, was that preserving special moments – or even ordinary moments – on film took a back seat to the more basic jobs in life, such as keeping your child alive.

'Ivy! Smile!' said Skye.

The baby, clocking Skye's phone, yanked off her sun hat, and posed for the camera, jutting out her bottom jaw to reveal two little teeth.

'Cheese, Ivy,' Clare encouraged, 'say cheese!'

'Eeee!' cried Ivy jubilantly.

Skye looked at the screen and beamed. 'Lovely. Listen, I'm going to get a coffee, do you want one?'

'Cappuccino please.' Clare automatically reached for her purse. 'Hold on, I'll give you some money.'

'No need, I'll get them.' Skye waved her away.

'I insist,' Clare held out a ten-pound note. 'I'll get them.'

'Why?' Skye said hotly. 'Just because my job isn't as well paid as yours doesn't mean I can't treat you to a coffee.'

'Keep your hair on,' Clare grumbled. 'I didn't mean to make you feel bad, I suppose I'm just used to paying my own way, that's all.'

'Meaning I don't, I suppose?' Skye shot back.

'No.' Clare stared back. 'Meaning exactly what I said; get off your high horse.'

'Says the woman who had a strop over which bedroom Liz gave her.' Skye gave her a sly look.

'Dear, oh dear,' said the man a few metres away busy building sandcastles for two little girls who were arguing over a pile of shells. 'And I thought sisters stopped bickering when they grew up.'

Clare and Skye looked at each other, sheepish smiles nudging at their faces.

'Can I have some chocolate too please,' Clare asked politely.

'Coming up,' Skye replied.

'OK, you . . .' Clare scooped Ivy up when she'd gone. 'Sunscreen time. Your favourite.'

She brushed the sand off her wriggling child, peeled off her T-shirt and shorts and began rubbing factor 50 into her skin. She'd just finished when Skye came back with the coffees.

'They didn't have chocolate, so I got you a brownie,' said Skye, handing her a paper bag before setting a drinks holder down with two coffees in it away from Ivy.

'Thanks.' Clare opened the bag. The brownie smelled delicious. Ivy heard the rustle of the bag and headed over, opening her mouth like a baby bird. Clare broke off a small piece and fed it to her.

'She's got gorgeous hair,' Skye commented, sipping her coffee, 'and lovely olive skin. Quite different to yours.'

Clare smiled. 'She has. I hope she keeps her curls as she gets older.'

Ivy crawled away and Clare took the opportunity to sip her cappuccino.

'Does she . . .?' Skye stopped mid-sentence and shook her head. 'Nothing.'

'It's fine, you can ask,' Clare said, knowing exactly what Skye was going to ask. Because everyone wanted to know the same thing: Who's the daddy . . .?

Skye bit her lip. 'I was going to ask whether she looks like her father. But then I realised I was being nosy. So if you'd rather not talk about him . . .?' She looked at Clare hopefully.

Clare gave a practised smile; she was used to this sort of question. 'When she was born, she came out looking like a little old man. My first thought was that she looked like Dad.'

Skye grinned. 'That must have been a shock.'

Clare's heart squeezed at the memory. The whole nine months had been one long shock.

'It was. But, to be honest, I was just glad she'd arrived, healthy and in one piece. It was a long labour involving a grumpy doctor and several pieces of equipment I'd rather never think about again.'

Skye cleared her throat. 'And are you still in contact with him, I mean does he see her?'

'The doctor? No, of course not.'

'I meant Ivy's father, is he still in her life?'

Clare's throat tightened. 'Never been in it at all. I mean, he was in, you know, briefly, but . . . the answer to your question is no.'

Skye's face was full of sympathy. 'I'm sorry to hear that.'

Clare caught hold of Ivy again and swapped her nappy. She wasn't entirely convinced it was robust enough to handle any serious business, but time would tell.

'He washed his hands of me – of us,' she said, telling Skye the same as she told anyone else who'd asked. 'Didn't want anything to do with us.'

Skye's face fell. 'That's terrible. To do that to you after giving birth.'

'It was even before that,' Clare said, grappling with Ivy to put her feet through the leg holes of the tiny sunsuit she'd bought her. It was like putting a pair of tights on a cat.

Skye grimaced. 'Are you sure I can't help with that?'

'I'm fine,' Clare panted, holding the suit by the shoulders and jiggling Ivy into it like a pillow into a pillowcase. 'Things cooled right off between us after Mum's accident. I don't think he could handle my grief. He couldn't reach me, I suppose.'

'You poor thing,' Skye soothed. 'I'm so sorry I wasn't around to help.'

Clare smiled ruefully. 'Thanks, but I probably wouldn't have let you even if you had been. Anyway, I found out I was pregnant, and whoosh. Gone. Never saw hide nor hair of him again.'

'What a shit!' Skye was agog. 'You are well rid of him. Poor Ivy. Poor you!'

Clare nodded gravely. 'His last words to me were, "Go, just go."'

The more times she told this story, the more real it became to her. Not that there wasn't some truth in it, she just tweaked it a bit.

Skye scowled. 'Well, if I ever meet him, I'll have some words of my own to say to him.'

Clare hid a smile; Skye had always seemed so shy growing up. It was quite comical to hear her so feisty.

'How long were you together?' Skye wanted to know.

Clare fiddled with the edge of the blanket, watching Ivy scoot back onto the sand. 'Long enough to know we're better off without him.'

'Good for you,' said Skye, moving closer to Ivy. She began filling the bucket with sand, handing Ivy the little rake to play with. 'I envy you. That certainty. Knowing what you want – or don't want – and sticking by it.'

'Hmm,' she replied vaguely, watching the two of them play together. She hadn't been certain at all, not in the beginning.

Finding out she was pregnant had come as a massive shock. It was the very last thing she'd expected. To the point where when she noticed that her boobs had morphed from the size of compact clementines to sizeable Sevilles, she'd been four months pregnant. Within days, she'd had her first scan and, if she had been wavering about whether she wanted this baby or not, that grainy image on screen of her child with a massive head and limbs which appeared to be waving at her had quickly made her mind up.

She was going to be a mother.

She'd always wanted a child, or children. Even when documentaries of childbirth had made her friends feel sick and vow that they would never ever put themselves through that, Clare hadn't wavered. Her relationship with her mum had been the strongest bond in her life. And, in the weeks after Jen died, Clare had felt untethered and lost.

The timing wasn't great, especially as she had only just taken on the job of head teacher.

But this baby, as unexpected as it might have been, felt serendipitously right. She and her child would form a new bond, a relationship just as strong as the one she'd had with Jen. Only this time even better, because there'd be no man to meddle with their heads, or let them down, or pretend he loved them, then, as soon as a better offer came along, he'd take it and jump ship. The more Clare had thought about it, the more she'd realised that solo parenting was exactly the sort of family that she wanted.

She'd flung herself into the pregnancy and embraced every heartburn-filled second of it. The new life growing inside her gave her something to focus her emotions on. It also made her cut down her gin consumption, which had crept up from a Friday post-work treat to a nightly drowning of the sorrows every time her thoughts returned to how much she was missing her mother.

She knew that being a single parent would scupper her chances of a future love life, but she'd never been great at lasting relationships anyway.

'It's like you were waiting for me to slip up,' James, one of her exes, had once said to her. 'You never wholly trusted me, did you?'

Clare could only admit he was right, and they'd parted ways – sadly on his part, relieved on hers.

She didn't need a counsellor to pinpoint the source of this mistrust; she already knew, right down to the actual day.

On the morning of her first day of school, when she'd left the house in a blue gingham dress and gleaming white socks, the Marriotts had been a family of three. By the time she'd made it back home brimming with stories to tell, it had withered to two: Mum and Clare.

'No wonder you're so self-sufficient.' Skye's voice cut into her thoughts.

Clare shrugged. 'Needs must.'

'I get that,' said Skye. 'But it's OK to cut yourself some slack, you know. Let other people help. Like me. I haven't even had a cuddle with Ivy yet.'

'Haven't you?'

Skye shook her head. 'Every time I try, you whisk her away.'

Clare felt her neck go red. 'It has been said that I have trust issues. With men.'

'Just men?' Skye's lips twitched. 'Can I take Ivy down to the water's edge and let her put her feet in the sea?'

Clare was torn. She ought to say yes, show Skye she was taking on board the criticism, but Ivy's first paddle was a special moment. She didn't want to miss that. 'We'll both go. We can each hold one of her hands.'

Skye smiled. 'Baby steps. Literally.'

The water was refreshingly cold, unfortunately Ivy hated it and let everyone know. Each time Clare and Skye lowered Ivy into the water, she lifted her knees up and screamed. After the third attempt, they gave up and walked back up the beach towards their things.

'I thought she'd love it,' Clare moaned, settling Ivy on her hip. 'She loves bath time.'

'I was always scared of the sea when I was little,' said Skye, sweeping her phone across the bay slowly to video it. 'Probably because once when I was swimming with Dad, he pretended that a piranha had brushed his leg. I was almost sick with fear and wouldn't go in again the whole holiday.'

Clare gave a snort. 'And there was me hoping he'd spend more time with us this summer. Maybe it's a blessing in disguise.'

'I'm sure he'll come if *you* ask him,' said Skye. 'He's so proud of you.'

Clare gave her a wry look. 'He didn't even spend time with me when I was a child, he's not going to change now. It was fine though,' she said casually. 'Mum and I had a good time. Holidays by the sea were the best bit of my childhood. And I want that for Ivy. Memories of endless summers, jumping over the waves, playing on the beach until dusk, trudging back up the hill with sandy feet and sunkissed skin.'

She settled Ivy back on their blanket and handed her a drink.

'Sounds lovely.' Skye sighed, stretching out in the sun. 'Most of my holiday memories are of Mum and Dad bickering and Dad would inevitably be called back to work, leaving the two of us on our own. I think my favourite holiday was to Disneyland Paris. When you came.'

'*That* was your favourite holiday?' Clare couldn't believe it. Personally, she'd hated every second of it. Although that was largely down to the fact that she'd been sixteen and all her friends had gone to Leeds Festival without her. She'd spent the week dawdling behind Dad, Frankie and Skye with her headphones in, pretending she wasn't with them.

Skye nodded. 'And even though it was obvious you hated every second of it, it was still nice to have someone to share a room with.'

'Good times.' Clare flushed, remembering how she'd brought a roll of sticky tape with her in order to mark a physical divide down the centre of the room, telling Skye that under no circumstances was she allowed to cross into her half.

Just then, Ivy recovered from her dip in the water, shuffled on her bottom across the blanket towards Skye and pulled herself up to standing.

'Have you come to say hello to Auntie Skye?' Skye said, taking hold of Ivy's hands to steady her. She quickly looked at Clare. 'Whoops, is that OK? Calling myself Auntie?'

Ivy reached up to Skye's face, pulled off her sunglasses and laughed delightedly. Clare watched her daughter interact with her half-sister. The baby had no idea, no interest in whether this new friend was a blood relative or not, she didn't care that Clare and Skye had different mothers, and it would be years before she showed any interest in knowing about her family. As far as Ivy was concerned, Skye was just here, spending time with her, having fun, making Ivy happy. Clare swallowed the lump in her throat.

'Of course it is,' she replied briskly. 'Half-Auntie Skye would be a bit of a mouthful.'

Skye blinked and, for a second, looked like she might cry. 'Thanks. Now she'll always know that I'm her family.'

Family. Clare's heart skipped a beat. 'I'd like that.'

Ivy suddenly scrambled back to Clare, held her breath and then gave a short grunt.

'Oh God,' Clare groaned, knowing exactly what that meant.

There was a high-pitched bubbling sound, followed by a hot sensation on her thigh.

'Do you know what,' said Clare, 'I think we're done with the beach for today. Shall we go?'

'Mmm.' Skye nodded, wrinkling her nose. 'Good idea.'

Half an hour later, they were back in town in the garden of the Ferry Inn. Clare and Skye were sipping cold lemonades, leaning on the wall. Across the estuary, the ferry unloaded one lot of passengers and boarded another. Clare kept an eye out for Liz, who'd be sailing back in this direction soon. Ivy was fast asleep in the buggy between them.

'Not quite the perfect first beach trip I envisaged,' said Clare. 'I had visions of her being a water baby. Oh well.'

'Will she remember it, do you think, being so young?' Skye asked, scrolling through the photos she'd taken that day.

Clare poked for a slice of lemon with her staw. 'I think memories are like layers of colour on a painting, you can't see them anymore but they're there. They're what make up the whole. I hope that whenever Ivy thinks of this place, she'll feel happy. It doesn't matter if she remembers individual things or not.'

'Like the volume of her shrieks when we dangled her in the sea, you mean?' Skye took a cube of ice out of her glass and crunched on it, making Clare wince. It had been ages since she'd visited a dentist, she didn't seem to have time for things like that anymore. 'Exactly. And I'd rather she erased the smell of those public toilets from her memory banks too. I should . . .' She left the sentence unfinished and sipped her drink.

I should have left her with you, as you suggested, she almost said. But that would admit that sometimes she needed help. And if she started relying on other people, going home to an empty flat on her own was going to feel even harder than it already was.

'What do you think about Dad demanding money from Liz?' she said, changing the subject.

'Demanding is a bit harsh,' Skye replied. 'It is his money.'

'But at such short notice?' Clare frowned. 'What can he need it for?'

'God knows. A new man bag?' Skye giggled.

'Facelift?' Clare joined in.

'A full set of those fake white teeth?'

'Brazilian bum lift?' They were both laughing properly now.

'Hair transplant?'

'He is very keen on maintaining his youthful physique; he's a proper gym bunny these days,' Skye confided. 'He was talking about being a vegan on Friday. And the bathroom cabinet contains far more of his face products than Nilla's.'

'Or maybe he'll just get himself a younger wife,' Clare teased. 'He has form for that. And Nilla has been away for a while. Maybe he'll get one off the internet this time, hence the twenty grand.'

'He wouldn't?' Skye looked horrified.

'I wouldn't put it past him.'

'Neither would I. I caught his assistant, Harriet, coming out of the bathroom the other day. She claimed she'd been taking a shower after going for a run, but you never know with Dad.'

'Oh God.' Clare shuddered. 'Let's hope he's got a good reason for making Liz pay the money back.'

'He and Nilla are coming up to their seventh anniversary.' Skye mused. 'What's seven? China or wood or something?'

'A sculpture for the garden? That might cost twenty thousand.' Clare shrugged. She hadn't really got to know his third wife. Nilla was twenty years younger than Dad, closer in age to her than him.

'Maybe.' Skye didn't look convinced. She sighed and turned her face out to the water again. 'Hey, is that Liz, getting on the ferry?'

Clare squinted, shielding her eyes from the sun. 'You've got better eyesight than me. Let's drink up and go down to the ferry landing to meet her.'

'Two ticks.' Skye leapt to her feet. 'That lemonade has gone straight through me.'

What she could do with twenty thousand pounds, thought Clare wistfully as she waited at the exit of the pub for Skye to come back from the loo. A deposit on a house most likely. Her flat in Bath was gorgeous – high ceilings, plenty of period features and original sash windows. She'd fallen in love with the sweeping stair-case. Looking down on it from the top floor where she lived, it curved like an ammonite, with its lovely iron balustrades and polished wood handrails. But after a year of lugging up an increasingly heavy child, thousands of nappies, hundreds of shopping bags, the staircase had begun to lose its allure. Then there was a lack of outside space. It had never bothered her before, but it would be nice to give the washing an airing at weekends – and Ivy, for that matter.

'Ready.' Skye appeared, rubbing hand sanitiser into her hands. 'Shall I help you lift the buggy down the steps?'

She shook her head. 'I can manage.'

Skye rolled her eyes. 'You should have that engraved on your tombstone.'

'Better than I *can't* manage,' Clare retorted. 'Look, the ferry has landed. Let's check if Liz was on it.'

Skye tapped along the length of Clare's arm as she bumped the buggy down towards the ferry landing.

'What are you doing to my arm?'

'Looking for a chink in your armour.'

Clare laughed. 'Did you find one?'

'Nope,' Skye replied. 'But I will. Everyone has a weak spot.'

'Really? So what's yours?'

'There she is!' Skye had started to wave. 'Liz! Wait there, I'll come and help you with the bags!'

She ran on ahead and Clare continued at a slower pace, wishing she'd waited at the top of the steps. Ivy seemed to double in weight when she was asleep. She stood to one side as a crowd of disembarking passengers and their dogs filed past her. By the time she'd reached the bottom, the ferry had reloaded and was already several metres away from the jetty.

'Do either of you know about Tinder?' Liz looked pink-faced and happy. 'Only I was thinking I might—'

'Hey!' There was a sudden shout from aboard the ferry and the three women looked round.

A man with dark hair staggered to his feet. The boat rocked and he wobbled. Several of the other passengers reached out to steady him. The girl next to him grabbed his leg and tried to pull him back down.

117

Clare stared, riveted to the spot. It couldn't be.

'Hey, it *is* you!' As he caught her eye and waved, she felt her face flame. 'Turn around please, driver, I need to get off.'

'Oh dear. Stevie, the ferryman, won't like that,' said Liz, shaking her head. 'No drunks allowed.'

'Is he drunk? I thought he was just waving.' Skye looked at the boat and then to Clare. 'Yes, he's waving at . . . *you*, Clare.'

'Take your seat please, sir,' boomed a stern voice from the helm of the ferry.

What the hell . . . Clare's mouth felt as if someone had filled it with dry sand.

'Saskia? Saskia! It's me!' she heard him shout. 'Wait there for me. I'll come straight back.'

Clare felt light-headed. No way. It couldn't be. But it must be because, well, because it clearly *was* him, and not only that, he'd called her Saskia. Only one person on the entire planet would do that. What the hell was *he* doing *here?* And, also, why was she still frozen to the spot. *Move, Clare, move!*

'Oh God, how embarrassing, poor guy. He thought you were someone else.' Skye took the other end of the buggy to help Clare lift it up the steps. 'No arguments please.'

Clare had no intention of arguing; it was all she could do to stay upright. 'Well, they do say everyone has a doppel-ganger,' she said lightly. 'Saskia must be mine.'

'Must be! What a shame, I thought my luck was in for a minute,' said Liz, with a giggle. 'How funny.'

'Hilarious.' Clare blew out a slow breath as she watched the ferry motor across the estuary; it looked as if she'd got away with it. Now to get as far away from the ferry landing as possible before Adam got back. She had a feeling he'd have questions which she wasn't ready to answer.

Chapter Eleven

Liz

'Et voilà,' said Liz, taking a step back from the seven-layer rainbow cake. 'It is finished.'

She'd done it; her first celebration cake in ages, and it felt great. The last couple of weeks had been great. Since the Delmarges' afternoon tea, they'd catered for a barbecue, a friends' reunion party at one of the apartments in South Sands and a surprise fiftieth birthday dinner.

It had been exhilarating but exhausting and she hadn't had time to think about anything other than the next booking. She'd been falling into bed with menus and timings and shopping lists whirring around in her brain. It was early days and there was a long way to go, but The Seaside Gourmet Girls was on its way to repaying its debts and she felt giddy with relief.

Skye came to join her. 'They're going to love it. Thanks, Liz. I know I offered to give it a go, but the nearest thing I've made to a cake in the last five years is a tray of no-bake coconut granola bars.'

'You can't be worse than your mum, Skye.' Clare shouldered her way in between them, Ivy held in front of her. 'Do you remember that Christmas cake she made once that turned out to be completely raw in the centre?'

'How could I forget,' Skye replied stiffly. 'You brought it up every Christmas after that.'

'Hardly *every* Christmas,' Clare scoffed. 'I stopped coming over when I was eighteen.'

'Much to Mum's relief.'

'Can you see the cake, Ivy?' Liz said, cutting across them. 'Isn't it pretty?'

'Oooh.' Ivy clapped her hands and they all laughed, putting an end to their bickering.

The smell of the Indonesian dishes that they'd prepared had suffused the whole house. All new flavours to Liz, but Skye had been so proud of her first booking and had then spent ages researching vegan food that she'd been happy to give it a go. There was a rendang curry, nasi goreng and gado gado and she'd even used tempeh for the first time. She hoped the birthday girl approved.

Liz wiped her hands on her apron and realised that they were a bit shaky. Anxiety was beginning to build. 'I think we'll get going, Skye. I know it's only two o'clock and we don't need to be there for another hour or so, but it's a long time since we've catered for anything this big and I'm as nervous as hell. Jen and I . . .' She swallowed. 'I'm going to miss her today, more than ever.'

'Me too,' said Clare, putting an arm round her, 'but Mum was in awe of your talents. "Liz has got the magic touch," she used to say, "everything else is just decoration." So The Seaside Gourmet Girls still has the magic.'

'She did used to say that,' Liz said with a sniff. 'I'd completely forgotten.'

'And you've got us,' said Skye. 'And I think we're doing OK so far, don't you?'

Liz nodded. She was so lucky to have these two young women cheering her on, even if they did still rub each other up the wrong way.

'Thanks, girls,' she said. 'You're right, Skye, we make

a wonderful team. I was dreading going back to work in earnest, but having you two to spur me on has made all the difference. You've both worked so hard, and you, darling Ivy, have cheered me up no end.' Liz stroked the baby's cheek 'ow Jen would have loved to be here, to be part of her granddaughter's life. 'It's made my world a much brighter place.'

'OK, enough,' Clare said, blinking. 'Or we'll all be in tears again.'

With Skye's help, Liz manoeuvred the cake into a box while Clare ran through the checklist of items they needed to take.

'So many things to think about,' Skye marvelled. 'Like allergies and intolerances and how many can't handle spice.'

'Not to mention checking every single ingredient to make sure it's vegan,' Clare put in. 'But I think we've cracked it.'

Between them, they loaded up Liz's van with cool boxes, crates of colourful crockery to complement the Indonesian theme and jam jars ready to be filled with the marigolds Skye had bought to decorate the table. Skye climbed into the passenger seat and Liz handed her the cake box before getting into the car herself.

'Wish I was coming,' Clare grumbled. 'I'm going to be having severe FOMO this afternoon.'

'Oh darling!' Liz frowned. 'That sounds painful.'

Skye and Clare laughed.

'What's funny?'

'It's not an illness,' Skye told her. 'It stands for fear of missing out.'

'Oh.' Liz laughed. All these abbreviations reminded her that she'd registered on Tinder a few days ago and had her eyes well and truly opened; she was having to learn a whole new language. 'Think of us sweating in someone's kitchen, eyes stinging from chopping chillies and onions for the garnish while drunk clients get in the way and add salt to things as soon as our backs are turned.'

Skye pulled a face. 'Do they do that?'

'You'd be amazed,' Liz replied. 'You have to have eyes in the back of your head.'

Clare grinned. 'You've convinced me. Ivy and I will head off to Kingsbridge for a big food shop instead.'

'On your own?' Skye said.

'Yes,' said Clare, tartly. 'Believe it or not, I have been shopping in the last year and I don't generally leave Ivy home alone.'

'No need to bite my head off,' Skye muttered. They'd got two more events to cater for later in the week and the shopping list Clare had compiled last night while Liz and Skye chopped today's vegetables was huge.

'Why don't you take her to the beach instead?' said Liz. 'You haven't been for ages. Wild horses wouldn't drag you away usually.'

Liz wasn't sure if she imagined it, but Clare's cheeks seemed to flush at her words.

'I'd rather go shopping, make myself useful,' Clare insisted.

'If you wait until this evening,' suggested Liz, 'one of us can go with you.'

Clare shook her head. 'Ivy will be in bed then and, anyway, I can—'

'You can *manage*,' Skye finished for her. 'We know. Fine. See you later.'

Clare waved them off and took Ivy back inside as Liz started the engine.

'Do you think something's the matter?' Liz looked over her shoulder as she reversed the van off the drive. 'She's barely left the house all week.'

'She seems OK, but I know what you mean,' Skye mused. 'Not that she'd tell me if there was.'

'I wonder if she's ever left Ivy with a babysitter?' Liz pondered.

Skye gave a snort.

'No, you're right,' said Liz, 'Of course she hasn't.'

'Persuading Clare to trust someone else with Ivy,' Skye said, narrowing her eyes. 'Hmm, that might have to be one of my goals for the summer.'

'One of?' Liz said, glancing at her as she edged towards the junction meeting the steep hill.

'I've got several.' Skye focused her gaze on the cake box on her lap. 'Being with Clare makes me feel as if I'm still a student on a gap year. She's exactly where she wants to be in life. Whereas I'm still dithering about, wondering what I want to be, *who* I even am. So I guess that's my main goal: to make some decisions about my future.'

She used to feel like that about Jen, Liz mused. Jen was a woman who knew what she wanted and went after it wholeheartedly. She, on the other hand, wasn't brave enough to pursue her heart's desire until it was too late. But that wasn't something she wanted to share with Skye.

'But you've been happy with your choices so far?' Liz asked instead.

Skye was quiet for a moment. 'Yes, mostly at least.'

'Then you're winning at life,' she told her. 'Comparing yourself to someone else will never end well. All you can do is make choices that serve you, that take you where you want to go. That's what Clare does, and you can do it too.'

'That's probably the best advice I've ever been given,' Skye said, looking thoughtful. 'But while I think about my next move, the most pressing job is to help you pay Dad his money back.'

'I'll drink to that!' Liz accelerated to get the little van up the hill. 'Thurlestone, here we come.'

The venue for the birthday dinner party was a charming cottage with thick whitewashed walls and a thatched roof.

As soon as Liz parked the van next to a trailer on the gravel drive, the front door opened. A young woman appeared in her dressing gown, her skin looking very orange.

'That must be Ele.' Skye quickly climbed out to meet her, still carrying the cake box.

Liz took her time, her fingers fumbling with the seat belt as a bout of nerves flooded through her.

'Showtime,' she murmured, opening the driver's door. 'Wish you were here, Jen.'

She was happy to cook anything in her own house, but she always experienced a wave of self-doubt when she arrived at someone else's. This was the point in any job where Jen would come into her own. She'd make light of any setbacks, smooth over any complaints and put Liz at ease in the kitchen.

Today, Liz was going to have to find a way to keep herself calm. A drink would do it. She swallowed, imagining ice-cold wine slipping down her throat. Maybe that was what she should do, where would the harm be if she just had a small one?

'Ele, meet my boss, Liz,' Skye said, when she eventually joined them.

'I'm so excited that we managed to book you!' said Ele, shaking Liz's hand. 'I went to a party, ooh must be three years ago now, and you did the food. I've never forgotten. Amazing. Anyway, I'd been ringing the number on your website, sent an email and nothing. I thought I'd give it one more go before giving up and then . . .' She spread her arms wide. 'Ta-dah! You answered! Couldn't believe it. Then we thought, in for a penny, in for a pound, let's go large and—'

'We're delighted to be here,' Liz interrupted as Ele took a breath. 'Can you show us where we'll be?'

'Of course.' Ele beckoned them towards the front door. 'And then I need to get in the shower and wash off this fake tan. I think you feel so much more confident when you've got a bit of a glow, don't you? I mean, look at your tan.' She pointed to Skye. 'You must be super-confident.'

Skye gave a tight smile. 'I'm working on it.'

She was just as capable as Clare, thought Liz, she just needed to believe in herself more. Have the courage of her own convictions. Skye was more introverted than Clare, but she had natural empathy, she was very much a team player and had an endless willingness to learn. She'd only been working for Liz for a couple of weeks but had already made herself indispensable. Maybe that could be one of Liz's goals this summer, to help Skye recognise her own talents.

'It's a very pretty cottage.' Liz noted the lovely oak settle in the hallway adorned with embroidered cushions.

'It's my parents' house, formally my granny's.' Ele waved a hand at the old-fashioned watercolours on the walls. 'Hence the 1940s vibe.'

'So you're not on holiday?' Skye asked.

Ele shook her head. 'I work remotely for a London company. Most of the guests are local too, including Angel, the birthday girl.' She directed them into the kitchen. 'Small, but perfectly formed, as they say.'

Crikey. Liz tried not to panic at the lack of room. At least they'd done most of the prep at home.

The kitchen consisted of free-standing cupboards and cooker, an original Victorian sink and a dresser with shelves full of pretty china. Other than a small table and four chairs, there was hardly any workspace at all. The biggest assets, without a shadow of a doubt, were the double doors leading out into the garden.

'Super,' said Liz, itching to get to work.

Skye put the cake on the table and opened the doors.

'It's not a surprise party, so I won't be asking you to hide in a cupboard or anything.' Ele gave a tinkly laugh.

Good job, thought Liz, eyeing up the size of the largest cupboard.

'Oh, there'll be twenty-one guests now. Is that a problem? Angel's brother is coming now too.'

'We've got mountains of food,' said Skye. 'Enough for several more last-minute brothers.'

'There is a cost per head, but we can waive one extra one.' Liz gave her a gently reprimanding look.

Skye mouthed an apology.

'Where will the guests sit?' Liz asked, noticing the lack of dining space.

'I've got a fold-up table to put outside which I thought you could serve from,' Ele said. 'I've left a pile of rugs out there too. Could you set those up in a long line please? We can eat cross-legged on the ground. Fingers crossed the rain holds off.'

Skye and Liz looked heavenwards, there was definitely a chance of rain later. Hopefully, the guests would have at least eaten dinner by then.

'Want to see the cake?' Skye lifted the box lid.

'Oh my gosh.' Ele clapped her hands. 'That is awesome! Thanks so much for being so accommodating, with the vegan thing and the cake and the extra person.'

'You're welcome.' Skye steered Ele firmly to the kitchen door. 'You relax and leave everything to us. See you in half an hour.' 'Where are we going to put everything?' she whispered, once they'd heard her feet thudding up the staircase.

'We'll just have to manage,' said Liz, tying on an apron and passing the other one to Skye. 'Let's crack on.'

Within a few minutes, they'd unloaded the car, stowed everything in the fridge and cleared away as much of the paraphernalia from every surface as they could to give themselves extra room.

Soon, the hot food was on the stove and Liz had prepped the rice cooker ready to go as soon as the guests arrived.

Skye was assembling ingredients for a salad when Liz felt the phone in the pocket of her apron buzz with a notification. She fished it out, took one look at the screen and dropped it back in her pocket.

'Oh my word, Barry.' Liz felt her cheeks flame. 'That's you struck off the list. Good grief.'

'What's that?' Skye glanced at her.

'It's that bloomin' dating app,' said Liz, fanning her face. 'I don't know how you young people cope. It's so stressful.'

'I've never used a dating app,' said Skye. 'I'd rather stay single than put myself out there.'

'I'm beginning to come to the same conclusion,' Liz huffed. 'I promised Patrick Delmarge I'd have a go at dating, but the men on Tinder all have a one-track mind. Some of the comments are so blue, I can hardly bring myself to read them, let alone reply.'

Skye looked bemused. 'You promised a client that you'd start dating. How on earth did that conversation go?'

Liz laughed. 'It was his elderly aunt and mother who started it. Dropping hints that Patrick and I should start "courting" because we're both single. He and I agreed it was about time we moved on from . . .' She stopped herself from telling Skye what she'd admitted to the Delmarges: that she'd been harbouring an unrequited love for four decades.

'From?' Skye prompted.

'Patrick's a widower,' she replied, dodging the question while removing fresh herbs from the cool box. 'I get the impression he loved his wife very much. Moving on must be difficult when your heart belongs to someone who's no longer there.'

Skye grinned at her. 'You do know they were trying to set you up with each other, not other people?'

Liz chuckled. 'Oh yes, they're completely transparent. Dropping hints about him rattling around the house by himself and asking whether I like his shirt.'

'So?' Skye poured them both some water. 'Why don't you give the old ladies what they want?'

Liz gave it some thought. 'Patrick is a perfectly lovely man. He's always been kind and considerate to me, especially after Jen died. He's devoted to his elderly relatives, pleasant-looking, lives in a beautiful house.'

'Yes, well, he sounds awful,' teased Skye. 'No wonder you aren't interested.'

'I'm not *not* interested, but he's a client.' Liz pointed out. 'It wouldn't be proper.'

'You're his caterer, not his counsellor, I don't think you'd be struck off for going on a date with him.'

Patrick and Liz. It wasn't totally ridiculous, she mused.

'He's never given me any indication that he's interested in me, and I've never thought about him in that way before because . . .' Because once Liz had decided that the only man she'd ever fall in love with was Mike, she didn't think of anyone that way. She couldn't say that, so settled instead for, 'He's not the usual type I go for.'

'So who is?' Skye demanded.

'Pff!' Liz gulped at her glass of water and tried not to think about Mike's lean body and the way her stomach flipped when he smiled. 'That's the million-dollar question. But as far as Patrick goes, you'll be able to judge for yourself. The Delmarges are having afternoon tea at my house soon. The old ladies wanted to see where I live.'

'I'll help with the catering so you can play the grand hostess,' Skye offered. 'If he's not right, he's not right. But you won't know until you try, will you?'

'I'll think about it,' she promised. 'It's got to be a better option than Barry from Babbacombe who claims to be VWE.'

Skye frowned. 'I might have to google that.'

'I wouldn't if I were you,' said Liz, handing her a knife. 'The images are hard to unsee. Now, chop this very well-endowed cucumber into slices for the salad.'

'Liz!' Skye exclaimed, shocked, and they both burst out laughing.

An hour later, most of the guests had arrived and everything was running smoothly. In theory, Liz could relax. The food was virtually done and the garden looked beautiful and there had been no catastrophes. Skye had done a brilliant job with the table setting – or floor setting, to be more accurate. Cushions spread along the rug acted as seats and she'd dotted the orange marigolds in a pattern down the centre instead of in the bud vases as planned. Bespoke menus and colourful napkins were tucked into water glasses and there were paper lanterns hanging from the trees.

But Liz couldn't relax. Goodness knows what her blood pressure was, but her head felt like it was about to explode.

She was having serious doubts about the vegetable rendang. Had she done enough? What if the first few guests took too much and there was nothing for the last ones. Or the rice? Why on earth had she agreed to cook rice for twenty people? Twenty-one, she corrected herself. And why had she allowed herself to be talked into this cuisine? She wasn't entirely sure where Indonesia even was, and she'd certainly never eaten half the food on today's menu.

She wished she was at home. Or with Clare and Ivy pushing a trolley around Tesco. What was that machine they had on *Star Trek* for transporting people? All she could remember was the command: Beam me up, Scotty.

'Are you talking to yourself?' Skye set the empty drinks tray down and began mixing another batch of cocktails. The birthday girl, Angel, had requested Twinkles made from champagne, supplied by her older brother, with vodka and elderflower and topped with a lemon-peel garnish.

'Habit,' Liz replied, eyeing up the drinks; they looked very refreshing. 'Some of my best conversations have been with myself. I'm so hot, Skye, I might self-combust.'

She'd been scraping the seeds from a pile of green chillies, and she was trying not to touch her face. There was a threat of a storm in the sticky air and not a breath of wind. The kitchen was like a furnace.

Skye added some ice to Liz's water glass. 'Keep yourself hydrated. I'm going to take another tray of cocktails outside.'

Liz sipped her water and watched as people helped themselves to drinks while Angel opened her gifts and hugged all her friends. They were mostly women, but there were a few men, including Viv's son, Noah, who was here with his girlfriend. All having a good time, all of them young and beautiful.

Liz had a sudden flashback to Jen and Mike's engagement party. They too had been young and beautiful, and head over heels in love. It had been sparkling wine rather than champagne back then, but the corks had popped just as loudly, the mood every bit as celebratory. As the first two of their peers to name the day, everyone had been overexcited by this big step towards growing up and settling down.

For Liz, the party was bittersweet; she was happy for them, of course she was, but two were about to become one and there'd be no room for a third person in their marriage. They were moving on without her, and despite the crowd and the noise, she'd never felt more alone. For the first time since the happy couple had got together, it had really felt as if she was losing Jen from her life. She remembered having a desperate urge to get really drunk and forget all about it for a while.

'Am I the last to arrive?' a voice came from behind her.

Liz jumped, sloshing her water. She put the glass down and smiled at a woman with a mane of soft dark curls. 'Hello! Not sure.'

'My apologies,' said the new arrival, grabbing a cloth to mop up the water.

'Not at all, I was miles away,' said Liz, realising that her hands were trembling. 'I can finish that, you join the others in the garden. Help yourself to a cocktail.'

'I'm driving, but thanks.'

Liz took a deep breath, annoyed with herself for letting such an old memory unsettle her. She counted the party: twenty-one. Everyone had arrived, so that girl had been the last. Time to start the rice. As she reached towards the rice cooker, she knocked against an open bottle of vodka and caught it before it hit the floor.

There was still some left in it.

Her mouth felt parched despite the water she'd been drinking; this was a thirst only alcohol could slake. She looked round to check no one was watching. One small sip wouldn't hurt, it would take the edge off her nerves, help her to settle. She swigged from the vodka bottle and gasped as the spirit hit the back of her throat. She closed her eyes and took a deep breath. That was better. Just one more little sip . . .

When Skye returned from the garden a few minutes later, Liz was buzzing. That little drop of booze had done the trick. Whoever said that alcohol was a depressant was totally wrong. The stress was gone, the nerves had subsided, and she'd managed to put all thoughts of Mike out of her head.

'What do you want me to do next?' Skye slid the empty drinks tray onto the work surface.

'The guests will mingle for another twenty minutes,' said Liz, checking the rice in the steamer. 'We'll put the food on the table outside where they can serve themselves. Clean down while they're eating. Load dishwasher. Serve dessert. Pack up as much as we can. Put the birthday cake on the platter and leave them to it. Bob's your uncle, Fanny's your aunt.'

Skye laughed. 'I don't know why you said you couldn't manage by yourself. Look at you, you're killing it.'

'The party mood must be infectious!' Liz threw her arms out, narrowly missing a bouquet of flowers which had arrived for Angel.

'They do seem a nice bunch,' said Skye, wistfully. 'And mostly my age.'

'Go and hand these round.' Liz gave her some bowls of nibbles, taking pity on her. 'It'll give you a chance to chat while you work.'

132

Her eyes lit up. 'If you're sure?'

'Go!' Liz flapped her away. 'Enjoy yourself. I'll be fine for a few minutes.'

Once Skye had gone, Liz added another slug of vodka to her glass and congratulated herself for having the fore-sight to add Skye onto the van's insurance policy. Not that she was planning on getting tiddly. Warm and fuzzy was fine, but she didn't want to risk overdoing it, not while she was working.

'Happy birthday, Angel,' Liz murmured under her breath and knocked the vodka back in one.

Chapter Twelve

Skye

Now that the hot food had been served, Skye's pulse was returning to normal speed. She hadn't said anything to Liz or Clare, but she'd had a sleepless night worrying about this, her first big event. She had so wanted it to be a success, and so far, it was.

She paused for a moment in the doorway, watching people laughing and chatting. She envied those who could relax at parties, simply wander up to a group and join in. She'd always been one to hang back on the periphery.

It hadn't helped that her parents could never understand her reticence. 'Go on, don't be shy,' had been her mother's refrain at social gatherings, as she'd try to push a young and nervous Skye into the fray. It had been a ridiculous approach; telling someone not to be shy was as futile as telling them not to be five feet four inches tall. Skye couldn't help it; it was who she was.

But today Skye had pushed herself out of her comfort zone for the benefit of Liz's business. Because if the party went well, then maybe they'd get more local jobs like this, instead of relying on tourists. Clare had tweaked the website and she had started to post her photos of Salcombe on Instagram, tagging the business. All good profile-building stuff, but they were going to need solid bookings to generate the profit to pay her dad back.

'Excuse me, may I get by?' said a voice from behind.

'Sure, sorry!'

It was Noah, the guy Liz had introduced her to. He passed her, carrying a speaker, which he set up at the bottom of the garden. Soon, music filled the air and people got up to dance.

The rain had held off until now, but the clouds were getting heavier and darker. If they could just finish eating before the heavens opened, it would make their job a whole lot easier, Skye thought. The only access to the house was via the kitchen and trying to clear away in the tight space with tipsy party guests charging in to get out of the rain was an extra obstacle they didn't need.

Skye left Liz decanting the passion-fruit fool she'd made for dessert into individual portions and went outside to clear the main course.

'Are these finished with?' She crouched down between Ele and Angel to collect their plates

'Technically, I should be finished,' Angel groaned, rubbing her stomach. 'But I might have to have seconds. It was all so delicious.'

'You're enjoying your birthday party, then?' Skye asked, thinking that Liz would be thrilled when she told her.

'I really am.' Angel held her glass out while the man next to her topped it up. 'I feel really spoiled. Especially as my big brother Adam has come down from Bath to spend time with me. We've got the summer together because he'll be working from Salcombe right through until September, so I'm really honoured.'

'Wouldn't have missed your birthday for the world,' Adam replied, grinning at Skye. 'Absolutely nothing to do with the thirty text messages you sent to remind me.'

'Sounds like your sister really wanted you here,' Skye replied, envious of their strong bond. She couldn't imagine Clare ever saying anything like that about her.

'We all do,' said Ele, with an exaggerated sigh, batting her eyelashes at Adam. 'But sadly to no avail.'

'My brother is famously picky when it comes to women,' said Angel to Skye, lowering her voice. 'He had his heart broken once and refuses to risk it a second time.'

Adam pretended to growl at his sister. 'Stop stirring. I'd rather be single than in a mediocre relationship.'

'Couldn't agree more,' said Skye. 'It's got to be right, for both parties, or else what's the point?'

'Hear, hear!' said a voice from further away.

Angel laughed. 'That's my best friend. I might have known she'd be listening in.'

A woman with long dark curly hair sitting further down the line of people leaned forward. She dazzled in a white sundress and a tiny diamond stud sparkled in her nose. Skye recognised her instantly. It was the woman she'd seen diving off the jetty on her first weekend in Salcombe. Marta.

'Oh hey, we meet again,' Marta said, smiling at Skye. She was sitting cross-legged; she was so flexible that her knees were flat to the rug.

'You two know each other?' Angel looked surprised.

'Not really. It was a brief encounter,' said Skye. Although she recalled every second of it.

'It was too early on a Sunday morning for you, Angel,' Marta added.

'Marta is the Sunrise Queen,' Ele explained. 'Swimming, yoga, general cheerfulness . . .'

'Whereas my sister rarely sees morning,' Adam teased. 'And is generally grumpy before noon.'

'Oh, shush. I work for a company in California, I'm allowed to start work late,' Angel retorted. 'Back to you, Skye, I'm guessing you're single too?'

Skye felt several pairs of eyes on her; heat rose to her face. 'Um, I . . . well, I suppose . . . Yes, yes I am.'

'Your food is incredible,' Marta interrupted her. 'I haven't tasted anything so fresh and authentic since I was in Bali doing my training.'

'Thank you,' Skye replied, her blush deepening. 'All Liz's work, I'm just the humble assistant.'

'Be sure to tell her from me,' said Marta.

'I will,' Skye promised. 'She'll be delighted – please spread the word if you know of anyone else who needs catering.'

She could see Liz now, through the doors into the kitchen, singing to herself, adding a swirl of fresh passion-fruit purée to the top of each dessert, stopping every so often to sip from her water glass.

'Wow,' Angel teased. 'Praise indeed coming from this one.'

Marta shrugged. 'Honesty is always good.'

There was a crash from the kitchen, reminding Skye that she hadn't done any work for ages.

'Whoops, there's my cue to help,' she said, scooping up a pile of plates. 'Excuse me.'

Skye found Liz kneeling in a frothy puddle of passion-fruit mousse, picking up shards of broken glass from the tiled floor.

'Liz! Be careful!' Skye gasped. She shut the doors from the garden for a second to make sure no one with bare feet came through and cut themselves while she found a dustpan and mop.

'It's fine, fine, fine,' Liz sang. 'I'd made some extras anyway.'

'I'll clear this up,' Skye offered. 'Why don't you wash your hands?'

Liz nodded, smearing her moussey hands over every conceivable surface as she staggered to a standing position. 'Good idea. Might just pay a visit while you do that.'

Skye had cleaned up, stacked the empty bottles in a crate and added the final garnish of baby mint leaves to the mousse by the time Liz returned.

'Are you OK?' Skye scanned Liz's face. Her pupils were dilated and her cheeks were pink. But then again, hers probably were too after that conversation in the garden about being single.

Liz beamed. 'Tip-top. I got a bit hot, that was all. Shall we carry these outside?' She gestured towards the rows of martini glasses filled with mousse.

'I'll do it,' said Skye, picking up the heavy tray. 'You have a sit-down. You deserve a break.'

'Thanks.' Liz sank onto a chair. 'I will.'

By the time everyone who wanted dessert had been served, Liz had fallen asleep. Skye felt guilty waking her, but they still had work to do.

'Liz!' Skye shook her shoulders.

'Wha—?' Liz's head jerked up and she took a moment to focus. Her eyes were bloodshot. Poor thing; she looked exhausted. 'Just resting my eyes.'

'Get Liz out here,' cried Angel from the garden, 'we want to give her a round of applause for her amazing food.'

'Come outside and take a bow!' Ele added and someone else whistled.

There was a bit of drool on Liz's chin. Skye handed her a tissue. 'Time to greet your fans.'

'Really?' Liz's eyes sparkled. Or, rather, one of them did, the other one was still having a job to open properly.

'Yes, really,' Skye assured her. 'Everyone has been asking me for recipes.'

'I've had such fun today, I was really nervous, but there was no need. Liz stumbled a little as she stood up.'

'Whoops. Not tipsy are you?' Skye teased. The smile dropped from her face as she caught a whiff of alcohol on Liz's breath. Oh no. *Oh no.* 'Bloody hell, Liz.'

'Of course not! I'm a profesh-niol,' Liz replied haughtily and flounced out of the kitchen.

Skye hurried after her. OK, maybe Liz had had a couple of drinks. But there was no need to panic. Skye could cover for her and finish the clearing away. All she had to do was make sure Liz didn't get her hands on any more booze.

Leaving Liz to chat with some of the guests, nursing a glass of water, Skye collected the dirty plates and glasses and took the leftover food to the kitchen. She worked as fast as she could, keeping one eye on Liz at all times. Most people were on their feet now, chatting in groups; a few more had joined in the dancing at the bottom of the garden.

'Normally there'd be fried egg in the rice, but with it being vegan I had to make a few substitutions,' Liz was saying. She was propped against the table, sloshing her water around as she spoke.

'And this curry . . . the flavours are mwah!' Angel kissed her fingertips. 'So much more intense than mine. What's your secret?'

'Skye and I devised the recipe between us' said Liz, flushed with success. 'Adapted it from beef rendang. Without the beef, of course.'

'You're a genius,' said Marta.

'You must have a drink, Liz!' said Noah, topping up everyone's glass with wine. 'Chef's prerogative, after all that hard work.'

'Well, if you insist.' Liz promptly tipped out the rest of her water on the grass and held the glass out for Noah to pour into.

Skye dashed outside. 'We've got to drive back, remember,' she said, aiming for a light tone.

'Oh, live a little. A small one won't hurt,' Liz said, accepting a drink. 'And you're insured to drive the van, so don't worry about that.'

'Cheers!' Ele chinked her glass against Liz's. 'You were saying, about your recipe?'

'Yes, sorry, my brain's gone,' Liz giggled. 'So, it's vegetables, coconut milk, then I made my own curry paste, of course. Oyster sauce, lemon grass and—'

Skye froze. Had Liz just said . . .

'Oyster sauce . . .?' Angel looked at the others and frowned.

Liz nodded. 'Gives it that lovely *umami*. Great word umami. Uuu-mah-mi. What?'

She lurched to one side with shock as Skye flung herself out onto the patio, squeezed in next to Liz and put a tight arm around her shoulders. 'The original recipe has oyster sauce. But we substituted it for something else didn't we, Liz?'

Liz looked blank. 'Er. Did we?'

Skye stared at Liz, hoping that the intensity of the look she was giving her would make its way through the fog clouding Liz's thoughts.

'We did!' Liz cried after a pause. 'No oysters were harmed in the making of this dish, I can assure you. Haha!'

'You had us going there, Liz,' Marta laughed. 'Good one.'

'I make my own vegan oyster sauce,' Angel said. 'Mushrooms and seaweed. Takes ages but tastes so good.'

'You've got too much time on your hands,' Adam said, bemused.

'Can I have a word, in the kitchen?' Skye whispered to Liz.

'Of course,' Liz replied, in a small voice. 'Excuse me, everyone, duty calls.'

It took her two attempts to set her glass on the table. Skye followed close behind as she stumbled inside.

'Oh no. Oh no. Oh bloody hell.' Liz clapped a hand over her mouth. 'I've fed oysters to vegans. What are we going to do?'

'What *can* we do, they've eaten it now?' Skye hissed. She ran over the recipe in her head; she was sure she'd crossed out oyster sauce.

'What if someone is allergic to seafood and their insides swell up and they die? I'll never forgive myself,' worried Liz.

'If anyone was going to have a violent reaction, they'd have had it by now.' Skye scanned the guests through the French doors. 'No one has been sick yet. Luckily.'

'This is bad, this is really bad.' Liz shook her head. 'I'm such an idiot. This would never have happened if—'

'If you hadn't been drinking?' Skye said flatly.

Liz flinched as if she'd been struck. 'If Jen had been here, I was going to say. I knew something would happen like this. I just can't do it without her. I just can't.'

She grabbed the vodka bottle and took a swig before Skye could wrestle it out of her hands.

'You *can* do it and you have,' said Skye, she needs to take the bottle back off Liz here first tipping the rest of the vodka down the sink. 'OK, you've made one small mistake.'

Liz shook her head and flopped down onto a chair. 'Two mistakes. There was fish sauce in one of the dressings, I remember now. I'm sorry, Skye.'

There'd been three mistakes if you counted drinking too much. Skye rubbed a weary hand over her face. Why would Liz jeopardise this event when allegedly it was important to her? What should she say to Angel about the compromised vegan food? And, most pressing of all, how could they finish their catering job when fifty per cent of the team could barely stand?

'Liz?' Skye began, but Liz hiccoughed loudly and slithered to the floor.

Chapter Thirteen

Skye

Skye got Liz back in a chair and forced her to drink some water before any of the party guests noticed anything was amiss.

'I don't suppose there's any chance of a coffee, is there?' Adam asked from the doorway.

'I bet he's VWE,' Liz sniggered, trying to nudge Skye.

'VWE?' he repeated, confused.

'Vegans with exceptions,' said Skye hurriedly. 'Coffee! What a good idea! One pot of coffee coming right up. I'll bring it out.'

'Is she OK?' Adam inclined his head towards Liz.

'Liz? Oh, she's fine,' Skye said lightly, stepping between them, as Liz seemed to be building up to a big burp.

'I feel a bit funny,' Liz moaned. 'I might just get some fresh air.'

She staggered up from her chair and Skye caught her as her knees buckled. Skye was mortified, as Liz would be when she sobered up. Hopefully, Ele would think it was hilarious and not mind at all, but they still had a summer of catering jobs ahead of them. The last thing they needed was word about this to get out.

'Oh dear, poor thing,' said Adam, kindly.

Skye looked at him, trying to work out if he was finding this funny or not. But his expression revealed nothing but concern.

'It's nerves,' Skye said, her eyes pleading with him not to tell anyone. 'This event means a lot to her. I think she may have overdone the Dutch courage.'

'Understood. Come on, Liz.' He tucked her arm through his. 'Let's have a turn around the garden and I can tell you my theory about saving versus spending in a bull market.'

Skye raised an eyebrow. She was about to make a comment along the lines of: I bet you're fun at parties, but seeing as he was doing her a favour, she kept quiet.

He grinned. 'I'm a financial advisor. That subject is guaranteed to sober anyone up.'

Liz blinked slowly at him. 'Do I have to?'

'Yes. You do.' Skye felt a wave of gratitude towards Adam. 'I'll finish making your coffee.'

'Let's start with the difference between bull and bear, shall we?' he said, leading a reluctant Liz out into the darkening afternoon.

As soon as they'd gone, Skye pulled out her mobile and called the only person she knew who could help. Clare answered immediately as Skye had known she would. Clare was too efficient to let a phone call go unanswered.

'Hello?' Clare's voice was loud and Skye could hear the noise of the car engine in the background.

'I need a favour. How difficult would it be for you to come to Thurlestone?' she asked.

'Why?'

'Liz has had too much to drink and I need help.'

'Shit.' Clare went quiet for a second. 'OK. I'm not far away, Ivy's asleep in the back. Give me the postcode and I'll put it in the satnav.'

Skye ended the call and took a deep breath. It was fine. It was all going to be fine. She did feel very guilty about the oyster sauce – oh God, and the fish sauce – but no one seemed any the worse for it and everyone had said it was one of the best meals they'd ever tasted. They would find a way to make it up to the vegans somehow. In the meantime, she needed to serve the birthday cake, clear up as much as she could, and when Clare arrived, she would pour Liz into the car and Clare could take her home. She could pack away everything and follow on in the van.

Skye left the front door on the latch so that Clare could let herself in, and returned to the kitchen. Ele and two of her friends had come in and taken the lid off the cake box. They were in fits of laughter, stabbing candles into the top of the beautiful rainbow cake Liz had made.

'Cake time!' Ele grinned squiffily at her.

'Good idea!' Skye gave her a bright smile. She heaped coffee into a cafetière, filled it up to the brim with water and found mugs, spoons and sugar. She glanced outside: still no rain, but in the distance towards the sea, she saw a flash of a lightning. Great; just what she needed. 'Should we take the birthday cake through to the living room, do you think, Ele?' Skye shouted to make herself heard over the hoots of laughter.

The birthday candles had come in a pack of one hundred. By the look of it, the girls had decided to use all of them. At this rate, Skye was going to have a fire on her hands as well as everything else.

'Outside is where the party is at,' Ele replied. 'Where are the matches?'

She started pulling out drawers.

'Wait!' said Skye. 'Liz has packed a little gas lighter somewhere. It'll be easier to use than matches.'

Before she could get as far as their equipment crate, one of the girls had slid her hands under the flimsy cardboard base and lifted it up.

'Bloody hell this is heavy!' she squealed. 'Ele, grab the other side!'

'We've brought a nice plate to serve it on.' Skye was feeling panicky; everything was getting out of control. Where was Clare? And what was that noise coming from the garden . . .?

Adam's grave face appeared at the open kitchen door. 'I'm sorry, Skye, I tried, but I'm no match for Liz's party spirit.'

Skye looked past him at the scene in the garden in dismay. Someone had produced a bottle of tequila and Noah was lining up shot glasses.

'Liz-Liz-Liz!' Angel chanted.

'Shot-shot-shot!' chanted someone else.

Skye didn't know whether to laugh or cry. 'Thanks for trying. Your coffee is ready.'

He stepped inside as the girls pushed past him with the cake, yelling, 'Coming through, coming through!'

Skye followed them outside in time to see Liz shimmying into position in front of a row of glasses. 'This is such fun! I've never done tequila shots before.'

Someone handed Liz a slice of lime and sprinkled salt on the back of her hand. The cake had been set down on the table. Ele and her friends were lighting matches, but a breeze had picked up and every flame was snuffed out before they could light a single candle. They were finding it very funny. Skye could hardly look.

'Try not to worry.' Marta's smooth voice materialised in her ear. 'We all have our own ways of letting our hair down. And something tells me Liz needs this.'

'You're probably right.' Skye glanced sideways at her. There was a calmness about Marta which Skye took comfort from. 'And, after today, I'm going to need a lie-down in a darkened room for a whole week.'

Marta laughed. 'You need to join me for some yoga. I'm a teacher.'

'Like classes?' Skye hadn't done much yoga in her life, but if there was a chance she could absorb some of Marta's serenity, it might be worth a shot.

She nodded. 'You should join us.'

'Us?' For a second, Skye was disappointed that Marta hadn't extended a personal invitation to her and flushed at the thought. She was instantly transported back to school and the crush she'd had on a girl called Luella, who she'd followed around like an adoring fan. But Skye was almost thirty, not a desperate-to-please teenage girl, and she gave herself a shake.

'In the summer, I teach sunrise yoga on the beach,' Marta explained, handing Skye a card. 'The schedule is in my Instagram bio. I'd love to see you there.'

'Thanks. Well, who knows, you just might.'

The two women smiled at each other. It had been a long time since Skye had a real connection with someone and she hadn't realised how much she'd missed it. She felt an urge to hug her, but before she had a chance to act on it, Marta tilted her face upwards and held out her hand.

'I felt rain.'

A droplet of cold water splashed on Skye's warm skin. Then another. 'Me too.'

There was a crack of thunder overhead and the heavens opened. Within seconds, everyone was screaming.

'Arrghhh!'

'Everyone in!'

'Grab the speaker!'

There was a stampede to get inside as people scooped up phones and bags and glasses. The door to the kitchen was a bottleneck and Liz was swept along with the crowd. The beautiful cake had been abandoned and Skye pushed her way to it, determined to rescue it.

'Skye! It's me!' came a voice from the midst of the crowd. Skye peered through the glass and caught sight of Clare waving frantically at her. 'Help me with Liz!'

'Two seconds!' Skye yelled back. 'Let me just get the cake.'

'Quick!' Clare shouted back. 'I've left Ivy in the car.'

Skye's clothes were already soaked and her hair was plastered to her head. The birthday cake was probably ruined, but Skye didn't care. All that work, all that money, not to mention the dozens of candles which now pierced it. She tried to pick up the cake, but the cardboard base had gone soggy.

'I'll help.' Adam appeared on the opposite side of the table; his shirt was wet through and she could see his nipples. 'Lace your fingers through mine.'

Skye dragged her eyes away from his chest and nodded. Their hands linked underneath the wet cake.

'Three, two one, lift,' he said.

They lifted it up and stepped sideways, clearing the table.

'I'll go backwards,' Skye offered.

Adam nodded and together they shuffled to the door. The icing was sliding off the cake, the candles floating down one side like slalom poles down a ski slope.

'Mmm, yum. Everyone's going to be clamouring for a slice of this,' Adam said, squinting at her, his face dripping wet.

'Don't make me laugh,' Skye said, trying not to giggle, 'I'm on the edge of hysterics already.'

'OK.' Adam looked over Skye's shoulder. 'Ready for the threshold. The step is right behind—'

Adam faltered as Skye lifted one leg to clear the step. The cake started to sag between them. Adam made a grab for it, but Skye tripped over the step and fell backwards into the kitchen. The cake landed with a splat on the kitchen floor.

'What the . . .?' Adam's voice sounded gruff as he stared over her shoulder.

'Ouch!' Skye hit her head on the corner of the dresser and landed on the tiled floor, one foot skidding in the cake. Pain shot through her. 'Adam, help!'

But she'd lost his attention.

'Saskia!' he cried. 'It *is* you. It's me, Adam. Remember?'

'Who?' Skye rubbed her head. Where had she heard that name recently? And who was Saskia?

'Oh my God. This is a bloody nightmare.' Clare shook her head in disbelief.

'Saskia, did you hear me?' Adam repeated.

Skye was going to have a massive bruise on her bum and her head was already thumping. Clare was right; this was a nightmare, and the sooner they could extract Liz, the better.

'Let's go.' Clare grabbed hold of her arm and tugged, but the combination of Skye's wet skin and the icing on the floor proved too much for her. Clare's shoe scooted sideways from under her, and she fell heavily onto her right arm, landing with a sickening crunch on the floor beside Skye. 'Oh-oh-oh. Noooo!' Clare gasped, her eyes wide in terror. 'I think I've broken my arm.'

Skye clambered to her knees, took one look at Clare's arm, which from the elbow down was facing the wrong way, and felt dizzy. 'Definitely not looking good.'

Adam knelt in front of Clare and studied her face. 'I can see this isn't a good time, but it is you, isn't it?'

'Skye, help me.' Clare's face had gone deathly white, and her voice had diminished to a whisper. 'Tell him to leave me alone.'

'Thanks, Adam,' Skye said firmly. 'I've got this. Come on now, easy does it.'

'*Clare*?' His brow furrowed, clearly confused. 'Please, can we talk?'

'I think I'm going to faint,' Clare groaned as Skye helped her to her feet.

'Let me help you get her to a chair,' Adam insisted.

Skye shook her head. 'She's my sister; I can manage.'

'Half-sister,' Clare murmured through her obvious pain. 'And we've got to get back to the car – I've left Ivy in it.'

Skye glanced around at the press of people, the mess on the floor and Liz weaving her way through the crowd. How could she possibly leave now? Then again, how could she not?

'OK, let's do it.' She manoeuvred Clare through the kitchen, clearing a path by waving an arm in front of her.

Together, they headed out of the front door and into the rain, where Clare had parked her car beside the van. Skye opened the car door for Clare to get into the passenger seat. Ivy was still fast asleep in the back.

Clare cradled her injured arm to her chest, her face still white. 'What the hell are we going to do?'

Skye's whole body was trembling, she was soaking wet, covered in birthday cake and her bum was going to be black and blue in the morning. 'I'm going to take you to hospital.'

'You can't drive my car!'

'Ivy certainly can't, and Liz is shit-faced, so have you got any other bright ideas?' Skye snapped.

'Fine!' Clare grunted. 'The keys are in my jeans pocket.'

She hitched one buttock off the seat and winced as Skye retrieved them.

Skye was so on edge that it took her a few seconds to get the key in the ignition and it crossed her mind that she probably wasn't in a fit state to drive at all.

Suddenly, Clare shrieked. Skye followed her gaze to see Adam flying out of the house towards them.

'I need to talk to you.' Adam knocked on the window. 'Saskia, I need to talk to you. Please!'

'Drive!' Clare yelled. 'Drive.'

'I'm trying!' Skye yelled back in frustration. 'But why does Angel's brother think you're called Saskia?'

Clare blinked at her. 'Because . . . I told him I was.'

Skye stared at her uncomprehending. 'You're not making any sense.'

'Adam is Ivy's father, OK?' she replied, dropping her chin to her chest. 'Now, please, can we go?'

'That is Ivy's father? The man who left you?' Fury raged through Skye, and before she was even aware of what she was doing, she sprang from the car and shoved Adam with all her strength. 'You bastard!' she yelled in his face. 'How could you?'

'What?' He looked bewildered. 'What have *I* done?'

She jabbed him in the chest. 'It's what you haven't done more like, you spineless piece of shit. How could you turn your back on her when she needed you?'

He held his hands up, as if surrendering. 'I'm so confused right now.'

Clare managed to wind the car window down. 'Skye. Get in. Now. *Please.*'

'I don't know what's going on, but I hope you're OK,' said Adam, taking a step away from the car. 'Maybe we can meet up soon, grab a coffee?'

Skye was overcome with indignation and anger. Seriously? How could he stand there, all casual, and say that? She leapt towards him and thumped him in the stomach as hard as she could. 'You stay away from her.'

'Oof.' Adam doubled over in pain. 'What was that for? I was only trying to help.'

'As if you don't know!' Skye gave him a look of disgust before jumping into the driving seat.

'Oh God,' Clare whispered, her face as white as a sheet. 'You shouldn't have done that.'

Skye put the car into reverse and put the wipers on fast.

'Yes, I should,' she said through gritted teeth. 'No one treats my family like that. Not even my half-sister.'

'That's just the point,' said Clare, watching Adam clutching his stomach. 'No one has.'

'No one has what?' Skye demanded. 'I don't understand.'

Clare closed her eyes. 'Long story. And not for today.'

Chapter Fourteen

Clare

'This has been a lovely treat, thank you.' Mum gave me a hug goodbye. 'I shall drift down to Devon on a cloud of bliss.'

We were in the reception of the Ivy Hotel and Spa at the end of a day of pure indulgence: swimming, saunas, massages, and best of all, hours of uninterrupted conversation catching up with each other's lives.

'Thank you for joining me,' I replied, wrapping my arms around her, savouring being with my favourite person on the planet for as long as possible.

'I'm so proud of my girl.' Mum pressed her cheek against mine. 'But it's nice to see you relaxed. You work so hard.'

'Er, pot, kettle,' I retorted with a laugh. 'And you're sure you can't stay for dinner? There's still money left on my voucher.'

Mum bent down to retie the laces of her Dr Martens boots. 'Tempting, but I daren't. We've got a big booking to prep for tomorrow. I need to be at Liz's bright and early or she'll get stressed.'

We both smiled. My godmother and Mum's best friend, Liz, had messaged her several times today checking up on details for their next catering event. Not that Mum would have it any other way. The Seaside Gourmet Girls succeeded because they both brought different skills into play: Mum being the unflappable hostess who could smooth over any bumps, and Liz, whose delicious food and attention to detail ensured that the bumps were few and far between.

'But you must stay,' Mum insisted. 'Make the most of your day off. Or else, knowing you, you'll spend the evening on your laptop and undo all the good work from today. Right, I'm off. I love you.'

'Love you too.'

We gave each other a kiss and I waved to her as she strode away in her fuchsia pink coat, out into the dark evening towards the car park.

I looked at the locker key in my hand, wondering whether to collect my things and go home. If I left now, I could unblock the kitchen sink, which had been harbouring a mysterious aroma for the last few days, or, as Mum had hinted at, I could squeeze in an hour of work.

But there was at least another twenty pounds to spend on my gift voucher (one of the best gifts from a pupil I'd ever had in my decade of teaching). I deserved this treat, I thought and headed to the bar for a drink.

'Ouch!' I gasped as someone barged into me, sending a plume of hot water out of the spout of the teapot I was carrying and over my hand. 'Shit.'

'Gosh, I am so sorry,' said a male voice behind me. 'Are you OK? Don't answer that. Stupid question.'

I stumbled back to my table quickly and set the pot down, squeezing my eyes shut against the pain. 'It's fine.'

It wasn't fine. I'd asked for a top-up for my mint tea and the water was approximately one million degrees centigrade.

'Ice! I'll get some ice.' He darted back to the bar.

I sat down, grabbed a napkin and dried my throbbing hand. There was already a livid red mark across the skin. I contemplated dashing to the bathroom to hold it under cold water like you're supposed to do, but there was a man fetching ice for me and I didn't want to appear ungrateful. Besides, he was already on his way back clutching a bundled-up cloth filled with ice cubes. He drew up a chair and sat down.

'Here.' He held out his hand for my burned one. 'Let me see.'

I put my hand in his immediately. Supporting my wrist, he lowered the makeshift ice pack onto the back of my hand. I let out a little moan.

'How's that?' he asked, worriedly. 'Better or worse?'

'Better.' I nodded my encouragement. This was weirdly very enjoyable. A stranger holding my hand, our heads almost touching. If I wasn't in acute pain, it would be quite romantic.

I'm ashamed to say this, but if some haggardy lizard had been invading my personal space like this, I'd have shaken him off and insisted that I could manage.

But he wasn't.

On a scale of one to ten in the looks department, he was hovering between nine and ten.

'Good.' He looked up at me and smiled, dimples appeared in his cheeks and I forgot about the stinging sensation on my skin.

Make that a strong ten.

He was my sort of age – that is to say, still young, definitely not at the 'your biological clock is ticking, better get a move on' stage. Average height, slim without being thinner than me – bonus. (Been there, got the 'my hips are stuck in your jeans' T-shirt.) Plus, thick dark hair with a bit of a kink to it; it would be nice to run my fingers through it, tug it a bit maybe. I blushed at the direction my mind was going in.

'You look really uncomfortable,' he said, apologetically, lifting the ice from my skin and releasing my hand. 'Shall I stop dabbing?'

I blushed some more in case he could read my mind. Already I missed his hand holding mine. And yes, it had been a while since I'd been this up close and personal with a man.

'Please don't stop,' I blurted out, indecently fast. 'I think it's helping, thank you.'

He leaned over me again, resuming his position as hand-holder and ice-pack provider. 'You're welcome.'

I flicked my gaze from my hand to him and cocked an eyebrow ever so slightly.

His eyes widened. 'I can't believe I just said you're welcome after giving you a third-degree burn on the back of your hand.'

'Not quite third degree,' I corrected him. 'But my days as a model for Tiffany are over forever.'

'Oh my God, please tell me you're joking.' He looked so horror-struck that I burst out laughing.

'Joking.'

This was fun. Hold the front page. Steady, sensible Clare with a five-year plan for everything was having some spontaneous fun.

I did have fun sometimes, I wasn't a total bore. Mum and I had had fun today. And I'd had fun two weeks ago, arranging all my jumpers in colour order in my wardrobe. But this sort of fun – having a laugh with a strange man in a hotel bar – well, that hadn't happened in a while. Or possibly ever.

A waiter glided over at that moment and interrupted us with a respectful bow. 'Are you going to be dining with us this evening?'

'I am, yes,' said my handsome first-aider. He looked at me. 'Are you staying at the hotel too?'

My heart skipped. He was staying overnight, which meant he wasn't local, which meant there'd be no chance of running into him at parents' evening and having an awkward conversation about tonight. Hurrah.

I shook my head. 'I'm a day guest at the spa. I was just grabbing a drink before heading off.'

His shoulders slumped. 'So you'd been feeling all zen before some klutz doused you in boiling water?'

I grinned. 'Pretty much.'

'Then allow me to buy you dinner. I owe you that at the very least.'

I opened my mouth to make a half-hearted attempt to protest, but he held my gaze.

'Please, you'd be doing me a favour, I never like eating alone.'

'But I don't even know your name,' I said, coquettishly. Not sure if I'd ever even been coquettish before.

'Adam,' he supplied. 'And you?'

At this point I'd usually stick my hand out to shake his and say, 'Clare Marriott, two Rs, two Ts.' In a confident, businesslike manner, as befitted a head teacher. (The head bit was new. I was in my first term and finding it thrilling and overwhelming, depending on what day it was.)

But I didn't. In the first place, he was holding my hand, pressing ice cubes to my burn, so shaking at this point felt a bit pointless. But there was something else going on here. Something very un-Clare like. Maybe it was because I'd had the best massage of my life earlier this afternoon from a Hungarian lady called Bella and my body felt languid and floaty. Or maybe it was because of the way we were leaning towards each other, eyes locked as if there were no one here but us.

Or maybe it was simply that there was no food in my fridge and the idea of pasta with Marmite again wasn't doing it for me. Whatever it was, I felt like stepping out of my life for a couple of hours and being whoever I wanted to be.

'Pleased to meet you, Adam,' I said, dropping my chin and looking up at him from under my lashes. 'I'm . . . Saskia.'

'Cool name.'

It was, I thought, pleased with my choice. I'd always slightly resented the ordinariness of Clare compared to my younger half-sister's name. 'Skye' suggested someone free-spirited, someone who threw caution to the wind and lived in the moment. Clare was someone who religiously saved ten per cent of her monthly salary, froze her leftovers in Tupperware boxes and filled the kettle before going to bed to save time in the morning. I was normally a complete Clare.

The waiter coughed, making both of us jump. 'Will that be two for dinner, sir?'

Adam raised his eyebrows enquiringly at me and I gave a slow single nod. A Saskia nod.

Because, of course, Saskia would say yes to an invitation like that.

Dinner was delicious.

'I've really enjoyed this evening,' I said, trying out a husky voice, ninety minutes later. 'I'm glad you bumped into me.'

Our table for two was in prime position near the window. Night had fallen, but the outdoor lighting gave us a magical view across the lawn to the lake beyond. It was the most romantic setting I think I'd ever experienced.

Our main courses had been cleared away and we were sharing the remains of a bottle of red wine and a cheese-board. My car would be staying here overnight and I'd be getting a taxi home, blow the expense. I'd hesitated less than a second before making that decision. Saskia wasn't the sort to miss out on a decent Barolo, and Clare found it a damn sight easier to flirt when her edges had gone a bit fuzzy. Although, at this point, I'd told so many lies that I'd have to switch to water soon before I started to contradict myself.

'Me too.' Adam's blue-green eyes flashed suggestively in the candlelight. 'Not literally, obviously. I'll forever feel bad about scalding you. But I've never met a location scout before. Such a cool job. You must have travelled all over the world?'

He speared the last sliver of Blue Vinny with his knife and offered it to me. *Phwoar.* He was getting sexier by the minute. I peeled it from the tip of the blade and put it on my tongue. Adam watched my every move. And I watched his. I was pretty sure he liked me. Either that or I had a smear of fig chutney on my face and he didn't know how to tell me.

To think I'd almost gone home at the same time as my mum. Imagine if I'd managed to persuade her to stay the night with me in Bath instead of dashing back to Salcombe. I'd have missed all this.

Adam swirled the wine around in his glass, still looking at me, and I realised I hadn't answered his question.

'I do get to visit some incredible places.' I shrugged nonchalantly. 'But, you know, the job still has its downsides.'

'Oh?' He waited for me to enlighten him, but I couldn't think of anything. I agreed with him; it *did* sound like a cool job. I only wished I knew more about it.

Fortunately, a member of staff picked that moment to collect our empty plates, saving me from digging myself into any deeper holes.

'Have you stayed at this hotel before?' I asked, taking control of the conversation once we were alone again.

Adam chewed his lip before replying. 'No, this is a first for me. Although it's been on my radar for a while.'

I studied him over the rim of my glass. 'It's my first visit too. I bet the rooms are gorgeous.'

'I could show you mine if you like.' His gaze was steady.

He was asking me up to his room.

I was no expert in these matters, but I don't think it was to look at the view from the window. Which was good, because it wasn't the view I was interested in. I'd liked what I'd seen of Adam so far and I was keen to see more. *Clare Elizabeth Marriott, you minx . . .*

'I'd like that.' I gave him an enigmatic smile.

I was actually doing this: picking up a man in a hotel bar and going back to his room. This was not like me *at all*. But I wasn't me, was I? I was Sexy Saskia the location scout. And we were two consenting adults who fancied the pants off each other.

Talking of pants. I wracked my brain to remember the details of mine. They were fine, I recalled with relief. I'd made an effort because I knew there'd be a communal changing room. I always darted into the cubicle if there was one. It pays to be careful in my job. This hotel was only a few miles out of Bath, there could easily have been parents from school here; I'd hate to have been caught in a state of shabby undress by one of the mums. I'd made that mistake before. Got stuck in a sports bra once in the changing rooms at my gym, only to be accosted by Izzie Millington's mum. I'd had to grapple topless with both arms in the air tangled in straps, with her giving me full barrels about the substandard lunch her daughter had been served the previous Tuesday. Once bitten, twice shy on that front. So, luckily, today's underwear was suitable for public consumption. Or private.

Adam stood up and offered me his hand. 'Shall we?'

I put my hand in his and got to my feet. A dart of pleasure ran up my arm as I felt his fingers close over mine. 'Just before we go . . . anywhere. Can I just check . . .' I swallowed, nervously. 'Are you . . . you're not . . .?'

He smiled, his expression open and honest. 'I'm not married or anything, if that was what you were worried about.'

'Good. And . . . um, you haven't got any kids?' I needed to be sure before this – whatever it was – went any further. He might not be local, but what if he had been once and he was here visiting his children and those children were pupils at my school and one day he turned up, took one look at me and said, 'Saskia? Is that you?'

'No kids,' he promised and then stepped closer to me and tucked a strand of hair behind my ear. 'Now, shall we get out of here?'

'Yes.' I nodded, my knees so weak that I wouldn't have been surprised if I'd dropped to the floor as soon as I started to walk. 'Yes please.'

We lay side by side in the vast bed, catching our breath. I could feel my pulse thudding at the side of my neck. I hadn't been this energetic since I won the teachers' race last sports day. Put me in a competitive situation and I'm compelled to aim for first place. I couldn't walk for a week afterwards, which served me right. Mind you, I had a feeling that might be the case tomorrow too.

'Was that OK?' said Adam beside me.

He sounded unsure of himself, which made me like him even more. Saskia would probably have said something provocative, like, not bad for starters, but I couldn't find it in me to tease him. He was too nice.

'More than OK.'

I turned to look at him. The room was mostly in darkness – I'd insisted on that – the only light was a glow from the bathroom. But I could see enough.

His face was inches from mine. He had nice lips, full and soft and the most perfect Cupid's bow I'd ever kissed. And I'd been right about his hair: it had felt gorgeous when I'd tugged it. I felt myself blush. I'd managed to keep up my Saskia persona throughout the whole act (or two acts, if you counted the one in the shower). But I was beginning to wish I'd never lied about my identity. Clare was beginning to emerge, and I was already worried about having to get out from under the covers naked and finding my knickers in the dark.

Maybe I'd just lie here a bit longer.

This whole night was so not me. I was sensible Clare, the one with the steady career, the one who worked hard at school and never caused her mother a moment's trouble. I've never even tried drugs, for God's sake, not one tiny whiff of a spliff, and I could always be relied on to drive on a night out.

I had this sudden image of myself writing tomorrow's post in my journal:

Dear Diary, last night I had sex with a stranger in his hotel bedroom. And bathroom, come to that . . .

I felt a giggle bubbling up in my chest.

'I just had sex with a stranger,' I said aloud into the darkness.

'Me too,' came the reply and we both laughed. 'We could swap life stories, if you like? So we're no longer strangers,' he suggested, trailing a finger up my arm.

I felt my body flood with desire.

'Or,' I said, pulling him towards me, 'you could just kiss me again.'

Words that would come back to haunt me, by the way.

He did kiss me again and I stopped worrying about finding my knickers.

We must have fallen asleep, because when I heard the soft vibration of my phone coming from my bag on the floor beside the bed, I sat up with a jolt.

The display on the clock beside the bed glowed red. It was after eleven and Adam was asleep. I slid out of the bed, wrapping myself in the damp towel I'd dropped on the floor after our shower, and pulled my phone from the depths of my bag.

I blinked at the screen, trying to work out what I was seeing. There were missed calls from an unknown number and several from Liz. Something was wrong. My blood started pumping even as I hit call on Liz's number.

She answered straight away. 'Oh Clare,' she sobbed down the line. 'I'm so, so sorry.'

'Liz? Oh my God, what's wrong?'

'It's your mum, darling. It's Jen.'

And just like that, the fun was over. Saskia vanished into thin air.

Chapter Fifteen

Clare

'Just drive, please.' Clare's voice trembled. 'Go!'

Skye complied.

They accelerated onto the road and Clare was pushed back against her seat. *The pain, the pain, the pain.* It was almost unbearable.

She forced herself to breathe as she watched Adam in the wing mirror. Hands low on his hips, shaking his head, he looked completely in shock. She was in shock too; not only from seeing him again, but from the crunching sensation going on in her upper arm. Her heart was thudding so erratically that it felt in danger of bursting right out of her chest.

Adam was in Salcombe of all places. She groaned out loud. Since hearing the name 'Saskia' being shouted from the ferry, she'd felt as if she'd been holding her breath. She'd deliberately stayed away from the beaches and the centre of town ever since to avoid bumping into him again, only to literally run into him at that party.

'I wish I'd never called you,' Skye said, her voice breaking. 'I should have just managed by myself. I've made everything far, far worse.'

'Not your fault,' Clare replied, although, truthfully, she wished the same. Her forehead was clammy, sweat prickled under her arms. 'You weren't to know.'

She closed her eyes to discourage any further conversation and her head was immediately full of him.

She'd never expected to see Adam again after that night. Never thought she'd be caught out like this, never thought she'd be confronted with the reality of Ivy's conception. Clare Marriott wasn't a liar, she was the sensible one. The sister who'd never made a misstep. The head teacher whose private life was completely wholesome. Clare was a woman who had it all, did it all and did it bloody well too.

Now she was going to have think fast; her past was catching up with her and she didn't know what to do about it.

And then there was Ivy. Oh God, *Ivy*, Adam's baby. A cold shiver ran down her back.

Had he seen her in the car seat? she wondered. Possibly not. Everything had happened so fast, and his attention had been on her. Father and daughter, separated by nothing more than a car window. Thank goodness she'd left Ivy in the car for those few minutes. Imagine if she'd walked in, a dark-haired baby on her hip. She shuddered. She'd just have to hope he didn't have a clue what – or who – was in the back of her car.

Adam. Her stomach flipped at the memory of him. Of what they'd done. Of what had come afterwards. If things had been different, if she'd met him on any night other than the one on which her mum had died, then maybe they'd have had some sort of relationship. But, as it was, she'd never seen him again.

It had been easy to write him out of the story, no one had questioned her. Dad wasn't interested enough, and Liz had been too bereft after Jen had died to want any more than the basic facts. As far as anyone else was concerned, Adam was an ex-boyfriend who was out of their lives. Ivy had Clare; she didn't need anyone else. His choice, his loss. They were better off without him. That was Clare's story and she'd stuck to it.

What she hadn't told anyone was that she'd never even known Adam's second name. The whole thing was just so sordid. How was it possible that the one night – *the one and only night* – she'd done something reckless and out of character could have set the course for her future? She felt confusion, shame and, above all, unbearable grief. But not regret, because to regret meeting Adam would mean regretting having her daughter, and Ivy was her world. Now her carefully curated life as a woman whose ex-partner had rejected the idea of co-parenting was in danger of coming apart at the seams. Her mind raced ahead to worst-case scenarios: he tracked her down; he demanded access to Ivy; he wanted joint custody. She knew she was catastrophising, but even so, her body started to shake with fear.

'No, no, no,' she whispered. 'Please, don't let that happen.'

'Sorry,' said Skye, oblivious to her real concerns.

Clare moaned as the car hit a pothole. Her whole left arm felt on fire. She had a flashback to falling in the kitchen. She remembered that she'd slipped sideways, her feet skidding in the cake. She'd fallen heavily on her side, but her hand had caught on something and she'd heard a crack. Looking down, she'd seen her forearm twisted outwards at an improbable angle. Without hesitation, she'd grabbed her wrist and wrenched the arm back towards her and clamped it to her chest. She hadn't let go since.

'I hope Adam's all right,' Skye muttered. 'I put all my strength behind that punch. I thought he deserved it.'

She left it hanging, clearly waiting for Clare to speak.

Say nothing, a voice in Clare's head whispered, *admit*

nothing. She'd already said more than she should have.

After a minute or so, Skye tried again.

'How's the temperature in the car? Too hot, too cold? Tell me if I can do anything to help.'

'The shopping in the boot of the car!' Clare remembered with a gasp, some stuff needs to go in the fridge.

'It's not important,' Skye said quietly. 'But you are.'

Clare turned her head away so Skye couldn't see her tears; neither of them had ever said anything nice like that before. 'Is Ivy OK?'

Ivy was directly behind her, making it impossible to check on her. She'd put the car seat there, diagonal to the driver's side, so that they could see each other.

Skye glanced quickly over her shoulder. 'She's fine, she's awake. Hello, Ivy!'

'Ivy, Mummy's here,' said Clare, forcing herself to sound normal. Tears of pain squeezed out of her eyes. 'We're going on a little trip with Auntie Skye. Actually, where *are* we going?'

'Kingsbridge hospital. It's the nearest A & E department.'

'Oh no.' Nausea surged through her. If she never went there again it would be too soon. 'Isn't there anywhere else?'

'Not for broken bones.'

It was on the tip of Clare's tongue to lie and say that it was only a sprain, but it would only delay getting pain relief and she wasn't sure how long she could endure this.

'I hate that place,' she whispered under her breath and, if Skye heard it, she didn't comment. Clare gave her a sideways glance; Skye had hitched the driver's seat as far forward as she could and was hunched over the steering wheel, shoulders up by her ears. 'Oh my God!' Clare cried suddenly. 'You're not insured on my car. Pull over, I'll have to drive.'

'With a broken arm? Are you insane?' Skye retorted.

'If we have an accident and Ivy gets injured . . .'

'We won't have an accident.'

'You're not used to Devon's narrow lanes and the high hedges. Slow down!' Clare screeched as a tractor came towards them. She tensed her body, trying to protect her arm from the movement of the car.

There was a passing place just in front of them. Skye pulled in tight, the branches of the hedge scratching the side of the car like nails down a chalkboard.

'It was you who told me to go fast,' Skye said as the tractor inched past them. 'And I've been driving a knackered old minibus in Uganda for years, where tarmac is a luxury. Relax.'

'Very funny.'

Skye winced. 'Sorry. But there's no way I'm letting you drive. Pretty sure that driving with a broken arm would invalidate your insurance, not to mention buggering up your arm for eternity.'

'Don't swear in front of Ivy. And it's an automatic. I could manage.' Clare could feel anxiety thrumming in her chest. 'Please. I'd just feel safer.'

'For an intelligent woman, you do say some ridiculous things.'

Clare looked out of the window. Her lips were trembling and she pressed them together. 'You have no idea.'

Saskia. My name is Saskia. Clare squeezed her eyes shut, blocking the memory, just as she'd been doing since that night.

'Sorry,' said Skye primly. 'But I'm driving. Get over it.'

'You love it, don't you?' Clare glared at her. 'Seeing me incapacitated.'

'What?' Skye replied, harshly. 'Why would you even think that? And, anyway, I am insured. Dad insured me to drive any car.'

'Of course he did,' Clare muttered under her breath.

'What's that supposed to mean?'

'It means that you're still Daddy's little princess even at thirty.'

'Twenty-nine.' Skye gripped the steering wheel. 'And if anyone was put on a pedestal, it was you – *Clare* this, *Clare* that.'

'Rubbish,' Clare scoffed. 'You were showered with gifts from the day you were born.'

'That's just stuff – I wanted attention, not stuff!' Skye bit back. 'Shit!'

A pheasant skittered into the middle of the road. Skye swerved around it, causing Clare to knock her arm on the car door.

'Ahhh, f—'

'Don't swear,' Skye jumped in. 'But sorry about that.'

'Oh for heaven's sake, stop saying sorry,' Clare said through gritted teeth. Her face was itchy with tears and she was dying to brush them away, but she daren't let go of her broken arm for one second.

They pulled up to a junction and Skye indicated to turn left.

'Could you . . .?' Clare squeezed her eyes shut; asking for help was so embarrassing. 'Could you wipe my face please. There are tissues in the glove box.'

'Sure.' Skye's touch was so gentle that more tears appeared. 'Oh Clare,' she whispered. 'I'm trying not to say sorry but—'

'You can go,' Clare nodded to the empty road.

'So, can I just ask.' Skye pulled away from the junction. 'About Adam.'

'No you can't.'

'OK.'

169

In the back, Ivy started to grizzle.

'Put her music on,' Clare suggested. 'That usually calms her.'

They drove the rest of the way to the sound of 'Old Macdonald'; Skye and Ivy joined in with all the animal noises while Clare did her best not to weep with self-pity.

When they arrived at the hospital, Skye stopped in the drop-off zone. An ambulance shot past them, sirens blazing, and Clare shrank down into her seat. Skye ran round to the passenger side and opened the door. She pressed the button to release Clare's seat belt for her and gently slid it over her body, taking care not to touch her.

Clare swung her legs out of the car and shuffled to the edge of the seat. 'Will you get Ivy out of her car seat for me please?'

Skye stared at her. 'If you dare tell me that you can manage Ivy with one arm, I won't be responsible for my actions.'

Clare swallowed. Skye had a point, but the truth was that she didn't want to walk in alone. 'What will you do if she cries?'

'What will *you* do if she cries?'

'Fine. Be quick,' Clare relented and stomped off towards the entrance.

'How are you doing?' the nurse asked. 'Has that pain relief kicked in yet?'

The nurse was called Pam. She was a jolly lady in her fifties, with greying blonde hair tied up in a ponytail and bright twinkly eyes. Ivy had rebelled against being held captive in her buggy and was now sitting smugly on Pam's lap, waving a fabric book around.

'Sort of.' Clare's voice was hoarse with the effort of not crying.

The truth was that Clare felt numb. As if breaking her arm wasn't enough, the trauma of the last time she was here kept washing over her in waves.

The nurse nodded kindly. 'Well done.'

They'd been here for an hour and a half. Skye had brought Ivy in her buggy and had remembered to bring her changing bag and an assortment of toys to keep her occupied. While Clare had been taken to be X-rayed, Skye had taken Ivy off to find some food.

Clare kept trying to smile for Ivy's sake. She'd been trying to smile for Ivy's sake for eleven months. More, if she counted the months of pregnancy when she'd rubbed her belly and told her bump how much fun they were going to have together. How loved the baby was going to be. She'd known she was expecting a girl. She'd found out as soon as possible. She'd had enough surprises to last a lifetime. First losing her mum, then finding out that she was pregnant. At a time when everything seemed so uncertain, she wanted to be sure of something.

'See here.' The nurse tapped the end of her pencil on the computer screen in front of them. 'Your humerus has what we call a spiral fracture. Quite a nasty break, I'm afraid. Poor Mummy,' she said to Ivy. 'Left-or right-handed?' she asked Clare.

'Right.'

'Well, that's something. What do you do for work?

'A teacher.'

'Head teacher,' Skye corrected, pride in her voice. Clare almost smiled at her.

'So you're on school holidays,' Pam said brightly. 'It'll be much better by the time you go back to school.'

'I'm not just a teacher though, am I? I'm mother to a baby.'

'Ah,' the nurse winced. 'True. A mother's work is never done. Just ask me, I've got four boys and a girl. I come to work for a rest. Right, I'm going to put you in a sling.'

'Not a cast?' Clare asked.

The nurse shook her head. 'A sling is the best thing for it. Allows gravity to do its thing.'

'Sounds a bit flimsy?' Skye looked anxious. 'What if she knocks it. Or if we knock it.'

Clare flinched. The thought of being touched by anyone or anything was horrific. It dawned on her then that this included Ivy. She wouldn't even be able to hold her little girl.

'Her birthday,' she rasped, huge tears forming in her eyes. 'It's Ivy's birthday soon. She'll be one and I won't even be able to cuddle her.'

Ivy stretched her arms out towards her, and all Clare could do was hold her daughter's hand.

'Oh darling,' she sniffed. 'Mummy can't hold you at the moment.'

'Mumma,' Ivy babbled, still reaching for her.

Clare gasped. 'She's never said that before. Yes, darling I'm your Mumma.'

And then it was too much to hold in and Clare let the tears fall. She sobbed and sobbed, her chest heaving as the pain in her arm gave way to the aching hole in her heart.

'My mum,' she wailed. 'I miss her so much.'

Pam laid a hand on Clare's knee. 'Let it out, sweet pea. Let it all out.'

'She died in this hospital after being in a car crash.'

'Shit,' murmured Skye. 'I had no idea. If I'd known, I'd—'

Pam silenced her with a wise smile. 'You did the best thing for Clare, don't worry.'

'Her car was ancient,' Clare sobbed. 'If she'd had an airbag, maybe she'd have survived. A lorry hit her on a narrow lane in the dark. The driver said one of her lights wasn't working and he clipped the front. That was enough to write it off. She had to be cut from the car, but they couldn't save her. And I didn't know.'

Pam handed her a tissue and she swiped it roughly at her face.

'I was out enjoying myself while my mum lay dying. I came to the hospital as soon as I could.' Clare closed her eyes. She could still hear the sound of her shoes squeaking on the linoleum floor, the smell of disinfectant. People striding down long corridors, everywhere so bright and busy even though it wasn't even light outside. 'My godmother, Liz, was here, waiting for me, but Mum had already gone by the time I arrived. I never got to say goodbye. And Ivy never got to say hello.'

'Oh, Clare.' Skye's eyes glistened with tears.

Ivy gazed at hersolemnly and Clare felt a pang of guilt. She had never cried in front of her before. She'd made a point of it, wanting her daughter's life to be filled with smiles and laughter. But she was so sad, and so tired of being strong.

'Well,' said Pam, when Clare's tears had finally halted. 'It sounds like that has been waiting to come out for a while.'

'Will the baby remember this, do you think?' Clare asked.

Pam opened a drawer in her desk and pulled out a bag of chocolate buttons. 'Is she allowed one?'

Clare nodded and then smiled as Ivy's face was immediately wreathed in smiles.

'Ivy will be fine. But you'll have to take it easy for the next few weeks and to do that, you are going to need help,' the nurse told her. 'Is the little one's dad around?'

Clare's chest tightened as she pictured the moment she and Adam had clapped eyes on each other in that kitchen earlier.

'I'm single,' she said gruffly.

'Let me take Ivy.' Skye leaned forward and plucked Ivy from Pam's lap, covering her cheek with kisses.

'That's a start.' Pam carefully took hold of Clare's good hand. 'Now, who's going to look after you?'

Clare looked down at her hand in Pam's and instantly she was transported right back to her childhood. To the days when her hand would be tucked into her mum's. *Never rely on anyone for anything, Clare. That's the best advice I can give you.*

'That would be me,' Clare replied determinedly. 'I can look after myself.'

Chapter Sixteen

Liz

Sixty-two years old and being driven home from a party like a disgraced teenager. Liz could have wept with embarrassment; instead, she let out a groan.

'Do you feel OK?' asked Marta, her eyes focused on the road. It had started to rain again, and her car windscreen kept steaming up.

'Anyone who gets really drunk at work could never say they're OK.' Liz attempted a weak smile. 'But thank you for asking.'

She turned her gaze to the dark green hedgerows, dripping with water. This was going to go down in history as one of the most humiliating days in her life.

Despite the drama caused by The Seaside Gourmet Girls, the party had continued once Skye and Clare had driven off. Everyone had appeared to be in high spirits and as soon as the storm had passed overhead, they had tumbled out into the garden again. Liz had been vaguely aware of Angel talking seriously with her brother, but Marta had sat her down with a cup of strong coffee while Noah and his girlfriend cleaned up the mess in the kitchen.

Two coffees later, Liz had been in the middle of sending Skye a text to ask how Clare was when Marta offered her a lift home. Her head felt like someone had taken an axe to it and her stomach was swirling ominously and she'd accepted gratefully. Now, she clung to the door handle and concentrated on not being sick.

'Want to talk about it?' Marta asked.

She shrugged. 'There's nothing to say. I often have a drink when I'm cooking. Today, I just had more than one.'

Marta didn't say anything.

Liz was hot, her heart was racing and she felt herself perspiring. She rolled down the window and felt cool air filter over her face. *Admit it, Liz*, said a little voice in her ear. *This isn't about today, this has been going on for months, years even.* She'd been kidding herself about her drinking. Excusing it, justifying it, laughing it off. But it wasn't funny, not anymore, not when she showed herself up like this. What must the girls think of her? And Noah? He was bound to tell his mum, and she wouldn't blame Viv if she never put any work their way again. Liz squeezed her eyes shut as a wave of nausea enveloped her.

'Stop the car please,' she groaned. 'I feel sick.'

Fifteen minutes later, they were on their way again.

Liz clutched the tissue Marta had given her, shame at what had happened making her head throb: the car swerving onto a grass verge, Liz stumbling out, this caring young woman rubbing her back while she threw up.

'That was probably for the best. The situation feels raw now,' Marta said softly. 'But there will be a lesson here. There always is.'

Silent tears made tracks down Liz's cheeks. This was a wake-up call. She'd relied on alcohol to get her through stressful situations for as long as she could remember. She was going to have to cut down, that was for sure.

'We can ignore it, or learn from it,' Marta continued. 'If you don't learn, there's a good chance it'll happen again.

Alternatively, what happened today can be a catalyst for you to change. That's the harder path, but in my experience, you never have to take that journey alone.'

Liz dried her tears. 'You sound as if you know what you're talking about.'

Marta nodded, her attention fixed on the junction, where she was waiting to turn right.

'I'm a yoga teacher now and I love my life. But a few years back, I had a career in London. I felt like I'd made it, but my body couldn't handle the unhealthy lifestyle. It was fast-paced, too much stress, too much alcohol, drugs even, on occasion. Not enough sleep, nothing to nourish me. I ended up having a stroke on the underground. I'd never been so scared in my life; I thought I was dying. That was my catalyst to change. Left my job, went travelling to southeast Asia, discovered yoga. And myself too, I suppose.'

'Wow.' Liz swallowed. She couldn't imagine changing her life so completely, not at her age. And, besides, was there any need? It wasn't as if she was an alcoholic. She could take it or leave it. It was just that she *took it* a bit too often. She pressed a hand to her head; all this thinking was making her brain rattle inside her skull. 'I admire you for taking control of your life like that.'

'I didn't have a choice,' Marta replied lightly. There was a calmness and a confidence to her that Liz had never felt. 'I rarely drink now. Everything in moderation. The important thing is to notice what your driver is, why you behave the way you do. It's not as easy to identify as you might think.'

'But you did it?' Liz asked.

Marta nodded. 'My driver was comparison. I compared myself to everyone else constantly and felt that I was falling behind: my bonus was smaller, I wasn't being promoted fast enough, I wasn't thin enough, I was still flat-sharing when my colleagues were on the property ladder. I drank as a way of ignoring my problems, I pushed myself to breaking point until I broke.'

Liz had said something similar to Skye only a few hours ago, about not comparing herself to Clare. 'You should talk to my god-daughter Skye, I think she needs to hear your story too.'

'I have spoken to her. I invited her to come to my sunrise yoga. You should both come. I think it might help you.'

Liz promised to think about it but in all honesty couldn't see herself contorting her body into uncomfortable positions in public.

Conversation between them stopped as they came into Salcombe. Liz's thoughts flew to Clare and Skye, and Ivy, of course. Tears pricked at her eyes again, the weight of her guilt heavy in her stomach. She owed them an apology, that much was certain. But an explanation too? Her heart thumped; could she even explain it to herself? What was her driver?

It was another hour before the girls returned. When Marta had dropped Liz off, she'd swallowed some tablets, forced herself to drink water and then fallen asleep on the sofa with the sound of the rain drumming down on the balcony outside the window.

The slam of a car door made her stomach tighten with dread. It was time to face the music. When she opened the front door, Skye was helping Clare out of the passenger seat. Clare was wearing a sling, her face was ash-white and her eyes red and puffy. In the back of the car, Ivy was screaming the place down.

'Your poor arm!' Liz swallowed a sob at the sight of them, they both looked exhausted. Shame ricocheted through her, this was all her stupid fault.

'Yep. Fractured. Two places,' Clare muttered, trying to retrieve her handbag from the footwell.

'Excuse me, Liz, can I get past?' Skye shunted Liz to the side and grabbed Clare's bag for her.

'Of course, sorry. What can I do?' Liz asked.

'Get Ivy out of the car, but be careful, she's been sick.'

'No!' Clare blocked Liz's access to the car door with her body. 'You've been drinking. Skye, you'll have to get Ivy. Liz, please can you get the bags out of the boot?'

'Of course.' Liz shrank back as if she'd been burned.

Clare tucked her head down and walked into the house, hugging her arm to herself.

'I'm so sorry about what happened,' Liz croaked.

'We can talk about it later. Sorry we didn't return your calls, it's been a bit manic,' said Skye, with a small smile. 'For now, Clare's in a lot of pain and Ivy needs a wash. Why don't you bring some of the shopping in, see what we can salvage?'

The air in the kitchen felt soupy with tension. Conversation was restricted to the absolutely necessary; mostly Clare telling Skye how to undo Ivy's clothes, Skye repeating that she could work it out for herself and Ivy making grunty noises as she tried to escape her aunt's grasp. Neither of her god-daughters were meeting her eye.

Liz unpacked the shopping and filled the kettle, wishing she could slide out of the room unnoticed and disappear to bed. But that was the coward's way out; if she did that, the problems would still be there in the morning. She wasn't going to go to bed tonight until she'd put things right.

Skye had to virtually force Clare into a chair and Ivy was at her mum's knees whining to be picked up. Clare fondled her daughter's curls, all the time talking to her, her lips curved into a smile. Skye bustled about, finding cushions to support Clare's arm and fetching the painkillers she'd been given.

Liz stifled a sob, wanting to help, but not daring to. These two wonderful young women had done everything in their power to get the business back on track since they'd arrived, and she'd thrown their help back in their faces. It was down to her to make amends, to prove to them both that their hard work hadn't been for nothing.

She finished making the tea, mustered up a smile and carried the mugs to where Clare was sitting in front of the patio doors.

'Here we are.' Liz set Clare's where she could reach it with her good hand and took a seat in an empty armchair, holding a mug for herself. 'I bet you're ready for a drink?'

'Not as ready as you were earlier,' Skye said pointedly.

Clare snorted gently.

'It's not funny,' Liz murmured, hiding her face behind her mug.

'This certainly isn't funny,' said Clare, indicating her arm.

'None of it is,' Skye added. 'I hope you don't mind, Liz, but I messaged Ele offering her a discount.'

'Absolutely,' she replied, her face hot with shame. 'It's the least we can do. Thank you.'

'She refused.' Skye continued, 'They all had a great time and even ate the part of the cake which was still intact. She also complimented your dancing.'

Liz exhaled, tears were close to the surface again. She'd been sure that the biggest order that the business had taken for almost two years had been about to end in financial loss.

'You were *dancing*?' Clare murmured. Her face was taut with tension and Liz could tell she was in pain.

She nodded and gulped her tea, which was too hot and burned her throat. She put it down where Ivy couldn't reach it and joined the little girl on the rug, where she was pressing the buttons on a musical toy. 'I'm mortified. I drank too much while I was at work. Someone drove me home, and I'm going to have to go back tomorrow to collect everything and face Ele again.'

'Male or female?' Clare demanded.

'Female. That pretty girl with the dark curly hair – Marta.'

'Thank God.' Clare sank back against her pillows and closed her eyes. 'If I wasn't in so much discomfort, I'd be really mad with you.'

Liz knew she deserved that. 'I'm already mad enough at myself for both of you.'

'I'm not mad,' said Skye. 'Just a bit confused. Why would you jeopardise everything for the sake of a drink?'

Liz's eyes stung; she didn't know what to say.

Ivy yawned and crawled into Liz's lap, rubbing her eyes.

'You're tired, sweetheart,' she said, gathering the little girl to her and holding her to her chest. It was a hug, of sorts, if a little one-sided, and it was just what she needed.

'It's way past her bedtime,' Clare said, shuffling herself up straight. 'And she needs a proper bath after being sick.'

Liz and Skye exchanged wary looks; this was going to be fun.

'Why don't we get you upstairs and comfortable in bed with some extra pillows,' Liz suggested. 'You need to rest and let your body recover.'

'I'm going to be in this sling for weeks, I can't sit in bed all that time,' Clare argued.

'No,' said Skye. 'And you can't be stroppy all that time either. OK with you if I bath Ivy and get her ready for bed?'

Skye was growing in confidence where Clare was concerned, Liz noted.

'Nobody but me has ever bathed her,' Clare said in a small voice.

'But I've helped before,' said Liz. 'And I'll be there.'

Clare opened her mouth to speak, but Liz got in there first.

'I don't blame you for not trusting me, but I promise you, I'd never put Ivy in harm's way, I love her as if she was my own flesh and blood.' Liz looked down at Ivy, curled up in her lap. 'As far as I'm concerned, she *is* family, you all are. And I'm completely sober now.'

Clare's eyes filled with tears. 'Of course you wouldn't, Liz. I'm not thinking straight. And I'm devastated by this.' She nodded her head towards her arm. 'What am I going to do? I'm helpless. I can't even hold my baby.'

'Oh, love.' Liz reached for Clare's good hand and squeezed it. 'You'll get through this. Your dad was right: "She can cope with anything, that girl," he said to me last time I saw him.'

Clare turned her head away and sniffed. 'Good job, isn't it.'

Liz's heart twisted. Jen had drummed into Clare the importance of independence and being self-sufficient, and there were merits to it, certainly. But there was a lot to be said for letting other people in. Everything in moderation.

Which applied to her too.

'Girls, before you go upstairs, I need to apologise properly.' Liz's heart raced. 'I'm so ashamed of my drinking. I've let you down, I've let myself down and I've let Jen's memory down too. I'm lucky that today's clients were so under-standing, but I was stupid to risk damaging our reputation.'

'What's going on, Liz?' Skye asked. 'Today wasn't the first time I've noticed you drinking more than . . . well, than everyone else.'

'And I've sometimes come off the phone from talking to you with the impression that you were a bit tipsy.' Clare finished her tea and Skye took the mug from her.

'Oh God.' Liz dropped her chin. Had it been that obvious? She'd thought no one could tell when she'd been drinking. 'You're right, I am drinking too much. I'm so ashamed. Your parents made a mistake picking me as your godmother. I'm supposed to set a moral example and I've failed you. If you'd both rather leave, I'll understand.'

Skye shook her head. 'Admittedly, today has been pretty shit, and I do think you need to cut down on your drinking. We can't risk that happening on another job. But you haven't failed us.'

'I agree,' Clare said. 'You're family. We're not going anywhere.'

'Good people make bad choices.' Skye slipped onto the floor to join her, threading an arm around her shoulders. 'Today was just a bad choice. Tomorrow's another day.'

'Jen and I always celebrated with a drink. Or commis-erated.' Liz gave them a wan smile. 'I'm not making excuses, but drinking has become a coping mechanism. A little pick-me-up here, a bottle of wine while watching a film there. Without Jen, life hasn't just become lonely, it's been joyless. So I drink to escape.' Her chest heaved as she finally admitted to someone how she felt.

'I get it,' Clare admitted. 'In the weeks after Mum's accident, I began drinking every evening. One gin and tonic became two, then a bottle of wine on a Friday night. Finding out I was pregnant was the catalyst for me. I stopped completely after that.'

Another catalyst. Perhaps, as Marta had suggested, this was hers?

'Oh darling.' Liz ached with sadness for her god-daughter. 'You've been so strong. Unlike me; I've known for months that I needed to get a grip, I just didn't have the motivation to do anything about it.'

'I had no idea that's how you felt.' Clare shook her head in dismay. 'I'm so sorry I wasn't there for you.'

'There was no way I was going to burden you with it,' Liz countered, 'you've had to deal with so much since your mum died. And yet, look at you, thriving, holding down a big job, bringing up a baby, doing everything on your own, while I've crumbled. I'm only telling you now because I think the only way to sort out my drinking is by being open about it.'

'Meanwhile, I've been thousands of miles away, existing in my own little bubble. I owe you both an apology. I should have been there for both of you,' Skye said.

Clare laughed softly. 'Don't beat yourself up – if you'd have offered to help me, I'm pretty sure you know what the answer would have been.'

'I can manage,' Skye said, mimicking Clare's voice, and they all laughed.

'Well, I can't manage alone. So will you help me,' Liz asked, feeling foolish even as she said the words. 'Cut down on the drinking, I mean?'

'Of course,' said Clare. 'I'm feeling a bit spaced out from the drugs tonight, but I'll come up with a plan tomorrow.'

'Thank you.' Liz's heart swelled. Some things never changed; Clare had run her life according to plan ever since she was a little girl.

'Maybe you need something to replace drinking with to keep you occupied,' Skye suggested. 'Like . . . knitting?'

Liz wrinkled her nose. 'Not for me.'

Clare chuckled. 'Me neither. How about something energetic instead. Like . . . I dunno—'

'Exercise?' Liz pulled a face.

'Sex?' Skye blurted out.

Liz was sceptical. 'Would that stop me drinking?'

Skye blushed. 'Don't ask me, I don't do much of either.'

'Well, it stopped me for a whole nine months.' Clare nodded at her daughter.

'Sex it is then,' said Liz.

'So, that's sorted,' said Clare. 'Now, bedtime for Ivy and probably me too. And much as I hate to admit it, I'm going to need help.'

Skye pretended to faint with shock. 'Wonders will never cease.'

Liz picked up Ivy and Skye helped Clare to her feet, and they headed upstairs. Clare protested at Skye's insistence that she support her from behind and Ivy tried to squirm out of Liz's arms. But, for once, it felt like the four of them were united. People who loved you didn't turn their backs at the first sign of trouble. They turned towards you, arms extended, and gathered you in. *We're not going anywhere*, Clare had said. Liz gave Ivy a little squeeze and felt her heart lift. It was going to be all right, after all.

Chapter Seventeen

Liz

Ivy had been bathed and Clare persuaded to rest in bed. She'd resisted, naturally, but when Liz listened outside her bedroom door, all was quiet. She knocked softly and opened the door.

Clare had Ivy at her breast, her gaze directed at her daughter. Her T-shirt was hitched up and Ivy was nestled into her, completely still, her little fingers splayed on Clare's chest. In an instant, Liz was taken straight back to a moment just like this, watching Jen feeding Clare. Mike had been sitting in a chair beside them, eyes closed and body wilting with fatigue. She'd been full of love and admiration for her best friend at the way she'd morphed from someone who could arrive in a foreign city and find the best club within an hour, to a mother so utterly in love with her child, she never wanted to let her go. And, at the same time, Liz had felt a pang of sorrow, knowing on some unknowable level that she would never get to experience that depth of love herself.

And yet, how fortunate she was, she thought now having watched from the sidelines as that small human had grown up, to have had a special place in her life, so that, now, here she was in Liz's house, with someone new for Liz to love.

She cleared her throat. 'Hello. Is it a good time?'

'Come on in,' Clare murmured. 'Join the party.'

'I've had enough partying for one day.' She attempted to smile, but her lips wouldn't work properly. 'Do you mind if I sit?'

'I'm on morphine,' Clare answered. 'I don't mind anything.'

Liz sat down on the edge of the bed, hyperaware that any movement might jolt Clare's arm. 'It feels like this is a precious moment.'

'It is,' Clare said with a sigh. 'I've been putting off dropping this last feed for months. I could have given up by now, but it's the best cuddle of the day. Or it was until I broke my stupid arm. I'm going to stop breastfeeding when she's one.' She looked incredulously at Liz. 'How is she already nearly one?'

'It's gone in a flash.' She had been to visit Clare in hospital the day after Ivy was born and the two women had cried bittersweet tears, both in awe of this tiny perfect bundle, this new life, but overcome with grief that Jen wasn't there to share the moment.

Ivy had grown so much since then, even since their last visit at Easter. Now, her body lay across Clare's, her feet dangling on Clare's thighs. It was such a lovely scene, but there was tension in Clare's face.

'If you're in pain, let me take Ivy off you.'

'Yes please, she's finished feeding now anyway,' Clare replied.

Ivy was heavy with sleep when Liz picked her up. She smelled delicious after her bath and Liz held her close, drinking her in.

'Goodnight, darling girl.' She kissed the baby's cheek and laid her gently in the travel cot beside Clare's bed.

'I'll be OK, you know,' said Clare, struggling to pull her T-shirt down to cover herself. 'This is the worst day.

Healing starts tomorrow. And as soon as they say I can start doing exercises, I will. I don't want you to think you'll be having to wait on me, hand and foot.'

'It would be my pleasure to look after you. I've been trying to do so since Jen died, but you've always rebuffed me . . . in the nicest possible way of course.'

'I do appreciate you, I promise,' Clare said meekly. 'But I can look after myself; Mum always said that needing others was a slippery slope.'

Liz shook her head fondly. 'It's OK to need people. Even your mum needed people. She needed me, she needed you. She even needed your father on occasion.'

'Dad?' Clare looked shocked.

Liz nodded. 'They still spoke regularly. Met up for the odd lunch.'

Clare's eyes were wide. 'Why didn't I know about this?'

'Because you'd have hoped it was a sign of them getting back together and your mother would never have entertained that. Children are very black and white in their thought processes, and there are many shades in between for relationships.'

'At least fifty.'

Liz laughed under her breath. 'I do love you, Clare Marriott.'

Clare smiled. 'Love you too, fairy godmother. I would have liked Mum to have met someone. Thirty years was a long time to be on her own.'

'Your mother had plenty of admirers,' Liz confessed, wondering how much to tell her daughter. 'There were one or two who I thought had potential and I said she should introduce them to you. Your approval would have been the litmus test for the relationship. But she would always chicken out in the end. I think she doubted her own judgement of character and, by then, she'd drummed it into you so firmly about the importance of being self-sufficient that admitting to her beloved daughter that she'd met someone seemed to her to be a sign of weakness.'

'That's sad.'

Liz gave her god-daughter a knowing look. 'It is sad. But it would be even sadder if you made the same mistake.'

Clare closed her eyes and groaned lightly. 'Ivy's got such a small team behind her. It's really brought it home to me today how her safety hangs by a thread, and that thread is held by me. What if it snaps, what if I let her down?'

Liz picked up her hand and kissed it. 'You won't let her down and if anything should happen to you, then you have people in your life who'll be there for her. Me, for example.' Which was another reason why she needed to get her act together, she thought.

'I haven't even had Ivy christened. I've always had you as my godmother, it isn't right that I haven't given Ivy the same privilege.'

Liz loved the idea of being classed as a privilege. 'I can help you to organise it, if you like?'

Clare wrinkled her nose. 'The last religious service I went to was Mum's funeral. I don't think I can face that sort of formality again yet.'

'I understand,' said Liz. 'There's no hurry. The important thing now is for you to get better. Something I heard recently stuck with me: illness begins with "I", wellness begins with "we". I think there might be something in that.'

Clare yawned. 'I like that.'

'Try to sleep.' Liz stood and kissed Clare's cheek. 'Yell if you need anything.'

'That applies to you too, Liz,' said Clare.

'Yelling?' she teased, as she reached the bedroom door.

'Wellness.' Clare held her gaze intently. 'Cutting back on your drinking, that's your wellness. Starting with "we".'

'Thank you, darling.' Liz's throat burned with the effort of not crying. She was a silly fool; telling Clare off for not letting others in when she was guilty of doing the same thing. 'I'll leave you to get some sleep. Goodnight. I love you.'

'Love you too,' Clare said sleepily.

It was love she needed, Liz thought, closing the door softly, not sex, as they were joking about earlier. Someone to share her everyday with. Someone to wrap an arm around her in the dead of night when she woke from a dream, someone to plan happy things with. That's what her life needed: someone to be her person. The summer would end, and the girls would go home, and her house would be silent again. Which meant she needed to get a move on and do something about it. There was no time to waste.

Chapter Eighteen

Liz

Early the following morning, Liz crept out of Clemency House so as not to wake the girls. The sun had only just risen and the lilac sky was streaked with peach and apricot. It was too early to go and fetch the equipment they'd left at the party, but that was fine, she needed some time to think, to get her thoughts in order. Skye and Clare had been kind to her last night, but that didn't stop her feeling ashamed of her behaviour. If yesterday had been a day of storm clouds and rain, today signified a fresh start and a chance to find her silver lining. She was determined to do better.

There were a million and one places in Salcombe which held happy memories for her. The terrace of Cliff House where she had celebrated her eighteenth birthday, or the alley by the Ferry Inn where she'd had her first proper kiss with Matthew Babington, (the one and only kiss; he'd kissed like a fish gasping for air), or maybe North Sands beach where she'd learned to swim in the gentle shallow waters of the bay, her feet kicking wildly as her mum shouted words of encouragement. There was even that day all those years ago at the Crab Shed, when Mike had taken her for lunch to cheer her up after Jonathan had left her.

★

'Come on, Liz, tell your old pal, what's been going on?' He reached for her hand across the table.

The kindness in his voice was almost too much to bear. Little did he know that the situation she found herself in was largely down to her feelings for him.

'I tried to make it work, but I've failed, Mike,' she replied in a wobbly voice. 'I thought I loved Jonathan enough for our marriage to last, but I don't.'

'But I was under the impression he left you?' Mike said, confused.

He was still married to Frankie at the time, and their paths didn't cross as often as they'd once done. He wasn't to know that she and Jonathan had been on the rocks for a while now.

'He did. Because he's a better person than I am. I've been burying my head in the sand, knowing he deserved better but not wanting to tell him how I felt.'

'We're a long time dead, Liz. It's all very well not wanting to hurt other people, but a relationship in which only one person is happy is not a good one. And, in time, Jonathan will find someone else who'll make him happy. As will you.'

'I won't,' Liz said. 'I know I won't.'

'There's someone out there for everyone, Liz. Yours is out there, you just haven't met him yet.' He brought her hand to his lips and kissed it.

But I have, she thought blinking tears from her eyes, and that's the problem.

Liz gave an exasperated laugh under her breath at the memory. Mike had his faults, but he'd been good to her over the years, and she'd appreciated those words of encouragement at the time.

But this morning she was craving the comforting memories of her father instead, and the carefree hours they'd spent together, when life had been one long, smooth, happy ride.

The quay at Whitestrand was busy all day and long into the evening, owners tinkering on their boats, tourists watching them longingly from the row of benches, daydreaming about jacking their jobs in to move here permanently. At this hour, however, Liz had her pick of benches and chose one close to the water's edge.

She sat down and closed her eyes, allowing her ears to tune in to the sounds around her: the tinkle of masts and the creaking of boats and the slap of gentle waves against the harbour wall. She breathed in the familiar smells, of the air, and the water, the faint seaweedy aroma of the fishing nets piled up to her left, and she let her mind wander back through time.

This place had been the centre of her father's social life. After work, at weekends, in the holidays and during his retirement before he passed away, he'd spent as much time here as he could. He'd had a succession of boats over the years, sometimes more than one at a time. She still remembered his excitement when they'd jumped in the tender and he'd taken her across the water to see his new Boston Whaler.

'One hundred and fifty foot long,' he'd boasted. 'You'll be captain of the high seas in this, Lizzie,' he'd said, jamming his cap on her head before breaking into 'I Am Sailing' by Rod Stewart. She must have been seventeen at the time and had pretended to be embarrassed, but secretly she'd loved singing at the top of her voice where no one could hear them.

She remembered buzzing with the prospect of adulthood, of leaving home for university, gaining her independence and making her own way in the world.

When had she stopped captaining her own ship and settled for being first mate of someone else's? She frowned irritably; she knew the answer to that one, but it was so pathetic that she didn't like admitting it to herself.

Liz cast her mind back to Jen's twenty-fourth birthday. It was late, almost midnight, when Jen had arrived back to the flat they shared at the dodgy end of Islington.

'Guess what?' Jen had been almost levitating with excitement.

'Er, you met George Michael on the night bus?'

She and Jen had been obsessed with the pop duo at the time. Jen was in love with George, while Liz was devoted to Andrew, because she thought it wasn't fair that George got all the attention.

'Ta-dah!' She'd stuck her hand in front of Liz's face and waggled her ring finger, on which sat a slim gold band and a trio of diamonds. 'I'm going to be Mrs Marriott.'

'Congratulations!' Liz had squealed, hoping she sounded as if she meant it.

Blood roared in her ears and she told herself to be brave, do the right thing and never let Jen know how she felt. Her best friend was getting married and the pain was unbearable.

Because, despite accepting Jen and Mike's romance since that first supper club at uni, she'd kept a corner of her heart solely for him. They might split up one day, she reasoned. And then maybe, once Jen had got over him, Mike would realise that the love of his life had been right under his nose all along.

And it wasn't just about Mike. Liz's relationship with Jen was bound to change once she was married. Jen was more than just a friend, she was the sister Liz had never had. And the thought that their closeness might diminish was worse than the prospect of losing Mike.

'Thank you! Obviously I want you to be my bridesmaid!' Jen had flung her arms around Liz's neck and the two best friends had cried tears of joy. Mostly.

★

So that was probably the moment, Liz reflected now. From that night on, she'd become the third leg of a stool and she had propped the other two up for the next three decades.

The sound of a boat engine being choked to death flipped Liz back into the present. Someone was having difficulty with their outboard motor by the sound of it.

'Damn and blast it!' A familiar male voice carried over to her from the jetty.

A man wearing a life jacket over his sweatshirt was sitting in an inflatable boat and muttering crossly to himself.

'Patrick?' Liz stood up to take a closer look. 'Is that you?'

The man looked over to her and waved. 'Liz! Hello, you're up and about early.'

'Couldn't sleep. What's your excuse?'

He grinned. 'I couldn't sleep either. I've been dying to take her for a spin and thought I'd better do it early before the water gets busy.'

She walked down the pontoon to join him. 'I didn't know you even had a boat.'

'I didn't until yesterday.' Patrick wiped his hands on a rag. 'Can you believe it? I've lived on an estuary for all these years and never set sail on my own before. I've relied on the ferry or water taxi until now. And I think I might be relying on it again at this rate.' His voice was light, but his normally easy-going features were wrinkled with frustration.

'Having trouble?'

He chucked down the rag and sighed. 'Is it possible to flood the engine in these things?'

She laughed. 'Want a hand?'

'Yes, please, if you . . .' He interrupted himself with a bark of laughter. 'I was going to say if you know anything about boats, but, frankly, the chance of you knowing less than me is virtually impossible. So, yes please.'

Patrick extended a hand to help her climb down into the inflatable boat.

'Welcome aboard the *Ecsta-Sea*,' he said with a flourish. 'Not my choice, I hasten to add. I might consider a rebrand. To *Mi-sery*.'

'You can't do that!' she said, feigning horror. 'It's bad luck.'

'I certainly don't need any more of that,' he grumbled. 'Can't get the old girl started.'

'You've got fuel?'

'Um. Yes.'

She hid a smile; he didn't sound too sure. 'Well, that's a good start. Let's have a look.'

She checked the fuel pipe was properly connected to the engine, squeezed the bellows to make sure it was primed and then popped open the cover concealing the fuel tank.

'I already bow down to your superior knowledge,' said Patrick.

'Save your praise until I've got the motor running,' she replied, secretly pleased to have impressed him.

The fuel line was secure, so she felt for the air screw. Closed. She smiled to herself; that was the culprit. Liz unscrewed it and dropped the lid again.

'The fuel tank has an air screw which should be open, otherwise it creates a vacuum and the engine won't start.'

'Of course. I knew that.' Patrick rubbed his nose and they both laughed at his obvious lie.

'Easy mistake. Try now.'

This time, the engine started easily.

'I'm glad you turned up or I'd have been swimming home,' said Patrick.

'Come on then,' she said, slinging on the spare life jacket. 'Let's take her out.'

'Now?' He looked pleased, but glanced back over to the bench where she'd been sitting. 'You aren't busy?'

She shook her head. 'I just nipped out for some air.'

'Luckily for me. Will you be captain, or shall I?'

'It's your boat.'

'Damn.' His eyes twinkled. 'I knew you were going to say that.'

He put the boat into reverse and they chugged away from the quay and out towards the sea. Patrick was taking it very steadily, but Liz didn't mind; she wasn't in any hurry.

It had been years since she'd seen Salcombe at dawn from the water. She'd forgotten how beautiful it was as the sun gradually came into view behind it, and she was filled with a sense of peace and well-being.

'This was exactly what I needed,' she said so softly that Patrick had to lean forward to catch her words. 'What a way to start the day.'

'It's definitely more enjoyable with someone to share the experience with.'

Like so many other things in life, she thought, trailing her fingers in the cold water. 'What changed your mind about getting a boat?'

He hesitated before replying. 'When Rachel and I moved into the house, we enjoyed the solitude. We'd look across the water at the flocks of people milling through the narrow streets in Salcombe and congratulate ourselves on living where we could enjoy the views but not get tangled up in the crowds. Since she died, the peace can feel mocking, and being remote isn't quite as idyllic as it once was. Instead of feeling smug about my solitude, I feel isolated. The views are still as beautiful, but now when I see the crowds, it highlights how alone I am. I thought a boat might help me feel more connected.'

Liz nodded thoughtfully; she'd never heard him talk like this. She'd assumed he was happy to be by himself, that his mum and aunt were pushing him to find a new partner against his wishes. But perhaps they knew more than she'd given them credit for.

'Then I applaud you. Although, in my experience, you can feel lonely even on the Salcombe side,' she admitted.

'Now you tell me,' Patrick said drily, making her smile.

It felt good to cast her worries aside for a while; she was so glad she'd bumped into him.

'My parents had boats here for years,' she told him. 'It was my father's hobby mainly, but it was great for me when I was a teenager. My friends and I would pile into the boat with fresh pasties and illicit cans of cider and go to the beach for the day. If we forgot something, we just jumped back on board and went home for it.'

'That explains your prowess at starting the engine. I can see I've got some catching up to do.'

'So, this boat is for social reasons, not because you've got an urge to captain your own ship and conquer the high seas,' she teased.

'Hardly.' He chuckled. 'At the moment, I'd be happy to conquer getting the damn thing to start without assistance. And it's a bit small for anything other than pottering up and down the estuary.'

'It doesn't matter about the size, it's about how it feels, whether it brings you joy.'

'Uh-huh.' Patrick drew his eyebrows together.

'And my dad's was small to begin with; he didn't go up in size until he was more experienced and he knew my mother could handle it.'

'Considerate of him.' Patrick spluttered and banged his chest. 'Excuse me, swallowed a fly.'

Liz cringed inwardly as it suddenly occurred to her what she'd said and why Patrick was making a hash of disguising his mirth. She didn't know whether to let out the giggle which was threatening to erupt or look away and wait for the moment to pass. Luckily, Patrick came to the rescue.

'But, to answer your question, it crossed my mind that if I'm to rekindle my—' He paused to clear his throat. 'Social life, then I'm unlikely to find a suitable person on my side of the estuary. So this was a pre-emptive move to broaden my horizons. What do you think?'

'Ah, so the *Ecsta-Sea* is your babe magnet.'

Patrick slid her a sideways glance. 'So far, it seems to be working.'

Liz felt a warm glow inside her and remembered the conversation she'd had with Skye about she and him 'courting', as his mother had put it. She could do far worse. But was that enough? Look at her and Jonathan. She didn't want another failed relationship on her hands. And she wasn't interested in casual hook-ups. Her next romantic encounter needed to be with someone she properly cared about. She and Patrick had joked about internet dating, but so far, her experience had been pretty dire and, if she was honest with herself, it just didn't suit her.

She drew in a deep breath. 'About dating—'

'That conversation we had about—' he said, in the same moment.

'Go on,' she urged, grateful to have been interrupted.

'No, no, you carry on, I insist,' said Patrick, clearly feeling the same.

'Not much to report, so far,' she admitted. 'I registered with one of those dating sites, but I feel as if I'm trying to sell myself on eBay, like a second-hand car. And I get asked for all sorts of details, things I wouldn't even want to discuss with my doctor, let alone a stranger on the internet. I think I'm going to delete it before someone decides to come round and "kick my tyres", so to speak.'

Patrick looked appalled. 'Now you've put it like that, I'm glad I didn't get around to doing anything about it.'

'Didn't you?' Liz was surprised by how much this admission pleased her. Patrick on a dating app would no doubt be snapped up in twenty-four hours and she wasn't sure that was what she wanted.

'Not online, at least. As coincidence would have it, Rachel's sister called and said she had a friend who she thought I'd get on well with. So she set us up on a date.'

'That's nice.' Liz tried to hide her disappointment. 'I hope it goes well.'

'It has already been and gone,' he said. 'There was no chemistry, at least not on my side. But at least I tried.'

'Oh dear,' Liz said in sympathy. 'When was this?'

'Last night.' He pulled a face. 'And she knows nothing about boats.'

Liz started to laugh.

'What's so funny?'

'Well, that was at least one thing you had in common.'

And then they were both laughing, and they carried on laughing until Liz thought they'd better turn the boat round and go back, especially as Patrick was a bit sketchy on how much petrol there was in the tank.

'So, I've told you why I was up at the crack of dawn,'

he said, once they were on their homeward journey. 'Why couldn't you sleep?'

Liz hesitated, wondering where to start.

He glanced at her. 'You don't have to tell me.'

'No, I want to tell you.' She chewed her lip. 'I suppose I'm worried that if I tell you the truth, you won't feel the same way about me anymore.'

'And how do I feel about you?'

She swallowed. 'I don't know.'

He held her gaze and smiled softly. 'Then you've got nothing to lose.'

'And you won't judge?'

He shook his head. 'Promise.'

'OK.' She took a deep breath. Talking about her problems, about any personal stuff, wasn't what she did. But then, bottling it up and escaping into the bottom of a glass hadn't done her any favours either. She had an unshakeable feeling that Patrick would be a good listener. Wellness started with we, after all. 'I'm afraid to say that I had too much to drink at work yesterday and I made quite a mess of things . . .'

As the boat puttered along back to Whitestrand, Liz told Patrick about the good, the bad and the ugly events of the previous day. About how nervous she'd been without Jen, how drinking had become her way of dealing with anxiety, about her oyster sauce crime, making a show of herself at Angel's party and how Skye had been forced to call for backup. And how the party had ended with a trip to hospital for Clare and a ride home for her with one of the guests. Above all, the deep, deep shame of knowing she'd let everyone down.

'Good grief, Liz, what a traumatic time you had.' Patrick reached across for her hand and squeezed it. 'Thank you for trusting me with that.'

201

'It's bad, isn't it?' Her throat felt tight, and she couldn't meet his eye.

'It's human,' he argued. 'I do feel differently about you now; I knew you were wonderful and now I know you're brave too.'

Liz felt her heart lift. He was so lovely and kind.

They were almost at the dock and Liz pointed out a space for him to head towards.

'Thank you, Patrick. They say every journey begins with the first step,' she said. 'And that's where I am now; right at the start of a new path. The girls have said they'll help. Although Clare is the one who needs the help. Poor thing, I've never seen her so defeated.'

'And you've got me. Any time you need someone to talk to, I'm your man.'

'And any time you feel remote over on your side of the water, I'm your woman.' Liz helped him secure a rope to the nearest cleat on the dock. It was time for her to disembark, but she was reluctant to leave him. 'Perhaps we should set up a code. Hang red flags out of our bedroom windows when we need a friendly ear.'

He gave a low rumbling laugh. 'It's a thought, but a red flag outside a lady's window might receive more than an offer of an ear.'

She giggled. 'Oh. That's true.'

'Goodbye, Liz.' He offered her a hand to climb out of the boat. 'Thanks for coming to my rescue.'

'You're welcome. Thanks for the boat ride.' She began to walk away but changed her mind and turned back to face him. He was still watching her. 'Patrick? Can we do this again sometime?'

A smile spread across his face. 'I'd like that.'

'Me too.'

She walked away then, thrilled with her own audacity. She listened to his engine roaring away across the estuary, and when she turned round a final time, her breath caught in her throat at the sight. The sun had risen high enough to crest the hill behind Salcombe and the *Ecsta-Sea* was bathed in light. Incredibly, there it was: her silver lining.

Chapter Nineteen

Clare

Clare lay awake in bed squinting. Whoever had shut the curtains for her last night had missed a bit and there was a sliver of light determined to find her face whichever way she turned. Not that she'd slept much. The nurse had instructed her to sleep upright propped up on pillows, but whenever she'd dozed off, her head had nodded, and she'd jolted awake again.

The pain in her arm was . . . well, she couldn't even find words bad enough, but given a choice between breaking her arm again and giving birth to Ivy, she'd choose that thirty-six-hour labour ending in a forceps delivery all day long. She felt guilty now for not giving enough sympathy to every child who'd turned up in her classroom over the last ten years with a limb in plaster. Although, thinking about it, the children themselves had seemed quite proud of their little casts. Maybe children's limbs were made of Play-Doh. Hers felt more like glass rods.

She looked down at her left arm. 'Ugh. That is bad.'

Her upper arm was double its usual size. She peered inside the sling and shuddered at the sight of the mottled purple skin of her forearm.

She loved Salcombe, she really did, but not being able to drive was going to be a killer. There wasn't even a big supermarket within walking distance. The little local one was fine for cooking for the four of them, but not when they had a booking to cater for. She knew that Liz or Skye could go shopping, but it had been one of her only contributions to the business effort. It had made quite a nice change, putting Ivy in the seat of the trolley and doing a big shop. At home, it was mostly nappies, coffee and finger food for both of them. She rarely cooked complicated stuff these days. Meals had to be quick and easy with minimal chopping; she'd learned that early on, when Ivy had suffered with colic. It was all right for you, Jamie Oliver, she'd thought, abandoning her cookery book in frustration. You try finely chopping an onion with a writhing baby on your hip.

Those early days had been so tough that sometimes she'd wondered if she'd done the right thing, going ahead with the pregnancy. And then there were others when the joy from something Ivy had done, or the way she'd smiled, or clapped, burst out of her like a firework and she knew that becoming a mother had been the right choice all along.

Her mind flitted back to the day she'd gone into labour. Forty-one weeks pregnant and getting seriously fed up. Clare didn't do 'late', but this was beyond her control. The day had started off with a call from Liz. This had been their morning ritual: Liz would call, ask her what sort of night she'd had and then offer to drive up from Salcombe to Bath to be on hand, just in case today was the day. Clare would promise she'd let her know the minute she felt a contraction. But that day, as they'd ended the call, Clare had flinched with the sensation of a steel strap tightening across her stomach.

The sensible thing to do would have been to call Liz back and ask her to come. But Clare wasn't feeling sensible.

Instead, in between contractions, she scrubbed every inch of paintwork in the flat, bleached the sink and put clean sheets on her bed. Then she phoned for a Domino's pizza, watched a Zac Efron film and dipped in and out of sleep. By seven o'clock, the contractions were so strong that she couldn't have held a phone conversation if she wanted to. Instead, she booked a taxi, picked up her hospital bag and used the fifteen minutes it took for the cab to arrive to make her way down from her top-floor flat to the front door.

'Maternity department please,' she'd said breathlessly as she opened the rear door.

The taxi driver had taken one look at her and panic flashed up on his face. 'Are you . . .?'

Clare had sucked in a breath and nodded. 'In labour, yes.'

The taxi driver had looked as nervous as she felt and had glanced over his shoulder at the front door. 'Are we waiting for anyone else to join us?'

'No. Only the baby. I hope you've got warm hands.'

It didn't take long to get to the hospital after that.

The taxi driver had most likely been wondering if the baby's father was coming. It wasn't Adam who was on her mind then but her mum. Clare missed her so much. The sound of her voice, the irreverent cackle of her laughter, the way she made up silly songs about nothing. She missed the way Mum made everything fun. She missed ringing her up on the way home from work to tell her the funny stories of the day. The little things that made her *her*, like the way her two front teeth overlapped ever so slightly so that she never passed a mirror without checking she didn't have something stuck in them and how she hated her second toes for being longer than her big toes. But, most of all, in that moment, Clare missed her mum's hand in hers on the most wonderful, most scary night of her life.

It had been the following afternoon before Ivy had deigned to put in an appearance. A full day and a half since Clare had had her first contraction. There'd been no one to brush Clare's hair off her sweaty forehead and whisper to her that she was doing brilliantly.

Instead, her daughter's welcome party consisted of Clare and a room full of strangers. No worries, Clare had told herself. She was all the baby needed, she'd love her enough for a whole army of relatives.

'I'm sorry it's just me. Sorry there's no man to cry tears of joy and promise that you'll always be daddy's girl,' Clare had whispered into the soft whorl of her tiny ear. Her lips were cracked after thirty-six hours in labour and they felt rough on the sweet skin of Ivy's cheek. 'But maybe it's better that way. You can't miss what you've never had.'

Now Clare held on to her broken arm, swung her legs down off the bed and walked to the window. Everywhere throbbed: her head, her shoulder, even her knee was bruised from the fall.

So much for the perfect summer holiday she'd been dreaming of. All because she'd slipped on that bloody cake.

Adam's face loomed up in her mind's eye. Adam's bloody gorgeous face. *Saskia, I thought it was you.*

Sorry to disappoint you, sweet cheeks, but it isn't Saskia, and it never was.

She sighed in despair. She couldn't change what had happened, but she did need to work out what came next. What she was going to do about the fact that the father of her child appeared to be living in Salcombe.

Ivy was starting to wake up. Having shared a room with her since she was born, Clare knew the signs: the fluttering eyelashes, clenched fists doing micro-movements, tiny lip-smacking noises. She'd worked her way out from underneath her sheet in the night and was at the top end, feet braced against the mesh sides, Winnie the Pooh tucked under her arm, damp curls at the base of her neck. A fierce love burned in Clare's chest for Ivy. She was completely and utterly hers.

Except that she no longer had the excuse of not being able to track down Ivy's father. It would be so easy to ring up the client from yesterday and ask for Adam's number. '*Tell him Saskia called . . .*'

If she did − and she wasn't yet sure if she could − everything would change. Her family would find out that she'd spun them a yarn about the 'ex-boyfriend' who'd abandoned her when he found out she was pregnant. And what if Adam wanted a role in Ivy's life and Ivy loved him and then, when she was five, he changed his mind and decided he didn't want to be a father after all and let her down, waltzing out of her life without a second glance? Like Mike had. What then?

Clare had to stay in control of this situation, she had to. Park her own emotions and do what was needed. There was no need to be hasty. Maybe now that she'd given him the brush-off at yesterday's party, he might not bother pursuing her. For all she knew, he might be in Salcombe with a significant other, someone who wouldn't be very impressed by her man hunting down another woman.

She racked her brains to remember what Skye had said to him, just before walloping him in the stomach. Clare sniggered under her breath. She'd seen a completely different side to Skye yesterday and she couldn't help but be impressed.

There was a rustling sound from Ivy's cot and, the next second, she was up on her feet, grinning at Clare and showing perfect little white teeth.

'Hello, darling girl.'

'Amamama,' Ivy chuntered, bobbing up and down, gripping the edge of the travel cot.

Clare tried to scoop Ivy up with one arm. A searing pain shot through her arm, and she bit down on her lip.

'I can't pick you up, darling,' she said, tears pricking at her eyes, 'I'm so sorry.'

While Ivy contented herself with an armful of soft toys which Clare managed to pile into the cot for her, Clare sat back on the bed and cried. She couldn't do this alone, she just couldn't.

Chapter Twenty

Skye

Everywhere felt clean and fresh this morning after yesterday's downpour. The sky was blue and the air crystal clear. A hopeful sort of day, thought Skye, powering towards the beach with her towel and water bottle.

Salcombe was mostly quiet. Dog walkers were out in force, runners pounded past her, adults of various ages strolled by pushing buggies containing little people in varying stages of sleep. As she passed them all by, exchanging a smile and the briefest hello, there was a shared feeling of smugness between them all that they still had this beautiful place all to themselves.

Skye's to-do list had got an awful lot longer in the last twenty-four hours, but she wasn't going to let it daunt her. She'd never thought about it before, but she was quite good at organising things, and people. When she'd arrived at the Hope Foundation, there'd been no filing system, no processes in place to keep track of the volunteers: who was arriving when and how long they were staying. Jesse was great at the big picture, but hopeless at detail. Skye had soon streamlined everything and created an induction programme. And it was because the charity project was in such good shape that she'd been able to leave at short notice, putting Terri, a capable girl from South Africa, in charge of keeping an eye on the volunteers.

Now, Skye was going to have to employ her organisational skills at Clemency House. Liz's admission about the extent of her alcohol dependency had come as a shock. Skye had never been much of a drinker herself and didn't know what it felt like to be incapable of resisting a drink. But she felt sure that the first step for someone getting to grips with any problem was a willingness to succeed. From what she'd seen last night, Liz seemed to be at that point and Skye was going to encourage her every step of the way. There would be loads of things they could do together that would help to distract her, and replace the buzz that alcohol had given her. Today was day one and Skye was confident that everything was going to feel so much brighter for Liz once they'd been to Thurlestone to sort out the mess from yesterday.

Clare however . . . Clare was another story. For her, it was also day one. But in her case, it was the start of a new reality and Skye had a feeling that Clare was going to struggle to accept it. Living with a one-armed, control-freak single mother whose chorus line was 'I can manage' was going to be a hoot and a half for the next few weeks.

It wasn't only her fractured arm that had rattled Clare. There was the whole Adam situation to come to terms with. Adam, the man Skye had walloped so hard that her wrist was hurting this morning. Figuring out how best to help Clare was going to be a lot more complicated than helping Liz, that was for sure.

As the beach came into view, Skye felt a frisson of anticipation. For now, she was leaving all the drama of Clemency House behind. She slipped off her Birkenstocks at the edge of the beach and picked them up. The sand was damp and coarse under her feet as she headed towards the water's edge where a group of people had already set up their mats and towels. Some were lying down, others seated, hands resting on knees as if they were meditating. Wandering between them was Marta. Skye felt a kick of pleasure at seeing her again. After the stress of yesterday, some time with a new friend, someone neutral who didn't need anything from her, was exactly what she needed.

Yoga was one of those things Skye had always meant to try but never got around to. She dug into the pocket of her hoodie and looked at the card Marta had given her again. *Sunrise Beach Yoga*. No indication of the level. She'd just have to hope that Marta wasn't one of those teachers who barked out instructions from the front of the class and assumed everyone knew what to do. Anything more complicated than a downward dog or a cat stretch and Skye would be all over the place.

Marta glided towards her. Her hair was loose, a cloud of brown curls ruffling in the breeze.

'Great to see you!' Marta's smile was wide and genuine, and Skye felt a weight lift off her shoulders.

'I thought it would be a good excuse to come and thank you for bringing Liz home last night. It was very kind of you.'

Marta waved her thanks away. 'Happy to help. And you'll stay to practise with us?'

'Is that OK? I don't need to book?'

'No, no. You are very welcome to join us.' Marta swept an arm out, indicating the wide beach. 'Plenty of room for everyone in my summer yoga studio.'

'You might regret that,' Skye grinned, handing her the money for the class. 'Is there a level under beginners?'

Marta laughed. 'You'll be fine, don't worry. How is everyone at home this morning?'

Her eyes were soft with kindness and Skye had an urge to put her head on the yoga teacher's shoulder and tell her everything.

She blew out a breath, unsure where to begin. Liz had been nowhere to be found this morning and she'd heard Clare crying as she'd passed her bedroom door. Guilt niggled her; perhaps she should have stayed at home and offered to look after Ivy for a while?

Marta held a hand up. 'Don't answer that. Yoga is about making time for you. We can suspend everything else for now. Just relax. Enjoy being with us and with yourself.'

'Thank you.' Skye swallowed the lump in her throat, realising just how good that sounded.

'You're very welcome.' Marta nodded. 'Set up your towel here at the front where I can keep an eye on you.'

Skye bit her lip. 'I'd rather go at the back where no one can see how bad I am. I'm a complete beginner. You'll have to go easy on me.'

'Always,' Marta smiled. 'But it's you who must go easy on yourself. My job is to guide you in your practice. There is no competition here, no ego.'

After Marta had moved on to the next person, Skye laid out her towel and peeled off her hoodie.

'Welcome to sunrise yoga, everyone.' Marta clasped her hands in front of her in prayer position and bowed to the class. 'As ever, I would ask you to turn your phones—'

Somewhere close by, a phone began to ring and everyone started to laugh. Skye congratulated herself on leaving her own phone on silent.

'—off,' Marta finished. 'So that we may focus.'

The phone carried on ringing. Heads began to turn in Skye's direction.

'I think it might be you?' The woman next to her pointed at Skye's tote bag.

She grabbed her bag, horrified to have brought attention to herself, and whipped out her phone. 'Sorry, everyone!'

It was Jesse. Skye groaned inwardly; they were supposed to be speaking to each other this morning and she'd forgotten. She quickly declined the call, turned the phone to silent and typed out a quick text message.

Sorry, can't talk now after all. I'll be in touch when I can.

A reply appeared immediately.

I feel like we're losing you to your UK life. You are coming back, aren't you?

Skye stared at the screen not knowing the answer to that and dropped the phone into her bag without replying. Instead, she recalled Marta's words from a few moments ago: she was going to make time for herself, everything else could wait. She turned her focus back to the front of the class.

'Thank you for joining me for beach yoga to welcome in this beautiful morning.' Their teacher extended her arms to include all of the group. 'Please take a seat, get comfortable and let's begin with some cleansing deep breaths.'

Skye sat, copying everyone else, feeling like she must stand out a mile as someone completely clueless. But breathing was nice. As she relaxed, she noticed the colours of the sky and the sea. She heard the call of the birds and the swish of the water. She became more aware of the beauty of her surroundings and her tiny place in it.

'Let us begin by setting your intention for today's practice.' Marta's voice was melodic and clear. 'What are your hopes for today, what is it you wish to achieve? Press one hand to your heart, and inhale, and exhale.'

Skye followed Marta's instructions, to stretch and twist and elongate the spine, her eyes shut as she dug deep to find the answers. Beside her, she was conscious of the deep, even breathing of the other yogis, all of them intent on their own practice, no one caring that her version of the lotus position was stiff and ungainly.

What did she hope for? A sign maybe? An end to her deliberations, to the constant balancing equation in her head. On one side was Jesse and her life in Uganda. Together, they could build the Hope Foundation, expand its reach, grow the services they offered, extend the education programmes to adults – there were so many possibilities. She could do something meaningful. And on the other side . . . Skye squeezed her eyes shut, trying to think what other sort of life she could have, one without Jesse, but her mind was blank.

There was a soft warmth at her shoulder, and she opened her eyes. Marta was crouched beside her.

'And now the other,' Marta instructed the whole class. 'Right hand to left knee, turn the head to look over your left shoulder. Breathe.'

Skye realised the class had moved on and they were all doing something new.

'Sorry, I . . .' she stuttered. 'I was miles away.'

'It's OK.' Marta knelt beside her, guiding her body into position. 'Breathing in positive energy, breathing out all that no longer serves you,' Marta intoned to the class.

What no longer served her? This was tough. Skye had thought the hardest bit was going to be keeping up with all the different positions. She wasn't expecting all this introspection. She looked around the group. There was a serenity to them all, a sense of peace and of unity. They even all seemed to be breathing in unison. She shut her eyes and focused.

Marta was back at the front of the group. 'Let's take in a few more deep breaths, inhaling as we reach our hands to the sky. Exhale as we bring them down to the ground. Let's make today's practice a celebration, focus on the good, on what we've achieved this week. On what we are proud of about ourselves. Imagine you are your own best friend. Congratulate yourself on something you're proud of.'

And then the class was on its feet and there seemed to be some sort of routine they all knew. Down dog, step forward, warrior two, forward fold, tabletop, mountain pose . . . or something like that; Skye wasn't too sure about the names of everything, she was concentrating on keeping up with them all. Considering she hadn't moved off her towel for twenty minutes, this was quite hard work. She was sweating and out of breath.

'Transfer the weight onto your hands,' Marta called.

Skye's mind crept back to Clare. She wouldn't be doing yoga any time soon. Last night, once the baby had been bathed and changed, Skye had helped Clare get ready for bed. And then she'd lowered Ivy slowly down into Clare's waiting good arm. She'd seen hundreds of women breast-feed their babies before. But to see her own sister . . . it had felt like such an intimate moment. It hit her suddenly now: Clare couldn't have done it without her. For the first time in their lives, Skye was going to be able to do things for her that Clare could not. Not that Skye was taking pleasure from that, but she, the flaky non-achiever, who'd so far failed at life, was going to be the one to step up. And that felt good.

Congratulate yourself on something you're proud of.

And there it was. Yesterday, Skye had held everything together. She'd taken control of a spiralling situation. Skye had coped with their biggest event so far, carrying on and working through it, while Liz had got steadily drunk. Then Clare had broken her arm and, even though the sight of it had been grotesque and she'd felt faint herself, Skye had climbed into a strange car and driven them to hospital. She'd looked after her niece for the first time ever, which she'd loved. And she'd got Clare and Ivy home and into bed. Small things, all of them. But she'd proved to them and herself that she was far more capable than they gave her credit for. And as temporary as it might be, Clare – stubborn, defensive, fiercely independent Clare – had needed her. For the first time since arriving back in England, Skye felt proud of herself.

Congratulations, Skye Marriott. Her family needed her and were going to need her for the foreseeable future.

'Back to downward dog now. Pedal through the feet, stretch those calves, gently. That's it, good.' Marta was moving around the group, assisting, guiding, encouraging. She was with the woman next to Skye now, trying to get her to step her feet in closer to her hands. Her downward dog was like a neatly inverted V, Skye noticed, legs and arms perfectly straight. Her own was more like a wonky picnic table.

'Keep the legs strong, push through the heels.'

Her hands were beginning to ache in this position. Most of the dogs she knew liked to be on their backs so you could tickle their tummies. She'd be good at that, flipping over and offering up her soft underbelly. She felt another giggle threaten to work its way out and tensed her stomach, not wanting to get told off again.

She felt a hand on her upper spine, pushing her towards the earth. 'Relax your head,' Marta was telling her, 'let it fall between your arms. That's better.'

Skye closed her eyes and took a deep breath, trusting her body to Marta's guidance.

'Push your hips backwards, straighten out your spine. Can you feel the difference?'

'Yes.' Skye's voice trembled. 'I'm still really stiff, but that's much better.'

Marta moved away and Skye collapsed onto her knees. So much for relaxation; this was a full-body workout.

'It is time for shavasana. Get yourselves comfortable, maybe put another layer on as we're going to be lying down.'

Thank heavens for that. Skye pulled her hoodie back on and lay down. She closed her eyes and let her spine mould itself into the sand beneath her; her fingers uncurled, her feet fell open and her body felt soft.

'What does your body need? The more we listen to our bodies, the more we can support not just others, but ourselves. To show up for others, we must first show up for ourselves. Caring begins with you. Invite kindness in. Are you listening to your body, your heart? You already hold all the wisdom you need, so listen deeply. Give yourself permission to ask for what you want.'

Skye focused on her breathing and did her best to listen deeply. Marta made it sound so easy. But the truth was that she couldn't ask for what she wanted, because she didn't know what that was. She'd been back in the UK for several weeks, yet she was no closer to making the decision that Jesse needed from her. Or maybe she had made it, and she just wasn't ready to admit it.

'When you are ready, roll onto your side, come up to a seated position . . .'

Two minutes later, Marta had wished everyone namaste and the class was over. People were already beginning to drift away.

'Did you enjoy that?' said the woman next to her, shaking the sand from her towel.

'Sort of,' said Skye. 'Although I was terrible at it, except for the lying down bit at the end.'

'It gets easier, I promise.' The woman smiled. 'See you at the next class?'

'Probably.' Skye felt someone's gaze on her and looked across the beach to find Marta waving at her. 'It's a great way to start the day.'

And a great way to get to know Marta better too.

Chapter Twenty-One

Skye

'Excellent! A new dinner party booking for a week on Friday.' Skye pressed 'send' on the email reply she'd written to a customer enquiry. 'No special dietary requirements either.'

'Straightfoward clients,' said Liz with a wry smile. 'Music to my ears.'

Skye closed the laptop, Sha and Liz had been to fetch the van from Thurlestone after she'd returned from yoga and there were no jobs for the time being.

Skye had known how much Liz had been dreading Ele, but unfortunately only the cleaner had been there and had handed the keys back without a glimmer of interest. From there, Liz had gone to the lock-up to put back all their equipment and Skye had raced back home to Clare and Ivy.

The plan was for one of them to be on hand to assist Clare for the next few days. If her arm was going to have any sort of chance of healing, she'd need to rest as much as possible. At the moment, whenever their backs were turned, she seemed intent on self-sabotage by attempting to do ridiculous things by herself.

For now, Clare was sitting perfectly still in an armchair, one eye on Ivy, the other on Liz in the kitchen, who was prepping for tomorrow night's champagne and canapés event. Clare had managed to pull on a strapless sundress with shirred bodice and, if it wasn't for her sad expression and the dark circles under her eyes, anyone would think she was ready for a day at the beach. Ivy was on the rug, riveted to something on the TV involving garish-looking puppets, and Liz was listening to a podcast about how to reduce alcohol intake which Clare had found for her.

Both she and Clare had told Liz that they were proud of her positive action to tackle her drinking. But, privately, Skye wondered if Liz was already brushing her drinking off as something she could simply choose not to do. Skye had read somewhere that a habit could take ninety days to break. It was unlikely that she'd be in Salcombe in three months' time, but they'd got another month together. Hopefully, Liz would have made progress by then at least.

Skye knelt down on the floor beside Ivy and tickled the back of her neck. The little girl giggled and crawled into Skye's lap, melting her heart as she'd done a hundred times at least over the last couple of weeks. Kids hadn't been ruled in or out of Skye's future, but Ivy was making a good case for 'in'.

'We could go out for a walk, Clare,' she suggested. 'I could push Ivy in the buggy?'

'I'd love to.' Clare's eyes were closed, but she shook her head. 'But walking hurts. Everything hurts, I just want to sit still and not move. And what if someone knocked into me?'

'Sure, good point.' Ivy stood on Skye's thigh, which was actually quite painful for a small person's foot, and smacked an open-mouthed kiss on her cheek. Skye forgave her for the pain instantly. 'I could take her out, get some fresh air?'

'You could take her to the p-a-r-k,' said Liz, not saying the magic word in front of Ivy in case it got her hopes up. 'You could watch from the balcony, Clare.'

There was a children's play area not far from Clemency House which Clare and Ivy had taken to visiting most days. Skye had gone with them once or twice and knew what to do and what Ivy liked best.

'She can be a bit funny about swings.' Clare wrinkled her nose. 'Maybe another day.'

Liz and Skye exchanged a look of mild exasperation.

Liz wiped her hands on a towel and sat on the chair beside Clare. 'You're going to be incapacitated for a while, love, and Ivy is still going to need to get out and about. Please let us help.'

'I know all of that.' Clare turned her head away and brushed at her eyes. 'I just . . . I'm so tired and sad and I can't stop crying. Everything has gone wrong. I wish Mum was here.'

'So do I, darling.' Liz touched Clare's leg gently.

Skye didn't think she'd ever thought that about her own mother. Frankie wasn't the maternal type and hadn't gone much beyond supplying the practical basics. And, once Skye had hit eighteen, Frankie had pretty much checked out of doing even that. Seeing the grief on Clare's face, Skye felt a pang of longing for the mother she'd never had.

'I know this doesn't help right now,' Skye said, 'but I was always envious of your relationship with Jen. You were so close; there was such a tight bond between you.'

'There was no one else.' Clare shrugged one shoulder. 'We only had each other. You had both your parents.'

'Hmmm,' she replied vaguely.

It sometimes felt as if Frankie was more interested in what her ex-husband was up to than her daughter. Since Skye had been back in the UK, her mother had claimed that her schedule was too crazy to commit to a date to meet up. Skye's offer to go and see her one weekend was met with lukewarm enthusiasm. Now, however, with Liz to counsel, a business to save and an injured sister, it was Skye who was too busy. She had a feeling her mum wouldn't be too disappointed.

'And me,' Liz put in. 'The two of you had me.'

'That's true,' Clare managed a weak smile. 'Best godmother in the world.'

It hadn't always felt that way to Skye. Liz might have been fond of Skye, and they had always got on well when they'd spent any time together, but it had been obvious that she was closer to Clare than her. No surprise given that Jen and Liz were best friends. There'd been times in the past when Skye had wished her parents had chosen someone without a connection to Clare to be her godmother, someone who'd have felt like 'hers', but Liz had come up trumps by offering her a job when she needed it, for which she'd be forever grateful. Besides, there was no point looking backwards.

'There was never much of a bond between the three of us.' Skye frowned. 'Mum and Dad were like a Venn diagram of two circles. The tiny part where they overlapped was me; for the rest of it, they were their own circle. I felt like I was the only thing keeping them together – and not in a good way. I always felt like a disappointment to Dad and an inconvenience to Mum.'

Clare blinked at her. 'But they doted on you. You got everything you wanted.'

Skye stared at her in disbelief. 'Like what?'

'Where do I start?' Clare scoffed. 'Your own pony?'

Skye winced. 'This is going to sound ungrateful, but I didn't ever want a pony. I wanted a BMX bike like you had.'

'That was a great bike.' Clare smirked. 'I bought it off my friend's brother for five pounds. Sold it a few years later for ten.'

'I was terrified of horses,' Skye recalled. 'Mum had this idea of belonging to the horsey set, owning a Range Rover and a pair of Dubarry leather boots and rubbing shoulders with all the other horsey mothers. It was a part she wanted to play. I had two winters of mucking out a pony before finally putting my foot down and refusing to take any more lessons.'

'OK, fine. But your birthday parties were off the scale. Mine were pizza, films and sleepovers, you had entertainers and caterers and DJs at proper venues.'

'Which gave me nightmares. I used to beg to have just my best friend over for pizza, but Mum said that would look cheap and people would stop inviting me to their parties if I didn't reciprocate. I argued that that would suit me just fine. But with Mum and Dad it was always about how things looked. Your parties sounded so much more fun.'

'Well, there you go,' Clare marvelled. 'The grass is always greener. It's a shame we're only talking about this now, we could have set each other straight.'

'Or swapped parties,' Skye suggested.

Clare shook her head. 'In all honestly, I loved my parties and my BMX. Mum always made sure I had fun. I suppose what I resented more was being the daughter that Dad forgot.'

'He never forgot you,' Skye assured her. 'I was the one who played second fiddle. Like my birthday weekend in London, he bailed last minute when he remembered it was your graduation. I was gutted. I would have understood if he'd told us in good time. Birthdays come around every year, but Mum and I had already checked into the hotel when he told us he wasn't coming.'

'What?' Clare sat up a little straighter. 'He didn't turn up to my graduation. He said he'd double-booked, and he had to be at a work thing. I've never forgiven him for that.'

'The lying rat!' Skye gritted her teeth.

'So where was he then?' Clare fumed. 'I can't believe he lied to both of us.'

'And if he was working, why not tell me and Mum the truth?' Skye remembered that weekend so vividly. It had cut her to the quick when she'd discovered he'd skipped her birthday to be with Clare. It had felt like the ultimate desertion on his part. 'Actually, I know why. Mum would have hit the roof if he'd bailed because of work. Dad knew she wouldn't make such a fuss if it was to attend your graduation.'

'Either way, he was dishonest,' Clare said. 'One person will always get priority and that's Mike Marriott.'

Liz sprang up off her chair and returned to making her canapés. 'I'm sure he has his reasons. And it's water under the bridge now.'

Skye raised an eyebrow at Clare as they watched Liz go.

'Bless her.' Clare smiled fondly. 'She sees the good in everyone. Whereas I can harbour a grudge for decades.'

'I'd noticed,' Skye replied.

'I still get cross when I think about that brand-new car you had for your eighteenth, while he and Mum went halves on an old rust bucket for me.'

'Understandable.' Skye had always felt bad about that. 'Again, I know this might not help, but the pressure of owning a new car at that age was awful. I pranged it in the first week and Mum and Dad were furious and told me that I didn't deserve it. On top of that, everyone at college demanded lifts to McDonald's at lunchtime and I couldn't say no. I'd much rather have had an old car.'

'Poor you,' said Clare drily.

'He's not perfect, your father, but he loves you both, I promise you,' Liz piped up. 'And he always tried to treat you fairly.'

'I guess at least on Clare's graduation he let us both down equally,' Skye yielded.

'Yay, go Dad!' Clare punched the air weakly with her good hand. 'Still doesn't excuse the car.'

'I don't know if I should tell you this,' Liz began hesitantly.

'You should,' Skye and Clare said together.

Liz bit her lip. 'OK. Well. He offered to buy you a new car, Clare, but Jen wouldn't have any of it. She thought it was ridiculous to give a teenager something so valuable when it would no doubt get covered in dents and scratches.'

Skye felt a pang of envy; she wished her mum could have been as practical. 'And she was right.'

'But also,' Liz continued, 'Jen wanted the present to be from her and Mike and that was all she could afford. Mike respected that, hence less money was spent on the car.'

'Oh, Mum,' said Clare, her eyes welling with tears. 'That was exactly the right thing to do.'

Skye nodded. 'Very sensible. I reversed mine over my girlfriend's foot and then shot forward in shock and hit her dad's car. She dumped me, unsurprisingly, and Mum and Dad went bananas. I ended up resenting that car.'

She steeled herself, waiting for a reaction. Not about the car but about the girlfriend.

'Gosh,' said Liz, widening her eyes.

Clare frowned. 'So, it was a girlfriend. I always wondered.'

Skye nodded. 'More of a crush really, nothing serious.'

'I had no idea,' said Liz. 'Your father only ever mentioned boys to me.'

'Sounds about right,' said Skye, flatly. 'I've had those too, and what he doesn't like, he ignores.'

'I'm sorry.' Clare sniffed. 'I should have been a better big sister to you. I was probably horrible.'

'Ah, don't cry.' Skye handed her a tissue. 'But, yes, you were.'

They shared a laugh, and weirdly, Skye felt closer to Clare than she ever had.

'Thanks for telling me all that stuff about Dad and Frankie.' Clare sniffed. 'I'm sorry about the Venn diagram thing. Me and Mum were a Venn diagram of two. But what linked us was . . . everything, I guess. I was the centre of her world, and she was the centre of mine. Even after I discovered boys, I told her everything. The night I met Adam, she was the one I wanted to tell.' Clare pressed her lips together, as if shutting the story down.

'Will someone put me out of my misery and tell me what a Venn diagram is and where I fit in,' Liz said.

The other two laughed.

'You link us all,' said Skye. 'You're the lynchpin of the family.'

'You turn our Venn diagrams into Olympic rings,' Clare put in. 'Although I'm not sure what Olympic event we'd compete at.'

'Oh, darling.' Liz pressed a hand to her chest. 'That's the nicest thing anyone's said to me in a long time. Well, except for . . .'

She didn't get to finish the sentence because her phone rang. She waved sticky hands at Skye and asked her to answer it, which she did. Her dad's number flashed up on the screen and it took all of her willpower not to call him out on his lie about the day of Clare's graduation and her birthday.

'Dad, hi, it's Skye. Liz is up to her eyes in pea and mint dip.'

'Fair enough. Is she well? How's it working out? Enjoying the job? Getting on with Clare OK?'

'Really well,' Skye replied, deciding to keep the small matter of Liz's drinking to herself. 'Or, I should say, business is good. Clare's had a nasty accident and broken her arm.'

'Oh dear,' Mike sucked in a breath. 'I broke my wrist once playing squash, I still won the game though. Tell her to do all the exercises they give her. She mustn't lose the mobility in her arm, she's no spring chicken anymore. I was back to full fitness in four months.'

Skye rolled her eyes. How did he always manage to make any subject about himself?

'I'll be sure to give her your love and pass on your good wishes,' said Skye, looking at Clare, who raised her eyebrows in surprise.

'Yes, yes, of course,' he replied warily.

Ivy pulled herself up using the furniture and sidestepped over to her, waggling her fingers.

'Dad, Ivy wants a word, I'll put her on.'

'Oh right,' said Mike without enthusiasm.

She held the phone to Ivy's ear. 'Say hello to Grandad.'

Ivy made a series of noises and tried to put the phone in her mouth. Mike remained silent. Skye rescued it from being licked.

'Dad! You didn't talk to her.'

'She didn't speak!' Mike said indignantly. 'What was I supposed to say?'

'Hello, Ivy, this is your grandad, I love you, maybe?'

'She doesn't know who I am, what's the point?' he said tetchily.

'Dad! The point is that you need to make an effort.' According to Clare, he'd shown little or no interest in his first grandchild. If she ever had kids, Skye was sure that *their* kids would instantly become the most precious creatures in her life.

'When you've had your own children, maybe then you'll be in a position to lecture me,' her dad replied as if he'd read her mind. 'Any sign of that, is there? Settling down and getting married? A good man could be the making of you. Just something to bear in mind. Now, is Liz free please?'

Skye was speechless. A man could be the *making of her?* What century was he in?

'He wants to talk to you,' she said grumpily, walking to the kitchen island where Liz was working.

Liz held up her sticky hands. 'Put it on hands-free, darling. Hello, Mike.'

'Hello, old girl.'

'Less of the "old", Michael Marriott, I'm six months younger than you.'

'You're only as old as the woman you feel, as the saying goes,' Mike laughed lustily.

Skye looked at Clare and they pretended to gag.

'So that makes you what, these days – thirty-eight?'

'Nilla's forty-five,' Mike retorted. 'Anyway, I'm calling about my business event.'

'What business event?'

'The one I booked you for, remember? Over lunch?'

'Just testing,' said Liz, wincing. She waved at Skye to pass her the diary. 'Remind me of the date.'

'Didn't Dad ask to speak to me?' Clare asked after Skye had passed the diary to Liz.

'He's tight for time,' she replied vaguely. 'But he was quite concerned about your arm.'

'You're a terrible liar.' Clare reached for her glass of water, sipped it and then closed her eyes. 'But thanks for trying.'

'How many people?' Liz was asking. 'And what time?'

Skye tuned out of the conversation and returned to what her dad had said about marriage. As if marrying a man was all she was good for.

That was why she never confided in him, or her mum, about her love life. Because whatever she decided to do, whoever she decided to spend the rest of her life with, she needed to be absolutely sure that it was what she really wanted. She knew that if there was any doubt in her mind, she'd be swayed by her dad's opinion. The desire to please her father, to make him notice her, had been at the heart of everything she'd done since becoming aware that she was being judged by a standard set by Clare. Clare wouldn't marry someone for Dad's approval, Skye mused. And when it came to it, neither should she.

The tone of Liz's voice brought her back to the moment.

'No, Mike. Absolutely not,' Liz was saying. 'Not at your house. You wouldn't have asked us to do that if Jen were still here, so don't ask me now.'

'What's going on?' Skye hissed to Clare.

'Dad wants Liz to cater for an event at his house. Liz says no.'

'Liz,' Mike's voice was cajoling. 'That's no way to run a business.'

'It's how I run *my* business,' Liz snapped back.

'Is now a good time to remind you that you owe me a lot of money?'

'He's unbelievable,' Clare whispered, shaking her head in despair.

Liz took a deep breath. 'If you're trying to bully me, I'll say goodbye.'

'Go, Liz!' Skye whispered back to Clare.

'Now don't go all stroppy on me,' Mike wheedled.

'Even if we did cover the Exeter area, which we don't,' Liz countered, 'I wouldn't do a job so far from Salcombe while Clare is still so incapacitated.'

'I'm fine,' Clare said.

Everyone ignored her.

'So now what do I do?' Mike muttered. 'I was relying on you. This is a big deal for me.'

'Oh for heaven's sake, you can hold your lunch here if it's that important,' Liz offered, irritably. 'That way, you'll be able to see your daughters and granddaughter at the same time. I know how you must have been dying to see them.'

Mike was silent for a long moment. 'What about parking?'

'You've got a brain in your head, man, work it out!' Liz barked. 'Up to you, take it or leave it.'

Skye and Clare exchanged impressed looks.

'I'll have what she's having,' Clare said with a grin.

Mike reluctantly agreed to take it, and after Liz had informed him that half of his booking was due up front, she ended the call.

'The man's worse than a spoiled child,' Liz said and stomped out of the room.

No sooner had she gone than the doorbell rang.

'I'll get it,' she yelled and thudded upstairs to the front door.

Skye strained to hear who was there and could just make out a low voice contrasting starkly with Liz, who'd seemed to have gone up an octave.

Footsteps pounded down again, and Liz reappeared looking flustered. 'It's Adam, from yesterday's party, at the door.'

The blood drained from Clare's face. 'You're kidding.'

'He said he wanted to see if Saskia was all right after slipping over yesterday. Why does he think your name is Saskia?'

'Don't panic, Clare,' Skye jumped in, concerned that the shock might be too much on top of everything else. 'I can get rid of him.'

Clare's jaw was set and she shook her head. 'No. Let's get this over with. Can you take Ivy to our bedroom and stay there until he's gone?'

'Sure.' Skye scooped up her niece, along with a handful of toys. Ivy kicked her legs in protest.

'I don't understand?' Liz said, bewildered.

'Liz, as soon as the coast is clear, show him in,' Clare added.

'Have I missed something here?' Liz looked from one to the other. 'Why are we hiding Ivy?'

Skye looked at Clare, waiting for her lead.

'Adam is *the* Adam.' Clare nodded at Ivy.

'Your ex? Oh, my good lord.' Liz clapped her hands over her mouth. 'In that case, he's not coming in, he can sling his hook, that good-for nothing toerag. And to think I was twerking with him yesterday.'

'The thing is,' Clare began, her voice shaking, 'I didn't tell you the truth about Adam. He knows nothing about Ivy. He didn't even know I was pregnant and, for now, I'd like to keep it that way.'

Liz's mouth dropped open. 'Oh Clare.'

'I'll tell you the whole story later, I promise.'

'I see,' Liz said hoarsely, then she rallied. 'Whatever you did, you'll have done for the right reasons, darling. So I'll be beside you every step of the way.'

Skye hesitated at the door. 'Me too. Clare, whatever this is, we're in this together, OK? Shout if you need me.'

Clare looked as white as a sheet. 'Thanks, sis.'

Sis. Skye scampered up the stairs two at a time, silently pleading with her niece not to start yelling at being parted from her mum.

Clare might be about to face her toughest challenge yet, but for the first time in her life Skye felt like she had a sister – a sister who needed her – and her heart might burst.

Chapter Twenty-Two

Clare

So, here's the thing. I'm the mother of your child, you have a daughter, you are a dad.

Clare's heart was pounding so hard that it had almost taken over the throbbing in her arm on the pain scale. She lowered herself into a deckchair and pulled her sunglasses down over her eyes.

The idea of Adam being here at Clemency House was too much for her poor brain to cope with.

What should she tell him? Nothing? Everything? Blurt out the truth that she was really sensible Clare Marriott, two Rs, two Ts, and burst the fantasy of their night together? Or could she keep up the pretence of being Sexy Saskia, the professional location scout?

Granted that last one might be a tall order today; braless and bruised, sweat pooling in every crevice around her injured arm, she had greasy hair and puffy skin from too much crying and not enough sleep. Hardly every man's fantasy – *any* man's fantasy, come to that. And then there was the entourage which accompanied Ivy wherever she went: the army of soft toys, the high chair, changing mat and the big pack of nappies at the bottom of the stairs. Would he register all that stuff as Liz brought him through?

Maybe the fact that she looked so awful would work in

her favour and he wouldn't be able to drag his eyes from the horror in front of him.

Out of the corner of her eye, she noticed the baby monitor plugged in, lights flashing, right next to the patio doors. It was kept there so they could hear Ivy even when they sat outside at night. Now it could well alert Adam to the presence of a small person in the house. She considered standing up to unplug it, but too late, Liz was showing Adam out onto the patio.

Oh God. Help.

'I'll leave you to it,' Liz said solemnly. 'Shout if you need anything.'

'Hey, stranger!' Adam's voice was higher-pitched than Clare remembered it. Or maybe he was nervous. That made two of them.

He stopped a few feet in front of her, phone in one hand, a bunch of keys in the other. He was tanned and well-dressed in a polo shirt, shorts and box-fresh white trainers.

Her heart skipped traitorously; no wonder she'd thrown caution to the wind that night. She'd thought that her memory might have embellished the truth of him during the intervening months. But, no, she'd remembered correctly. He was hot.

'Hey,' she replied. She felt a tug in the pit of her stomach.

'It's good to see you.' His mouth curled in a smile.

'It's *weird* to see you.'

He nodded. 'Weird just about covers it. It's been a while.'

'Twenty months.'

His eyes flickered. 'Very precise.'

'It's a skill.' When you'd been pregnant for nine months and had an eleven-month-old baby, these things tended to stick in your mind. It was also the day her mum had died, a date that would be forever etched in her memory.

She was glad she'd been sitting down when he arrived, because he'd have almost certainly noticed how much her legs were trembling.

'Look.' He rubbed a hand through his hair and chewed his bottom lip distractedly. 'Sorry to come by unannounced, but since seeing you from the ferry, and then bumping into you yesterday, I haven't been able to stop thinking about you. So I thought I'd ask Ele for the address of the caterers and take it from there. And here I am.'

'And here you are,' Clare swallowed.

His voice was exactly as she remembered it. Not that that should have come as a surprise, but it was incredible how simply talking to him brought the memories of that night into clear focus.

'I don't want to give you the impression that I meet someone once and get obsessed with them and try to track them down, but . . .' He jingled his keys. 'Do you mind if I sit down for a minute?'

'Sure.' She waved him towards the other chair to avoid him coming any closer and then cradled her sling with her good hand, an automatic gesture of protection at the approach of another person.

'Looks painful,' he said, indicating her arm with a nod of his head.

'It is. Terrible. The worst pain I've ever had, even worse than . . .' She brought herself up short before saying child-birth. 'I can't even think of anything. That's how bad.'

'What did you actually do?' he asked. She gave him such a sharp look that he recoiled. 'To your arm, I mean, after you slipped on my sister's birthday cake?'

'Angel is your sister?' Clare gasped. Her mind instantly leapt to *Auntie Angel* before reminding herself that they were a long way from going down that road, if they ever did at all.

'My little sister. That's why I'm down in Salcombe, I didn't want her not to have any family with her this year. I'm staying for the summer while my mum is away in Australia visiting her best friend. And my dad . . . isn't here either.'

He cares about his family, a little voice said, in her head, *good sign*. She brushed it away. Her dad had been a family man until one day he wasn't. Not her family, at least.

'Fractured in two places,' she said. 'Not a day I ever wish to revisit.'

Adam winced. 'That sucks.'

'Yep, so much for my plans for swimming and lazing on the beach.'

'Sorry to hear that.'

She felt herself growing hot under the weight of his gaze. She checked her strapless dress hadn't slipped down under one boob and surreptitiously wiped a fingertip below each eye to remove any traces of yesterday's mascara. 'What?'

He laughed softly, shaking his head. 'All this time, I've wondered if I'd see you again and you turn up at my sister's birthday party.'

'So, you'd thought about me?' She'd thought about him too. A lot. But it had never once occurred to her that he might have been doing the same.

'That sounds a bit creepy.' He gave her a crooked smile. 'But, yes, I guess I have. It felt like that night ended too soon.'

Clare felt her cheeks grow warm. 'I thought it went on quite a long time.'

'I wasn't referring to . . .' His face flushed beneath his tan. 'I mean that I was disappointed when you left. You got a phone call about your mum. I was worried about you. And I kept thinking about you, wondering if everything was all right with her.'

Clare looked down at her lap. 'Mum was in a car crash that night. She didn't survive.'

'Oh my God, I'm so sorry. That must have been horrendous for you.' Adam shook his head, his eyes full of sympathy.

'Another day I'd rather not revisit,' she said wryly.

'Not looking good for me, is it? Two meetings, two bad endings.' He swore under his breath. 'Sorry, that sounded flippant, and it wasn't meant to be. I guess this is just . . .'

'Weird?'

His eyes met hers and for a moment he said nothing. 'I've been thinking back to that night, remembering how much I enjoyed meeting you, wishing I'd done things differently, at least taken your number, while for you . . . it ended with you losing a loved one. I'm so sorry. I wish I'd known. I wish I could have been there for you.'

A wave of emotion surged through her. Clare had never felt as alone as she had during the long hours of that traumatic night. Even Liz, who she'd known all her life, couldn't fill the void. She remembered feeling as heavy as lead and yet as light as air all at the same time. Weighed down with grief, but barely tethered to reality, as if any second she could be lifted from the ground and carried away like a seed from a dandelion clock.

'Hey?'

She felt his fingertip briefly touch her leg, feather-light and non-threatening. Just long enough to jolt her back to the moment.

'I appreciate that, thank you,' she said. 'But we didn't know each other. Not really.'

He didn't even know her real name.

She should tell him the truth, she owed him that at least, and it wasn't as if she could hide from him now that he knew where she was staying, where *they* were staying. In the room above, possibly even looking out of the window – she didn't dare check – was their baby.

'I know that.' The corner of his mouth lifted into a smile. 'But that was because of the circumstances. If things had been different—'

'You mean if we hadn't met in a hotel bar and ended up in bed together almost immediately?' She tilted her chin up and met his eye.

He looked down at his hands and then back at Clare. 'It sounds sordid when you say it like that. But it didn't feel that way at the time. At least not to me.'

Her stomach twisted. It hadn't felt like that to her either. She wondered how things might have played out if . . . if . . .

'The thing is, I can't think about you without connecting it to Mum and imagining the terror she must have felt in the split second before the collision . . .' A sob formed in her throat, and she squeezed her eyes tight.

Adam groaned softly. 'I'm so sorry. That sounds lame, but I really am. Do you have siblings, other family around you to support you?'

She shook her head. 'My godmother, Liz, who I believe may have shown you her dance moves yesterday?'

He nodded, conceding a small smile.

'My dad is around, but my parents divorced nearly thirty years ago. He was shocked, naturally, but he didn't grieve, not like me.'

'My dad died last year,' said Adam. 'The circumstances weren't as traumatic as – what was your mum's name?'

'Jen,' Clare supplied. Which was also his daughter's middle name. *Ivy Jennifer Marriott*.

'Not as traumatic as *Jen's*,' he continued. 'But it's ripped a hole through our family. He was . . .' He faltered and

239

took a moment to breathe, as if trying to find the words. 'He wasn't just a brilliant dad, he was the best man I knew. Probably the best I'll ever meet. So I understand what it feels like to miss someone you can't imagine ever living without.'

'I'm sorry for your loss, Adam,' Clare said. 'I really am.'

She held her hand out to him. His eyes reached hers and there was a moment of such connection between them that she could have sworn her heart stopped for a second. He scooted his chair closer so that their knees were almost touching and took hold of her hand.

'This reminds me of when we met.' He looked down at their joined hands.

'You mean when you doused me with boiling water?'

He screwed his face up. 'Not my finest moment. Although as a ruse to get to hold a beautiful woman's hand, it did me proud.'

She raised an eyebrow. 'So you make a habit of picking up women in hotels?'

'No! God no!' he proclaimed. 'Seriously. I never normally stay in hotels.'

Her lips twitched. 'You pick them up in other places?'

'No!' He slapped his free hand to his forehead and groaned. 'I think I'd better shut up before I get myself into more hot water.'

'Instead of just me,' she deadpanned, and they both laughed.

She'd gone all fluttery. He was lovely. Not just hot. But actually a nice human. Or was this her abandoned sex life talking? She hadn't dated once since that night. With Mum's funeral, then realising that she was pregnant and then having Ivy, there'd been no space in her life for men. This was probably the first conversation she'd had like this with a man since she'd met Adam.

'I don't make a habit of meeting men in hotel bars either,' she said softly. 'In case you were thinking that I did.'

'I wasn't, but good to know.' His fingers tightened around hers. 'But I bet you do stay in a lot of hotels. You're still a location scout, I assume?'

And here it was; the moment of truth, quite literally.

She couldn't bring herself to lie again. What if Ivy wanted to know about her dad when she was older? Clare wouldn't be able to lie then, it wouldn't be fair. She'd have to tell Ivy the truth. The thought made her heart race.

Her mum had brought her up to be wary of men, of letting them in, trusting them not only with your heart but with your most precious thing – your child. And her own father had been at the root of that mistrust. He had let Clare down, and Skye too it turned out, time and time again. And Adam? Was he the same?

Clare glanced through the patio doors, where she could just make out Liz in the kitchen. Her gaze flicked quickly upstairs to her bedroom window. Skye had closed the bedroom curtains, but was peering out through the tiniest gap.

Maybe she could tell Adam the truth in pieces, bit by bit as he earned her trust. He deserved to know that he had a wonderful daughter, just as Ivy deserved to know about her dad. But, at the same time, she needed to protect Ivy from potentially being abandoned by a man, as she had been. Clare drew in a breath and prepared to start telling the truth.

'Actually, I'm not a location scout,' she admitted with a sheepish smile. 'Nowhere near as exciting as that. I'm just a teacher.'

'Oh.' He sat back, confused. 'Wow.'

She winced. 'On the day I met you, I'd had a spa day at the hotel with my mum. After she left to drive back to

Salcombe, I decided to stay for another drink. I was putting off going back to my flat, where I'd have ruined the effects of my de-stress massage by opening up my laptop for yet another game of guess the government's new shiny idea for buggering up the education of our kids.'

Adam looked bemused. 'You sound like my mum.'

'Thanks. That was exactly the tone I was going for.'

'By which I mean that she's a teacher,' he corrected himself swiftly. 'Or was. Now she's a retired head teacher. Four decades of biting her tongue and muttering that if politicians spent as much as one hour in a school before meddling with the system, then education would be a much calmer ocean to navigate.'

Clare grinned. 'I'd probably like your mum.'

'She'd probably like you.' He held her gaze. 'And, for the record, I'm much more impressed with teaching as a career than a location scout. What made you make up something like that?'

Her face flooded with heat and she dipped her chin. 'Look, it's ridiculous and I'm totally embarrassed to admit it. But "normal, sensible me" would have turned down the offer of dinner with a good-looking stranger and dashed off home. And I thought that, for once, I'd try on a different personality. So,' she cleared her throat, 'I became Sexy Saskia for the night. I just made her up on the spot.'

Adam stared at her. 'So your name's not even Saskia?'

She shook her head. 'It's Clare.'

He gave a laugh of surprise. 'That explains why we couldn't find any trace of you online. Do you have any idea how many location agencies exist? How many Saskias there are on LinkedIn?'

'Not a clue,' she said, trying to keep the smile from her lips. He really had tried to look for her.

'So if you were there for the day, do you live near Bath?'

'Yep, right in the centre.'

'Cool.' He nodded. 'I live—' He broke off and gave a sheepish laugh. 'I live within walking distance of the hotel.'

'OK, so you were there because . . .?' She eyed him quizzically. A row with his partner, maybe, and she'd kicked him out. She'd put money on it.

'This is embarrassing,' he laughed under his breath.

'Go on, what did you do?' she prompted. Expecting, but not wanting, to hear the worst.

'I locked myself out.' Adam bit his lip and grinned.

A bubble of laughter burst out of her. 'No way!'

He nodded sheepishly. 'I was having the house renovated and had just come back that day from visiting my parents. I had a row with the builder on the front doorstep. He stormed off site and the door slammed, leaving me locked out until the next morning. I was too annoyed with him to ring and ask him to come and let me in.'

Her lips twitched. 'So you booked into the hotel. Why didn't you tell me that?'

'Well, *Saskia*,' he teased, 'I was already the clumsy oaf who'd knocked into you, I didn't want to be the loser who'd also managed to lock himself out of his own house.'

'I might have thought it was endearing.'

'And I might have thought taking your mum on a spa date was endearing, Clare.'

He'd said her real name. A shiver ran down her spine. Was this flirting? It felt like flirting. After twenty months of being a grieving daughter, a pregnant head teacher, a single mum, she felt like Clare again. Granted, she was sensible Clare this time around, not Sexy Saskia, but still, it felt good.

'We can't change anything about that night,' said Adam, his voice low. 'But we—'

A loud screeching noise interrupted him. Over his shoulder, Clare saw the lights on the baby monitor flashing all the way up to max, her mouth went dry. *Turn it off*, Clare willed Skye. *Move away from the monitor.*

'What was that?' Adam said, his ears pricked.

'I don't know,' said Clare. 'A cat maybe?'

'It must be stuck somewhere.' He got up and walked around the edge of the balcony, looking below for signs of an animal in distress. 'I can't see anything.'

Ivy squealed with laughter; it sounded as if she and Skye were having fun. Auntie Skye, Clare thought absently, the unexpected bonus of this summer's trip to Salcombe.

Adam stood still and strained to listen. 'It's coming from over there.' He pointed to the patio doors, just as Skye's voice came through as clear as a bell.

'Shush-sh-sh. We'll go down and see Mummy in a minute, sweetie.'

Adam crossed the patio in three short strides, picked up the baby monitor and looked at her, puzzled. '*Mummy?*'

Her heart pounded; this wasn't how she'd planned it. Not that there was a plan, but if she'd had time to formulate one, it wouldn't have been this.

Clare licked her dry lips. 'That's me.'

'You're Mummy?' His face was unreadable.

'Yes, I've been busy since we last met.' She nodded, guilt flooding through her as she watched Adam process what she'd said. 'I had a baby.'

He smiled stoically. 'Congratulations. That's brilliant news, Sask— I mean Clare.'

'Thank you.' She gave a shaky laugh. 'It came as a bit of a shock, but she's the best thing that's ever happened to me.'

'She? A daughter?' Adam's eyes softened. 'It never occurred to me that . . . Of course, I mean, it's been a long time since we met, of course you've moved on. We all have; I dated someone for a while myself. Not that that's relevant. Look, I should go. I hope me turning up like this hasn't been embarrassing for you. He's not here, is he?'

'Who?'

'Your new man, the baby's father?'

'Oh him? Um, no, he's not in the house, no.' Technically Ivy's father was outside on the patio, so not a complete lie, but certainly disingenuous of her. She had a terrible feeling that her face was scarlet. 'Would you like to meet her?'

Adam paused and ruffled his hair for a second. 'I'd better get going, actually.'

The strength of her disappointment took her by surprise. 'Right. Of course. Not everyone is a fan of babies.'

'It's not that, I just—' He stooped to kiss her cheek. 'You've moved on and I'm happy for you, Clare, and I'm glad we got a chance to meet again.'

'Adam?' She bit her lip. She couldn't let him go. Not with so much still unsaid between them. 'Do you think we could meet up again?'

He took a step back and looked at her warily. 'Is that wise?'

'As a friend, I mean. Especially now I've broken my arm. I'm going to be really bored stuck in the house. If you're going to be around for a while . . .?' She held her breath; praying he said yes.

He gave her a twisted smile. 'Sure, why not. Give me your number and I'll give you mine.'

'Great,' she smiled with relief, as he swiped his phone screen. 'It's Clare Marriott, two Rs and two Ts.'

Chapter Twenty-Three

Liz

As soon as Liz was sure that Clare could handle Adam
without her being there, she collected her bag and slipped
out of the front door. After the last hour of conversation
with her god-daughters, her brain felt as if it might explode.
The urge to escape from the house for a while and untangle
her thoughts was too strong to ignore.

Clare and Adam.

So that was Ivy's father; what a hunk! No wonder Ivy
was such a beautiful child, even accounting for Liz's bias.
With those looks, he could be an actor or a model, or
the lead singer of a band. And it wasn't just his face, it
was his manner, so charming; he looked at you as if you
were the most important person in the room. Liz put a
hand to her face, aware that she was getting warm just
thinking about him.

She wouldn't interfere, no matter how much she wanted
to. There could be any number of reasons why Clare hadn't
been honest with that lovely young man about Ivy's existence. But her heart couldn't help but skip a little; wouldn't
it be wonderful if the two of them got together, a lovely
romantic ending to the summer . . . Liz gave herself a little
shake. It wouldn't do to get carried away, and hadn't she
just promised not to meddle?

And then there were the girls. Her god-daughters. That earlier conversation had had its awkward moments.

She was used to being caught between Mike and Jen, but this was the first time it had happened between Skye and Clare. She loved them both dearly, always had. But this last couple of weeks had brought her so much closer to Skye. She'd always thought of the younger of Mike's daughters as being the shy one, the least likely to step up to the plate. But, boy, had she got that wrong! Skye had turned out to be such a support to her, and now to Clare too. And thank goodness at least one of them had an uncomplicated love life.

Liz hoped she had done the right thing, telling Clare that Mike had offered to buy her a new car. It felt like a betrayal to Jen's memory to be telling her daughter things which Jen hadn't wanted her to know, and she sent up a silent apology to her best friend. But she thought of Clare's reaction on learning her father hadn't treated her any differently and decided it was worth spilling the beans. It had been healing for Clare to know that she wasn't thought of any less than Skye. There'd been a touch of defiant pride on her face too, to discover how far Jen was prepared to go to stick to her principles. Not only had her first car been perfectly adequate, but it had been a gift from both of her parents. Clare respected that.

And then there was Skye talking about having had a girlfriend. Liz didn't care a jot what her sexuality was; she was a delightful girl and Liz hoped whoever she fell in love with was good enough for her. However, the fact that Mike had only ever mentioned boyfriends to Liz was disappointing. Supporting your children in their biggest decisions in life was what made you a good parent.

She turned left at the bottom of the hill, called into one of her favourite shops and bought both girls scented candles for their rooms. On the other side of the road, the display in the wine-shop window caught her eye. There was a special promotion on pink wine: three bottles of Provence rosé for the price of two. Two days ago, she'd have been straight in there, telling herself that she was supporting a local business by buying from them. Not to mention justifying treating herself to a couple of bottles because it was a bargain.

She turned away. And then turned back. It *was* a bargain. Also, she reasoned, it wasn't as if she was planning on giving up wine forever, just long enough to retrain her drinking habits. She could get three bottles and keep them; it was always good to have some in, just in case.

Oh sod it; she couldn't resist. Liz went inside, smiled at the shop assistant, who recognised her, and loaded three bottles into a basket. As she walked to the cash desk, adrenaline flooded her system, making her heart race. What was she doing in here? Why was she so weak and pathetic? How could she have gone back on her promises so soon?

'Is everything all right?' asked the concerned assistant.

'Got to go,' Liz mumbled, her face already breaking out into a sweat. 'Sorry.'

She dumped the basket on the counter and fled.

It was a full five minutes until she could breathe properly. She felt wobbly and tearful, but underneath it all, there was a tiny spark of pride that she'd done the hard thing. The wine habit had been years in the making, starting right back in her student days. All she had to do was manage the cravings one day at a time, and that was what she'd done. She didn't want to let the girls down, not after yesterday's performance. There was Patrick too; he'd been so kind to her when she'd confessed to him, she didn't want to disappoint him.

As she passed the pasty shop, the one solitary chicken and leek pasty in the window called to her and she stopped to buy it. Never underestimate the power of a flask of tea and a warm pasty, her dad used to say when they were out sailing and a storm took them unawares. There was no rain today, the air was crisp and cooler than it had been after yesterday's clouds. But she still drew strength from her dad's words.

She wandered up to Whitestrand again and stopped at an empty bench overlooking the water.

The pasty was delicious. Just the hit of carbs she needed, and as she waited for it to cool between bites, her thoughts meandered back to Jen and Mike.

Liz had sometimes found it hard to stand back and watch when Jen's pride had stood in the way of accepting help from her ex-husband. Jen had acted that way to snub him, but more often than not, it had been Clare who'd suffered. Was it any wonder their daughter had an independent streak as wide as the Salcombe estuary? Liz had stepped in this time and opened up about the car, because she couldn't bear there to be any resentment between Clare and Skye. Especially when it wasn't based on the facts. For all his faults, Mike had tried to treat them fairly when he could.

And from her position as their godmother, she'd had a bird's-eye view of the extended family. Like an umpire at Wimbledon, perched on her high stool, overlooking the whole picture: Mike on one side of the net, Jen on the other, with Clare bouncing backwards and forwards between them.

Liz had been the obvious choice for godmother to Clare. It had been a role she'd assumed would be hers but, nonetheless, had been delighted to be asked. With Skye it had been a different matter entirely and Liz could never recall her acceptance of the job without a flush of shame.

She cast her mind back to a day not long after Skye was born. She and Jen had been catching up over a glass of wine one night after Clare had gone to bed.

'I've got something to tell you,' Liz had said, topping up Jen's glass.

Jen's eyes had sparkled expectantly. 'Please let it be something good.'

'Mike has asked me to be the baby's godmother.' She'd held her breath, knowing how hard it was for Jen to hear about Mike and his new family. He'd sent Liz a photo of Frankie and the new baby, taken while they were still in the delivery suite. Frankie was a beautiful young woman and even just after giving birth she'd glowed, her smile dazzling. How she was going to take to motherhood was anyone's guess – on the few occasions Liz had met her, Frankie had seemed rather self-absorbed.

'Course he bloody has,' Jen had muttered bitterly.

Liz had pulled her friend into a hug as tears leaked from her eyes.

When Mike had first left Jen, Liz had hated him so much, she couldn't bear to think about him, let alone see or speak to him. What he'd done to her best friend was unforgivable. To cheat on Jen, to get another woman pregnant when at home he had what thousands – no, millions – of men would have given their right arm for. Jen was funny, intelligent, kind, loyal . . . And Clare – how could he walk away from his delightful little girl?

The Marriott family had been an extension of Liz's own. Now that their little unit had been torn apart, Liz had felt the loss of it deeply. Mike's defection had meant the end of so many things; making up a foursome with the Marriotts was something she and whomever she'd been seeing at the time had done ever since her best friend and former crush had got together. Mike walking away had altered that dynamic forever.

But – and Liz would never admit this to anyone – Mike being no longer in her orbit had done her a favour. Her feelings for him should have gone by now. They were still close as friends, still got on well, but he'd never shown any interest in her since that one celebratory kiss at uni when they'd got top marks for their joint project. He'd dated her friend, married her friend, had a baby . . . if she'd needed a sign that her love for Mike would be forever unrequited, the universe had answered repeatedly. And yet . . .

'And?' Jen had said, after blowing her nose.

'I said no, obviously,' Liz had assured her.

'Say yes.' Jen had a glint in her eyes. 'Ring him up and say you've changed your mind, you were in shock and didn't think it through, but you're flattered, et cetera, et cetera.'

'Hold on.' Liz had blinked in surprise. 'You *want* me to be a godmother to Frankie and Mike's baby? Why?'

'Think about it,' said Jen, digging into the bowl of crisps in front of them. 'You can be my spy in the camp. Well, not spy, just, you know, find out what she's like. Clare is going to be spending time with a woman who's not me or you. I mean, should I be worried? And . . .' she'd hesitated, looking vulnerable for a moment, 'I know I shouldn't care, but I want to know what she's got that I haven't.'

And because Liz would do anything for Jen, she'd agreed, thus keeping both Mike and Jen happy. But that didn't stop her feeling uncomfortable about the whole thing as she'd stood beside the font at Skye's christening promising to perform her duties as godmother.

As it had turned out, Liz's opportunities to report back to Jen had been few and far between. Frankie had seen to that, understandably not welcoming the ex-wife's best friend into her home. As the years had rolled by, Jen had been less interested in what Mike was up to and more determined not to let him buy Clare's affection with expensive gifts. What their daughter needed, Jen would supply herself, or from the child maintenance payments he made to her.

Liz admired her for that; it was a good feeling to know that what you had you'd got on your own merit. But there was a graciousness to receiving help when it was offered that had passed Jen by.

Liz remembered the day she'd realised that when her parents died Clemency House would belong to her. She'd been consumed with guilt, knowing that she was going to receive such a wonderful gift and feeling that she'd done nothing to deserve it.

Her father wasn't having any of it.

'Don't underestimate the joy your mother and I will get from knowing that our family home will one day belong to our only daughter,' he had said. 'Smoothing the way for your children is as much a gift for the older generation as it is for the younger. Don't deny us that happiness by feeling guilty about it.'

After she and Jonathan had parted ways, it had been to her mother and Clemency House Liz had returned. Her father had already passed away and the two women had comforted each other. The house had been her sanctuary and her happy place ever since.

Mike had been frustrated by Jen's stubbornness not to allow him to spend money on Clare. It had been up to Liz to remind him that when he'd walked out on his wife and child, he'd forfeited the right to criticise her choices.

Liz had always been there for him. Always. She'd never been able to say no. Like that day the girls were talking about: Clare's graduation and Skye's birthday treat. Liz had felt sick with terror earlier when they'd been discussing it. What a risky game Mike had played, assuming that neither of them would ever discuss the day when he'd let them both down. He should have told Frankie and Skye the same story as he'd told Clare and Jen: that he had an unavoidable work commitment. Silly man.

Anyway, regardless of the lies he'd told back then, her lie by omission felt much worse. She knew exactly where Mike had been that day because he'd been with her. She'd never told a soul and she never would. Mike had sworn her to secrecy; she wouldn't let him down.

Liz folded the empty paper bag, brushed a few stray crumbs from her chest and left her spot. She picked up a little beach toy for Ivy and then the sign for the bookshop caught her eye, and she dipped into the little alleyway and headed inside.

She'd known the owner a long time; Jess had a knack of finding exactly the right book for every customer. Liz gave her the brief: something a new mum can escape into, nothing dreary or grim. Five minutes later, she was back on Fore Street with a copy of Maeve Binchy's *Circle of Friends* and a list of suggestions for what Clare might like to read next.

'Liz!' She turned at the sound of a woman's voice and spotted a raised hand waving to her from across the tourist-packed street.

'Viv! I owe you a drink,' said Liz, greeting her old friend with a kiss on the cheek. 'For putting all this business my way. I really appreciate it.'

Viv took her hands. 'Darling, I owe *you* a drink for coming up trumps with your marvellous cooking. All my properties are fully booked and I've got waiting lists for several of them.

The thing about Salcombe holiday homes is the views are so gorgeous that my clients would rather stay in to eat, albeit have dinner cooked by someone else, of course.'

'And who can blame them,' Liz agreed. She felt the same about her lovely house, except, in her case, her favourite thing was to cook in her own kitchen.

'You and I make a fabulous team.' Viv squeezed her hand. 'I missed you last summer, Liz, I really did. I'm so glad you're making a go of it again.'

'Me too.'

Liz repeated her offer of a drink, but Viv shook her head.

'I'd love to, but I have an appointment. Although I have to say,' she lowered her voice and tittered, 'I'm surprised you can even contemplate alcohol today.'

'Why?' Liz felt her face redden. 'What do you mean?'

'Oh, come on, Liz.' Viv nudged her arm. 'Noah told me all about it. I must admit I was quite shocked.'

'Oh that,' Liz laughed uneasily. 'It was a one-off. I think someone spiked my water glass.'

Viv raised an amused eyebrow. 'From the photos of you doing tequila shots, it looked as if you really got into the party spirit.'

Liz was mortified. If only the ground would swallow her up so she could terminate this awful conversation. 'I let myself get pressured into it,' she said feebly. 'It won't happen again.'

'Good,' said Viv, all business. 'Because I'd hate my clients to think I'd recommended someone to them who gets drunk on the job.'

'Oh totally. Let's say no more about it,' she replied hopefully.

'Mum's the word.' Viv smiled. 'Now, I'm due at the beauty salon before a hot date with a gorgeous man. Mani, pedi, facial and a short back and sides.'

Liz folded her own stubby nails into her palms. 'That sounds quite a radical haircut.'

Viv put a hand to her mouth and whispered behind it, 'Waxing my lady garden, darling. Next time you see me, you won't recognise me, I'll be a new woman.'

'You're already gorgeous as you are,' said Liz, thinking that a generous compliment or two wouldn't go amiss under the circumstances.

'Bless you,' Viv said coyly. 'But you know what it's like in the early days with a new man; us girls have to make an effort.'

'I wouldn't know, it's been so long,' replied Liz. 'Noah mentioned you'd started dating again, who's the lucky chap?'

Viv's eyes softened. 'It's a guy called Patrick Delmarge. My friend set me up with him. We had our first date last night. He's quite a catch.'

'You were with Patrick last night?' Liz had to stop herself from gasping out loud. This was the woman he'd been talking about? He'd said there'd been no chemistry between them and that he wouldn't be seeing her again. Viv seemed to think otherwise. Had Patrick lied to her? That seemed unlike him.

'You know him?' Viv's smile froze.

Evidently not as well as she'd thought, Liz mused.

'He's a client,' she replied. 'That's all.'

'Thank goodness for that! I'd hate us to be rivals.'

'No, no,' Liz assured her brightly. 'No chance of that.'

'We just had a drink yesterday.' Viv twirled a strand of her hair girlishly. 'But today I'm going to his house.'

'He's got a lovely house,' said Liz, unable to stop herself from adding, 'Five bedrooms. He can see my bedroom from his.'

Viv gave her a sharp look. 'Can he now? Anyway, I must dash. Wish me luck.'

Liz couldn't bring herself to do that, so she said goodbye instead and sighed with disappointment as Viv sashayed away.

Viv and Patrick. So much for waving flags to each other from their respective bedroom windows. Only this morning she'd been thinking of him as her silver lining, but suddenly her mood had clouded over. Flippin' men. Would she ever understand them?

Chapter Twenty-Four

Clare

'Sh-sh-sh-sh,' Clare murmured, leaning into the travel cot to stroke Ivy's forehead. It was afternoon nap time and Ivy was almost asleep. The room was dark, and a warm breeze drifted in through the partly open window. Gradually, Ivy's breathing slowed, and her fingers loosened their grip around Winnie the Pooh's paw. Her nap would last about an hour; a little pocket of time which, at home in the flat, Clare would spend tidying up or catching up on washing or ironing. She had kept their daily routine as close to normal as possible since being in Salcombe, although now, of course, she couldn't do much in the way of housework and was having to rely on Skye and Liz to help her do everything.

It was two weeks since she'd broken her arm, and being so useless was driving her bonkers. She could just about manage to pick Ivy up, but she was on edge all the time, in case she moved suddenly and knocked against her. And as for nappy-changing, forget it. The one occasion she'd insisted she could manage had ended very badly; everyone involved had had to have a bath. Auntie Skye had been given the job for the time being. Every cloud and all that, thought Clare now, smiling to herself.

Satisfied that Ivy was asleep, she checked the baby monitor was switched on, closed the bedroom door and carefully descended the steep stairs, holding onto the rail. She did everything slowly and carefully now.

Breaking her arm had scared her. And not just because attending the weekly fracture clinic at the hospital brought back bad memories of losing Mum, but because the self-sufficiency she was so proud of had vanished in a puff of smoke. All it had taken was one slip-up, one accident, to turn her life upside down, Ivy's too. Their summer holiday wouldn't create the idyllic memories she'd envisaged; but at least they were at Liz's, with other people around to help. Clare shuddered every time she thought about what it would be like at home, trying to manage with a broken arm. She'd been upgraded from a simple sling to a brace, at her last appointment it was more difficult to get on and off, and bulkier, but it made it easier to be close to Ivy because her injured bones were better protected.

Clare was never ill. She couldn't remember taking a day off sick from school in years. In all her internal monologues about her desire to succeed, her determination to remain independent and not rely on anyone else, she'd never considered that one day she might be incapacitated.

Now, she felt vulnerable; Clare Marriott wasn't invincible after all. She had to learn to let people in, if not for her own sake, then for Ivy's.

She found Skye and Liz in the kitchen putting the finishing touches to afternoon tea for the Delmarges. They were due in the next hour and the house smelled deliciously of vanilla and sugar and fresh baking. Liz had unearthed her parents' beautiful Limoges tea service, which Skye was setting onto a tray. Liz was decanting scones from a baking sheet onto a cooling rack.

'Little Miss Marriott is asleep,' Clare announced, joining them. 'Which should mean she'll be all sweetness and light when our guests arrive.'

'I shall try to take a leaf out of her book then,' said Liz. She put the baking sheet in the sink and washed her hands. 'I would have cancelled on them, but Patrick's mother and aunt would be so disappointed. They don't get out of the home very much and it wouldn't be fair.'

'It wouldn't be fair on us either,' Clare replied. 'I want to meet the man who's got you all riled up.'

'I'm not riled. Just confused. Patrick told me one thing and Viv gave me a completely different story.' Liz took the butter dish from the fridge and slammed the door.

'Shall I move the tripod and binoculars from the balcony in case he takes a look through and notices that they're zoomed in on his house?' Skye said innocently.

Clare smothered a snort.

Liz flushed. 'Might be a good idea.'

'Ask him about Viv,' Skye suggested. 'There might be a perfectly valid explanation as to why he hasn't told you about her.'

'I agree,' said Clare.

A couple of weeks had gone by since then but Liz was still grouchy about it. The sooner they could get to the bottom of it, the better. 'Although I'm surprised he hasn't been in touch with you himself,' She added.

'He has been in touch,' Liz admitted sheepishly. 'He suggested going for a drink. I said no, of course.'

'Why *of course*?' Skye asked. 'That would have been the perfect opportunity to clear the air.'

'I couldn't,' Liz murmured. She handed Skye the cutlery to add to the tea tray.

The slump in her godmother's body language made Clare's heart squeeze.

'Because of the temptation to drink?' she asked gently. 'Was that why?'

Liz nodded. 'I don't think I'm strong enough to say no to a glass of wine yet. Especially on a date with a man. I can't remember the last time I went to a bar and didn't have an alcoholic drink.'

'Ah, sorry,' said Skye contritely. 'I didn't think.'

Liz smiled at her. 'It's fine. Anyway, I've decided to keep out of the way during afternoon tea. Clare, I wondered if you might sit with them, see if you can pick up any clues about him and Viv?'

'Leave it with me.' Clare narrowed her eyes. 'I'll give him my special head-teacher stern look.'

Skye laughed. 'You had that down a long time before you became a head teacher. Remember when you thought I'd taken your iPod? I thought you were going to burn holes in my skin.'

Clare remembered it well. She'd taken her best Christmas present to Dad and Frankie's on Boxing Day and had spent most of the day with her headphones plugged in. At bedtime, she'd stuffed the iPod in a sock, forgot she'd done it and blamed Skye, who'd been hovering over it enviously all day. She didn't find it until she'd gone back home to her mum. 'I did apologise.'

'Actually, you didn't at the time,' Skye said airily. 'But apology accepted.'

'And perhaps don't stare at him too hard,' Liz teased. 'He is a paying customer, after all.'

She dropped the oven gloves to the floor and Clare automatically bent down to pick them up for her. Her broken arm swung forward away from her body, and she felt the two parts of her fractured bone move independently of each other.

'Oh God.' She closed her eyes as nausea hit her. 'I hate it when that happens. That's karma for the iPod.'

'Please sit down.' Liz's face was as pale as Clare's felt. 'You give me the dithers when you do that.'

'Me too, to be honest,' said Clare, clambering onto a stool at the island with Skye's hand to steady her.

'Can I get you some painkillers?' Skye asked. 'Are you allowed some?'

'Please.' Clare nodded.

She had finished her course of morphine. She'd been taking that at night and once she'd managed to get herself comfortable, she'd slept really well, better than she had since before her mum died. Ivy had started sleeping through the night too – a new development which had happened with perfect timing.

She was still in a lot of discomfort. The swelling in her arm hadn't gone down much yet and the bruising was horrendous – she could hardly bear to look at it. Liz certainly couldn't. Skye seemed to take everything in her stride, from adjusting Clare's arm brace to helping her get dressed. There was no dignity and very little privacy, she had learned, when you'd broken a limb.

'Can't you give me a job?' Clare said mournfully, watching Liz cut cucumber into thin slices. 'Just something easy?'

'No,' Liz and Skye said in unison.

'I need to do something to take my mind off Adam.' She couldn't stop thinking about him: his muscular frame, those dark curls and how happy she'd felt when he'd smiled at her.

She'd had second thoughts about contacting him after he'd gone, deciding to leave the ball in his court. She was aware that she was backtracking on what she'd thought at the time. But old habits die hard; she didn't want anyone in her and Ivy's life who wasn't fully committed to being there. And maybe she'd been right to be cautious, because he hadn't been in touch with her since.

'Talk to us about him,' Skye said, passing her some tablets and a glass of water. 'You can do that.'

'Yes,' Liz agreed. 'You've quizzed me about Patrick, I want to know all about the man who's got you worked up into a lather.'

'Touché.' Clare was amused by their inquisitive faces. 'What do you want to know? I've already told you the gory details.'

'You've told us the facts,' Liz clarified, counting them off on her fingers. 'Where and when you met, that you left the hotel without swapping numbers, and that by the time you found out you were expecting, you'd left it too late to track him down. What I don't understand is why you didn't tell us the truth in the first place?'

Clare paused before replying, getting her thoughts in order. That night after Adam had been round, she had given Liz and Skye the bare bones of their history and admitted they'd only ever had one night together and not a full-blown relationship after all, but she wouldn't be pressed on the rest. She hadn't been ready to let down her guard; but she was leaning so heavily on these two women in every practical aspect of her life at the moment, it didn't seem right not to trust them with her emotions too.

'Embarrassment?' she admitted. 'Shame, I suppose? Because I don't do mess, or failure, or letting myself down.'

'You haven't done any of those things.' Skye looked appalled. 'I think you're amazing. You've coped with so much over the last couple of years. A lot of people would have crumbled under the pressure. You're an inspiration to me.'

Tears pricked Clare's eyes. 'Really?'

'Skye's right, darling.' Liz gave Clare such a warm look that two tears broke free and rolled down her cheeks. 'You have high expectations of yourself, which is not a criticism, but, sometimes, I think you need to cut yourself some slack.'

Clare gave her a weak smile. 'I've always tried to show Dad that I could succeed at anything I put my mind to – school, university, my career. I'd assumed I'd be in a steady, suitable relationship before I even considered starting a family. Ivy was a result of a one-night stand and it was an unwanted pregnancy, at least at first. As soon as I decided to keep the baby, I thought I could only face going through with it if I had a good cover story. Hence Adam getting the role as the bad guy who dumped his pregnant girlfriend.'

'And he's not a bad guy?' Skye said hopefully.

'I don't know.' Clare shrugged. 'He's little more than a stranger.'

Liz raised an eyebrow. 'A stranger with benefits. That's a new one.'

Clare managed a half-smile. 'I like to be different.'

'He was a real gentleman at Angel's party,' said Liz.

'I got on well with him too,' Skye agreed. She pulled her phone out of her apron pocket, looked at the screen and put it away. 'Right until the moment I punched him. Obviously.'

'I'm not sure I'm ready to share Ivy with anyone.' Clare bit her lip. 'Although, as her father, I know he has rights.'

'You liked him enough to . . . you know what.' Liz couldn't bring herself to say it. 'So I'd give him a chance.'

'Could you get to know him first? Treat him like you've just met,' Skye suggested.

'As opposed to being the father of my child?' Clare groaned. 'How did I manage to cock this up so badly? Also, I'm not sure that he even likes children. I asked if he'd like to meet Ivy and he made his excuses and left. I gave him my number and since then, radio silence.'

The three of them pondered that for a moment.

'Who does he think her father is?' Liz asked.

'He didn't hang around to find out,' Clare replied. 'He asked if her father was inside the house and I said no.'

'That's why he hasn't been in touch! He's assuming he was encroaching on a happy family,' said Skye. 'He's acting honourably, that's all.'

'Send him a message,' Liz suggested. 'Tell him you'd like to talk to him and invite him over.'

'We've got a wake for Mr Barton next Sunday, so you'll be on your own,' Skye remembered. 'Ask him then and you'll have the house to yourself.'

Clare mulled it over. Should she? It felt dishonest not telling him he had a child. It was one thing being economical with the truth about him to her own family, but it didn't sit well with her to keep such a big thing from him. Then again, was she ready for his reaction – good or bad? There was only one way to find out. 'OK, I will. Would someone mind passing my phone? No time like the present.'

Skye obliged and Clare managed to scroll, one-handed, to his number.

Hi Adam, this is Clare. Just wondering if you wanted to come over next Sunday afternoon, if you're free? Liz and Skye are out working, so Ivy and I will be at a loose end. No worries if not.

'I've sent it,' she said, letting out a deep breath. 'And now we wait.'

They didn't have to wait long; her phone beeped almost immediately.

Hi Clare, sounds great. Just to clarify – you'll be on your own at home?

She exhaled to steady her nerves; this was really happening. 'He said yes,' she told them, already typing her response.

Yes, just the two of us.

'I thought he might.' Liz arranged the warm scones on the cake stand, a smug smile on her lips.

OK. Fancy going for ice cream at the Winking Prawn instead?

I'd love to, but you'd have to push Ivy's buggy. I've tried doing it one-handed – impossible!

I think I can manage that :)

Full disclosure, there's a small chance you might have to change a nappy. Feel free to pull out now . . .

So this is the real reason you want me to keep you company?! Never changed a nappy in my life, so would you mind starving her for a couple of hours beforehand to lessen the chances? Joking. Sort of.

Lol. There's probably a tutorial about it on YouTube.

Thanks, but I've only got my work laptop with me and I'd rather not have that pop up in my search history.

Don't you mean poop up?

Very good. See you Sunday.

Looking forward to it x

Me too x

When Clare looked up from her phone, Liz and Skye were watching her eagerly.

'Looks as if that went well,' said Skye.

'We're going for ice cream together!' Clare's stomach flip-flopped from excitement, to dread and back again. 'I can't believe how easy that was.'

'Well done, darling.' Liz rubbed her back. 'You've done the right thing.'

'Are you sure you'll be OK on your own?' Skye frowned, looking at her own phone again.

'No, but I'm doing it anyway.' Clare smiled at her sister's concern; how far they'd both come. Only a couple of weeks ago, a comment like that from Skye would have really grated. Now, she was simply grateful. 'Thank you both for your support, I probably wouldn't have been brave enough to do it otherwise.'

'Expecting a call, love?' Liz asked Skye.

'Nothing important.' Skye went pink and put her phone face down. 'I had a call come through from my boss in Kampala when I was at my first yoga class, and had to cancel it. I've left a couple of messages since but not had any response. It's just unusual, that's all.'

Clare studied her sister. She was getting attuned to Skye's body language and mood. Skye had talked a lot about Uganda and the charity she worked for and the children at the school. But there was something missing, something she wasn't telling them. The one thing she did talk about was her sunrise yoga classes; she raved about how amazing it was to greet the day stretching on the sand.

Clare didn't want to pry, but she hoped in time that Skye would open up to her. Whenever she pressed her about what had made her leave Uganda earlier this summer, she muttered vague excuses about needing a break. But that didn't ring true; she wasn't having a break, she was working really hard.

'What time is it over there?' Clare asked. 'Could that be the problem?'

Skye shook her head. 'Two hours ahead. This is the time we normally catch up with emails and admin.'

'I'm sure there'll be a perfectly valid explanation,' Clare said. 'Maybe try again?'

Skye wrinkled her nose. 'Maybe later. Our guests will be here any minute.'

Liz checked her hair in the mirror. 'I feel a bit queasy. I'm normally very comfortable with Patrick. But if he has misled me about Viv, this is the last time I'll be buttering his scones.'

'Confront him,' said Skye. 'There might be a perfectly valid explanation for that too.'

'Flippin' men,' Clare grumbled. 'We're probably better off without them.'

'Agreed,' Liz and Skye replied unanimously.

Chapter Twenty-Five

Clare

The Delmarges had arrived on time; Patrick had parked at the front door and Clare, Liz and Skye had gone out to greet them. The car doors were open and Clare caught the scent of lavender and rose perfumes as the two old ladies scrambled to get out.

'Welcome to Clemency House,' Liz said.

Patrick appeared not to detect the frostiness in her voice, but it was obvious to Clare.

'You're very kind to invite us,' he said, his eyes firmly locked on Liz.

Clare took an instant liking to him: he was dressed in crumpled linen shorts and shirt and had the sort of deep creases at the side of his eyes which implied he'd spent a lot of his life smiling.

'I hope it's not an imposition?'

'Not at all,' Liz said, tartly. 'Let me introduce everyone . . .'

There was no mistaking Liz's tone this time as she explained who was who and that Ivy would be joining them shortly, and Patrick did a wary double take.

'It's lovely to finally meet you and your family,' Clare said, deciding to step into the role of hostess. 'I've heard so much about you from Liz.'

'Really?' His face lit up. 'Good I hope?'

Liz smoothed her hands on her apron, remaining tight-lipped.

'Oh yes,' Skye confirmed.

'I'm thrilled to have company,' Clare added, and indicated her arm. 'I haven't dared venture too far since this pesky accident.'

'How was your journey?' Skye asked Patrick's mother. 'Pleasant I hope?'

'Would have been better if my son wasn't a spoilsport.' Camilla clung on to the car door while Patrick lifted her walking frame out of the boot and set it in front of her.

'How so?' Clare asked, protecting her arm as Camilla took a step towards her.

'We wanted to come by boat. We'd have been no bother,' she said with a sniff and then jerked her head towards Patrick. 'But misery guts said no.'

'It would have been such fun,' said Agatha, already seated in her wheelchair on the pavement with her bag perched on her lap.

'For whom?' Patrick chuckled.

'He's lovely,' Skye murmured in Clare's ear.

'Perfect for Liz,' Clare whispered back.

'I'd have loved to have been on the water on a day like today,' Camilla sighed.

'It's years since I've bounced about on an inflatable. Sadly,' Agatha added with a mischievous twinkle at Skye, who offered to push the wheelchair inside.

'Either of you might have fallen overboard,' said Patrick smoothly, adding under his breath, 'and I might have been tempted not to rescue you.'

'Very droll,' his mother replied, driving everyone out of her way with her walking frame so she could reach the door.

'Besides I'm not a good sailor yet, as Liz will testify; I still need someone to help me navigate.' Patrick gave Liz a hopeful smile.

Skye and Clare exchanged dreamy glances; the man was smitten, it was adorable to see.

'Let's get everyone comfortable,' said Liz, ignoring him and waving them down the hallway towards the living room. 'Your afternoon tea awaits.'

'Can't wait, something smells delicious,' said Patrick, rubbing his hands together.

'Liz has been whipping up delicious treats for you all morning,' said Clare, standing aside to let the guests go in first.

'And I still have plenty to do,' Liz announced, 'so I'd better get back to the kitchen.'

'Before you dash off . . .' Agatha produced a bunch of peonies from her bag and handed them to Liz. 'These are for you, Elizabeth.'

She took them from the old lady and buried her nose in the flowers. 'How gorgeous!'

'Patrick chose them,' Agatha added.

Liz gazed at the flowers and then met Patrick's eye directly. 'You needn't have, but thank you.'

'A bit romantic for my taste, but you know what he's like,' said Camilla. 'Always has to get his own way.'

Patrick simply shook his head fondly. 'Would you like some help, Liz?'

'Not today, thank you,' she replied, primly. 'Do take a seat.'

'You have a beautiful home,' said Camilla, clasping Liz's hand, before she had a chance to leave the room. 'It's even lovelier close up.'

'Oh it is,' Agatha was quick to add. 'Patrick showed us through his binoculars, but we couldn't pick out the details.'

Patrick let out the tiniest sigh and strode to the French doors. 'Do you mind if I open these?'

'Yes, do, darling,' said his mother. 'You look a little hot under the collar.'

'I'll go and put these in water,' said Liz, slipping out of the room.

Ivy chose that moment to wake up, and Skye ran upstairs to fetch her.

'Tell me, Clare.' Agatha gestured to Patrick to pull the wheelchair up to one of the armchairs. 'How did you break your arm?'

'I slipped on a birthday cake, would you believe?' Clare smiled wryly.

'Oh, I do love an amusing anecdote,' Agatha clapped her hands.

'There's really nothing to tell.' Clare shuddered as an image popped into her head. Adam carrying Angel's birthday cake inside out of the rain with Skye and the flood of shock which had rushed through her when they'd both realised who the other was. The fall, the pain, the panic . . . maybe one day she'd find it amusing. But not yet.

'You're a head teacher, I understand,' said Patrick, helping his aunt transfer from the wheelchair to the armchair. 'Your family must be very proud of you.'

'Thank you.' Clare breathed a sigh of relief at the change of subject. 'And I'm not sure really, I don't have a large family.'

Skye entered the room with Ivy on her hip. Ivy's cheeks were flushed and her body still soft with sleep. She was clutching one of her favourite fabric books.

'Here she is!' said Camilla, putting her glasses on over bright eyes.

'A baby,' Agatha gasped. 'What a treat.'

'*I'm* very proud of my sister,' said Skye, kneeling on the rug to put Ivy down. 'I'm not even sure what I want to be yet and I'm nearly thirty.'

'Thank you. And I'm proud of you,' Clare replied, taken aback. 'Skye has worked for a children's charity in Uganda for the last five years,' she said for the benefit of the others. 'Off she went to the other side of the world, on her own, and made a life for herself. I think she's very brave.'

'Running away isn't brave,' Skye murmured, stroking Ivy's hair.

Clare didn't know what she meant by that, but before she could quiz her any further, Ivy pulled herself up, holding on to the coffee table, and turned to face her, looking as if she was about to take her first step.

'Mumma-mumma!' she babbled and then dropped comically onto her bottom again. 'Ooh.'

Everyone laughed and clapped.

Liz arrived with the tray and poured tea from the pot into cups for everyone.

'Is there anything else to bring in?' Patrick rose from his chair.

'Skye will be assisting me today,' Liz said, with a polite smile. 'Thank you all the same.'

'If you're sure.' He sat down, his eyes full of disappointment as he watched her leave again.

Skye excused herself from the room and Ivy tottered towards Camilla, supporting herself as usual on an assault course of furniture.

'Oh my,' Agatha warbled. 'What a little dote. Who does she look like?'

'Not Clare,' Camilla put in, scrutinising mother and daughter. 'Clare's skin has a pinky hue. The child has lovely olive skin. Her father perhaps?'

'She's very like him, yes.' Clare had never admitted it before, even to herself. But since seeing Adam again, there was no mistaking the similarities between them. The curve of her eyebrows, the dimple which appeared when she had a proper belly laugh, the shape of her nose, even her square fingernails were so different from Clare's oval ones. The more she looked at Ivy, the more she recognised Adam in her daughter's features. Would he pick up on the likeness? she wondered.

Ivy continued her journey around the room, still clutching her book, until she reached Patrick and held out her arms to be picked up.

'Don't feel obliged, or you might be stuck with her for hours,' Clare warned him. 'A comfy lap and a book is her idea of heaven.'

'What a coincidence. It's mine too.' His eyes softened. 'I'd have loved children.'

'And I'd have loved grandchildren,' Camilla sighed dramatically as if he'd denied her on purpose.

'It simply didn't happen for us.' He smiled at Ivy, carefully lifting her onto his lap. 'But we were happy anyway.'

'Didn't happen with my third husband either, poor chap,' Camilla sighed regretfully. 'He'd have loved enough for a rugby team, but he didn't score a single try.'

Clare didn't know what was funnier: the old lady's euphemisms, or the horror on her son's face.

'Do you think you'll have more children?' Agatha wanted to know.

'Auntie.' Patrick cleared his throat. 'Let's not pry.'

'I wanted enough for a rugby team too,' Agatha said wistfully. 'The nearest was kissing the boys' school rugby players one New Year's Eve.'

'What, all of them?' Clare choked on her tea.

'Every last one,' Camilla put in. 'We got sent home from the party in disgrace because of her.'

'Worth it,' Agatha whispered. 'I'd do it again given half a chance.'

'You should,' said Camilla. 'Not you, Aggie. I mean you, Clare. You make beautiful babies, I'd have more if I were you. Not now, of course – you have your hands full. Or hand, I should say.'

'Apologies, Clare,' said Patrick. 'My mother has a unique perspective on personal boundaries.'

'I'm content for it just to be Ivy and me,' Clare replied. 'Her father's not on the scene.'

'Was he a bounder?' Agatha tightened her lips. 'I've had my share of those.'

Clare shook her head. It was on the tip of her tongue to say that he seemed lovely, before realising that that would reveal that she barely knew him. A truth she'd rather not share with these lovely old ladies.

'He's a good man,' she settled on. 'But it's complicated.'

'Say no more,' said Patrick, giving his mother and aunt a warning look.

'It happens,' said Agatha. 'Better a happy child with one happy parent than an unhappy child with two unhappy parents.'

'As the long saying which doesn't roll off the tongue goes,' said Camilla with a chuckle. 'But at least you tried, dear. Aggie wouldn't even do that.'

Except with the rugby team, thought Clare.

'Our father was a wonderful man,' said Agatha. 'He and our mother were blissfully happy for their entire married life. They set the bar high.'

'That didn't stop *me* trying to reach it,' Camilla pointed out. 'Took me a couple of attempts. Patrick's father, for example. A wet lettuce if ever I met one.'

Patrick met Clare's eye and shook his head. *Such a good sport,* she thought Clare, *never rising to the bait.*

'Or you could take a leaf out of my book,' said Patrick, addressing her directly. 'Set your own bar. Don't let your parents' experiences colour your own. Happy families, broken families, blended families . . . just because your parents did something well or badly doesn't mean you'll do the same. We're all human, we don't expect perfection from ourselves, why expect it from others, especially our parents?'

Camilla gave him a haughty look. 'I'm not sure whether I'm offended or not.'

Clare thought about what Adam had said about his father: *He wasn't just a brilliant dad, he was the best man I knew.* Another man who'd set the bar high for his family. Maybe Patrick was right. Maybe she should stop using her parents' broken marriage as the cornerstone on which to build her own relationships. Perhaps she should start from scratch, trust her own instincts, instead of assuming that every love affair was doomed to fail.

'Don't be offended,' said Clare. 'Your son is very wise. And look, he's also a baby whisperer.'

Ivy had fallen asleep again, her head tucked under his chin, her fingers clasped around his thumb. Everyone cooed and Patrick went pink with pleasure.

The old ladies fell into conversation about the shortcomings of someone called Eddie Sprigg while Clare sighed longingly, wishing her own dad was more like Patrick. But life didn't work like that, you couldn't wish people were different because it suited you. Mike didn't want to be a hands-on grandfather. Maybe it was time she accepted that and stopped willing it to happen. Ivy should be surrounded by people who delighted in her presence, not those who merely tolerated it. And Adam, she mused, which side of the fence would he fall on?

When he'd come round to see her, she'd been disappointed that he hadn't wanted to meet Ivy. Did that mean he wasn't into kids? Or was it, as Skye suggested, that he'd assumed that Clare and her baby were part of a little family unit, and he hadn't wanted to cause any awkwardness.

Whatever his thoughts, she'd find out tomorrow. She hoped he'd adore his daughter. She hoped he'd find Ivy's every sound, her every gesture, every hair on her head as amazing as Clare did. Because if he did, she'd feel much happier about letting him into their lives.

Her stomach somersaulted as she processed how much her opinions had changed. What had happened to her desire not to share Ivy, to not put her daughter in a position where she might be let down by anyone?

Perhaps because, eventually, people need people, she thought. Even she, who'd doggedly pursued independence at all costs, had had to accept that.

Liz and Skye arrived with trays of food: triangular-shaped sandwiches filled with the Delmarge ladies' favourites, Viennese fingers dipped in chocolate, scones with jam and cream. Ivy woke up, much to everyone's amusement, and soon she and Patrick were covered in bits of chewed-up sandwich. Clare couldn't think about food, her stomach was churned up and her head was too full of Adam and what was going to happen tomorrow.

Eventually, tea was finished and the Delmarges readied themselves for their departure. Clare and Liz escorted them to the door while Skye took Ivy down to the kitchen. Once Agatha and Camilla were in the car, Patrick hovered awkwardly in front of Liz.

'Goodbye then, it was lovely to see you.' Liz took a step back indoors.

'Liz,' Patrick stuttered, 'I was wondering if you fancy coming out on the boat with me on Wednesday. I could pack us a picnic lunch, let me cater for you for a change.'

'What a lovely idea!' Clare dived in to encourage her. 'I'd be nagging you for an invite if it wasn't for my arm.'

'It's kind of you,' said Liz. Clare held her breath, willing her to give him a chance. 'But, unfortunately, I'm meeting an old friend for lunch.'

That was the first Clare had heard of it.

'Ah OK. Another time perhaps?' He raised an eyebrow hopefully.

'Perhaps.' Liz folded her arms. 'The person I'm having lunch with is Viv. I think you might know her?'

'Ah.' His smile froze. 'Yes, we've met.'

'Last time I saw her, she was looking forward to a date with you. Was that a picnic on your boat too?' she asked coolly. 'Oh, no, silly me. You invited her to your house.'

'I'll go inside,' said Clare meekly. 'Goodbye, Patrick, nice to meet you.'

'Likewise.' He smiled faintly as she retreated into the hallway.

'Salcombe is a close-knit place,' she heard Liz say. 'It's hard to keep secrets. Like lunch dates.'

He held his hands up. 'Liz, please let me explain.'

'No, Patrick, I will not. Because the fact that you even feel the need to explain tells me all I need to know. I confided in you, and you weren't honest with me. You know I've been hung up on the same man for forty years.'

What? Clare had started to go downstairs, but her ears pricked up at that. She turned and crept back up and stood hidden behind the front door.

'Liz, I don't know what to say, but I assure you—' Poor Patrick was floundering by the sound of it.

But Liz wasn't in the mood to listen. 'I was trying to break the power he has over me because *you* said I deserved better. And you were right. I do.'

'But . . .' he stammered.

'Goodbye, Patrick.'

Clare leapt out of the way as Liz stepped inside the house and shut the door.

'Sorry,' she blustered, embarrassed at being caught eavesdropping. 'I didn't mean to overhear.'

'Never mind,' Liz replied briskly, two red spots like warning signals flashing up on her cheeks. 'I think he got his answer.'

She skirted past Clare without another word, charged upstairs to her room and shut the door with a thud.

He certainly had, thought Clare. But she hadn't got her answer: who on earth had Liz been 'hung up on' all these years, who was she trying to break free from? Clare's brain crackled with possibilities, but she drew a blank

Her own secrets had come out in the open this summer, it sounded as if Liz's could be next.

Chapter Twenty-Six

Clare

There was a knock at the front door. Clare left Ivy sitting on the rug, checked her face in the mirror – she was a bit rosy, but there was nothing she could do about that now – and opened the door.

Adam.

She felt her chest heave as a mix of pleasure and apprehension stole her ability to speak. She was so glad he was finally here. Not that he was late, but Skye and Liz had gone out half an hour ago to cater for the wake and she'd been like a child with ants in her pants ever since, unable to sit still for more than two minutes.

'All good?' He smiled at her. The same friendly smile she'd been attracted to on the night they'd met.

'Yep.' She gestured to him to come inside, returning his smile.

An awkward moment followed in which they leaned towards each other in anticipation of a kiss, both thought better of it and leaned out again. Good start, thought Clare, that was like the mating ritual of two shy flamingos.

'You?' she asked.

'Yeah, great. Lovely day.' He put his hands in his pockets.

'It is,' she agreed. This was painful, where was her witty

repartee? Her funny one-liners? And why was she riveted to the spot, staring up at him?

He cast an eye down at her dress. 'You look nice.'

'Thanks.' She was wearing her favourite sundress over a bikini. 'I chose it because it's easy to get in and out of.'

'OK,' he nodded, chewing the inside of his cheek to stifle a smile.

'Oh no! That came out wrong.' She pointed to the brace on her arm and laughed. 'With this, I mean, not . . . Anyway, come in and meet Ivy.'

'Can't wait,' he said with a grin.

She led him into the living room, surreptitiously wiping her arm across her hot forehead. Was he as nervous too? she wondered. He was hiding it well if he was. So much was riding on this trip to the beach. She wanted to like him, she wanted Ivy to like him, and she hoped he would enjoy spending time with them. Then, if all those stars aligned, maybe, at the end of the day, she could tell him the truth about who'd he'd spent the day with.

But she was getting ahead of herself. He had many tests to pass, the first of which was to load up the buggy with everything they'd need and help them all get out of the house.

'And this is Ivy.' Clare knelt down and Ivy came scampering over, looking up at this new man with curiosity. 'Say hi to Adam.'

Adam squatted down to their level, picked up a Peppa Pig soft toy and made it wave to her. 'Hey, Ivy,' he said in a squeaky voice which didn't sound anything like the TV character.

Clare suppressed a smile; he'd clearly never seen the show. Lucky him.

Ivy smiled and did a little bounce of approval.

Adam handed Peppa to her and straightened up. 'Ready then?'

Clare nodded. 'Can you help me pack up? Here's her drink.' She handed him a sippy cup. 'And there's a change of clothes and couple of towels on the table. They all need to go in the main bag. There's a net bag with her beach toys which should hang off the handles and—' She stopped mid-flow, realising that Adam was grinning at her. 'What?'

'Nothing. Just, wow.' He ruffled up his hair. 'I think I've done well if I've remembered my wallet.'

'Welcome to a day in the life of a parent.' Her heart stuttered. This was literally his first day as a parent and he didn't even know it. For a split second, she had serious doubts about her plan; was she playing a dangerous game with his emotions? No, no, she'd thought it through carefully; she had to protect her daughter. She wasn't trying to deceive him, this was simply the safest way to introduce them to each other.

'I can go and fetch my car, if you like?' Adam offered. 'Save us carrying all this stuff.'

Clare was tempted; walking any distance made her arm ache. But he was here now, and she was desperate to be outdoors enjoying the sunshine. Besides, he'd have to work out how to fit Ivy's car seat and she'd be worried the entire time that he hadn't done it properly.

'Let's walk,' she said. 'It'll be fun. The beach, Ivy! Mummy and Adam are taking you to the beach!'

'Bee bee bee!' Ivy joined in enthusiastically, scrubbing her hands through her hair just as Adam had. She did that quite a lot, Clare realised. Coincidence, or could that sort of mannerism be passed genetically? She had no idea, but then Adam picked up his daughter for the first time and jiggled her up and down and she could think of nothing else but how incredible this moment was. A moment she'd never, ever imagined would happen.

Ivy put a hand on his face and touched the faint stubble on his jaw. Clare was fascinated by her reaction; Ivy had been held by men before, but not often, and she was growing up now, noticing more things.

Adam grinned. 'Does that sound good, hey?' He turned to Clare. 'I can't get over how light she is, she weighs nothing at all.'

'She's the perfect weight for her height and age,' Clare leapt to her daughter's defence.

'I don't get to hold many babies, that's all. I can't even guess how old she is.'

Clare slipped her sunglasses on strategically to buy herself some thinking time and hide her eyes. If she told him Ivy would be one in a couple of weeks, surely he'd put two and two together and work it out? She wasn't ready to face that conversation yet. She opted for a white lie. 'She'll be one, later in the summer.'

'Right.' Adam looked at Ivy thoughtfully.

'What's the matter?' Clare felt panic rise in her chest, how good at maths was he?

'Nothing, it's just . . .' He shook his head as if getting rid of the thought. 'It sounds silly, but she reminds me a bit of my dad.'

'Really?' Her voice had gone abnormally high. 'How funny.'

Just then, Ivy yawned, making them laugh.

'Sorry, am I boring you?' said Adam. 'Let's go.'

'Can you?' Clare gestured towards her crossbody bag.

'Yes, sure.' Adam picked up the bag, looped it over her head and carefully settled the strap under her injured arm. His fingers were light on her skin, his breath warm on her cheek, and she found herself holding her breath. 'Is that OK?'

She nodded and picked up her water bottle. 'Perfect. Thank you.'

They headed out of the house, Adam locking the door for her.

'I'll walk this side of you,' he said, steering the buggy so that her brace was next to him. 'Then anyone who comes near us won't be able to bump you.'

'Thank you,' she replied, mentally awarding him points for his thoughtfulness.

Did people assume they were a family, she wondered, a young couple and their baby walking down the street? It struck her that she and Ivy had never been anywhere with a man like this.

'I've never pushed a buggy before. Apart from helping people on and off buses and trains and things. How am I doing so far?' he asked.

'Not bad.' She sipped her water. 'Although you have just run over her sock.'

'What?' He spun round and spotted Ivy's little ankle sock on the ground. Now he was in the way of a trio of teenage girls and he gave them a crooked smile. 'Sorry, ladies.'

They went giggly and then cooed over Ivy. 'Cute baby!'

'Thanks,' Adam said proudly as he scooped up the stray sock.

'Finished showing off?' Clare teased.

'Sorry, couldn't resist it. OK, you tinker.' He crouched down in front of Ivy, catching hold of her bare foot. 'Whomsoever this sock fits will be my princess. Look at that – it fits!'

Ivy squealed with pleasure as he blew a raspberry against her skin.

'Glad you didn't offer to marry her,' said Clare.

He grinned up at her. 'That would be a bit weird.'

On so many levels, she thought, unable to stop herself from smiling as Adam pretended to eat Ivy's feet while tugging on her sock. He was winning her daughter over effortlessly so far. And she was feeling pretty happy with the situation too.

'Although I'm hoping for better things for her than being somebody's princess,' she told him as they started walking again.

'What do you mean? Isn't that a good thing to be?'

'You're either born a princess or you marry a prince and become one,' Clare shrugged. 'I'd rather she achieved something on her own merit.'

'You're so right. I didn't think of it like that. So what would you like her to be?'

'Anything that makes her feel fulfilled.' That was easy, she never wanted her daughter to feel pressured to be something that didn't feel right for her. 'Like she's doing the best job in the world. Whether that's an artist, or an archaeologist, or an astronaut.'

'Careers beginning with other letters of the alphabet also available,' said Adam, putting on a funny voice. 'Location scout, for example.'

'Very funny.'

Half an hour later, they were descending the final slope towards North Sands beach. Their progress had been slow, Clare was hot and sweaty, and her arm inside the brace was aching. This was the longest she'd spent out of a chair since her accident, and she was ready to sit down and rest her elbow on a pile of cushions. She'd drunk almost a litre of water too and could have wept when the sign for the toilets came into view. The tide was out and although the beach was busy, as it always was in August, there was plenty of room for everyone.

'Ice cream first or sit on the beach?' Adam asked.

'Toilet,' said Clare, stowing her empty water bottle in the basket of the buggy.

'OK.' He stopped pushing Ivy and took a seat on the wall. 'We'll wait for you.'

Clare bit her lip. 'I should probably take her with me.'

Adam frowned 'I thought she wore a nappy?'

She snorted. 'Not because she needs to go, but because I never leave her with people.'

She never left Ivy alone with anyone, let alone a relative stranger.

Adam nodded slowly. 'I understand. You don't trust me with her.'

Clare shrugged awkwardly. 'It's not that. OK, it is that a bit. But what if she wakes up and freaks out because her mummy isn't there? She might look cute now, but, honestly, those lungs can wake the dead when they get going.'

'Then I'll lift her out of her buggy, gatecrash the ladies' and dangle her over the cubicle door.'

'You'd do that?' She looked at him, amused.

'If it helps keep the peace, then yes.'

'OK, how about you come as close as you can so I can still hear you?'

'Deal. Let's go.' Adam pushed the buggy right to the entrance of the ladies' toilets and Clare went inside.

'Everything OK out there?' she yelled out to Adam, hoisting her dress up. She'd got the hang of one-handed toilet trips now. The key was loose clothing without any fastenings and comfy underwear which lifted and lowered without snagging anywhere, or, as in the case of today's outfit, a bikini with a triangle top with ties and a pull-on sundress.

'Tickety-boo,' Adam called back. 'And the aroma is to die for.'

Clare giggled to herself; she was having a good time. Just like their first date, even without Sexy Saskia's help.

She wriggled back into her clothes, washed her hands and re-joined him outside.

'Still asleep,' he replied, pointing at Ivy. 'Crisis averted.'

'Thanks for being patient with me,' she said. 'I'm used to doing everything for Ivy without help from anyone.'

He regarded her curiously. 'Not even from her father?'

Her face flamed; she'd walked right into that. 'Not even him,' she said in a quiet voice. 'I had it drummed into me from an early age to be self-sufficient.'

He held her gaze thoughtfully as if there was more he wanted to say, or perhaps ask.

'Ice cream time, what do you reckon?' He pushed the buggy away from the public toilets.

'Good idea,' she said, happy to change the subject.

They'd only gone a few paces when two tiny socks, one after the other, were flung from the buggy, making them both laugh. This time, Adam picked them up and shoved them into one of the many bags hanging from the handles.

'Hello, sweetie. We're at the beach!' said Clare, peering into the buggy to see Ivy's blue-green eyes wide awake.

'Obviously she heard the magic words – ice cream. A girl after my own heart.'

'Either that or being parked in the doorway of the toilets acted like smelling salts in front of her delicate nose,' she replied.

'I prefer my theory. Let me guess your favourite flavour.'

'OK,' Clare smiled smugly. He wouldn't get it. No chance.

286

'OK, let me think.' He narrowed his eyes. 'Definitely not chocolate, or strawberry, or coffee. I'm going to say cherry.'

She shot him a look of surprise. 'How did you know?'

'Your dessert choice the night we met.'

She shook her head, frowning. 'I had lemon posset.'

'You did,' he confirmed, 'but the cherry clafoutis was your first choice and they'd run out of that.'

'I'm . . . I'm . . .' She gave a laugh of disbelief. 'Flabbergasted.'

Adam smirked. 'So what's mine?'

She cast her mind back to their dinner. He'd opted for the cheeseboard rather than a sweet dessert and when they'd got up to his room, there'd been chocolates on the pillows, and he'd swept them into a pile saying she could have them both because he didn't like chocolate much.

'You don't really have much of a sweet tooth,' she began, pleased to see him look impressed. 'So ice cream is something you enjoy to cool you down rather than for the flavour, so I'm going for the classic. Vanilla?'

'Yes!' He lifted a hand and she high-fived him and they both laughed. 'Although bang goes my theory that I'm a man of mystery.'

'Mystery is overrated,' she said kindly.

He grinned. 'True. I mean meeting Saskia was great, but getting to know Clare Marriott is miles better.'

Clare was brimming with happiness. They walked towards the ice-cream kiosk together, Adam in charge of the buggy, her keeping close to him, protecting her arm as small groups of people passed them by. She stole a look at him as he pulled a wallet out of the back pocket of his shorts. He was good company, good-looking and, so far, good with Ivy. This was going well, too well. There had to be a catch.

'Do we get one for Ivy?' he asked, nodding to the list of flavours on the board inside the kiosk.

Clare shook her head. 'She's never had ice cream.'

He pretended to look appalled. 'That's practically child abuse. A beach trip with no ice cream? And I thought you were so nice.'

'Did you really?' She gave him a sideways look, her voice feeling thick in her throat.

His eyes fixed on hers. 'Sorry, was that too personal?'

'Not at all. Because I am nice. She gets lots of treats, like raisins and yoghurt and rice cakes . . .' She broke off to laugh at Adam, who was looking at her in horror.

'Poor child,' he murmured and squatted down to Ivy's level. 'Hey, kiddo. If Mummy says yes, I'm going to treat you to your first ever ice cream.' He gave Clare puppy eyes. 'Can I?'

Kiddo. God, he was gorgeous. Her chest tightened and she hid it by pretending to sigh. 'It's like having two kids. Tell you what, we'll get her a spoon, she can try both of ours, let's see whose she prefers, mine or yours.' *Mummy's or Daddy's.*

He brightened. 'Deal. She'll like mine though, because she's got good taste.'

They bought their ice creams and sat on the wall to eat them, with Ivy in her buggy in front of them: a tub of vanilla for Adam and a cone of cherry ice cream for Clare because she couldn't manage a tub and a spoon.

Adam cheered when Ivy shuddered at the taste of the cherry and then instantly felt bad about celebrating her puckered little face. Luckily for Clare, Ivy didn't care for the vanilla either, so they pronounced it a draw. Not only that, but she pounced on the box of raisins Clare had packed, which meant she was the winner overall.

'I admit defeat,' said Adam, dropping his tub and the supply of napkins they'd got through in the bin. 'But I'm not giving up yet. Ivy clearly needs my bad influence in her life.'

'How so?' said Clare, sipping from her newly replenished water bottle.

'Look at her,' he protested. 'Ploughing through those raisins. It's not natural for a child to prefer wizened fruit over ice cream.'

Clare shrugged playfully. 'What can I say, she's a sensible child. She must take after her mother.'

'Not her father?' Adam probed. 'You haven't told me much about him – in fact almost nothing.'

Her pulse started to race. He'd given her the perfect opening, she could just come straight out with it. But the moment wasn't right, this felt too off-the-cuff, not special enough. She wasn't going to tell him. Not yet.

'Can we leave it,' Clare said quietly. 'Please?'

He held her gaze as if deciding whether to push her and then gave her a small smile. 'Sure.'

For the next couple of minutes, they focused on getting onto the sand and finding a spot. Clare wanted to be by the rocks as usual, but Adam wanted to be closer to the water.

'Then I can take Ivy to paddle, and you'll still be able to watch us.'

'Or maybe I'll come and paddle too.'

He sucked in a breath, looking dubious. 'What if a wave knocked you over? Or your feet sank in the sand, and you lost your balance. Or one of those kids playing frisbee ran into you.'

She snorted. 'Looking on the bright side.'

'I just feel, you know, responsible for you.' Adam unrolled the blanket, spread it out for Clare to sit on and then piled the bags around the edge. 'And I want you to enjoy yourself.'

'I always do when I'm . . .' *when I'm with you*, she'd been about to say, but changed it to 'on the beach. It's my happy place.'

'And let's keep it that way.' He pulled his T-shirt over his head.

That ought to do it, she thought, unable to drag her eyes from his naked torso. She could vividly remember the feel of his taut body, the touch of his skin on the night they'd spent together in his hotel room. The lights had been turned off then, but now, under the summer sun, she could see every muscle, every contour. His body was even more beautiful than she remembered.

'Clare?'

'Yes, sorry?' She snapped herself out of her thoughts and watched him unstrap Ivy from the buggy.

'Does she need sunscreen on?'

She shook her head. 'Already done. Just her hat from the bag.'

Hat on, Ivy crawled over to her, and Clare automatically shifted position to cuddle her to her side, kissing the little girl's cheek. She smelled of baby shampoo and sunshine.

'Mummy loves you,' she murmured before Ivy wriggled away and onto the sand.

Adam tipped out the bag of beach toys and Ivy picked up the spade and started scraping it backwards and forwards across the sand.

'What are you thinking about?' Clare asked Adam, trying to decipher the distant look in Adam's eyes.

'My dad, I miss him,' he replied. 'The beach was his happy place too. He was like a big kid. He'd start building boats or elaborate castles in the sand. Angel and I would help in, but before long, he'd got all the other kids on the beach joining in too. Or he'd get us to bury him with just his face sticking out and then when he finally broke out of his coffin, as we called it, he'd roar like a monster and chase us all into the sea. Children were drawn to him, you know. Days like today were his favourite. He'd have loved this.'

'He sounds like the best sort of father,' said Clare, softly, thinking that she had very few memories of her own dad doing anything like that.

'I know there's no point in having regrets,' said Adam, turning over the bucket to make a sandcastle. 'But I do wish he'd lived long enough to have grandkids. I know my mum will throw herself into the role, but he'd have been a great grandad.'

'That's exactly how I feel about my mum,' said Clare, tugging her sundress down with one hand over her chest. Thank goodness for shirred bodices, she'd never have been able to get in or out of her clothes without Adam's help otherwise. 'I'd love her to see this.'

Adam glanced at her and then shielded his eyes. 'Um, Clare, I think something has come adrift.'

Clare looked down. Her bikini top had come loose at the back and was hanging down between her boobs. She flattened her arm across her chest, but had no way of doing it up by herself. 'Don't look,' she yelped.

'Not looking. But, as you know, it's nothing I haven't seen before.'

'It was dark then. And it was a lifetime ago,' she muttered, mortified.

'Maybe, but I still remember it well.' Clare felt a pang of longing. So did she. But this was neither the time nor the place to take a trip down memory lane, however much she wanted to.

Ivy had no idea what was going on but scooted back over to join in the drama, her eyes trained hopefully on Clare's boobs. *She was definitely giving up that last breastfeed, thought Clare, trying to fend the baby off.*

'Biscuit!' she cried.

'What. Now?' said Adam uncertainly.

'No, not me, Ivy. One look at my boobs and she thinks it's snack time.'

Adam said nothing, for which she was very grateful. He rummaged in the bag as directed by Clare and produced a pink wafer biscuit. Ivy couldn't get over to him fast enough.

'Da,' she said, grabbing it off him.

'Ta! She said ta!' Clare gasped. 'Can you get your phone out and video her please.'

Adam took his phone from his shorts pocket and swiped the screen. 'Have I just witnessed a first?'

'Yep. Ivy,' Clare prompted, 'say ta! Ta, ta, *ta.*'

'Buh–buh–ba,' said Ivy, swishing the pink wafer through her hair.

They looked at each other, disappointed.

'Oh well,' said Adam with a shrug, moving the focus off Ivy and inadvertently onto Clare.

'Will you stop pointing your camera at me please,' she yelped. 'And would you mind doing me up?'

Adam crouched down behind her. She leaned forward, trying to pass him the ties of her bikini top. His hand skimmed the side of her breast, and she breathed in sharply.

'Sorry,' he said, tightening the straps behind her. 'I'm trying not to touch you, but it's very hard.'

'The jokes are writing themselves here.' She felt her breath hitch. 'Don't worry about it. Thanks for helping me. And thanks for being here.'

He sat beside her, so close that she could see the flecks of green and blue in his eyes, and rubbed a hand through his hair. A gesture she was beginning to recognise as something he did when he felt uncomfortable.

'Clare, what are we doing. What is this?' He waved a finger between him and her. 'Not that I'm not happy to be spending time with you, I am. With both of you. But you and I have history. I know things have moved on for you since then.' He inclined his head towards Ivy. 'But for me . . .' He broke off and inhaled. 'It feels like we're picking up where we left off.'

She swallowed. He was close enough for her to feel the warmth of his body and smell the coconut scent of the lotion he'd applied to his skin. Her stomach fluttered. 'Me too.'

He reached a hand to her cheek and slid his fingers into her hair. 'Clare,' he murmured, his mouth no more than a breath from hers.

'Bi–bi–bi–bi!' Ivy chuntered.

Clare and Adam moved apart, the moment broken as Ivy pulled herself up using the buggy and attempted to reach the bag containing the biscuits.

'Ivy! Be careful.' Clare rolled from sitting over onto her knees, terrified that Ivy was going to pull the buggy down on top of her.

Adam jumped to his feet and held out his hands. 'Ivy! Wait, I'll get you a biscuit.'

Ivy gave him a gummy smile, reached her arms out to him and took a few tentative steps towards him before plopping down on her bottom and clapping her hands.

Clare gasped and clutched Adam's leg. 'She walked, she actually just walked!'

'Bloody hell!' he laughed. 'Don't tell me that's a first as well?'

'Yes, those were her first steps.' Clare smiled at him, tears clouding her vision as she felt a lump form in her throat.

She didn't know what would happen tomorrow, or the day after that, or when term started again in September and she and Ivy were back in Bath. But right now, on North Sands beach, both of Ivy's parents had witnessed their baby take her first steps.

'Can we see if she'll do it again?' Adam asked.

Clare nodded, loving the way he checked in with her, never presuming anything.

'OK, kiddo, you've got this.' Adam crouched down and lifted Ivy to her feet, steadying her before resting his cheek lightly on the top of her sun hat. If there was ever a picture Clare wanted to freeze in time to look back at over and over again as one of life's perfect moments, this was it. 'Ready to walk to Mummy?'

'Bi-bi-bi!' she demanded imperiously.

'And then a biscuit, yes, I promise,' Adam laughed.

'Wait! I need to capture this.' Clare reached into her bag for her phone, held it up and started to video. 'OK, we're good to go.'

'Good luck,' said Adam in a serious voice. 'The hopes and dreams of the whole country are behind you now.'

'Ivy!' Clare beamed at her. 'Come to Mummy.'

Adam, very slowly, released his grip on her. Ivy, grunting with effort, staggered in her direction.

'Good girl!' Clare encouraged her, trying to hold eye contact and video her at the same time. 'Come on, keep going.'

Adam was right behind her, his hands hovering, ready to catch her if she fell, Clare was only a step away, holding her breath, willing Ivy to make it across the blanket. The three of them united, caught up in each other, a triptych of concentration.

Which was why nobody was aware of the dog until it was too late.

It all happened in a blur: kicked-up sand, the whip of a leather lead against Clare's back, the thud of a furry yellow body sending Ivy crashing to the ground. Her little face registered shock then she let out an ear-piercing yell.

'What the hell! Is she OK?' Adam shouted as he threw himself onto the dog to catch it.

The animal, a young Labrador, was panting with excitement, its tail thumping against Adam's body. Adam dodged it as it tried to lick his face.

'She will be. It's all right, darling.' Clare checked her over; her tears were from shock and not pain by the look of it. She kissed her and brushed the sand from her little cheeks.

'Sorry! Sorry!' A man in a back-to-front baseball cap sauntered across, holding his hands up. 'He just wants to play, he's only a puppy.'

Adam stood up and handed the end of the lead back to the owner. 'Tell that to the little girl he's just knocked to the ground.'

'All right, mate.' The man ruffled the energetic Labrador's head. 'I've said I'm sorry. Come on, Storm.'

'If you're going to bring your dog to the beach, keep control of it.' Adam was bristling with fury, his hands curled into fists. Clare had never seen him look so sexy. 'That sort of incident can traumatise a child for life.'

'Slightly dramatic.' The man stared at him like he was crazy. 'But point taken. Is the baby OK?'

He addressed this comment to Clare, who nodded.

'She'd just taken her first steps,' she explained. 'So it was a big moment. Is Storm friendly?'

The man rolled his eyes. 'Too friendly. Wants to meet everyone and join in every ball game on the beach. Which

295

is great until he slips his lead and comes into contact with protective dads.'

'It's not the dads that I have the problem with, it's contact with vulnerable children that's out of order,' Adam growled.

He looked so put out that Clare was finding it hard not to laugh. She reached out to the dog, who licked her hand.

'Look at his soft tongue, Ivy,' she murmured. 'It tickles.'

Ivy flapped her own hand up and down in front of the dog's face and Clare caught hold of it, not wanting her to scare the dog.

'Gently, darling.'

The pink crumbs of Ivy's wafer were too much for the dog to resist and she giggled and wriggled as the dog's tongue licked the palm of her hand.

'There you go, you see,' the man said smugly. 'Storm wouldn't hurt a fly.'

He sauntered off and Adam shook his head in disgust. 'Arsehole.'

Clare snorted with laughter. 'Language.'

'Sorry.' He dropped down next to them, sitting cross-legged, and Ivy crawled off to investigate the sand again, none the worse for her ordeal.

'You were brilliant,' he said softly. 'Cool as a cucumber.'

'Thanks. I think it's being a teacher,' she mused. 'I've seen every sort of accident, from vomit to broken bones. Sometimes it's hard to stay calm, but it's always best if you do. The kids pick up on our signals.'

Adam let out a sigh as if irritated by himself. 'I over-reacted, didn't I?'

He'd reacted like any protective father would have done, she thought, without even knowing that that was what he was. She couldn't have asked for more.

'It's instinctive, the desire to protect,' she said mildly. 'And I think you were brilliant too. Did you know you're bleeding?' She pointed to the bottom of his foot.

Both of his feet were sandy, but there was a dark red patch on the ball of his right foot. He brushed off the sand and winced. 'There's something in it, I think. Can you see?'

It was really awkward to bend forward with the big brace on her arm, so Adam lifted his foot close to her face.

'This is pleasant,' she giggled, squinting at his foot.

'Oh yeah, I know how to treat a woman.'

'It might be a shard of glass or a piece of shell. You need to wash it. I'll go and fill Ivy's bucket with sea water.' She started to get to her feet, but Adam beat her to it.

'I'll do it.' He hobbled to Ivy. 'Mind if I borrow your bucket, Ivy?'

'Bic-bic,' Ivy babbled.

He looked at Clare over Ivy's head. 'She drives a hard bargain this one.'

He passed the bag to Clare and left her to dole out another biscuit. She felt a warm glow as she watched him limp down to the sea. He was lovely, really lovely.

She imagined his face when he found out that Ivy was his daughter. She was sure he was going to be over the moon. Not that she expected him to drop everything and build a new life with them. She didn't need or want that. But she'd like him to be part of her life and if that wasn't possible, then at least part of her daughter's.

She wasn't going to reveal her secret now. They needed to get back home so he could bandage his foot up and get it looked at. Instead, she was going to make a special occasion of it, make it a moment to remember.

She waved to him, her heart soaring as he hobbled back up the beach towards them. Why had she ever thought that they would be better off without him? Life was never going to be perfect, but this felt pretty damn close.

Chapter Twenty-Seven

Liz

Liz stacked the dishwasher with Mrs Barton's crockery while Skye loaded The Seaside Gourmet Girls' equipment into crates.

The wake was almost over, most of the mourners had left and Liz and Skye were clearing away as quickly as they could. They were both dying to get back to Clemency House to find out how Clare had got on with Adam at the beach. Liz had high hopes for the two of them, if they could get over their shaky start, that was. He seemed such a nice young man; Jen would have approved. What would Mike think of the situation? she wondered.

He'd only find out if Clare chose to tell him, of course – he certainly wouldn't find out from Liz. She'd always been good at keeping the Marriotts' secrets.

Her thoughts meandered back to when Jen had found out she was pregnant. How excited she'd been. She and Liz had spent an entire day window shopping for baby clothes, cots and prams, discussing what it was going to be like having a baby in the family.

Mike's reaction had been more understated; he'd asked to meet Liz for a chat one day and, of course, she'd agreed. She'd found him slumped at a table stirring sugar into his coffee cup.

'Hello, father-to-be,' she'd greeted him playfully.

He'd exhaled woefully. 'Hi, Liz.'

She'd sat down with a bump. 'Has something happened? Is Jen OK, the baby?'

'They're fine,' he'd said wearily. 'Well, Jen's fine and there's nothing wrong with the baby as far as we know.'

'But?' She'd waited patiently for him to work out what he needed to say. He'd always been the same: tongue-tied when it came to expressing his emotions.

'Jen's too good for me.'

She'd groaned. Not this again. 'Jen adores you. And, if she doesn't think she's too good for you, then you needn't either.'

'I don't want to let her or the baby down.'

It was moments like these, when he showed his softer side, that made it hard for Liz to quell her own feelings for him.

'Mike.' She'd patted his hand. 'You're having a wobble. This is a classic Mike Marriott move. Remember your wedding day? These are the same thoughts.'

The groom had gone missing just before the service and the best man and two of the ushers had been despatched to locate him (or, as Jen had put it: to chop his balls off if he was even thinking of jilting her). But it had been Liz who'd found him. She'd nipped to the loo for a nervous wee and had found it already occupied. The door was eventually opened by a very pale Mike, who'd confessed that he didn't deserve Jen and he was scared of messing up her life. Liz had given him a pep talk, threatened him with bodily harm if he dared let Jen down, before hugging him and sending him to the altar. The ceremony went ahead without any further hitches, and she never told Jen what he'd told her.

Mike had given her a lopsided grin. 'You're right. But I think I'm right too. She'll be a brilliant mum.'

'She will,' Liz had agreed, unequivocally.

'Do you think I'll be a brilliant dad?'

'Well . . .' she'd begun, determined to be positive and tactful and perhaps give him a few home truths about the selflessness involved in parenting.

'Exactly,' he'd interrupted her, holding his hands out. 'Not quite such an immediate "yes", is it?'

'Just do your best, Mike, that's all Jen will ask of you.'

'I will, I promise,' he'd said.

And because Liz had wanted to believe him, she did.

'Liz? Liz?' Skye waved a hand in front of Liz's face.

'Sorry, miles away.' Liz blinked away the past and focused on the present. 'Do you mind doing one last sweep for crockery and I'll go and bring the van up onto the drive?'

'Sure.' Skye picked up a tray to collect any stray cups and saucers.

Liz let herself out of the front door and walked down the road to where she'd left the van. They'd unloaded right outside the house earlier, but moved the van to keep the drive free for the funeral cars. She was unlocking the driver's door when she heard her name being called.

She looked further down the hill and saw Patrick jogging towards her, his hand raised in greeting.

Her stomach pitched, remembering the hurt and confusion on his face when she'd tackled him about his date with Viv.

'Patrick.' She opened the van door and summoned up a tight smile. 'Hello.'

'Liz, I'm so glad I caught you.' He gave her a wary look, as if not quite sure of the reception he was about to get. He was wearing shorts and walking boots and had a rucksack on his back. He looked a picture of health and wholesomeness and she felt herself soften towards him. 'I feel I owe you an explanation.'

Not an apology, she noted. She nodded for him to continue. 'I'm working, so I mustn't be long.'

'Of course,' he said, the relief evident in his voice. 'I've been for a walk around Overbeck's Garden. Have you been?'

'I have.' It was a beautiful National Trust place not far away. The last time she went had been for afternoon tea in the café with Jen for her birthday. 'Although not recently.'

'I kept thinking how much more I'd have enjoyed it if you'd have been with me.'

She raised an eyebrow. 'Not Viv?'

'Definitely not Viv,' he said, emphatically. 'Liz, I'm sorry there has been a communication problem here. I had no intention of misleading you. Yes, I did go on a date with Viv. She was the one I told you about who my sister-in-law had set me up with. I had no idea she was a friend of yours.'

'That doesn't matter, but what does matter to me is honesty.' Liz folded her arms. 'You said there was no chemistry there and you wouldn't be seeing her again.'

'Which was correct,' he said eagerly. 'I'm sure she's a very nice women, and a good business contact to have on your side. But we didn't click.'

'That's not how Viv recalls it,' Liz pointed out. 'In fact, when I saw her, she was on her way to the beauty salon getting ready for her second date with you.'

Patrick groaned softly. 'I'm sorry. No wonder you were annoyed with me.'

'Disappointed,' she corrected him. 'I have no claim on you, nor you on me. But there was no need to lie to me.'

'As far as I was concerned, it was strictly business and not a date at all,' he assured her. 'You know the annexe?'

'Of course,' said Liz, beginning to realise where this was going.

When she and Jen had first met the Delmarges, Patrick had shown them the self-contained annexe beside his house. Rachel had had plans for it once, but they'd never got around to doing any of them before she died.

'Viv believes that it could be suitable for a holiday let. We talked about it briefly that first evening, but she contacted me the next day, saying she had a proposal for me. So I agreed. I must admit, I was surprised at the sort of money we're talking.'

'It can be very lucrative,' she agreed. 'And a simple way to earn an income.'

Viv had suggested it to Liz as an option once. Apparently, if she moved out of Clemency House for the summer months and allowed Viv to let it out for the holiday trade, she could earn enough to live on for the whole year.

'Unfortunately, I don't think Viv and I will be doing any business.' Patrick ran a finger around his collar. 'Only moments into our conversation she tried to hold my hand across the table, at which point I had to put my foot down and set her straight.'

Liz had to suppress a smile at the affronted look on his face.

'I said that I had met someone else,' he continued.

'Have you?' she said, feeling her heart start to thud.

He nodded. 'That someone is you, Liz. I was happier on that short trip in the *Ecsta-Sea* than I've been in a long time. I have no plans to see Viv again, either socially or professionally. And I apologise again for the misunderstanding. I hope we can remain friends?'

To his surprise, Liz pulled him in to a hug and kissed his cheek. 'Of course we can.'

She let go of him and was pleased to see that the twinkle in his eyes had returned.

'I've known Viv a long time and she's a difficult woman to say no to,' she said. 'I'm sorry for jumping to conclusions, but Viv was so sure that she was on a date with you that I was completely taken in. Let's forget all about it.'

'With pleasure!' He looked genuinely relieved. 'Does that mean you'll join me for a trip on *Ecsta-Sea* sometime? I wasn't kidding when I said I could use your expertise and it goes without saying that I'd love to have your company.'

This time, Liz didn't hesitate to accept his invitation. 'That would be lovely. We've got a big lunch event at Clemency House tomorrow, so how about the day after that. I'll need a day off to recover by then.'

Patrick was grinning from ear to ear. 'It's a date.'

She kissed his cheek and said goodbye before driving the few metres to Mrs Barton's house. This had worked itself out beautifully. Whether Viv would feel the same was a different matter entirely.

Chapter Twenty-Eight

Skye

Skye took off her apron and folded it. She and Liz were finally leaving the wake. They'd spent the last five minutes packing leftover food into the fridge while Liz had repeated word for word what Patrick had told her about Viv and how they were friends again. Judging by how girlish Liz was being, Skye would bet money on them being more than friends before long.

Mrs Barton came to the door to wave them off; she looked tiny standing on her front doorstep.

'Thank you for your hard work. You made it so much easier for me.' She held out an envelope to Skye addressed to The Seaside Gourmet Girls. 'Here's the balance of your fee.'

'It's our pleasure, Mrs Barton,' said Liz. 'Thank you for using our company.'

'Ken would have loved it.' Mrs Barton dabbed her eyes. 'He always liked a party.'

'You did him proud,' said Skye. 'Your husband's wake struck exactly the right note.'

'I've known him all my life, you know.' The old lady gave them a watery smile. 'We grew up on the same street. I can't remember a time when I didn't love him. He's such a big part of me, I'm not sure who I am now he's gone.'

After managing well all afternoon, Skye was now struggling to hold back tears. She'd never felt like that about anyone. What a privilege, to love and to be so loved by another person that your whole existence becomes one, that you grow into each other so completely that you feel inseparable.

'He sounds like a very special man,' said Liz, her eyes looking shiny too.

Mrs Barton seemed to gather herself. 'Anyway. Are you sure you won't take any of the leftover sherry – I bought far too much.'

Skye noticed the hesitation on Liz's face and jumped in quickly. 'That's very kind, but no thank you. Why don't you go and put your feet up for an hour, perhaps pour one for yourself.'

The old lady nodded, and they said goodbye.

Skye looked back as Liz started up the van and turned out of the driveway. Mrs Barton stood to the side of the doorway waving. Skye imagined that that was her side, that Ken had always stood on the other, the two of them having waved off their guests a thousand times over the years.

As they headed back towards the lock-up, Skye gave a sigh. 'That was sad, but so happy too.'

'I was thinking the same,' Liz agreed. 'Better to have loved and lost and so on. And thanks for stepping in about the sherry, darling, I was tempted. It's going to be a long time before I stop automatically reaching for a glass of something to relax, or relieve stress, or to celebrate. But alcohol wasn't doing me any good, I see that now. I feel so much better for not drinking; I'm sleeping better, I've got more energy and I'm getting my zest for life back.'

'I think you're doing brilliantly. You ought to come to yoga with me,' Skye suggested. She was sure Liz would love it. 'You'd learn to meditate, and Marta says that's a good way of coping with stress.'

Liz didn't look convinced. 'I'll think about it. In the meantime, I'll just have to distract myself with elderflower pressé. And dates with Patrick Delmarge.'

Skye laughed. 'That works too.'

'It's good to hear you laugh.' Liz smiled at her. 'You've come out of your shell since being here. I know you and Clare got off to a shaky start, but you seem a lot closer now.'

'We are.' Skye looked out of the open window, gazing at the loveliness of her surroundings: the pastel-painted houses, the narrow streets, the glimpses of the sparkling sea over rooftops and through the trees. She'd left Uganda in June in order to give herself the time and space to think about her future. To decide whether the life Jesse was offering was really what she wanted. Getting to spend six weeks in Salcombe with Clare, Ivy and Liz was an added bonus which she couldn't have foreseen. And now that she had them back in her life, she wasn't ready to let them go. Ironically, it had been her family who'd made her want to escape her home, but it was also her family who'd helped her to make the next big decision.

She turned to her godmother. 'Liz, I love it here. I mean, I really love it. Salcombe, my job, you three. I'm having the best summer.'

'Oh darling!' Liz reached for her hand across the gearstick. 'That's fantastic to hear. Maybe we can make this a regular thing? I'm sure Clare and Ivy will be back next summer. Although . . .' She paused and chewed her lip.

'What?'

'Nothing. Yet. Speaking to Patrick has given me food for thought, that's all. But Salcombe is Clare's second home, I can't imagine a time when she won't want to come. And you must too.'

Skye beamed. Whether it was intended or not, she'd always felt like the outsider. 'I'd like that. I'd like being part of the traditions. Like cream teas, and fish and chips on the first night.'

'We usually do breakfast at the Winking Prawn and lunch at the Crab Shed too. And Jen always liked a beach barbecue and beers.' Liz pulled a face. 'Maybe not the beers this time. But let's try to fit the rest in before you go back to Africa.'

'I'm not going back,' Skye blurted out. 'I've thought and thought about it and it's not what I want.'

Liz slowed down as the car in front put its brakes on. 'Then lucky us!' she said, smiling. 'I'm really pleased for you if it's what you want.'

'It is what I want. When I came back earlier in the summer I didn't expect to feel like I fit in in this family. But I do. And I owe that to you. If you hadn't asked me to work for you, none of this would have happened.'

Skye let out a breath, relieved to have finally said it out loud. It had been a game of tug of war for her heart: the friends she'd made, the beauty of Kampala, the year-round warmth, not to mention how purposeful her life had been during the five years she'd spent there. And love, of course, she'd found love in Uganda. But she knew now without a doubt that that life, that love, was over. She'd found a new purpose here, among her own family; there were adventures she wanted to have, she wanted to put down roots, perhaps love again . . .

'You've been such a help to me,' Liz said. 'I'm glad I've been a help to you in some way too. Is that why you were trying to get hold of your boss, to resign?'

308

'Exactly.' Jesse wasn't going to take this well. They hadn't managed to speak to each other for a couple of weeks now and Skye was getting edgy. The conversation needed to happen as soon as possible. 'I know you originally said six weeks,' Skye ventured, 'but do you think I could work for you a little longer?'

Liz sighed. 'You can stay with me as long as you like. But as for working for me . . .' She gave Skye a look of apology. 'I'm not sure I want to run a catering company anymore, so there may not be a job for you.'

'But you love cooking.' Skye gave her a look of surprise.

'I love cooking in *my own* house. Doing afternoon tea for the Delmarges was the perfect job, it didn't feel like work. Today, working in Mrs Barton's kitchen was a chore. The oven didn't get hot enough, the fridge wasn't cold enough and the dishwasher was one of those half-sized ones designed for fairy folk.'

Skye smiled. 'I see what you mean. OK, I'll work for as long as you need me and then I'll have a rethink.'

'Deal. I'd been considering retirement earlier in the summer,' Liz admitted sheepishly. 'But I've got my mojo back now, so that's not going to happen. I've got a few ideas, and once I've paid your dad what we owe him, I'll be making some decisions of my own. Why aren't we moving, I wonder?'

Salcombe streets were always busy, but the queue of traffic they were in appeared to be completely stationary, and motorists were starting to toot their horns.

Liz turned the engine off. 'Looks like we aren't going anywhere for the time being.'

Skye poked her head out of the window. 'I can hear raised voices. Perhaps there's been an accident?'

'I pity the ambulance or police car that has to get through the gridlock.'

Skye spotted a familiar figure coming towards them. 'There's Marta, we can ask her.'

Marta was wearing her hair loose, with sunglasses pushed back on her head, and her curls bounced on her shoulders. She was so beautiful. Skye felt more nervous the closer Marta got. She gave a low laugh, chiding herself – it was about time she got over her girl crush, she was a grown woman for heaven's sake.

She leaned further out of the window and waved to get Marta's attention.

'Oh bugger.' Liz slipped down in her seat. 'The last time she saw me I threw up on a grass verge when she drove me home. She must think I'm a complete lush.'

'Marta's lovely,' Skye replied. 'She won't think that at all.'

'Hey!' Marta's face split into a smile and she touched Skye's arm. 'Good to see you both.'

'Thank you again for bringing me home the other week.' Liz gushed. 'I misjudged my limits badly and I'm very embarrassed about it.'

Marta dismissed her apology with a hand gesture. 'Please, don't worry about it. You were under a lot of pressure at the time. As well as man trouble, I remember? I hope you've managed to smooth things over with him now? Tell him how you feel?'

Liz turned puce. 'Well, I . . . I . . . yes, thank you, I did,' she stammered.

'She's got a date,' Skye said slyly. 'With a lovely man, who Clare and I approve of, so things are looking up.'

Marta looked delighted. 'That's great news. I think it's always better to be honest with those we care about. Even if feelings are not reciprocated, it will help the other person to understand you better and to be more sensitive around you.'

'Good advice. Thank you.' Liz turned an even deeper shade of red. Ahead, the cacophony of car horns was getting angrier. 'Any idea what's going on up ahead?'

Marta pulled a face. 'There's a tourist going in the wrong direction down a one-way street. Plus, a delivery van blocking the road and a group of pedestrians all trying to direct traffic but getting in the way of the vehicles. I offered to help, but the driver waved me away. Poor guy.'

Liz groaned. 'Not again. That happens all the time in summer.'

'Sounds like he needs to de-stress at sunrise yoga with us,' said Skye.

'So you're coming tomorrow?' Marta asked her.

Skye nodded. 'Definitely. Best way to start the day.'

'Wonderful – in that case, would you like to go for breakfast afterwards?' Marta's gaze flicked away into the distance and then back to Skye. 'I'm always starving after I teach a class and I'd love to hear more about your time in Africa.'

'Oh.' A blush crept over Skye's face. She'd love that. In fact, she couldn't think of anything she'd love more, but she managed a calm response. 'Sounds great!'

'Then it's a date.' Marta covered Skye's hand with her own. 'My parking ticket is about to run out, I'd better dash. See you tomorrow, Skye.'

She leaned into the car and touched her lips to Skye's cheek. Skye's breath caught in her throat at the unexpected gesture as the scent of patchouli and sandalwood filled her nostrils.

'I look forward to it,' Skye said, excitement buzzing through her.

'That's two of us with dates,' Liz teased after Marta had walked away.

But Skye couldn't bring herself to join in the joke. Her feelings for Marta were so confusing. It was just an invitation to breakfast; Marta wanted to talk to her about Africa, that was all. *But if it was a date,* a voice in her head asked, *then how would you feel?* Was it possible that the reason she felt so drawn to Marta, was that she wanted to be more than friends?

Her mouth had gone dry and suddenly she felt too confined inside the van. 'I'm just going to go and see the drama for myself.'

'OK. If we don't move soon, I'm going to park up and walk home; we can empty the van later.'

Skye set off towards the cause of the traffic jam. Her feet picked up pace as she saw a crowd of people around a Volkswagen Golf, guiding the driver with hand signals as the car inched forward and then backwards on the narrow street in an attempt to turn round. Pedestrians squeezed through, some stopping to shout complaints at the stranded car.

'Excuse me, excuse me!' Skye pushed through the throng, hoping to do something to speed up clearing the traffic jam.

A blond head appeared through the open car window, and she froze to the spot, her breath leaving her lungs in a whoosh of shock.

No way.

Was this real or were her eyes playing tricks on her?

She blinked and focused again. Definitely him. Her stomach, her legs, her chest. . . everything felt weak as her brain processed the sight of him. He was as tanned as ever, his muscled arm resting on the open window as he manoeuvred the car forwards.

'Jesse!' Skye yelled, clapping her hands over her mouth.

The brake lights of the car came on and he turned to her, his blue eyes wide in surprise. And then he was out of the car and sprinting towards her.

'Skye! It's you!' He scooped her up and swung her round, his mouth finding hers. 'I've missed you so much.'

He tasted of mint and cola and she could smell the faint eucalyptus scent of the soap they used in Kampala. The smell of home-her old home.

'I've missed you too,' she said, her voice choked. 'You look great.'

'You too.' He pulled back to scan her face as if he was trying to absorb every detail of her. He caught hold of her hands. 'You look . . . radiant, glowing, gorgeous.'

She couldn't take her eyes off him. She *had* missed him. He was probably the best friend she'd ever had – and the last person she'd expected to see here, causing chaos in this little Devonshire town.

Her brain kicked into overdrive. What was she going to say to him? And – oh God, Liz and Clare, what was she going to tell *them*? She had no choice but to take him to Clemency House. But should she talk to him alone first? Tell him her decision?

'Mate?' the driver of the van wedged behind Jesse's car yelled out of the window. 'This is all very romantic, but can you move your bloody car?'

'Of course.' Jesse held his hand up apologetically and then nodded to the assembled crowd. 'Sorry, everyone. I'm used to African dirt roads – these narrow streets have defeated me.'

'Excuse me, let me through!'

Skye turned towards the voice to see Liz, elbowing her way to the front of the crowd. She stopped in her tracks and stared, no doubt surprised to see Skye holding hands with a strange man in the street.

'Skye? Ooh hello, who's this?'

Oh hell. This wasn't how she'd planned it; Skye felt her knees tremble, but thankfully Jesse had his arm around her waist.

Skye swallowed. 'Jesse, this is Liz, my godmother. Liz, meet Jesse.'

Liz extended a hand for Jesse to shake. 'So *you're* Skye's boss! Welcome! We've heard a lot about you.'

Jesse's gaze slid from Liz to Skye, a look of confusion on his face. 'Her boss? I'm a lot more than that. I'm the man who wants to marry her. Her fiancé, if she's decided to say yes.'

'Fiancé?' Liz stared at her in amazement. 'Skye, is that right?'

'Well.' Skye opened her mouth to speak, but there was nothing there. No words, no excuses, no explanation. She couldn't do this to him. She couldn't be so heartless, not while Liz was looking at her, while Jesse was waiting for her to confirm that he was telling the truth. 'Yes. That's right. Jesse's my boss *and* my boyfriend.'

But you don't love him, a voice in her head yelled at her.

Marta's words flashed up in her mind: *It's always better to be honest with those we care about.* So why had she just lied to the ones she cared about most in the world?

314

Chapter Twenty-Nine

Skye

JUNE 2022

Someone cranked up the music and within seconds we were all on our feet, whooping and clapping to the beat. Friday nights at the Hope Foundation Camp in Kampala were often like this. School was finished for the week, and it was a time to blow off steam. Someone would light a fire, a speaker would be rigged up, and a cooler filled with bottles of beer brought outside.

It was impossible not to dance to African music. Everyone joined in. Even the new gritty-eyed volunteers who'd only just arrived and were disorientated and dazed and still trying to work out if the crackling noises were coming from the fire or from the thick bush which bordered the camp.

Jesse appeared at my side, ready to party. He smelled of his lime shaving oil and smoke from the fire; his eyes were shining as he twirled me around, much to the amusement of the children from the village who'd crept into the party as soon as they heard the music.

'Remember how shy you were when you arrived?' he shouted over the music.

I laughed, recalling being mortified as someone had pulled me to my feet and forced me to dance, my stiff, self-conscious body refusing to unwind. 'You helped me to step out of my comfort zone. Now I'm the first up to dance. Although I'll never be as good at it as those two.'

I pointed to our friends Aster and Apolo. They were in the middle of the circle, showing the new arrivals how to twerk.

'But you're the most beautiful woman in the whole of Africa, especially in that dress.'

'Thank you.' I kissed his cheek before giving him a twirl.

I didn't normally change out of my T-shirt and shorts in the evening, but Dembe had suggested wearing my new dress. It was a traditional batik print, bold bright colours and a tight bodice which did wonders for my meagre cleavage.

'You look like a princess,' Dembe had said, tucking a flower behind my ear.

Was Jesse my prince? I wondered now, as he kissed me and went to fetch a drink. He was my best friend and probably my favourite human.

We had a lot in common, both of us from privileged backgrounds, unremarkable grades at school and neither of us had had a clear idea of what we wanted to do for a career. His parents had assumed he'd follow his father's footsteps into the financial sector, but Jesse hadn't wanted to be tied down to a desk, he wanted to be physically active. Running the Hope Foundation, as we now did together, suited us both.

We'd been happy as just friends. But one day he'd kissed me, and everything had changed. He'd confessed that he'd wanted to kiss me since the moment we met. I hadn't known what to say; I loved him, but not in that way. Somehow I got swept along with the excitement of it all. As time had gone on and his love had become more passionate, I felt more and more like a fraud.

I knew at some point I would have to be honest with him about my feelings. But not yet. Why rock the boat? We were both happy and I wasn't hurting anyone. For now, life was happy and fulfilling and I didn't want to do anything to spoil it.

I pushed away my worries and lost myself in the music once more. I was a different person now. Free and relaxed. I caught sight of Jesse through the dancers. He'd moved to the outer edge of the crowd and was sipping from a beer bottle, just watching me. His eyes soft with love. I grinned at him and turned away to dance with one of the new volunteers.

Suddenly, Jesse raised a hand and gestured to Apolo to pause the music.

'What's the matter?' I said, as he caught my hand and drew me into his side. 'Is something wrong?'

'Everything's fine,' he said and then yelled to the group. 'Can I have your attention, for just one minute?'

'Quiet!' Someone rattled a spoon against a beer bottle and gradually the noise level lowered.

I caught Dembe's eye and frowned. 'What's going on?'

We'd already done the induction speeches to welcome the new volunteers. Why was he interrupting the party?

She shrugged and then grinned mischievously. Aster joined her and they started to giggle. I didn't know what was coming, but a sixth sense sent a shudder of fear through me.

'Skye,' Jesse began.

He stepped away from me, holding my hand at arm's-length. I felt exposed, with all eyes on me, and my heart, already racing from the dancing, felt too big for my chest. I stared from Jesse to my friends, wondering what this was all about.

'Since you walked into this camp five years ago, you have brought sunshine into the lives of hundreds of volunteers and over a thousand children and their families here at the Hope Foundation. But, most of all, you've brought joy, happiness and love into mine.'

He turned to face me, taking hold of both of my hands.

'That's so sweet, thank you,' I said, my face burning with embarrassment. Jesse knew I didn't like the limelight. What was he playing at? 'I'm very grateful to be here, let's dance again, shall we?'

'Skye, I can't imagine my life without you. And I hope, if you feel the same, that I won't have to.'

Suddenly, Jesse went down onto one knee and pulled a square box from the pocket of his shorts. His eyes were locked on mine as he lifted the lid of the box to reveal a diamond set into a white-gold band. I registered the mix of exhilaration and love and total confidence – on his face. And then time slowed down to a grinding pace as my brain processed what was happening right in front of me and adrenaline coursed through my veins. *Please, no.*

'Skye Marriott, I love you with all my heart. Will you marry me?'

Keep smiling, I urged myself, *don't ruin this for him.*

I was hyperaware of my surroundings. Above us, a jet-black moonless sky sparkled with stars. Twists of smoke and tiny embers like fireflies filled the night air. Around us, our friends were holding their breath, their faces alight with excitement. Even the new volunteers had given up trying to connect to the Wi-Fi and put their phones down for a second. And kneeling in front of me, his face wreathed in smiles, was the man I loved. And I truly did love him.

'Oh Jesse!' I gasped, pressing my hands to my face. My cheeks were wet with tears.

Jesse got to his feet, took the ring out of the box and everyone whooped and cheered as he slid it onto my finger.

'It's beautiful,' I said. 'I love it. And I love you.'

He put his arms around my waist and drew me to him. As I wrapped my arms around his neck. He kissed me to a round of raucous applause. Phone cameras flashed as our proposal was recorded for prosperity.

And then we were descended on by our friends and staff and the kids, everyone squealing and hugging and kissing as the music was cranked up again and the party resumed, the mood euphoric. Jesse and I danced too, our bodies pressed against each other, my eyes glued to the rock on my ring finger.

'You didn't say yes,' Jesse murmured once we were no longer the centre of attention.

My mouth felt as dry as the sun-baked soil and I swallowed. 'I know.'

If you feel the same, he'd said.

And that was the issue. I didn't.

Chapter Thirty

Skye

The morning after Jesse's surprise appearance, Skye reached for her phone on the nightstand, taking care not to wake him. Five o'clock. Too early to get up. She'd hardly had any sleep and her eyes felt gritty. She hadn't come to bed until 1 a.m., busying herself with prep for Dad's business lunch later today and catching up with admin and emails. None of which were strictly necessary but meant that Jesse was bound to be asleep by the time she joined him in her bedroom.

Skye suppressed a moan. What an almighty mess.

She rolled over to study him. His breathing was soft and even, his arm was thrown back above his head, his tanned face so dark in contrast to his blond hair. There was a scar on his shoulder from an operation he'd had after a football accident at school. She knew his body intimately: where his birthmarks were, how to make him convulse with laughter by tickling him on the side of his neck, and she understood the meaning behind all of his smiles.

She'd probably always love him. She'd spent the happiest years of her life so far with him. He was her best friend, but that wasn't enough; he deserved to marry someone whose very soul lit up when he was in the room. She blamed herself entirely for not being honest with him. If she'd only been brave enough to tell him that she wasn't in love with him before he proposed, then maybe all this heartache could have been avoided.

And now, having decided he'd waited long enough for an answer, he was here in Salcombe, in her bed. Was it better or worse to be face to face with the person you loved while they broke your heart? Skye felt sick at the thought of what she was going to have to do to him. Last night had been bad enough.

'Your *boss?*' he'd said in disbelief once they were alone together. 'What's going on here, Skye? Are you ashamed of me.'

They were back at Clemency House, standing in the hall. A few metres away, she could hear Liz humming inside the downstairs loo and the sound of running water.

'Of course not,' she'd whispered, squeezing his hand. 'I just needed some time to think about us. I didn't want advice or anyone else's opinion. This is something I wanted to decide by myself.'

'I understand, but you've had time,' Jesse had said, running his thumb softly down her cheek. 'You must know what the answer is by now. That's why I've come, to hear it.'

He was right, she did know. She'd blinked at him, fear ricocheting around her stomach like a marble in a pinball machine. But she couldn't simply dissolve their relationship in the hall, just after he'd stepped into the house, while Liz was going to the loo within earshot. 'Jesse, I don't—'

At that moment, the door had opened, and Liz had appeared.

'Why didn't you tell us you're getting engaged?' Liz had said, hugging them both. 'This is wonderful news. You'll stay with us, of course, Jesse,' she'd continued, blithely unaware of the tension between them. 'There's plenty of room; the more, the merrier, and Skye's got a double bed. I'll fetch you some clean towels.'

'Thanks, Liz.' Jesse had given her a flash of his devastating smile. The one which all the female volunteers at the Hope Foundation went weak-kneed over. 'If you're sure I'm not imposing? I should have called ahead, but that would have ruined the surprise.'

'He's an absolute babe,' Liz had added, pretending to whisper behind her hand, nudging Skye. 'No wonder you wanted to keep him to yourself.'

'Yep,' Skye had said faintly.

Clare had welcomed him warmly and Jesse had ingratiated himself by insisting on cooking everyone dinner and carrying Ivy upstairs for her.

'Nice guy. Are you happy?' she'd asked Skye in a quiet moment.

Her reply, while gathering up some of Ivy's toys and stowing them in the toy basket, had been non-committal. 'It's great to see him.'

'Bit of a shocker, though. I got the impression you were single.' Clare had whistled under her breath. 'But engaged?'

'I know, I know.' Skye had felt awful for misleading her sister, just when they'd started to develop a proper sibling relationship. 'I wanted to say more but I couldn't.'

Clare had held her gaze and nodded. 'OK, but I'm here if you want to talk.'

Those words came back to Skye now as she lay in bed. Gently, she peeled back the covers and slid out of bed. She tiptoed along the corridor to Clare and Ivy's room and listened at the door. All she could hear was the distant squeal of seagulls. She turned the doorknob and poked her head into her sister's room. Clare was sitting up in bed, her left arm resting on a cushion. Skye could just make out the shape of her niece pressed against the mesh side of the travel cot.

'Can I talk to you?' Skye whispered.

'Thought you'd never ask.' Clare nodded to the empty half of the double bed.

'I used to fantasise about us having midnight chats when I was younger.' Skye confessed as she climbed in next to her sister. 'I used to peer into your room when you stayed over to see if you were awake. You never were.'

Clare pulled a mock-guilty face. 'I was. I just didn't want you in my room.'

'You cow.' Skye gave a soft laugh.

'I know,' she replied with a snort. 'But, hey, here we are. I'm beginning to realise that keeping myself at arm's-length from other people isn't fully living. I thought I was protecting myself from getting hurt and being let down, but I was also preventing myself from enjoying other things. Important things like sisterhood.'

'That's very deep for this time in the morning.' Skye's throat felt thick with emotion. 'But also the nicest thing you've ever said to me.'

'I know,' Clare grumbled. 'I must have bumped my head when I broke my arm. I don't recognise myself. So what's the story with Mr Muscles? Why didn't you tell us about him?'

'Because . . . because he's a lovely guy: kind, gorgeous, fun, hard-working. On paper he's a great catch.'

'Ah,' Clare nodded. 'The old "on paper" situation. Still doesn't explain why you couldn't speak about him.'

Skye chewed the edge of her thumbnail. 'Because I couldn't risk Mum and Dad finding out and them trying to convince me to marry him.'

Clare shuffled up the bed, wincing with pain as she made herself more comfortable. 'Let me get this straight. You kept his proposal a secret because you know they're going to approve?'

Skye's lips twitched. 'Sounds mad when you say it like that. But I needed to make my own mind up and not be influenced by what they think. Correction, what *Dad* thinks. I'm pretty sure, as far as Mum is concerned, I'm an adult and no longer her problem. The thing is, unlike you, I've never achieved anything noteworthy. I've never had a proper career or passed exams or stuck at anything.'

'Well, that can't be true,' Clare scoffed.

''Fraid so – as far as Dad is concerned, anyway. And although he rolled his eyes when I went travelling, since then, I've held down a job and been in a stable relationship. Getting married will be the first time I've ever actually surprised him by doing something well.'

'Marriage isn't some sort of gold-medal situation,' said Clare, tutting. 'And if there's one thing Mike Marriott should pipe down about, it's other people's marriages. He's hardly an advert for matrimony, is he?'

'Maybe not, but when he called to talk to Liz about today's business lunch, he told me that a good man could be the making of me.'

'Idiot,' said Clare.

'Agreed. So I knew if I told Dad that Jesse wanted to marry me he'd try to persuade me that I should. The safest thing to do was to keep everyone in the dark, make my decision and then let Jesse know as soon as I could.'

Clare gave her a gentle smile. 'And you've been trying to get hold of him, so that must mean you've made your decision?'

'Yes.' Skye stared at her hands. 'I do love him, but I'm not *in* love with him, I can't marry him.'

'I could tell that straight away.'

Skye glanced at her sister. 'Really?'

'When you turned up with him yesterday, I thought he must be someone you'd met while travelling.' Clare laughed softly. 'It was quite a shock when he said he was your fiancé. There was something missing between you – a spark.'

Skye nodded. 'I've always thought so too, but we get on so well that I told myself it didn't matter, that sparks go out over time anyway.'

'So what changed?'

'He proposed in front of all our friends and colleagues and the new volunteers. Even if the answer had been an easy yes, he should have known me well enough to know that that sort of thing was my worst nightmare.'

'You know what that reminds me of?' Clare shook her head. 'That time Dad made you stand up in the restaurant so that everyone could sing happy birthday to you. Anyone could see how much you hated it.'

'My God, you're right.' Skye looked at her, amazed.

'So, basically, you're engaged to a man like Dad. I think there's a name for that – the *something* complex.' Clare reached for her phone. 'I'll google it.'

'Please don't.' Skye shuddered. Was that what she'd done? Inadvertently found herself a man like her father? This was getting worse by the second. Jesse was always so definite about everything, so sure that his way was the right way. She'd taken refuge in that at one time, but she couldn't do it anymore. She needed to strike out on her own. 'Anyway, there was no way I could stay in Kampala after that. Everyone walking on eggshells, not knowing whether we are actually engaged or not.'

'You did the right thing coming back.' Clare put her phone down. 'And you've had the bonus of Ivy and me with you during your period of self-examination. Win–win!'

They grinned at each other. It felt good, this new relationship with Clare. Skye hoped it would last long after summer ended. It would, she decided; she'd make sure it did.

'Very true,' she replied. 'But now I've ruined the one chance I had to impress Dad. For once, I wanted to make him as proud of me as he is of his other daughter.'

'Our father has a lot to answer for,' Clare tutted. 'Can I confide in you about something?'

Skye nodded; she'd been waiting for this all her life. 'Of course.'

'I really like Adam. But I'm scared of letting him in. What if it goes wrong? What if Ivy gets used to having him around and then he does a disappearing act? I'm big enough to handle the disappointment, but I don't want to put Ivy through the heartache that I went through with Dad.'

This wasn't about Adam at all, Skye realised; Clare was worried about history repeating itself. Her heart twisted. She'd always thought Clare was so confident, turned out she had just the same self-doubts as she did.

'Take it slow,' she said. 'Think butterfly in a china shop rather than bull. Let him prove he can be trusted and explain to him what you're worried about. My friend Marta says it's always better to be honest with those we care about.'

Clare picked at the sticky tape keeping her brace in place. 'Good advice. The thing is, I was absolutely convinced that my parents were madly in love with each other. Dad let me and Mum down, and a part of me will always expect that if I let my guard down with a man it'll happen to me too.'

'You were what, four? Five? When Dad moved out?'

Clare nodded. 'My first day of school. I came home bursting with stories to tell him and I never got the chance.'

Skye reached for her sister's hand and held it lightly. 'It must have been terrible for you. And your mum. But do we really ever know what's going on in someone else's relationship, let alone when we're only children? I'm pretty sure I've cherry-picked my memories, most of which are the dramatic ones. But there must have been boring days when Mum and Dad just got on fine and didn't argue.'

'Of course there were.' Clare grinned. 'I can remember being bored out of my skull some weekends at yours, so it can't all have been arguments. Anyway, look at us now, both keeping secrets from Dad. Who'd have thought we'd got so much in common?'

'You mean pretending you had an ex-boyfriend who dumped you when you were pregnant?'

Clare nodded. 'If Mum had been alive, I'd have told her everything, but I knew I'd never be able to tell Dad. So I decided it was easier to lie to everyone. There were dark times when I really wanted to tell Liz, but she and my dad go way back, and I wasn't completely sure she'd be able to keep my secret.'

'And why couldn't you tell Dad?'

'Because all my life I've tried to do well at everything,' said Clare, tilting her chin defiantly. 'I wanted him to see that I haven't needed him, that he might have set fire to our family, but that fire gave me the spark to succeed. Picking up a random guy in a hotel bar and sleeping with him was not the way I'd intended to start a family. I didn't want Dad to spot a chink in my armour.'

'Ivy isn't a chink in your armour,' Skye chided her. 'She's the shiny breastplate.'

They both turned and watched Ivy fast asleep in her cot with not a care in the world.

'Adam's a lucky guy,' Skye murmured.

'Let's hope he thinks the same.' Clare puffed out her cheeks. 'I think today's the day.'

'You're going to tell him the truth?'

Clare nodded. 'I've been sitting here thinking about it since I woke up. I'm going to take it slowly, like you said. But he deserves to know that he has a child. He might be heading back to Bath soon, for all I know, so I'm going to send him a message, ask if he's free tonight.'

'How do you think he'll take it?'

'God knows. *Well*, hopefully.' Clare bit her lip. 'I was thinking early supper at the pub, taking Ivy with us to defuse any tension. Plus, she's the greatest advert for parenthood I've got to offer.'

'I like him, he gives off good vibes,' said Skye, remembering how kind Adam had been at Angel's party.

'He does. He adores Ivy already.' Her face went dreamy. 'You should have seen them together at the beach. He played with her. Dad never did that with me. Then when a dog gatecrashed our rug and knocked her over, I thought he was going to punch the dog's owner, he was so cross.'

Skye whistled under her breath. 'You've got it bad.'

'Shut up.' Clare side-eyed her, nonetheless turning a pretty shade of pink. 'It's just . . . He could have been someone who doesn't like kids, and he isn't and that makes me feel so much better about him. And he was there when she took her first steps, which is such a major thing in her development – literally, her first steps on earth. I'll never forget that moment – the look of surprise on Ivy's face that she was finally doing it, and the look of elation on his. It feels like a sign.'

'I'm really happy for you,' said Skye. There was a lump in her throat just looking at the happiness on her sister's face. 'So, your date with him tonight. Is this about Ivy connecting with him or you hooking up with the sexy hotel guy again?'

Clare pulled a face. 'Can it be both?'

Skye laughed. 'It might be easier to be romantic if you don't have a small person to look after. Besides, if you have Ivy with you, your focus will have to be shared between him and her. Go by yourselves and you can gaze lustily into each other's eyes without distraction.'

'Go out without Ivy?' Clare looked as appalled as if Skye had suggested going out in her birthday suit.

'I'll babysit. She knows me well enough now. Go out *out*. Get dressed up – well, as much as you can with that big thing on your arm.' Skye watched a variety of thoughts cross Clare's face. 'Go on. See if the chemistry is still there.'

Clare took a deep breath and blew it out slowly. 'OK.'

'Yes!' Skye raised her hand and Clare high-fived her. 'I repeat, Adam is a lucky guy.'

'And your lucky guy is out there somewhere too,' Clare replied. 'You just haven't met him yet.'

Skye's heart thundered against her ribs; she held Clare's gaze, daring herself to say it aloud.

Clare's eyes widened. 'Oh my God. Have you met someone else?'

'Shush, keep your voice down.' Skye looked at the door nervously.

'You have!' Clare's smile was triumphant.

'What you said about a spark missing between me and Jesse.' Skye wet her dry lips with her tongue.

'Yes?'

'I think I may have found the spark.' She chewed her lip. 'But it's not a man.'

It wasn't a secret that she'd dated boys and girls in the past, it wasn't that that was making her heart race.

It was the strength of her feelings towards Marta which shocked her.

'That's OK, isn't it?' Clare nodded encouragingly.

'Oh God.' Skye pressed her hands to her cheeks; this was crazy, what was she thinking? 'I'm nearly thirty and I've never felt this way about *anyone* before. Everything until now feels like a silly crush in comparison. This feels, I don't know, real, different.'

Her sister twisted so she could reach Skye's hand and squeeze it. 'I don't think there's an age limit on falling in love, or finding someone who ignites the spark, and there's certainly not a rule book on who we're allowed to fall for. If Marta makes you happy, then that's all that matters.'

Skye's eyes pinged open. 'How did you guess?'

'Marta this, Marta that,' Clare teased.

Skye blushed. 'Am I really that bad?'

'No comment.' Clare mimed zipping her lips.

'She's amazing,' Skye exclaimed quietly, shaking her head. 'I've had crushes on girls before, but never a proper relationship. I guess, deep down, I always assumed that the big serious love of my life would be a man. But now I'm not so sure. What if she doesn't feel the same? I'm going to feel such an idiot. And what will Dad think? And Liz?'

'Whoah.' Clare laughed. 'One step at a time.'

'True,' Skye winced. 'Before I can even think about this, I need to tell Jesse that I can't marry him.'

'No use pulling the plaster off slowly. Do it soon, for both your sakes.'

Skye climbed out of Clare's bed. 'I will. He's a lovely guy and he doesn't deserve to be badly treated. But first I'm going to beach yoga to get my head straight. And then I'm having breakfast with Marta.'

A dart of excitement pinged at Skye's heart; it would be the first time they'd met up without one of them being at work. She wouldn't be able to stay too long; it wasn't fair to keep Jesse waiting, but there'd be time to get to know each other, and hopefully work out if that magic spark was there for Marta too.

'Your eyes shine when you talk about her. Promise me you'll tell all when you get back.'

Skye's stomach twinged with nerves; she so wanted it to go well.

'Promise.' She got as far as the bedroom door when something occurred to her. 'Marta said something odd to Liz yesterday. She must have been referring to their conversation in the car on the way back from Angel's party. She asked Liz if she'd sorted out her man trouble and said something about feelings not being reciprocated. Any idea what she meant? I don't think it was Patrick.'

Clare shook her head. 'No, but I overheard her saying something odd to him. She said that she'd been hung up on the same man for over forty years, that he still had power over her and that she was trying to get over him.'

'Bloody hell.' Skye widened her eyes. 'Poor Liz. I wonder who that could be?'

'I've racked my brains but can't think of anyone. Mum would have known.'

'Why don't you just ask Liz,' Skye suggested. 'She'll tell you.'

'Maybe.' Clare didn't look convinced. 'But I think I've had enough family revelations for one day and it isn't even seven o'clock yet. See you later, go and sort out your chakras.'

'Oh shut up.' Skye laughed under her breath as she left the room. She loved her sister; she'd be teased mercilessly if she admitted it to her, but she did.

Chapter Thirty-One

Liz

Liz turned on the laptop while she waited for the kettle to boil. She wasn't the only one up early, judging by the whispers she'd heard coming from Clare's room as she'd come downstairs. Hopefully, she'd get a few minutes to herself before someone joined her.

Lunch for eight people, no expense spared. Normally, catering for such a small number wouldn't have Liz breaking into a sweat, especially as she didn't even have to leave Clemency House to do it. But this was Mike. She'd never be as tall and beautiful as Jen, Frankie and Nilla, but she was a brilliant cook, and everyone knew the way to a man's heart was through his stomach.

She clenched her jaw, realising that she was doing it again: sticking Mike Marriott on a pedestal and worshipping at his feet. She'd promised herself that phase of her life was over. Why was it so hard to remember?

Everything pointed her towards breaking away from the unhelpful obsession she had with him. She was seeing Patrick tomorrow, lovely, gentle Patrick. A man who'd loved his wife until she died and beyond. A man who worked hard, looked after his mother and aunt and was always kind and thoughtful, his eyes never roving to check he wasn't missing out on something better when they were together. She'd accepted Patrick's excuses about Viv very easily, she admitted to herself; she'd be far less likely to have believed Mike if he'd fed her the same lines. But she was sure Patrick was telling the truth; she could well imagine Viv not taking no for an answer straight away. She'd been on the receiving end of Viv's persuasive powers often enough herself.

Viv would be a good match for Mike, she thought idly, pouring boiling water into the teapot. She laughed softly. Except for one thing – they were of a similar age; Mike's taste in women got younger and younger as time went by.

'Silly arse,' she muttered, splashing milk into a mug.

'Charming.' Skye wandered in and kissed Liz's cheek.

She was dressed in a pair of orange leggings and a multi-coloured tie-dye T-shirt, her hair held back with what looked like a strip torn off one of Liz's old tea towels.

'Not you, darling, your father,' said Liz.

Skye rolled her eyes. 'Don't tell me we've had more alterations from him?'

'I haven't checked my emails yet. But it's too late for any more changes. I've got lobster for eight and that's that.'

Skye chewed her lip. 'Ah. Nine, I'm afraid, he's bringing his assistant now. Harriet.'

'He is the absolute limit. He really is.' Liz shook her head in dismay.

'You love him really.' Her god-daughter laughed, filling her water bottle from the tap. 'Am I still OK to go to yoga? I can give it a miss if you need me.'

'Yoga?' a gruff voice said from the door. 'Are you going now?'

Jesse leaned against the door frame, wearing nothing but a pair of cotton boxer shorts.

'Jesse!' Skye jumped. 'I thought you were still asleep. You don't mind, do you? I'd pre-booked before I knew you were coming.'

'But I've hardly had any time to talk to you.' He strode across the kitchen, wrapped an arm around her waist and kissed her cheek. 'Morning, Liz.'

Liz felt her face redden. 'Morning, Jesse. Can I get you a cup of tea?'

He thanked her, said yes and began playing with Skye's hair. 'I missed you when I woke up.'

Skye twisted away from him. 'I don't think Liz needs to see that in the morning.'

Liz found it impossible not to stare at Jesse. He was an Adonis. She couldn't remember ever seeing such a beautiful man in Clemency House before. Bronzed, muscled, broad, with a smattering of golden hair on his chest. He was the epitome of youth and masculinity.

The work phone beeped with a text message; Skye scooped it up, putting space between her and her fiancé.

'Oh, that's a shame.' Skye scanned the screen and handed the phone to Liz. 'A cancellation. The booking for that big family party.'

'Working already,' said Jesse, spooning sugar into his tea. 'Maybe you could miss yoga today, especially as you've got your father's lunch coming up later?'

'I'd rather not,' Skye replied quietly.

'Yoga is a great idea,' Liz said, sensing the tension shooting back and forwards between them like laser beams. 'You've already done so much prep, Skye, you deserve an hour or so to yourself.'

'OK.' Jesse conceded defeat. 'But how about I meet you afterwards for breakfast? We can talk, and I get to see some more of this beautiful place.'

Skye sat down to pull on her trainers. 'So sorry, Jesse. I've already made plans for breakfast with a friend. I'll be back as soon as I can.'

'Really? Can't you cancel it?' Jesse looked terribly disappointed and Liz's heart went out to him.

She gave Skye a beseeching look to take pity on him. She'd only made the arrangement with Marta yesterday and that was before her boyfriend arrived; surely things were different now.

'I won't be long,' Skye muttered, not meeting Liz's gaze.

He exhaled, clearly frustrated. 'I know you're avoiding me.'

Skye's eyes shone with tears. 'Jesse, don't make me do this now.' She touched his cheek. 'I'll be back soon. I promise, we can talk then.'

Jesse sighed as he watched her leave and then, without another word, took his tea back upstairs.

Liz felt awkward for the pair of them. It just went to show that you never could tell. Only a few days ago she'd thought that Skye had such an uncomplicated life. How wrong she had been.

She settled down to compose a reply to the message which had just come in. It had been one of Viv's clients – a buffet lunch for twenty at a glass-fronted holiday house in East Portlemouth – and then turned her attention to the accounts.

For the next twenty minutes, she tried to put Skye and Jesse out of her mind and focused on the business. Mike was bound to ask for an update on the loan repayment later and she wanted to have the facts at her fingertips. Bookings had been incredible over the last month and there were plenty more in the diary. But while they'd made a profit, they were quite a way off her twenty-thousand-pound target.

Liz closed the laptop again and sighed. She'd paid herself virtually nothing and Mike had covered Skye's pay as promised, but even so, they were going to need a few more big jobs in the next few weeks.

She thought about Viv. Was it worth doing a flyer to her holiday guests? she wondered. Offering them something special, a discount on a repeat booking perhaps?

She was still mulling it over when her phone rang. Her heart gave a start when she saw Mike's name flash up.

'Mr Marriott,' she drawled, 'are you ready to be wowed by the culinary expertise of The Seaside Gourmet Girls today?'

'Hey,' said Mike.

'Is for horses,' she teased, rolling her eyes. 'Hey' coming from a man in his sixties sounded faintly ridiculous.

'What? You're losing your marbles, old girl,' he chuckled. 'Just ringing to check everything's on course for today. It's a biggie for me, this one, Liz. Don't let me down.'

'When have I ever let you down?' she replied.

'All right, no need to be so touchy, I don't want you having a hot flush.'

'Michael, I am perfectly capable of serving a restaurant-quality lunch in my home to your guests. However, if you're having doubts, then feel free to go elsewhere.'

'No, no,' he said hastily. 'It's cool.'

Cool. What a plonker. Just who did he think he was? Patrick wouldn't ever use the word cool because . . . because he knew how to age gracefully, whereas Mike seemed intent on hanging on to his youth.

'You've added an extra guest,' Liz said shortly. 'Harriet?'

'Yes, Harriet.' His voice softened. 'My assistant. Smart as a whip. Charms the pants of anyone that girl, a real asset.'

Liz could imagine, she thought wryly. 'The garlic prawn salad will stretch to an extra portion. The problem is the lobster. I only bought enough for eight, as previously agreed.'

'Oh, don't worry, she's vegan,' Mike casually informed her.

'What?' Liz almost dropped the phone.

'Vegan,' he repeated. 'No meat, fish or dairy.'

'I know what it is!' she bristled. Oh God, she was having a flashback to that bloody oyster sauce. She shuddered. At least she wouldn't make that mistake again, tempted though she might be. 'But we dealt with dietary requirements in an earlier email. You're an absolute birdbrain, Michael Marriott, and I'll be very tempted to shove your lobster where the sun don't shine.'

'Oh, Liz.' He laughed then, properly laughed, and suddenly she was right back in that lecture theatre when they'd done that killer presentation together and he'd picked her up, whirled her around and kissed her.

Then she joined in the laughter and for the next couple of minutes they hooted and wheezed until he couldn't speak, and she had tears running down her cheeks.

Finally, she got her breath back. 'Look, leave it with me, I'm sure I can rustle up some deep-fried tofu balls.'

'Ouch,' Mike sniggered. 'Sounds painful.'

And they were off again.

'Haven't laughed like that in ages,' said Mike once he'd recovered enough to speak. 'I bloody love you, Liz.'

Heat rushed through her and before she could think about all the things he did to wind her up, her reply was out. 'I love you too. See you later.'

'Love who too?' Clare called from the stairs.

'Your dad,' she said, still smiling as Clare entered the kitchen.

'You love my dad?' Clare looked bemused. 'Aww.'

'Of course I do.' Liz felt herself redden. 'But not like that. He's my oldest friend. We've been in each other's lives for forty years.'

'Gosh, yes, I suppose you have,' Clare said in odd voice.

'Right.' Liz pushed herself from the table. 'Time to get cracking. I'm going to impress Mike Marriott today if it kills me.'

'You've just said he's your oldest friend. Surely you don't need to impress him.' Clare headed for the coffee machine and switched it on.

Something in her tone made Liz anxious. 'Today, he's a paying customer. I want him to be happy. That's all.'

Her stomach flipped as she recognised her own white lie. She knew she was meant to be falling out of love with him, but some habits were hard to break.

Chapter Thirty-Two

Skye

'I wish you all a beautiful day.' Marta bowed to her class, her hands in prayer position over her heart space. 'Namaste.'

Skye and everyone else repeated the blessing back to Marta and the session was over. People took their time to get to their feet; some stretched, others stayed where they were, eyes closed and faces tilted to the sky. She didn't blame them; there was something about the setting and the feeling of togetherness and the sense of well-being Marta created in this class that made you want to stay longer and eke out every second of it before flipping the reality switch and rejoining your day. But this time Skye wished they'd all pack up and disappear so that she'd have Marta to herself.

Ele was here too. Skye caught her eye and she came over.

'I'll miss this class when summer ends.' Ele shook the sand from her towel and folded it into a neat square.

'But Marta has a studio for the winter, doesn't she?' Skye said, gathering her own things together.

'She does, but there's a magic to sunrise yoga when it's on the beach.'

'I think this class will be magical wherever it takes place,' Skye replied, watching as Marta said her goodbyes to members of the group. 'I love the beach, but I'm quite looking forward to seeing the change of the seasons in Salcombe.'

'Sounds like Marta has a new fan.' Ele grinned.

'*This place* has a new fan,' Skye corrected her, trying not to blush as Marta joined them.

'Hey, you two, thanks for coming to practise with me,' she said, greeting them both with a kiss on the cheek.

'Just what I needed.' Skye pressed her hands to her lower back and stretched. 'I didn't sleep much last night.'

'Same,' said Ele, yawning. 'Angel and Adam came over. He's going back to Bath soon, so I cooked them dinner. May or may not have overdone the red wine.' She grimaced.

Skye's stomach dipped; he'd be finding out he had a child tonight. What a shame he wasn't going to be around for long to get to know her.

Marta laughed. 'You need some carbs to soak it up.'

For one awful moment, Skye thought Marta was going to invite Ele to come along with them.

Ele groaned. 'Yes! A sesame bagel with peanut butter awaits at home. See you soon.'

She gave them both a hug and waved goodbye and then it was just the two of them.

'Shall we go?' Marta said, her brown eyes twinkling at her.

Skye nodded. 'I'm starving.'

'My scooter is just over there.'

'I thought we'd be walking,' Skye said, surprised.

'Nope.' Marta laughed at the look on her face. 'I live inland; it would take me an hour to get here. Walking to the beach is fine for tourists, but we're not tourists.'

'We're not,' agreed Skye, feeling oddly proud of the fact.

'This is my baby,' Marta grinned, leading her to a blue scooter parked by the sea wall. 'I've got a car too, as you know, but it's much quicker to get around on this.'

She packed both of their belongings into the pannier at the back, handed Skye a helmet and leapt on. Skye climbed on behind her.

'Scoot up a bit more,' said Marta, turning her head to speak to her. 'And hold on tight.'

Nerves fizzed through Skye as she inched forward and placed her hands on Marta's hips. She could feel the heat of Marta's skin through the Lycra of her yoga leggings, smell the scent of her hair, and she felt giddy with the nearness of her. She'd often gone on the back of scooters in Uganda and never once had she found it as intimate and intoxicating as this.

'Ready?' Marta asked before turning the key.

Skye took a deep breath and pressed herself closer to Marta's body. 'Ready.'

'That was amazing.' Skye's eyes shone as she pulled her helmet off outside the coffee shop. 'So fast compared to a car, and such a great view too.'

'Glad you like it. I much prefer it to driving a car. I like to feel the sun on my face and the salty air on my skin. The throb of an engine between my thighs,' she added cheekily.

'I'm sold,' Skye replied, feeling warm inside her yoga gear. 'If I end up living here, I might treat myself.'

'You mean you might be staying?' Marta raised her eyebrows. 'I thought you were just here for the summer.'

Skye held her gaze. 'I was. But now I'm not sure what comes next.'

'Breakfast comes next,' said Marta decisively, pointing towards the door.

No sooner were they inside than Jade came over and embraced them both. Skye had only met her briefly at

Angel's party but had been grateful for her help when things had got out of hand towards the end.

'Welcome, welcome, I knew you two would get on. This is amazing. What can I get you? Skye, I know you like your coffee and I've got a new blend in that you should try, and Marta I've made the most amazing caramelised-onion marmalade, you're going to love it! Sit down, sit down.' She released them and flapped her hands towards the table in the window.

Skye and Marta exchanged smiles and sat down opposite each other.

'I love that girl,' said Marta, watching Jade tip coffee beans into the grinder. 'She and Ele have been good friends to me. When I first arrived here, I was an exhausted, broken wreck. They held space for me while I mended; they nurtured me and brought me back to life.'

She had a haunted look in her eye and Skye wondered what could have happened to her. She wanted to ask but knew better than to pry. Some stories took time to tell; Skye was content to wait.

Instead, she reached across the table and placed her hand on top of Marta's. 'I'm sorry to hear that. Jade's a ray of sunshine, that's for sure.'

Marta smiled and covered Skye's hand with her other one; Skye did the same so that all four hands were stacked together, and they laughed at their childishness.

'And she makes great coffee too.' Marta peeled her hands away just in time for Jade to place a French press of coffee on the table.

Skye decanted hot milk into two mugs for them, Marta pressed down on the plunger and poured the coffee while they ordered some breakfast. Jade scurried away with their order.

Marta and Skye sipped and savoured their coffee in amiable silence for a few moments.

Skye exhaled with pleasure. 'Delicious.'

'How is the coffee?' Jade piped up, clearly having been watching for Skye's reaction. 'It's from Africa!'

'Best coffee ever!' Skye replied, laughing as Jade punched the air.

'Tell me about Africa,' Marta said, sweeping her hair back over one shoulder.

Skye smiled. 'Well, for starters, coffee plants grow wild everywhere.'

'I'm sold already,' Marta grinned. 'You must miss it?'

'I love the life out there, I love Kampala, I love the weather and the landscape and the feeling of being so aware of the natural world, with national parks and wild animals right on our doorstep. I miss my friends, and the kids at school and their families. The Hope Foundation is like a family. I think that's what I loved most about being in Uganda – the sense of belonging. I hadn't felt that at home in the UK.'

Marta nodded thoughtfully. 'I always spend the month of January in a new country; it fills me up and gives me a fresh perspective on the world. Maybe I need to go and visit.'

'You should,' Skye said, loving the idea of one month of the year travelling. Perhaps it was something she should consider. 'I'm sure you'll fall in love with it.'

'From what you've said, it sounds as if your heart lies in Kampala?'

'It's more complicated than that.' Skye picked up a spoon and stirred her coffee absently. 'Right now, all I know is that I've felt happier during the last few weeks than I have in a long time. But that might all end today.'

'That sounds like the start of a good story,' said Marta. 'Talk to me. Tell me as little or as much as you want.' She held her hands up. 'No judgement from me, I promise.'

343

Skye felt something inside her loosen. *No judgement* was something Marta said at the start of her yoga classes and it never failed to resonate with her. It helped her to be free from the pressure of doing things perfectly. Not just free from the opinion of others but from herself too.

'I appreciate that.' And she hoped Marta meant what she said, because she wasn't proud of what she was doing to Jesse.

'Excuse me,' Jade whispered, sliding their plates on to the table. 'Enjoy.'

They smiled their thanks.

'Take your time,' said Marta, handing her a napkin.

Over a pot of coffee and cheese and caramelised-onion toasties, Skye told her everything. About her weird relationship with her parents, her new bond with Clare and how even though she wasn't sure about having kids herself, she was besotted with Ivy. She told her how she'd escaped the embittered Marriott family home to go first to university and then travelling, ending up in Uganda, and how her parents were divorced within the year after she'd left home.

'I don't know whether I did them a favour or not by leaving,' she said, sipping her coffee.

'Maybe without you there to glue them together, they were like two pieces of a broken mug,' Marta pointed out. 'Are they both happier now?'

Skye wrinkled her nose. 'Dad remarried – naturally. I think he's allergic to being alone. Although Nilla, his third wife, has been staying with her mum in Copenhagen for weeks. My mum seems happier now than she was – still obsessed with what my dad is doing though. She picked fault with me a lot when I was growing up. Wanting me to be as outgoing as she is, which was never going to happen.'

'OK,' Marta said perceptively. 'You've told me about everyone else, tell me about you. Why do you think your happiness is about to end? And please let it not be because of our breakfast date.'

'Of course it's not that.' Skye felt the weight of tears forming in her eyes and looked straight at her. 'I've made a bit of a mess of everything. My past has caught up with me and taken me by surprise. I've got to do something terrible today and I feel really guilty.'

Marta slid her hand across the table. Slowly, Skye reached hers to meet it until their fingertips were touching.

'This past, is it a person?' Marta asked and Skye nodded.

'Jesse. He arrived unannounced yesterday. We've been together for three years.'

'He?' Marta raised an eyebrow.

She nodded. 'He's my boss. He was the first friend I made in Africa.'

'But he turned into a friend with benefits?'

Skye felt her face flush. 'Exactly. But I was happier without the benefits.'

'I understand,' Marta said softly. 'Some relationships work better as friendships, while others are destined to be much more.'

Skye lifted her eyes to meet Marta's as butterflies danced in her stomach. Neither of them spoke for a moment until Marta broke the spell by pouring them both more coffee.

'So, tell me about you and Jesse.' Marta took Skye's hand in hers and held it lightly.

'I've always had a niggling feeling that Jesse wasn't my happy ever after, but I was too cowardly to do anything about it. Breaking up with him would have meant breaking up with my life in Uganda and I couldn't bring myself to do it, I had so much to lose.'

'But something happened to change that?'

Skye nodded. 'He proposed. He wanted – *wants* – to spend the rest of his life with me and suddenly I saw my freedom vanish in a puff of smoke. Looking at him down on one knee holding out a ring forced me to face the truth. I wasn't sure I wanted a future with him. Even then, I couldn't come out and say it. That's why I came back to the UK.'

'You ran away?' Marta frowned.

'No, no, he accepted my decision to go,' she clarified. 'I thought that time away from him would help solve my dilemma. Deep down, I thought I'd go back to him. The love I have for him might not be the electric kind you see on TV, but I thought it would be enough to sustain a life together. But I know now that it isn't enough. It isn't fair on him, and we both deserve a love that sweeps us off our feet.'

'And now he's here and wanting a decision from you?' Marta withdrew her hand to cut a piece off her toastie.

Skye nodded. 'He was so sure that I'd change my mind and come back with him. He's got our future all mapped out. More travel, develop the Hope Foundation in other areas . . . and I'd have liked to do that if we were just friends.'

'But no more benefits.'

'No,' Skye agreed. 'I don't feel that way about him and I can't pretend I do anymore. But I do love him, and I feel like the worst person alive to have to tell him.'

'He loves you and this is going to be hard for him, but he needs to hear the truth. You're a good person, Skye, you have a good heart, you can do this.'

'You make it sound so easy,' she sighed.

Marta shook her head. 'It's not, but we've all been in difficult relationships. Once it's over, you'll feel like you can breathe again.'

Skye nodded and felt a tear run down her face.

Marta touched her cheek, wiping away the teardrops. 'Don't cry, it'll work out.'

Skye looked into Marta's eyes, so kind and full of warmth. She'd thought earlier that her feelings for Marta were confusing, but they weren't at all. The spark that had been missing between her and Jesse was here, now, arcing between the two of them.

Skye turned her face into Marta's palm and kissed it. 'Thank you.'

Marta leaned across the table and grazed Skye's lips softly with hers. 'You're welcome.'

There was a sharp knock on the glass, making them both jump. Skye sprang back from Marta and looked through the window. Her face burned as she saw Jesse staring at her, his eyes unblinking. He looked devastated.

'Jesse!' Skye stumbled to her feet, her chair making an angry screech across the floor. 'Shit-shit-shit. I'm sorry, I have to go. The bill—'

'Hey, it's fine, you go, don't worry.' Marta grabbed her hand, forcing her to make eye contact. 'Good luck. Text me when you can.'

'Thanks. I will.' Skye nodded, scooped her bag from the floor and flew out of the café.

Jesse was waiting for her outside, his face taut with shock. 'What the hell, Skye? I don't even know what to say to you right now.'

He shoved his hands into the pockets of his shorts and walked away towards the harbour, head hanging low.

'Wait,' Skye cried, following him. 'Let me explain.'

'I just saw you kissing a woman.' He held his arms out in defeat. 'I don't think that needs much explanation.'

'Jesse.' Skye put her hands on his arms – strong, tanned arms which had held her a thousand times. 'I feel terrible about this, please can we talk?'

'*You* feel terrible?' He gave a humourless laugh. 'What about me? I came back hoping my girlfriend had decided to marry me. But instead I found she's got a girlfriend of her own.'

'It's not like that,' she said, dry-mouthed and conscious of the interest of passers-by.

'Is this the real reason why you came back? To be with her?' His eyes were stony and Skye hated herself for what she was doing to him. 'Nothing to do with me – *with us* – all along?'

She shook her head. 'No. I promise. This – what you just saw – this is brand new to me. I haven't lied to you, I wouldn't. I love you too much for that.'

'You love me, huh?' he said flatly. 'That's strange, because I arrived to find no one knows about us, you've avoided touching me, even talking to me, and then this morning, rather than cancel your plans, you tried to leave the house before I woke up. Forgive me if I find it hard to believe that's love.'

Skye's whole body flamed with shame. 'I'm so sorry.'

They were standing in the middle of the street and a car was heading their way. She looped her arm through his and tugged him to the pavement.

'I came back because being with you all the time made it hard for me to think straight. I loved working with you. I loved being at the Hope Foundation; my life was good. That all changed when you asked me to be your wife.'

His shoulders slumped. 'It changed for me too. I thought our life was going to be even better.'

'You'd had time to think about it. The proposal came totally out of the blue for me. I had to press pause before giving you my answer, because before I committed my whole life to you, I needed to know I was doing the right thing – for both of us.'

Jesse hung his head. 'I suppose I knew you didn't want to marry me as soon as I held out that ring. I could see the panic in your eyes, like you wanted to run. I'm sorry I pushed you this far. But I thought love would be enough.'

Skye took a step closer to him, he leaned down and touched his forehead to hers. 'You're a lovely guy, Jesse. I've had the most amazing time with you, you've taught me how to love, how to be a family, even when none of us actually were. You deserve someone far better than me, and I have absolutely no doubt you'll find her.'

'I thought I had' He shut his eyes and groaned. 'I feel like such a fool.'

'No, I'm the fool,' she insisted. 'I've let you down and I can't forgive myself for that. But honesty is important too. I love you as a friend and I always will.'

'And what about her?' He nodded back towards the café. 'You've never looked at me like you looked at her.'

It was true, Skye realised, and it was all down to the elusive spark. But Jesse was hurting enough, she didn't want to make it worse by admitting it. Skye thought about Marta, about what she'd be doing right now and felt guilty about her too; dashing out and leaving her like that.

'I wasn't expecting to feel that way about a woman,' she murmured, forcing herself to look him in the eye. 'I don't know if this is the new me or whether it's temporary, but right now, it feels . . . it feels like something I want to explore.'

Jesse gave her a half-smile and pulled her into a hug. 'Whatever life holds for you next, I hope you'll be happy. Maybe we can stay in touch, as friends?'

'Friends,' she said, returning his hug. 'I'd like that.'

But no more benefits.

Chapter Thirty-Three

Liz

'Everything's ready.' Liz ushered Mike from the hall into the kitchen. 'And Skye's laid the table outside for nine places, like you asked.'

'It all looks great.' He nodded appreciatively, his eyes roaming across the row of lobsters prepped on the kitchen island.

'Hi, Dad.' Clare walked towards him, holding her broken arm out in front of her like a shield. 'Look at the state of me. Ivy, come and say hello to Grandad!'

Ivy, who'd had to have her dress peeled off after a mushy avocado accident, dutifully staggered a few paces towards him.

Mike kissed Clare's cheek. 'You and Ivy will make yourselves scarce, I hope?'

He patted Ivy's head, which was enough to make her lose her balance and drop back onto her nappy-cushioned bottom. For a second, she looked as if she was going to cry, but Liz quickly scooped her up and shook her head in despair at Mike.

'I wasn't planning on it, no,' Clare replied, reaching for Ivy's hand and kissing it.

'Come on, Clare. This is a business meeting.' Mike's tone was exasperated. 'I can't have an injured woman and a baby dressed in nothing but a nappy at a business meeting.'

'An injured woman?' Clare looked at him in disbelief. 'Is that all I am?'

Liz tutted. 'Mike, you're in my home and this isn't a woman and a baby, this is your daughter and granddaughter. Have some manners.'

Mike rubbed a hand through his silver hair and smiled. 'I apologise. I'm tense, I want this to go well. There's a lot of money in it for me.'

Good, thought Liz, maybe that would keep the wolf from the door, and he'd be able to give her more time, or, even better, let her off some of the debt. She'd had another two cancellations this morning, which was odd and, more importantly, disastrous for her bottom line.

'I need to be seen as agile and energetic, a man on board with forward thinking and new ideas. Being a grandad isn't cool,' he explained matter-of-factly. 'I need to look cool.'

'For heaven's sake, Mike.' Liz felt anger flare in her chest.

'I tell you what isn't cool.' Unsurprisingly, Clare looked hurt. 'A man in his sixties who's too vain to admit he is a grandfather, who refuses to have anything to do with his granddaughter. Now, *that* isn't cool.'

'Dad.' Skye shook her head sadly. 'That was a terrible thing to say.'

Liz was quite worried about Skye, she looked washed out. Things had been so busy this morning that they hadn't had long to chat. No sooner had she and Jesse arrived back at the house than it had been full steam ahead to get on with this lunch. But Skye had told them that their relationship was officially over. Jesse would be heading back to Africa as soon as he could arrange a return flight.

'Women,' Mike growled, storming out to the patio.

'He is so annoying,' said Clare through gritted teeth.

'He is,' agreed Liz, 'but for the next three hours he's paying the bills, so let's at least try to be nice.'

By the time the rest of his party had arrived and were seated outside, Ivy was upstairs taking her nap. However, Clare was adamant that she wasn't going to be banished up to her room and Liz didn't blame her. Jesse had made a brief appearance to get some water and Mike had pounced on him, wanting to be introduced. Skye had been flustered and ended up introducing Jesse as her boyfriend and Mike had pumped his hand vigorously.

Liz had had the dubious pleasure of meeting Harriet, Mike's assistant, who'd inspected the food, given her precise instructions of when staff were allowed out onto the patio, made them all sign a form to promise that they wouldn't talk about today's meeting to anyone and generally managed to make herself very unpopular. If Liz never set eyes on that abrasive young woman again, she'd be happy.

Skye was serving drinks when Liz made her way out onto the patio with an armful of hats, as per Mike's last-minute request. She wouldn't have recommended eating outside today; the sun was beating down and even though she was in her coolest sundress, sweat was trickling down her back and his guests were squinting in the light, their forearms and faces getting pinker by the second.

She set the assortment of headwear down on the table, trying not to catch Skye's eye. 'Sorry, everyone, this is the best I can do.'

She'd found several saucer-like affairs she'd worn to weddings, a bucket hat, a straw boater and a floppy hat she'd bought after being influenced by Kate Middleton, and a matching pair of baseball caps she and Jen had bought at a Magic Mike concert. Skye scuttled away, barely able to contain her mirth as the group – five men and four women – muttered their thanks, rooted through the pile and each pulled on a hat. Mike managed to grab one of the Magic Mike ones and looked very pleased with himself.

Harriet shoved her sunglasses up into her hair, examined the bucket hat and curled her lip. 'Seriously?'

'You don't want your guests to get sunstroke, do you,' Liz replied sweetly.

'I think it's fun.' One of the women laughed beneath a wide-brimmed hat Liz had bought for Mike's wedding to Frankie. 'Does anyone have any sunscreen?'

The question wasn't directed at Liz, so she didn't answer.

Mike's nostrils flared and she could tell he was getting impatient for the meeting to start.

'Harriet?' he asked. 'Let's get everyone looked after and then we can get down to business. Finally.'

Harriet pursed her lips and produced a small tube of what looked like very expensive sunscreen from her bag and handed it reluctantly to the other woman, who smeared it down both of her bare arms, then passed it around to the others.

Skye returned with plates of appetisers and set them in the centre of the table. 'Shall I throw this away?' she asked, holding up the empty tube.

'Yes please,' said Harriet through gritted teeth, adding to Mike in a low voice, 'I'm putting that on my expenses.'

'Let's start with the introductions.' Mike cleared his throat. 'Tessa, would you like to kick off.'

'Sure.' A woman wearing a green wedding hat sat forward. The peacock feather in her hat began bobbing and brushing the tip of her nose. 'Tessa Field, head of investments for . . .'

She looked so ridiculous that Liz had to dash back inside before she gave herself away.

'Look at them all in those hats,' Clare sniggered. She was tucked away inside keeping an eye on them all. 'How can they take each other seriously dressed like that?'

'Serves them right. Getting us to sign non-disclosure agreements, for heaven's sake. I've never done that in my life,' said Liz with a chuckle, joining her. She didn't know whether to be insulted or impressed that Mike had chosen her house to host such a sensitive meeting. 'As if we're going to tell anyone.'

'Perhaps it's a top-secret project,' Skye suggested. She was on her way out, carrying two heavy water jugs.

'Or illegal,' Clare waggled her eyebrows suggestively.

'It better not be,' Liz huffed. 'If he's chosen to hold a clandestine meeting in my house for anything dodgy, he won't be getting any of his twenty grand back and that's a fact.'

Skye delivered the water and came back inside. She looked tired, Liz thought.

'I'm sorry I can't manage without you, love.' Liz rubbed Skye's arm. 'It's not easy on you or Jesse, this.'

'I don't mind,' Skye smiled faintly. 'It's better to have a distraction.'

'What's Jesse doing now?' Clare asked. 'I haven't seen him for a while.'

'He's upstairs packing. I don't think he wants to come down. Especially with Dad being here. I should have said he was my boss, not my boyfriend, but I panicked. Once the guests have gone, we're going to go out for one last drink for old times' sake, then he's leaving.'

Harriet looked round and caught all three of them staring. She leapt to her feet and stomped inside.

'Can I just remind, everyone,' she said, haughtily, 'that this is a very important meeting. We're talking high stakes

355

and an extremely prestigious scheme. We need to know that we can count on your professionalism, and we do not need an audience.'

'What is the meeting about?' Clare asked. 'I'm his daughter, I'm sure he won't mind me knowing.'

'Or me, his oldest friend,' Liz added, enjoying the look of discomfort on Harriet's face.

Harriet gave them a Cheshire Cat smile. 'I'm sure if Mike wants you to know, he'll tell you himself. And so lovely that he keeps in touch with his *old* friends,' she said to Liz. 'It's important to our company that we support small businesses like yours and make sure we put back into the community.'

Our company, Liz noted. Since when? She wasn't too keen on being thought of as some sort of charity case either. 'That's very kind of you,' she replied, biting back her true thoughts on the matter.

'I know.' Harriet nodded. 'We'll have the starters now, please.'

'Of course, madam,' said Liz, bobbing down to curtsey.

Harriet didn't seem to pick up on the sarcasm; she inclined her head and went back to join the meeting.

Skye whistled. 'That is some attitude.'

As Harriet sat down, she squeezed Mike's arm. He in turn stood up, topped up some glasses and turned to come inside.

'Did you see that?' Liz's eyes widened. 'If she's his assistant, then I'm Mary Poppins.'

'You are kidding me,' Clare murmured.

'Unbelievable. I knew she was lying when I caught her coming out of the bathroom at Dad's.' Skye strode off to fetch the starters.

'Excuse me, ladies, little boys' room,' Mike announced, striding through the room and out to the cloakroom.

'Harriet seems . . . *ambitious*,' said Liz when he reappeared.

Mike nodded; his eyes were focused on his assistant. 'She's great, isn't she?'

'Hmm,' Liz said. 'And she's young and attractive. How fortuitous.'

Mike pulled a wounded face. 'Her talents got her the job and nothing else.'

'How old is she, Dad?' Skye piped up.

'Twenty-five. Almost. It's her birthday in a couple of weeks.' There was a smug tone to his voice, which made Liz want to shake him.

'What a dedicated employer you are, memorising her birthday,' Clare said, over-brightly. She slurped loudly from her water bottle. 'Good for you, Dad. Right, I'll be upstairs if anyone wants me, shielding my injured arm from our delicate guests.'

'You lot are scary when you're all together.' Mike blinked nervously and ran a finger around his collar. 'I'd better get back out there.'

Liz shook her head; he didn't change.

With the starters out of the way, Skye cleared the table while Liz plated up the main course.

Mike was in full flow as she and Skye carried out plates of lobster and bowls of Jersey Royal potatoes tossed in herb butter. There were grilled asparagus spears for Harriet. Liz had had second thoughts about the deep-fried tofu balls because of the last-minute cooking requirements. She was glad she hadn't gone to too much effort now that she'd met Harriet.

'Family is very important,' Mike was saying to his guests. 'Both to us as individuals and to the Good Vibrations company. I'm a family man myself, as you know. Skye is my youngest daughter.'

'Hi.' Skye nearly dropped the tray; Liz knew she hated to be the centre of attention like this.

'Skye has been working in Uganda with her boyfriend, helping families who haven't had the same advantages she had,' Mike said proudly. 'Just back for the summer. And I'm sure she'll be starting a family of her own soon.'

Oh no. Poor Skye, talk about bad timing.

Liz coughed in an attempt to attract Mike's attention, but he simply looked at his daughter and nodded encouragingly. 'Isn't that right, darling?'

Skye swallowed as everyone looked at her, waiting for her to respond.

'Skye?' Mike gave an awkward laugh and Skye seemed to shake herself.

'Actually, it's not right. I've left Uganda and my job,' Skye said. 'And I've left my boyfriend too.'

'What?' Mike's eyes bulged in surprise. 'Ah well, perhaps that's something we can talk about later.'

'No, it's fine. Seeing as you asked, I'm not sure about starting a family,' Skye said, ignoring him. 'Because it's early days with my new relationship and I'm not sure how she feels about kids.'

Liz felt a squeeze of panic; Skye was rigid with tension and after the stress of the last twenty-four hours, she wouldn't be surprised if she let rip at her father.

'Shall we leave our guests to eat their lunch,' Liz suggested quietly, as people around the table began to shift awkwardly in their seats.

'How *she* feels?' Mike stuttered. 'Don't you mean—'

'I meant what I said,' Skye replied. 'Now, a question for you, Dad. How old am I?'

Mike looked at Liz for help. 'Er . . .'

Liz shook her head in dismay; he was on his own in this.

'And Clare? When's Ivy's birthday? Hmm? Thought as much.' Skye set a plate in front of him with a thump.

He brushed off the moment with a laugh. 'A bit of memory lapse, chaps. Must up my cod liver oil tablets.' But the colour had drained from his face, and he was suddenly very intent on attacking his lobster with the crackers.

'Ew.' Harriet winced, an asparagus spear hovering by her lips as she watched him ripping into the lobster.

A man in a straw boater leaned forward. 'Gay. How interesting. Can I ask you where you go to buy *intimate* items?'

'I beg your pardon!' exclaimed Liz. She looked at Mike for him to intervene, but he was too busy slurping the juice out of a lobster claw. 'You don't need to answer that, Skye.'

Skye blinked at him uncertainly. 'Like underwear?'

'Well, underwear and more intimate items for the bedroom.'

Liz inhaled sharply as Skye picked up a water glass and threw the contents over him. 'Pervert.'

Harriet gasped and Mike made a gargling noise as if someone had winded him.

Liz ushered Skye back inside as everyone else started talking at once.

'I shouldn't have done that.' Skye was shaking.

'He'll dry,' said Liz.

Mike was on his feet, saying something to pacify the group. Someone laughed and the others joined in. Whatever he'd said seemed to have worked.

'I can't believe I just said that out loud,' Skye groaned, covering her face with her hands. 'About having a new relationship.'

'Is it true?' Liz asked, still with her arm tightly around her god-daughter.

She nodded miserably. 'And bang goes my chance of ever making my dad proud.'

'Forget your dad for a minute,' Liz chided, kissing her cheek. 'You've just done an exceptionally brave thing and I'm proud of you.'

'Really?' She looked sceptical.

Liz nodded. 'Would this be Marta you're talking about?'

Skye smiled bashfully. 'I think I've known I had feelings for her beyond friendship since I met her. But today . . . today confirmed it.'

'And she feels the same?'

'She didn't come out and say it, but I think so. But then Jesse turned up and caught me with her. I had to run off in the middle of our breakfast. Once Jesse has gone, I'll call her. So we can talk properly.'

'I'm really happy for you.'

Skye heaved a sigh of relief. 'That means a lot to me, thank you.'

'Are you going to tell Frankie?' Liz asked.

'Eventually.' Skye pulled a face. 'But not yet. Knowing her, she'll plaster it on social media, start going to Pride marches and make it all about her and how accepting she is. I need to get used to this myself first.'

Liz smiled to herself; that was exactly what Frankie would do.

'Excuse me, Skye?' The man in the straw boater had come inside but was hanging back awkwardly.

Liz bristled and took a step forward. 'If you've come to make inappropriate remarks to my staff, I'm going to have to ask you to leave.'

He held his hands up in defence. 'My apologies. I assumed you knew where we are from. I'm Iain Banks from *Good Vibrations*. We're seeking investors to allow us to expand into Alaska and Northern Canada.'

'The sex shop!' Liz's hand fluttered to her throat.

'We prefer to use the term adult entertainment,' said Iain. 'And we tend to be a bit broad-minded in our discussion. I'm sorry for any distress caused.'

'No harm done,' said Skye, scratching a mark off her apron, avoiding his eye. 'Apology accepted. But my private life isn't up for discussion.'

Iain nodded. 'Understood.'

As soon as he'd gone, Liz and Skye hooted with laughter.

'Sex shops,' Liz gasped, holding her side. 'So much for Mike being involved with something extremely prestigious. I thought it must be something for the royal family. What a let-down!'

'He needn't have asked us to keep it a secret either,' Skye spluttered. 'My dad in sex shops! I'd rather never even think about it again, let alone tell anyone else.'

'Come on,' said Liz, handing her a tissue to dry her tears of laughter. 'Let's get this over with. Only one more course to go and then we can all relax.'

Ninety minutes later, Mike's guests had gone. Harriet remained outside making notes and tapping at a laptop. Skye and Clare were upstairs with Ivy, who'd woken up from her nap. Liz was cleaning down the kitchen surfaces when Mike came to talk to her.

'This has been such a success, Liz, even with Skye throwing water on the top dog at Good Vibrations.' Mike took hold of her shoulders and planted a kiss on her forehead. 'You've done me proud.'

'I've enjoyed it. Most of it,' she said sternly. 'Why didn't you tell us who your guests were?'

He frowned. 'Didn't Harriet?'

Liz shook her head. 'I think the power went to her head today.'

He looked through the open patio doors to where she was sitting and grinned. 'She's young.'

'Younger than your daughters,' Liz warned. 'Both of whom you upset today, by the way.'

He leaned back against the kitchen worktop and sighed. 'I know. I'll make it up to them.'

'Good,' she said firmly. 'And do it soon. Mend those bridges. Those two young women look to you for approval.'

He looked surprised. 'Do they?'

'Of course they do, idiot, always have. Not that you deserve it.'

'You're probably right.' He looked around to check they were alone. 'There's something I need to tell you.'

'There's something I need to tell you too.'

Liz had come to a decision. She wasn't going to beat herself up about not being able to repay him the money by his deadline. She was doing her best and that was all she could do. And she'd realised something else too; while she'd enjoyed working with Skye and getting to know her better, she definitely didn't want to run the catering business anymore. She'd changed since she and Jen had started it and she was ready to move on.

'Oh.' He tucked his chin in, looking put out. 'You go first then.'

Liz swallowed. 'OK. Business has been very good over the last few weeks.'

'See! I knew you could go it alone.' Mike leaned on the edge of the kitchen worktop and folded his arms.

She shook her head. 'I couldn't have. If it wasn't for Skye and Clare, I wouldn't have been able to take on the work physically or mentally. I'm still grieving for Jen. This was our business; it isn't the same without her. And I'm not going to keep it going.'

He frowned. 'We had a deal, you agreed to repay the twenty grand.'

'I haven't forgotten. I'm some way short of the full amount. But I'll give you what I can.'

'Oh well, it's better than nothing, I suppose,' he grumbled.

She blinked at him in surprise; she'd been expecting more resistance than that.

'Shall I transfer it to your personal account?' she asked, relieved.

'No, don't do that!' He cleared his throat and looked around to check no one was listening. 'To be honest with you, what would really help is if you could pay a bill directly for me. Avoid the paper trail coming back to me.'

Liz narrowed her eyes, smelling a rat. 'I'm confused.'

He checked on Harriet again. 'As I said, it's Harriet's twenty-fifth birthday coming up and she's always wanted to fly business-class to New York.'

'Who hasn't?' said Liz drily.

'So I said I'd treat her. I need the money to pay for the tickets.'

For a long moment, Liz was so stunned that she couldn't speak.

'So . . .' Mike looked warily at her. 'Would that be OK if I use your bank card to pay for the tickets?'

Finally, she spoke, fury making her voice shake. 'You mean to tell me that I've been slaving away all summer rather than enjoying time with Clare and Ivy to pay for flights to New York for a twenty-five-year-old girl?'

'You do owe me the money,' he said indignantly.

She shook her head. 'You are the limit, you really are. And what does Nilla think about this?'

Mike grimaced. 'That's the other thing I need to tell you. Nilla and I are splitting up. She's met someone else, so she won't give two hoots.'

'I'm sorry to hear that.' Although Liz wasn't in the least surprised. Every time her name came up, he'd either squirm or change the subject.

'Don't be. We stopped getting what we wanted from the relationship long ago. It's time for us both to move on.'

'And what *do* you want?'

Mike released a satisfied breath and let his eyes roam to the young woman sitting out on the patio. 'Harriet's sexy and sassy and she makes me feel young. Walking into a room with my hand on her waist does wonders for my ego.'

'You don't need any help with your ego, Mike, you never have.' Liz shook her head in disappointment. 'I've stood by you for years, even when you behaved abominably towards Jen and Clare by swanning off with Frankie, but this . . . do you know, I think we may have come to the end of the line.'

'We both know that's not true,' he laughed, taking a step closer. 'You've always had a thing for me.'

'I have not,' she spluttered, feeling herself getting hot.

'Oh, come on. When I started going out with Jen, you looked like you were about to burst into tears every time I came to pick her up.'

'That's not true.' It was true, but only the first few times; she couldn't believe he'd remembered that.

'You cried at our wedding.' Mike smirked.

Liz's heart squeezed, remembering how glowing Jen had looked, what a beautiful bride she'd made. She couldn't have loved her more if they'd been sisters. 'Everyone cries at weddings. What is your point?'

He stepped closer and took her hands in his.

Liz sucked in a breath. In another time and place, she would have loved this, but now all she could think was that she didn't want him near her. That he wasn't worthy of her, or Jen, or even that young girl who was – as Mike had so eloquently put it – doing wonders for his ego.

'My point is,' Mike continued, smoothly, 'that you have always been there for me. Wives come and go.'

'Mike!' She was appalled. That was a callous thing to say about the women who'd given birth to his children and shared his life, his home. Not to mention the fact that one of those wives had been her dearest friend. 'How dare you?'

He batted her protests away with a casual shrug. 'But remember that day? It was you I needed. I wanted your arms around me. You felt like home, Liz – you feel like home.'

'Which day?' She shook her head. 'The day you married Jen?'

'No, silly.'

Liz thought she heard a noise on the stairs. Her eyes flicked towards the door, but there was no one there.

Mike's eyes were locked in hers. 'I'm talking about the day of Clare's graduation.'

'Which clashed with Skye's birthday treat in London,' she sniffed. 'You lied to both of your daughters, and you made them both feel they weren't important to you. That's unforgiveable.'

'And that's not the only thing that's unforgiveable here, is it?' came a sharp voice from the doorway. 'Look at the two of you. It's disgusting.'

Liz and Mike whirled round as one to see Clare in the doorway. Standing next to her was Skye. Liz felt faint with dread and guilt, and she stepped forwards until her hands could grip the edge of the sink.

Mike shook his head, staring down at the floor, hands on his hips. 'Oh God.'

'I don't think he is going to be much help with this one, Dad,' said Clare.

Liz looked at the girls, sisters united in their contempt for her and Mike.

Clare's eyes were narrowed, chin held at a defiant angle, but despite the bravado, Liz knew just how much she'd be hurting inside. Skye clung to her sister, tears threatening to fall. In that second, she'd never hated herself more. Whatever happened next, her priority was them, not their father, not this time.

Chapter Thirty-Four

Clare

'Girls!' Liz gasped. 'How long have you been standing there?'

'Too long,' said Skye, in a wobbly voice.

'So, can I get this straight?' Clare's lungs felt so tight she could scarcely breathe; she couldn't drag her eyes away from Liz. Her beloved Liz. How could this be happening? She'd loved Liz all her life. In tough times, it had been Liz she'd turned to. She'd always been there for her, unconditionally on her side, no matter what. Clare hadn't felt this devastated since her mum died. 'The man you told Patrick about, the man you've been hung up on for more than forty years, is my dad?'

Liz didn't answer. Not that she needed to, the rabbit-caught-in-headlights expression she was wearing did it for her.

Mike frowned. 'We were having a private conversation. At your age, I shouldn't have to either answer to you or remind you to respect someone's privacy.'

'Respect?' Skye virtually spat at him. 'That's rich.'

'Did Mum know?' Clare demanded. 'About the two of you. On her wedding day?'

Despite Clare's turmoil, the presence of her sister comforted her. Skye was a far stronger character than Clare had given her credit for. Upstairs just now, while she'd been changing Ivy's nappy, she'd started humming a song by Katy Perry. It had taken Clare a while to catch on; in the end, Skye had had to sing loudly in her face that she'd kissed a girl and she'd liked it. Then the whole story had come out. They'd hugged and laughed quietly so as not to upset Jesse. The cloud which had been hanging over her sister had gone. Only now, coming downstairs into this shitshow, the cloud was back and over both of them.

'And the big lie,' Skye said in a low voice, folding her arms. 'The double-booked graduation-slash-birthday weekend. I'm really looking forward to hearing the truth behind that.'

Liz looked at Mike, waiting for him to speak, but he had shielded his eyes with his hand under the pretence of rubbing his forehead.

'Will one of you do the decent thing and own this mess, please?' Clare said, exasperated at their lack of action.

'There's nothing to tell.' Liz looked at Mike, panic written all over her face. 'Tell them.'

'So there is something to tell?' Clare looked from Liz to Mike and back again. 'Or nothing?'

'Make your mind up,' Skye added.

Mike beckoned Clare and her sister into the kitchen. 'Can we all sit?'

Clare exchanged looks with Skye. They'd have to be quick. They'd left Jesse reading books to Ivy in the upstairs lounge; neither of them looked particularly comfortable with the situation.

'I can't believe this is happening,' Clare murmured to Skye as they took a seat at the dining table.

Harriet chose that moment to enter the room too. She had her bag on her shoulder, a portfolio case clutched in her folded arms.

'Mike?' She looked at them all gathered around the table and gave him a puzzled frown. 'Are you ready?'

He sucked in a breath. 'You carry on. I'll see you at home.'

'Home?' Skye and Clare exclaimed in unison.

'Office,' Mike stuttered, his neck flushing bright red. 'I mean at the office.'

Harriet nodded. 'Understood. Goodbye, everyone, and thanks for catering for us. It wasn't quite restaurant standard, but our clients seemed to enjoy it.'

Clare gritted her teeth; Harriet was the most patronising, annoying woman she'd ever met. And she'd met a lot of annoying people in her time. Parents at school mostly.

'You've moved your assistant in to the house?' She looked at her father, gobsmacked, as Harriet let herself out.

'Does Nilla know?' Skye asked. She gasped. 'Is that why you wanted me out of the house this summer? So you could conduct your affair in secret?'

'Enough!' Mike brought the palms of his hands down on the table. 'Stop firing accusations at me for one second and allow me to answer them.'

Clare's head swivelled away from him to focus on Liz. 'I stopped expecting anything but disappointment from him long ago, but you . . . I just can't believe you'd do this behind our backs.'

Her anger was still burning like acid in her stomach, but it was the sadness that felt overwhelming.

Liz swallowed. 'Clare, Skye, my darling girls. I know your minds are racing ahead filling in blanks and visualising things they don't want to see. There are answers to everything, I promise.'

Beside Clare, she felt Skye shudder.

Liz stretched across the table to take their hands, but both snatched them out of reach. 'I'm going to start with one thing. I'm begging you, trust me.'

Clare's stomach twisted. 'I don't think I can hear this.'

Skye touched her arm. 'I want to trust Liz.'

Clare looked at her younger sister. Skye had such a good heart, maybe she should follow her lead on this one. 'Fine.'

'I promise you, I have never gone behind your mum's back, Clare, or yours, Skye,' said Liz in a small voice.

'That's not what we just heard,' Clare retorted.

'I fancied Mike long before he met Jen. And, to my eternal shame, I never really got over it. I was heartbroken when they got together. Jen was closer to me than a sister could ever have been and deep down I knew that it wasn't going to work, I knew he didn't deserve her. But I still carried a torch for him myself. The sensible thing to do would have been to move away completely, get him out of my system.'

The look of sheer desperation on Liz's face tore Clare's heart into pieces. She wanted to say that she was glad that Liz had hung around and played such a special role in her life. But she couldn't, not yet. She needed to hear the full story, reassure herself that Liz hadn't been the reason her parents' marriage had failed.

'But instead I hung around on the sidelines,' Liz said, looking down at her hands. 'Always keeping an eye on Jen, but also staying a bit in love, always comparing Mike to other men. None of my relationships worked out, not even my marriage.'

'Good grief!' Mike exclaimed. 'I didn't realise this was how you felt. I thought it was just a silly crush.'

'It was a silly crush,' she agreed. She looked at her god-daughters. 'Jen has always been more important to me than your father. I promise you, other than friendly pecks on the cheek, we've only had one proper kiss. And that was before he met Jen.'

'I don't remember that.' He turned the corners of his mouth down and shook his head, nonplussed.

'When we got our grades back from that group project in final year? You picked me up, spun me round and then we kissed.'

'If you say so,' he said, bemused. 'All I remember is having to carry the group so that we got decent marks.'

'Oh for heaven's sake.' Liz folded her arms, lips pinched.

'But what about Mum and Dad's wedding?' Clare asked.

This time, Mike did look sheepish. 'I got cold feet.'

'I found him in the loo, crying like a baby,' Liz supplied. 'I threatened to come after him with my meat tenderiser and mash up his manhood.'

'Now that I do remember. I loved Jen very much.' Mike looked at Clare. 'I didn't think I was good enough for her.'

'You weren't.' She stared back at her father mutinously. 'Watching what you put Mum through nearly broke her, and me.'

'I'm not proud of the way the marriage ended,' he said, meeting her eye. 'But I don't regret you, or you, Skye, for a single moment.'

'My birthday weekend in London,' Skye said quietly. 'I'd been looking forward to that for weeks. You and Mum were arguing so much at the time, I hoped that doing something fun together would bring us closer as a family. You even came up to London with us. And then the next minute, you vanished in a puff of smoke.'

'You lied to all of us,' Clare agreed. 'Except Liz apparently.'

Liz clasped her hands in front of her and stayed silent.

Mike twisted the gold ring on the little finger of his right hand. Clare had a vivid memory of sitting on his lap twisting that ring while he was watching something boring on TV. It had belonged to her grandfather.

'My dad, your Grandad Tom, died when you were small, Clare. Skye, you never knew him at all. He was only fifty-eight. His dad, your great-grandfather, died even younger, he didn't reach fifty. I come from a line of men who die young. For the last ten years, I've felt like I'm living on borrowed time, expecting to get ill, panicking whenever I get heartburn in case it's really a heart attack.'

A spark of comprehension lit up inside Clare; she'd known this about her grandfather and great-grandfather but had never given it much thought.

'The month before that weekend, I found a lump,' said Mike quietly. 'In my testicle. And I freaked out. Thought this is it. My time was up. Just like Dad and Grandad, I'd never make it to old age.'

'I didn't know that, did you?' Clare looked at Skye, who shook her head.

'No one knew,' said Mike. 'I'd fast-forwarded my brain to the worst-case scenario, and I didn't want anyone to see how scared I was. I paid to go to a private hospital in London for tests. When the results came back, I couldn't even bring myself to open the envelope.'

'He called me, and I opened it with him,' said Liz.

Skye's eyes were still shiny with unshed tears. 'Not Mum. That's so sad.'

'Was it cancer?' Clare's heart was in her mouth. As much as she was angry with him now, she didn't want to lose him. She wanted honesty from him, that was all.

He nodded. 'It had been caught early, but they wanted to perform surgery as soon as possible.'

372

'I did offer the use of my meat tenderiser again,' Liz said, risking a smile.

Mike smirked at her and, for a second, Clare saw them both as old mates from uni who'd grown up with each other, been there for the good, the bad and the downright ugly.

'The surgery was the weekend of my birthday and Clare's graduation,' Skye realised.

'Your mum had already got tickets to a show, and you were so excited,' he said. 'I knew if I warned Frankie that I couldn't go before the day, she would cancel and rearrange. I didn't want to do that to you. I knew the two of you would still have fun without me.' He turned to Clare. 'There was so much going on at the time that I did get the date of your graduation wrong. It was in my diary for the following week. It wasn't until Jen called me the night before to arrange lunch for the three of us in Bath before the ceremony that the penny dropped. I cocked up, love, and I'm sorry.'

'Mike needed someone to be with him after surgery because of the anaesthetic,' said Liz. 'He asked me to go with him, so I did.'

'I'm glad he had you to turn to,' said Clare grudgingly. 'Although I'm still annoyed by the secrecy and lies.'

'And I'm still annoyed about Harriet,' said Skye, sitting back in her chair. 'Bloody hell, Dad, she's young enough to be your granddaughter.'

'Which is ridiculous, given the way you behave to your *actual* granddaughter,' Clare added.

'I feel like I'm being attacked by my own children.' Mike squirmed and looked pleadingly at Liz.

'Don't look at me for protection,' she huffed. 'You're a serial adulterer with an embarrassing habit of trying to make yourself look and sound younger than you are.'

'Thanks a bunch.'

'What do you expect,' Liz said indignantly. 'You've just informed me that all our hard-earned money this summer was going towards flights to New York for Harriet's birthday.'

Skye gasped. 'That's outrageous. That's where the twenty thousand is going – on flights?'

'You're kidding,' Clare muttered. 'You pressurised your oldest friend to repay a debt for that?'

Mike scratched his chin. 'It was a loan which had become due, that was all. And anyway, it worked out well for everyone. Liz got her mojo for work back. Skye got a job for the summer and a new lesbian girlfriend by the sound of it.'

'Dad,' Clare warned. 'Not appropriate.'

He raised his hands in apology. 'And you two girls have made friends at last. You don't know how happy that makes me.'

'No thanks to you,' said Skye. 'Nothing I did was ever good enough for you. All I wanted was to feel like I mattered to you.'

Clare reached out to her sister and held her hand. 'You are the sweetest, kindest, most thoughtful person I know. And you matter to me.'

Skye looked at her sceptically. 'Is there a punchline?'

Clare smiled. 'Only that you're my favourite sister.'

'Your *only* sister.'

Clare nodded at their dad. 'As far as we know. I wouldn't put it past him to have another few kids stashed away.'

Mike pushed his chair back with a scrape and stood up. 'If you're going to be ridiculous, I shall see myself out.'

'Bye then.' Clare didn't look at him.

'Bye, Dad,' said Skye, following suit.

Mike dithered on the spot, clearly not expecting that response. He balled his hands into fists. 'Of course you matter to me. Both of you. I'm proud of you both. And, Skye, I wouldn't have offered to pay your wages this summer for Liz if I hadn't thought you could do the job.'

'Oh Mike.' Liz lowered her head into her hands. 'That was unnecessary.'

Skye froze. 'Is that true, Liz? Dad's paying my wages, not you?'

'It was the only way I could afford you, love,' she said, her voice no more than a whisper.

'So you didn't offer me the job because Dad recommended me, but because I was free labour?'

'That makes it sound underhand and it wasn't like that,' Liz pleaded with her.

'Does it matter?' Mike said, exasperated. 'You've had a good time, haven't you?'

Skye jumped to her feet. 'Yes! Yes, of course it matters. I thought you really wanted me to work for The Seaside Gourmet Girls, Liz, but instead you were just doing what Dad wanted, like you always have. And, Dad, tell me you weren't just treating me like you do all your problems, by throwing money at it to make it go away?'

'Nilla's left me,' he blurted out. '*She* left *me*. I'm single again, I had a chance to live like a bachelor, recapture my youth and I wanted to take it.'

'With a twenty-four-year-old,' Clare added, not at all surprised to find out that he and Nilla had parted ways. 'You cliché.'

'I'm sixty-three, who knows how long I have left. If I want to flirt with women younger than me and they're amenable, why not?' he said crossly. 'I could hardly do that with Skye in the house.'

'And to think I was worried about you being lonely.' Skye looked down at her feet. 'When the truth was that I was cramping your style.'

'But I *was* lonely,' said Liz. 'And I have loved having you here.'

'I wish you'd been honest with me,' Skye said.

'I was honest with you when I arrived to find you here,' Clare said with a mischievous smile, trying to lighten her sister's mood.

Skye's lips twitched. 'No one would ever accuse you of being dishonest.'

Except Adam, Clare thought wincing, although in a few hours from now she hoped she'd have smoothed over that bump in the road too.

'Are we done?' Mike looked at his watch.

'No,' said Liz firmly. 'You can pay my bill before you go. There's a supplement for vegans, a hire charge for sun hats and a premium for signing non-disclosure agreements.'

He sighed irritably. 'I suppose I asked for that.'

'You and I are done, Dad,' said Skye in a level voice. 'I'm *done* trying to impress you and I'm *done* with your indifference. I'm going to be staying in Salcombe, you'll be happy to learn. Not in a high-flying career, but doing something I love; but don't worry, I'll be staying out of your way.'

'Skye,' Mike began wearily, holding his hands out in a placatory manner. 'I think—'

'I'll stop you there, Dad, because I don't care what you think.'

'Are you OK?' Clare asked Skye as they left the room, leaving Liz to squeeze more money out of Mike.

'"Let go of what no longer serves you,"' she said, throwing a glance over her shoulder. 'Something Marta says in yoga meditation. So I'm letting go of trying to please him. He's going to have to work very hard to get in my good books.'

'Mine too. And I'm going to give up trying to get him interested in Ivy too. He doesn't deserve her.'

As they set off up the stairs to relieve Jesse of babysitting duties, there was a ring at the doorbell.

'I'll get it,' Jesse yelled.

'It'll be a shame to see him go,' Clare teased. 'Easy on the eye, babysitter, butler . . . there's no end to his talents.'

'Shush,' Skye whispered. 'Don't give him any ideas.'

By the time they'd reached the top of stairs leading to the front door, Jesse, with Ivy on his hip, had opened it to reveal Adam waiting on the other side.

'Adam!' Clare exclaimed in panic. 'Hello!'

He was over an hour early. She hadn't done her hair or changed her clothes and the mascara she'd applied this morning was probably all over her face after the last emotional hour. She'd so wanted to impress him, rekindle the feelings they'd had that first night. Fat chance of that now.

'Someone's keen,' Skye murmured in her ear before slipping away into the living room.

Clare pushed herself into the gap next to Jesse, careful as always not to hit her arm against the doorway. She smiled at Adam, but he didn't smile back. Instead, he was struggling to drag his eyes from Jesse and Ivy.

'I know, sorry, I'm early. But I can see it was a mistake.' He took a step back from her.

'It's fine,' Clare said, flustered. 'Come in and wait while I—'

'You're Ivy's father, I take it?' Adam said to Jesse, talking over her. 'None of my business. I'll go. I'll leave. Sorry to have disturbed you.'

377

Adrenaline pulsed through her. This was not how it was supposed to be. She couldn't blurt out the truth, not here, not in front of Jesse. Adam deserved more than that, so much more.

Jesse gave a bark of laughter. 'Very funny, good joke. I love it.'

'What's funny?' Adam shook his head. 'Sorry, I don't get it.'

Jesse grinned and he held Ivy in his outstretched arms, nodding at Adam to take her. 'Here you are, Ivy, go to Daddy.'

Fear burned like acid in Clare's stomach, rising through her, burning her throat, stinging her face. She opened her mouth to speak, but nothing came out. It felt like one of those dreams where you were screaming and screaming in terror but couldn't make a sound.

Ivy babbled delightedly at the sight of Adam and dive-bombed directly at him, forcing him to take her from Jesse.

'There you go.' Jesse clapped him on the shoulder and retreated out of sight.

'Clare?' Adam studied his daughter's face while she grabbed bits of him: his lips, his ear, tufts of hair.

'I'm so sorry.' It felt as if the blood had drained from her body. One tiny gust of wind and she'd collapse.

'I'm her dad?' Adam spoke the words slowly, almost under his breath. 'He said *I'm* her dad?'

She nodded. Her heart was thrashing against her ribs; this was a disaster. 'It's true.'

He stared at her, uncomprehendingly. 'Ivy is mine? I'm a father? And all this time you let me believe it was someone else?'

'I was going to tell you.' She swallowed. 'Tonight in fact. That's why Skye is babysitting, so we can talk properly.'

'I can't take this in. I tried to ask you about him when we were at the beach, I gave you loads of opportunities to tell me.' He shook his head, the look of confusion on his face made her feel nauseous. 'And yet you said nothing.'

'I know, I know.' She licked her dry lips. 'I wanted to, but I needed to know what sort of a person I would be letting into her life. I thought we should all get to know each other first.'

Adam gave a huff of disgust. 'So you could just spring it on me like a big surprise. Is this some sort of weird power game to you?'

'No!' she cried. 'Not at all.'

He held Ivy close, inhaling her baby smell as if imprinting it into his memory. 'It feels like it to me. And I'm not here to be played, Clare. This was a shitty thing to do. Really shitty.'

He brushed his lips to Ivy's cheek and handed her back to Clare, waiting until she'd got a grip around the little girl's body with her good arm. And then he turned to go.

'Is that it?' Clare said, feeling the tears running down her face. 'You're walking away from us?'

He whirled round and Clare was shocked to see that his eyes were moist too. 'Do not put this on me. This is your doing, Clare, yours.'

Clare watched him walk away until he'd disappeared from view, sobbing silently so as not to alarm her daughter. She couldn't very well argue with that, could she. Because it was true. It was her doing. All of it.

Chapter Thirty-Five

Liz

The house was quiet. Liz was alone. Jesse had left and the girls had gone out with Ivy for a walk. It had been weeks since Clemency House had had just her in it.

She flopped down on her bed, relishing the softness of her mattress, exhausted from the tensions of the day. What was that line from *A Midsummer's Night's Dream*? Something about what a tangled web we weave, when something-something to deceive? Whatever the words were, she was in agreement with Shakespeare. Secrets, lies, disappointments, discoveries. Who knew so much could happen during one executive business lunch? At least the lobster was a triumph.

She could swing for Mike, she really could. She finally saw him for what he really was, a selfish, self-centred lothario who'd put his own vanity before love for his children and grandchild. And to think she'd wasted all those years lusting after him. What a tosser. Harriet was welcome to him.

And the money he'd asked her to pay back. Even that had been part of a bigger deception. He hadn't wanted a paper trail for the New York tickets, otherwise the expense would have shown up in the financial statement he'd no doubt have to produce for the divorce proceedings. She was annoyed with him about many things, but in the end, him requesting the repayment of the loan had worked in her favour. Skye, Clare and Ivy being here had filled the house with happiness again.

Right now, she couldn't imagine Mike ever having that sort of relationship with his two girls.

She'd never had sisters, but she understood what sisterhood meant. She'd stood by and watched as Mike had loved and left first Jen, then Frankie and now Nilla. She'd picked up the fragments of Jen's broken heart, gathered Clare into her arms and done her utmost to heal them.

'I always loved you more, Jen,' she said aloud. 'He was right on your wedding day when he said he wasn't good enough for you. You deserved better than him. I still miss you so much. I wish . . . I wish . . .'

Wishing Jen was still here wasn't going to help; the words choked her throat and tears began to leak from her eyes. Grief enveloped her, tightening its grip around her chest as it had done time and again since Jen had died. She felt the return of the urge to drink which she'd been fighting so hard against for the last few weeks. Marta had said that *her* driver was to escape from comparing herself to others. And this was Liz's: her love for Jen. When Jen had lost her life in that car crash, a void had opened up in Liz's and she'd used alcohol to fill it. The world accepted grief for family members, for spouses, but nobody had recognised the depths of Liz's grief for Jen. She might have been 'just a friend', but to Liz she was the most important person in her world.

She was reaching for a tissue to dry her eyes when her phone rang.

She glanced at the caller ID: it was Viv. She contemplated ignoring the call, but remembered the bookings that had been cancelled today and wondered if she knew anything about it.

'What did you expect?' Viv snapped when Liz asked her.

'I don't know what you mean?' she replied, stunned.

Viv gave a steely laugh. 'Pinching Patrick Delmarge from me like that. So underhand. And after all I've done for you.'

Liz sat bolt upright. 'You're the one behind the cancellations?'

'I might have dropped a few of them a note, expressing your sorrow but that you'd got in a muddle and double-booked them.'

'But I'd never do that,' Liz exclaimed. 'And as for taking Patrick from you, that's not true!'

'I could have ruined your business, Liz,' Viv said in a tone which implied that Liz should be grateful that she hadn't. 'I still could. Getting pissed out of your skull at a catering event? I can't imagine many people would want you sniffing around their wine racks if that got out.'

Liz felt sick. 'Viv, you wouldn't! It was a one-off and the event wasn't even for one of your clients.'

'I can't believe you'd go after Patrick after I told you that he was a catch. So much for the sisterhood. You've lost me an attractive man and the possibility of a new property on my books.'

Liz's hackles rose; from what Patrick had told her, Viv had been responsible for both of those losses herself.

'After Jen died,' Viv continued, 'I covered for you, rang round all of my clients who'd got bookings with you to explain what had happened. You owed me, Liz, and how did you repay me?'

'Look, Viv, I'm sorry, I really am. I hadn't realised that you were so keen on him. Noah gave me the impression that you were seeing people casually.'

Viv was quiet for a moment, obviously not sure how to respond to that one.

Liz carried on while she had the chance. 'I haven't even been on a date with him, so I really don't think I'm to blame for what has or hasn't happened between you.'

'So I gather,' Viv bit back. 'But I dropped by on the off chance he was there this afternoon and he wouldn't even let me across the threshold. Kept blathering on about going for a picnic with you.'

Liz couldn't hold back her smile, imagining Patrick fending Viv off. She couldn't wait for tomorrow. It suddenly dawned on her how much she was looking forward to seeing him and how foolish she had been. She had almost let him slip through her fingers; she could so easily have lost him to Viv, as she'd lost Mike to Jen all those years ago. Although perhaps in Mike's case that had worked out for the best in the end. Patrick seemed impervious to Viv's charms, but even so, there was a distinct whiff of déjà vu about the situation.

'Anyway, I've said my piece.' Viv appeared to be running out of steam. 'Under the circumstances, you'll understand that I'll no longer be recommending your services to my clients.'

'Oh that's a relief,' said Liz, summoning up the backbone she should have relied on a long time ago.

'Excuse me?'

'I was going to let you know that I won't be taking any more bookings; you've saved me a call.'

'Why ever not?' Viv sounded most put out.

'This is not public knowledge,' Liz lowered her voice to sound mysterious. 'But I've decided to set up a supper club. Very exclusive, small numbers, gourmet food cooked and served here at Clemency House.'

'Oh, I see.'

'You're the first to know, Viv, and I'd rather no one else knows for the time being.'

'Of course,' Viv purred. 'You can count on my discretion.'

Liz bit back a giggle, she could virtually hear the cogs in Viv's brain deciding who she was going to call and tell first.

'I don't expect you'll want to come,' said Liz airily, 'but as a gesture of my gratitude, I'd love you to come to the first supper club, as my guest of course.'

There was a pause and then, 'With a plus-one?'

Liz pulled a face. 'Naturally.'

That was a quarter of her eight places accounted for. Still, if it meant repairing her relationship with Viv, it was worth it.

'Excellent.' Viv sounded smug. 'Let me know the dates and I'll see what I can do. I met a divine chartered surveyor at a property viewing yesterday, he might do nicely. Bye for now.'

Well, that went rather well, Liz thought to herself proudly. She'd been thinking about reviving the supper club idea for a while, but it had taken Viv's provocation for her ideas to fall into place.

She pushed herself off the bed, ran her fingers through her hair and put her feet back in her slippers.

This called for a celebration. She could sit outside and watch the world go by with a glass of wine.

The thought brought her up short. No. She mustn't. She'd been doing so well.

Her heart started to race. No one would know. She could open a bottle, just have one glass and pour the rest away, no one would be any the wiser. She deserved it.

Liz laughed at herself and shook her head. She wasn't even sure why she was being so puritanical about it, she was a grown woman, for heaven's sake. And drinking to celebrate something was a completely different thing from drinking to escape.

She almost ran down the stairs, her mouth watering at the thought of that delicious first sip. There was a bottle of Sauvignon Blanc in the cupboard under the stairs which the girls didn't know about. It wouldn't be cold, but an ice cube would soon remedy that. Liz dived into the cupboard head first, shifting stuff out of the way until she found the wine.

'Jackpot.' She shimmied backwards out of the cupboard.

She got as far as dropping an ice cube into her glass and opening the drawer to find the corkscrew and froze.

'No, Liz. No way.'

She was shocked at how easily she'd almost slipped back into her old habit. Boredom, loneliness, grief or, as in this case, celebration; she'd promised herself she wouldn't use drinking as her go-to response anymore and yet here she was.

She slammed the drawer shut, annoyed with herself. She wasn't going to succumb. She had to break this cycle. She couldn't rely on Clare and Skye to police her drinking, it wasn't fair on them. She had to hold herself accountable.

She pushed the bottle of wine away unopened, filled the glass with tap water and drank it down.

Take a minute, Liz, think about what your body really needs right now. Instead of drinking alone, how about celebrating in a different way, a better way?

A face flashed up in her mind. Patrick.

She liked him very much and it seemed that he liked her. And he had said that he was her man, any time she needed him. So what if he wasn't expecting to see her until tomorrow?

'What do you reckon, Jen?' she mused. 'Shall I go for it?'

Liz smiled, knowing exactly what her best friend would be yelling at her right now. She scribbled a note for the girls, telling them where she was going, grabbed her car keys and left the house.

Fifty minutes later, Liz arrived in East Portlemouth, belatedly realising as she caught a glimpse of herself in her visor mirror that perhaps she should have at least washed her face and brushed her hair.

Too late, she thought, getting out of the car. She was here now, and he'd have to take her as he found her, and vice versa.

Her nerves were zinging about all over the place as she waited for Patrick to answer the door.

'Liz?' His gentle, kind face broke into a smile when he saw her.

'Surprise!' she said with a hopeful smile.

He looked over her shoulder, checking she was alone. 'A lovely one!'

He was in his usual uniform of crumpled linen shirt and shorts, his feet were bare and he had some sort of white powder on his chin and in his hair.

'I know I'm meant to be seeing you tomorrow, but I wanted to give you something.' She took a step towards him.

He looked amused as his gaze dropped towards her empty hands. 'Give me what?'

She took another step and closed the gap between their bodies. Placing her hands on his shirt, she tilted her face up to his. 'This,' she said, kissing him.

'Wow, thank you,' he whispered.

To her relief, he gathered her to him, bringing his hands to her hair, and they kissed again.

'That was a good kiss,' she whispered back, looking into his dark blue eyes.

'It was. Would it be very presumptuous of me to invite you in?' Patrick murmured against her lips.

'You mean over the threshold?'

He laughed at her turn of phrase. 'That's exactly what I mean.'

She smiled to herself, as Patrick took her by the hand and led her inside. Liz one: Viv nil.

Chapter Thirty-Six

Clare

Clare was sitting at the dining table with a pad of paper in front of her and a stack of party invitations already sealed in their envelopes. There was only one left to write, and it was to the person she wanted at Ivy's first birthday party more than anyone. She'd ripped up two invitation cards already, not satisfied with what she'd written, and had now resorted to practising on paper before ruining another card.

> Dear Adam,
>   I've tried calling and texting and it's pretty clear you don't want to talk to me. Marta is going to pass this on to Angel for me in the hope that she gives it to you. Please give me a chance to explain.

Too negative.

> Dear Adam,
>   I'm not sure whether you're interested. Or even whether you're still in Salcombe . . .

This one sounded like she didn't care one way or the other.

Dear Adam,

It's Ivy's birthday on the 29th and we're having a party at the house. It would be great if you could come?

Too stilted.

She scrubbed the words out and made a growling noise under her breath. This was hopeless.

'You ready?' Skye walked in jiggling her car keys.

Clare felt a pang of envy at Skye's freedom to jump in the car and head off at will. She couldn't wait to drive again. Absolutely could not wait to get this uncomfortable brace off her arm either. She'd never take for granted again the ability to scoop her daughter up and give her a proper cuddle.

'Yeah.' She stood up with a sigh. 'I'll finish Adam's invitation later. I still can't work out what to write.'

'Maybe close your eyes and take some deep breaths, listen to your heart,' Skye suggested. 'That's what—' She stopped abruptly and smiled at Clare sheepishly.

'Marta would say?' Clare finished for her. The gospel according to Marta, as she now playfully referred to her sister's constant referencing of her girlfriend.

'Can I bring Marta to the party?'

'Of course you can!' Clare replied, surprised she even needed to ask. 'Bring all the lesbians. The more, the merrier.'

'Stop,' Skye groaned, laughing. 'You can't tease me about it yet. It's all too new.'

'My little sister floating about with a big goofy grin on her face?' Clare said. 'Too right I'm going to tease you. Besides, I'm a bit jealous of you and your happy ending.'

They made their way out of the house, locked the door and got in the car.

'Don't give up on him just yet,' Skye said, helping her with her seat belt. 'Jade heard through Angel that he's really cut up. Maybe he'll come round.'

'I hope so.' Clare gave a half-smile. 'But maybe he's like every other man in my life – the cut-and-run type.'

'Jesse wasn't like that.'

'Bless his golden muscles,' said Clare.

'And neither is Patrick, from what I can see.'

'True.' Clare smiled at that. Patrick Delmarge was an old-school romantic and Liz was giggly with the newness of their relationship. He sent flowers, he phoned at bedtime to wish her goodnight and he escorted her to the door after their dates, even when it meant driving for fifty minutes back to East Portlemouth when they'd gone out in his car. It was early days with them, but she'd never seen Liz so happy, and she really hoped it worked out for them.

Then there was her supper club idea, which Clare absolutely loved. She still remembered the stories her mum used to tell her about Liz and Jen's student days and how much the pair of them had loved entertaining their friends in their tiny student flat. This seemed like the perfect next step for Liz, combining all the things she loved: Clemency House, cooking and company; and she knew that her mum would approve too.

While she and Skye were at the hospital this morning, Liz and Patrick were taking Ivy over on the ferry to the beach. Three whole hours where Ivy would be out of her sight and out of her control and she wasn't even panicking about it. If there was one thing that breaking her arm had succeeded in doing, it was to give her the freedom to start accepting help. Which was fortunate, seeing as she'd be going back to Bath soon for the start of term and her arm wouldn't be strong enough to manage everything by herself.

She'd thought about asking Skye to move in with her for a few weeks, just until her arm was mobile again, but it wouldn't be fair on her. Not now that she and Marta were growing closer.

Clare watched Skye fondly as she started the car and reversed out of the drive. She was unrecognisable from the timid creature who'd rocked up to Clemency House, weighed down by decisions she didn't want to make, trying to please everyone and putting herself last. Now look at her, blossoming, confident and in charge of her life.

'What?' said Skye, catching her eye.

'Nothing,' she replied. 'Just looking at my amazing sister. Right, let's get to my X-ray appointment to see if my broken arm is mended. I might get them to take a look at my heart while they're at it. See if there's any chance of that getting unbroken any time soon.'

Clare looked at the X-ray of her arm which the doctor had pulled up onto his computer screen. There was a thicker bit where the fracture was, the bones laying down new calcium deposits apparently.

'It's healing nicely,' said the doctor. 'Well done. Time to remove that brace, put you in a collar and cuff. I'll leave you with the nurse.'

The nurse was Pam, who'd looked after her when she'd first had her accident. Pam fixed a neoprene sling around Clare's neck with Velcro, adjusting it until it felt comfortable.

'You can start to remove it for periods of time now, let your arm hang. You need to retain as much movement in your elbow as possible,' she told her.

Clare winced. 'OK.' The idea of removing all protection when Ivy was anywhere near her gave her the collywobbles.

If she ended up undoing the healing of her arm, she didn't know what she'd do.

'And we need to arrange some physio, but I can see from your home address that you're not local?' said Pam.

Clare nodded. 'I'll be going back to Bath soon.'

The nurse studied her. 'I'd have expected you to be happier about your progress, but you seem a bit down. Major trauma such as you've been through can lead to depression in some cases. Have you been having dark thoughts?'

'Not depressed. Just . . .' Clare swallowed, horrified to find she was on the brink of tears. Bloody hospital, her emotions always made their way to the surface when she was here.

'Talk to me,' said the nurse, handing her a tissue.

Which was how Clare came to tell Pam about a one-night stand in a hotel which led to a baby who was born while she was grieving for her mother and the surprise discovery of the baby's daddy, who she still had feelings for and with whom she'd completely blown it.

'I want him to be there at Ivy's first birthday party – not for me, but for her.'

Pam raised her eyebrows. 'Really?'

'OK, a bit for me. But I can't find the words to invite him. He's missed out on a whole year of her life and if I could turn back the clock I would, but I can't.'

'Can't you just tell him that?'

'I've tried.' She sighed and her eyes roamed over the desk. There was a framed photograph of Pam looking absolutely knackered holding a newborn baby.

The nurse followed her gaze and smiled. 'My son, Marcus, just after he was born. I look at it every day and I still can't believe how lucky I am.'

392

A light bulb went off in Clare's head. 'Oh my God. I can send him photos! Let him see her entire first year in pictures. I can't turn the clock back, but I can show him what she's been up to since she was born. Thank you, nurse!'

Pam looked bemused. 'Any time.'

Clare stood up and opened the door, before remembering where she was. 'Oh sorry, are we done?'

'We're done,' Pam said with a laugh. 'Good luck.'

It took Clare a couple of hours once she'd got back to Salcombe to sort through her phone and get everything together for her letter to Adam. This time, she wrote it without hesitation.

Dear Daddy,

I was born on 29th August last year at three-thirty in the afternoon. Mummy was starving because I'd taken my own sweet time to arrive. I had thick dark hair when I came out and Liz said I looked like a chimney brush. Mummy didn't say anything, but she wasn't very happy about it and, when Liz left, she told me that I had lovely hair just like my daddy.

We live in a flat in Bath and Mummy has had great fun carrying me and the buggy up four flights of stairs every day. She kept saying that she couldn't wait until I could walk. But now that I can, she seems to be scared of me doing it. I was really glad that you were there when I took my first steps, even if that huge dog did knock me to the sand straight afterwards.

If I was to tell you everything that has happened to me over the last year, this letter would be very long, so I'll just give you the highlights.

I love bath time and I especially like trying to eat the bubbles. I pooed in the bath once and Mummy said some naughty words, but on the whole she keeps her potty mouth away from me. My favourite food is toast. I can carry a mushed-up crust in each hand for hours. I'm starting to talk now: bic-bic and mama being my two favourites. I'm not a fan of ice cream, but I'm open to persuasion – maybe we can try again one day. I go to nursery while Mummy's at work where we sing songs, make a mess and eat a meal approximately once every two hours. I have lots of friends but not a lot of family.

I'm having a birthday party on my actual birthday at Liz's house and I'd really like you to come so that when I'm older, I can look back at the photographs and see that you were there. You don't have to talk to Mummy if you don't want to. She'll understand. But I'd like you to talk to me please.

Lots of love

Ivy xx

PS Here's a memory stick full of photos from my first year. There are 363 – one for every day of my life so far. I'd really like one of you and me together on my birthday. Hope you can make it.

Chapter Thirty-Seven

Clare

It was Ivy's birthday and her party was in full flow. Wearing her gift from Skye, a batik print dress and matching headband and knickers over her nappy, the birthday girl was the star of the show. Clare brimmed with maternal pride as she followed Ivy's progress from guest to guest, pinching crisps from plates and wiping sticky fingers on clothes and getting away with it due to her impossible cuteness.

Clare stood leaning against the glass of the balcony, taking a moment to imprint the day on her memory. The sun was bright overhead, and a blue sky and shimmering water dotted with boats formed the glorious backdrop to the party. Despite this afternoon's heat, she could feel summer coming to an end; there was change in the air, an autumnal nip, and she felt the stirring of anticipation that school would soon be back in session. New children, new families to get to know, new challenges for her school, and she couldn't wait to get started.

There were changes afoot for her and Ivy too. Leaving the lovely flat she'd owned for several years was going to be a wrench, but there was no outside space, not even a communal area she could use. Now that Ivy's sole purpose in life seemed to be to move as fast and as far as she could at a moment's notice, Clare had decided to find a house with a garden. A new home for the two of them. She was excited for that too.

A burst of applause brought her back to the present; she turned to see Ivy centre stage, bending her knees and wiggling her bottom, her head waving side to side to the music, Marta, Skye, Ele and Jade giving her encouragement. Patrick had brought a couple of portable speakers with him and was in charge of the music. Motown, he'd decided, would bridge the generations and start Ivy off early on her journey to musical appreciation. Ivy, giving it her all while The Supremes sang about baby love, seemed to approve.

Clare's gaze lingered on her sister and Marta. The two women were so good together, joy seemed to radiate from them. Skye had taken to coming into Clare's room last thing at night for whispered conversations so as not to wake up Ivy. They talked and talked now, making up for lost time, sharing bits of their lives previously withheld. Skye was still getting used to falling in love with a woman, constantly questioning herself and her emotions. From what Clare could see, Marta was the gentlest and wisest of humans and, if she had to entrust her sister's heart to anyone, Marta would be her top choice.

Clare let the sounds wash over her: the gentle burble of conversation; spoons tinkling against china cups; the hoot of Liz's laughter coming from indoors. Her heart thrummed with gratitude: her hotchpotch Salcombe crew, the friends and family who cared enough to come together to celebrate her daughter's first year and the start of her second.

She'd invited not only Patrick, but his mother and aunt too, much to their delight. The two old ladies had declared themselves not fans of buffets and preferred to be in the middle of the action, which apparently meant pulling their chairs up to the table. For such slender creatures, they could certainly put away a decent amount of food.

Liz had been to their retirement home herself to fetch them so that Patrick could sail across from the other side of the estuary. He was obsessed with that boat, Liz was fond of saying, as if the two of them were already an old married couple instead of the starry-eyed, touching-each-other-at-every-opportunity couple which they actually were. Any awkwardness about Liz's friendship with Mike had evaporated. Clare and Skye loved her too much to harbour any grudge and, as Liz had said, she'd done nothing wrong other than fall in love with someone who hadn't loved her back.

The song changed to 'My Guy' and Liz whooped with delight. 'Where is he? This is my favourite?'

Patrick gathered her into his arms in seconds and the rest of the party watched, misty-eyed, as the two of them began to dance with eyes only for each other. Across the room, Skye caught her looking and both of them pressed their hands to their hearts. Bless them. Clare smiled at the two old ladies swaying and clapping in time to the music. How happy they were to see Patrick finally get his girl. How long would they each stay living on opposite sides of the estuary? Clare wondered. They'd seen each other every day since their first date and were already planning to rent out their properties as holiday lets and move into each other's houses when they got bookings.

Ivy spotted her mum and tottered across to her.

'Ah-ah.' She held her arms up to Clare.

'Come on then, hang on to Mummy's neck.' She reached down and Ivy held on tight, settling onto her hip and tucking her head under Clare's chin.

She fits perfectly, thought Clare, kissing her daughter's hair. *We fit perfectly*. She breathed in the scent of Ivy's shampoo, of her skin – smells she could identify without hesitation. Her baby. She'd had the honour of having her precious daughter in her life for one year today; she'd been a mother for a whole year.

Motherhood, she thought with a pang, what a lot it had brought her. A bond she'd have forever, a feeling of belonging, a love so immense and unconditional that just thinking about what it meant to be Ivy's mother made her well up. Clare cast her mind back to the day she realised she was pregnant and the overriding fear that she couldn't do it alone. But she had.

Skye approached carrying two champagne flutes. Elderflower pressé they'd gone with, rather than alcohol, and it was the perfect choice for a summer's afternoon. Clare was still having to manage one-handed, so she had to make a choice: either put Ivy down or decline the drink. She chose to keep hold of Ivy and Skye set the glass down on the table for her.

'Happy with everything?' Skye asked, nodding to the party decorations which she and Marta had put up earlier.

'Very,' Clare replied. 'It's gorgeous, you've done a brilliant job. I think Ivy may have peaked too soon in terms of good parties. She's going to be appalled next year when she sees what she gets when I'm in charge of the décor.'

The colour scheme was a pastel rainbow: ivory, pale pink, baby blue and lilac. Skye had gone to lots of effort to keep everything to theme. Tissue-paper honeycomb balls hung from the ceiling as well as from the newly erected sail-shaped sunshade on the patio. A helium balloon arch spelling 'Happy Birthday Ivy' bridged the gap between inside and out and a tiny throne (an old chair which Skye had discovered in a skip) was wound with fronds of real ivy picked at dawn that morning, and looked like something from a fairy tale. Vases of fragrant stocks, daisies and lisianthus adorned the table among plates of food. Liz had handled the catering, naturally, managing to create a menu both delicious and whimsical to suit the occasion, including bowls of Ivy's favourites – Wotsits and Quavers.

'Don't worry,' Skye laughed. 'I'll help at the next party too. I'll always help if you want me to.'

Clare touched her head on her sister's shoulder. 'I'd like that.'

'Are you sure you're happy?' Skye peered at her sister. 'Because I'm sensing a "but"?'

Ivy decided she'd had enough of being cuddled and wriggled out of Clare's grasp. She set her free and picked up her glass, taking a sip before replying.

'The "but" is nothing to do with the decorations and everything to do with the people missing from the party.'

Skye nodded, understanding. 'Your mum?'

'She'd have loved this,' Clare replied wistfully. 'She'd have made such a fuss of Ivy and she would have gone way overboard with presents.'

'And I'm sure Dad will turn up,' said Skye. 'Late, obviously, but he will come.'

Clare paused. 'Dad's not invited.'

'What? Really?' Skye said, shocked. 'But he's Ivy's grandad.'

She shrugged. 'I didn't want to give him the opportunity to let us down. To make promises to come and then forget. Also, he's never shown an interest in her, so why should he come to her party. When he's ready to be a grandfather, we'll be waiting. But I'm not forcing him into it. He's the one missing out. The sad thing is that I'm not sure he even realises it. Anyway, you said you were – and I quote – done with him, I didn't want him to turn up and spoil the day for you.'

Skye shook her head, marvelling at her sister. 'You really don't take any prisoners, do you? I'm in awe. I'd have crumbled and ended up begging him to come.'

'Maybe one day he'll grow up, but until he'll refer to himself as Grandad and not Mikey, I've decided I'm not going to waste my time on him.'

At that moment, Liz appeared from inside, carrying a plate of cupcakes with sugared flower decorations on them. Or rather, where the decorations had been, there were gaping holes in the top of the icing.

'Was this you, you little monkey?' Liz said, tickling Ivy's tummy. 'Did you vandalise all these cakes?'

Ivy collapsed onto her bottom in a fit of giggles before grabbing one of the naked cakes and biting into it, paper case and all.

'The little minx!' Skye gasped. 'Did you see that!'

'She gets that from you,' said Clare. 'Do you remember Dad's birthday party when you bit the cherry off every single Bakewell tart and put them all back on the cake stand.'

'I did not.' Skye pressed a hand to her mouth. 'Why didn't you stop me?'

'Stop you? Who do you think helped you reach the table?' Clare said mischievously. 'Frankie was furious.'

Skye grinned at Clare. 'We've got more shared past than I realised.'

'And more shared future to come.'

'I'll drink to that.' Skye tilted her glass towards her. 'To the future.'

Clare raised her glass and suppressed a sigh. There was someone else she'd hoped to share a future with, but it looked as if that was wishful thinking on her part. There had been no word from Adam – not an RSVP, not a please leave me alone, not a joyful acceptance, nothing. Which she guessed told her everything she needed to know. It was her fault, and she could live with that for herself, but she felt bad about it for Ivy. At least she hadn't spent too much time with him this summer. Maybe it was for the best that they made a clean break before she started to depend on his presence, before Ivy formed a bond with him. What you've never had you can't miss, right?

'I'm going to miss you when you leave,' Skye nudged her, bringing her out of her thoughts.

'I'll miss you too, and Ivy will miss having so many servants at her beck and call. But I'm ready to go home to Bath. I love it here, but Salcombe will always be my second home; it's my summer place. I associate it with sunshine and playing on the beach, swimming in the sea, although not so much of the latter this year, obviously.'

'Salcombe is going to be my proper home, I think.'

Marta chose that moment to join them. 'I'll drink to that.'

'But you'll come and visit us in Bath, both of you?' Clare asked. They'd have fun, she thought. A girlie weekend. She smiled just imagining it.

'Just try stopping us,' said Marta, taking hold of Skye's hand.

'I've been thinking about how to earn a living and I've got an idea,' said Skye.

'Yay!' Clare grinned at her. 'Come on then, spill the beans.'

'I'm still in the planning stage,' Skye confessed. 'But Marta knows and she thinks it's a good idea.'

Clare pretended to be insulted. 'One month as your confidante and I've already been usurped.'

'Not going to happen,' said Marta. 'All I hear is Clare this, Clare that.'

'Funny that,' Clare waggled a teasing eyebrow at her sister. 'All I hear about is you.'

'Stop ganging up on me,' Skye groaned. 'I need both of you.'

Marta pulled her in for a hug. 'I'm glad to hear it, but sisters are special.'

'Agreed.' Clare held up her glass. 'To sisterhood.'

'Sisterhood.' Skye and Marta chinked their glasses to hers.

'Come on, what's your idea?' Clare tried again.

Skye's eyes sparkled. 'Yoga Brunch. Basically, Marta and I will join forces to do joint events. A yoga class followed by a delicious nutritious brunch.'

Clare raised her eyebrows. 'That might even tempt me into lotus position.'

Marta laughed. 'I get clients asking all the time if I'll do refreshments, especially in the studio in the winter. I think people enjoy the connection and want the class to go on longer.'

'I'll keep the food simple,' said Skye, cheeks pink with excitement. 'And Liz is going to help me with the menus to start with, and lend me her equipment.'

'So, basically, I'm the last to know.' Clare pretended to be offended. 'Well, I think it's a great idea and I think you'll make a brilliant success of it.'

'See?' Marta kissed Skye's cheek. 'You needn't have been worried about telling her.'

'True,' Skye grinned. 'She's not as scary these days.'

'Oi!' Clare laughed.

'Girls? Look who I found loitering on the doorstep,' Liz called them from inside. 'Come in, come in!'

'Oh my God.' Clare stiffened, a pulse beating urgently at her throat. 'I daren't look, is it Adam? Please say it is.'

Skye turned towards the doors and where Liz's voice was coming from. 'No. I'm sorry. It's Dad.'

'*Dad?*' Disappointment hit her like a blow to the stomach. Today was an almost perfect day; the only thing she'd needed was for Adam to come through for her. To act on that letter she'd written on Ivy's behalf. What she didn't need was her dad turning up uninvited and rubbing her, Liz and Skye up the wrong way like he had the last time he was here.

Clare set her glass down and marched inside to where he was waiting in the kitchen; he was rocking on the balls of his feet, hands in pockets.

Mike took one look at her and held his hands up. 'Don't worry, I'm not staying. But I wanted Ivy to have a present on her birthday.'

He pointed to a stuffed toy on the kitchen island: a pug dog with wings and a unicorn horn. Not even wrapped.

Clare couldn't help but let out a derisory snort. 'OK. Well, thank you.'

'And this.' He pulled a small envelope out of the breast pocket of his shirt.

'Thanks.' Clare set it beside the unicorn pug to open later.

'Can I get you a drink, Mike?' said Liz, hovering in the background.

'He's not staying, apparently,' Clare answered for him before he could get a word in.

'I didn't realise you were throwing a party for her.' He looked wounded.

'Why would you?' she said lightly. 'You never take any interest in her life.'

He hung his head. 'Ouch.'

A dart of guilt pierced through her. She was better than this. Whatever he'd done, whatever water had flowed under the bridge, he was here now, he'd remembered Ivy's birthday, and he was family.

'Sorry, Dad, that was rude.' Clare sighed, pushing her hair out of her eyes. 'Would you like a drink?'

He gave her a half-smile. 'Love one. Have you got a kombucha?'

She gave him a 'What do you think?' look and he laughed sheepishly.

Liz put a glass of pressé into his hand, touched his arm and left them to it, wandering over to check on Patrick's mum and aunt, who were eyeing up Mike speculatively.

'Clare, I've done a lot of thinking over the past few days. I've realised I could have done better with you and Skye.'

'And Ivy,' she put in.

'And Ivy,' he agreed. 'But hopefully if I buck up my ideas quickly enough, I can avoid getting it wrong with her too. I haven't earned my place at the birthday table this year, but that's going to change. Next year, she'll probably be talking and maybe she can phone me and invite her old grandad herself.'

It was such a lovely image that Clare permitted him to see her smile. 'Sounds good.'

He sipped his drink. 'So how do I make it better? What do I need to do?'

Clare felt exasperation tighten her chest, but when she looked at her dad, she could see he was being serious.

'Take time to get to know us. Learn what makes us tick. And in Ivy's case, be her grandfather, instead of a silver-haired man who wishes to be known as Mikey.'

He nodded. 'OK.'

'When we try to tell you something, listen without judging us first. And when you talk to us, treat us like adults.'

He nodded again. 'OK, I can—'

'I haven't finished,' she jumped in. 'Make Skye feel like she matters. Don't compare the two of us; we're different people with different life views. But she's amazing, Dad. She's funny and feisty and incredibly kind. And one last thing: stop chasing women half your age. It's embarrassing.'

The corner of his lips curled upwards. 'Don't pull any punches, will you? You sounded exactly like your mother then. And I hear what you say. Harriet's gone. I lost my head there for a while. But she's gone.'

There was a whoop of laughter and Mike glanced outside to where Patrick was holding Ivy in one arm, the other around Liz.

'Hmm. That chap seems to have got his feet under the table.'

'Patrick?' Clare smiled fondly. 'Liz loves him and so does Ivy. Don't you dare pull that jealous face. Lots of kids have two sets of grandparents. There's room for everyone.'

Her throat burned then, thinking about her mum, about Adam's family and how things could have been different if she'd only been brave enough to tell him the truth and let him into their lives sooner. Not for her sake, but for Ivy's.

'Ivy has barely any family; if Patrick wants to be in *loco grandparentis* as it were, I'm not going to stop him.'

'What about Ivy's father?' Mike asked shrewdly. 'And his family, don't they want to stay in touch with her?'

Clare ran the tip of her finger along the kitchen island. This was the moment. Whatever he thought of her, she ought to tell him. She couldn't expect him to change if she didn't demand the same of herself.

'I cocked that up, Dad.'

He looked surprised. '*You* did?'

She smiled. 'I know. Unheard of, right?'

His face softened. 'Darling, we all cock up occasionally. It's part of being human.'

405

She dipped her head, feeling the sting of tears in her eyes. He stepped closer and engulfed her in a hug. She couldn't remember the last time he'd done that. It felt nice.

'Thanks, Dad,' she mumbled into his shirt.

'Want to tell me about it?'

Not really, she thought, but as Marta said, our loved ones deserved honesty and when it came down to it, her dad fell into that category. So instead of clamming up as her body was screaming at her to do, she nodded.

'Ivy's dad *is* called Adam. But he was never my boyfriend. I met him the night Mum died . . .'

Mike held her and he listened, properly listened, while she told him the whole story: about how she'd pretended to be brave when she'd found out that she was pregnant. About how she had no way of contacting Adam because they hadn't exchanged numbers. She missed out the bit where she'd pretended to be Sexy Saskia the location scout, but she told him how she'd met up with him again in Salcombe unexpectedly and how lovely he was and how brilliant with Ivy. How she'd known she had to tell him that he was Ivy's father, but that she'd been scared.

'Scared?' Her dad pulled back to look at her.

She nodded. 'I was worried that if we let him in and he left us that Ivy would get hurt.'

He let out a sigh and smiled sadly. 'I can guess where that has come from. But history doesn't have to repeat itself. And he sounds like a decent chap, especially as he seems keen to get involved with a baby who he doesn't think is related to him. I'd have run a mile if a girlfriend of mine had a baby.'

Clare frowned. 'Not helping, Dad.'

'Sorry,' he said meekly. 'Carry on.'

'I decided to tell him.' She continued to tell him about Jesse and the doorstep disaster and how Adam had gone quiet ever since and hadn't responded to Ivy's party invitation. 'So that's the story of how I cocked up my daughter's relationship with her father and upset the only man I've ever really—' She brought herself up short before saying 'loved' because she couldn't possibly love him based on the limited time they'd spent together. But they might have made it that far if she hadn't been too slow to tell him the truth.

'So?' Her father took a step back, his sharp eyes watching her.

'So what?' Clare shrugged. 'That's it. I tried, I failed. I can't force him to take an interest in his child, can I?' She returned his stare defiantly, but he refused to break eye contact.

'If you could see him now, what would you say?'

'Where to begin. I'd say . . .' She hesitated, her face softening into a smile, eyes prickling with tears. 'That I miss him, and I'm sorry and I'd like another chance and even if he can't give me a chance, that Ivy doesn't deserve the cold shoulder and that if there was any way he'd consider being a part of her life, I'd like to make that happen.'

'OK, Clare, listen to me,' he said urgently. 'Turner Investments, who came here for that lunch the other day, weren't sure about working with Good Vibrations to begin with. It took days and weeks of emails and phone calls and pitches to them to get them to take that meeting. But I persevered, I kept knocking on their door until finally . . .' He held his hands out, eyes sparkling. 'I cracked it.'

'Are you seriously comparing the expansion of a chain of sex shops with me reconnecting with the father of my child?'

He opened his mouth, clearly about to protest, and then laughed. 'Point taken. But what I'm saying is that you're a Marriott and Marriotts don't leave any stone unturned.'

She blinked at him, not comprehending. Hadn't she done that? 'That letter written from Ivy to him *was* the last stone.'

Mike tutted fondly. 'Do you have his address?'

'Marta's got his sister's address.'

He held up his car keys and jingled them. 'Ready for one last shot?'

'Now?' she spluttered.

'Right now.'

She looked outdoors to where Ivy was holding court, the centre of attention and loving every second of it. She wouldn't be missed for an hour or so.

Her stomach churned with excitement and nerves as she met her dad's hopeful face. 'Let's do this.'

Chapter Thirty-Eight

Clare

Clare and Mike ran to his Range Rover and climbed in. He started the engine and pulled away before she'd even managed to do up her seat belt. This felt so exciting. She grinned at her dad, who grinned back.

'Thanks, Dad.'

'I feel like I'm in a car-chase scene in a film. Where one half of a couple is about to fly off and the other person has minutes to get to the airport or lose them forever.'

'You old romantic.'

He raised an eyebrow. 'Beneath this steely exterior lies a big softie. Postcode?'

She gave him Angel's address and he tapped it into the satnav. They were fifteen minutes away.

Every nerve ending thrummed with possibility. Adam might not even be there, but at least they were taking action. It felt good to be doing something positive rather than constantly straining to listen for the doorbell on the off chance that he turned up.

'Dad?' she said suddenly. 'Is this a good idea?'

'It's my idea, so yes, of course it is, why? Are you having second thoughts?' He looked sideways at her, gently teasing, but concerned too.

She puffed her cheeks out. 'Just worried I might look a

bit desperate. It's Ivy's first birthday and he's a no-show to her party. This is his way of turning us down.' She swallowed the pang of hurt on her daughter's behalf.

'Possibly,' he said, frowning. 'Or he didn't get the invite. Or he did get the invite, but he needs more time to figure out how he feels. Or, perhaps, he wants to talk to you but not in front of a crowd. Maybe he was on his way but got a puncture. Or—'

'OK, OK, I get the message,' she replied, mollified. 'You've convinced me. Carry on, Driver.'

'Right you are, madam.' He switched on the music. Smokey Robinson's voice filled the car.

She shot him a look. 'Mum's favourite. Or are you going to pretend you'd forgotten, again?'

'How could I forget,' he said wistfully. 'I remember everything about her. I was thinking about her on the way to Liz's, about how she'd have been a fantastic grandparent and would have been furious with me for being useless.'

Clare stared at him. 'You still loved her.'

'I loved her more than anyone else in the world,' he said softly. 'I messed it up with her. And I've never forgiven myself.'

'Oh Dad.' She reached across the console separating them and touched his arm. He smiled at her sadly and her heart ached for him. Beneath all his bravado and bluster, he was as vulnerable to heartache as everyone else.

'Remember this one?' He skipped through the tracks until he found the song he was looking for.

'Yes!' Clare's eyes danced, picturing the three of them in the car together. 'Happy times.'

Mike nodded. 'The best.'

And for the first time in almost thirty years, father and daughter sang along at the tops of their voices to 'I Second That Emotion'.

As they left Salcombe behind, the roads narrowed, the hedges grew higher and the traffic slowed down to a crawl. It was even worse in the opposite direction heading towards Salcombe and, a couple of times, Clare caught a glimpse of bickering couples and crying children who looked as if they'd encountered one too many snarl-ups today.

'This is why I could never live here,' Mike growled as he pulled into a tight passing place, the twigs of the hawthorn hedge squeaking against the paintwork of his car like nails down a blackboard.

'Unless you swapped your posh car for something smaller,' said Clare, winding the windows up to stop the hedge snagging her hair.

'Or a tractor. Finally,' he grumbled as the last in a long line of cars inched past them.

'So what happened with you and Harriet then?' Clare asked as they picked up their speed to a heady old twenty miles per hour.

Mike ran a hand over his chin. 'I was flattered by her. It was a ridiculous situation, as you pointed out. I've extricated us both admirably, and there are no hard feelings. I pulled some strings and got her another job with more pay. At Good Vibrations, incidentally. So, all's well that ends well.'

'I can't say I'm not relieved,' she replied. 'I'm not sure I could have stomached a twenty-five-year-old stepmother.'

He chuckled. 'There was never any danger of that. *Harriet Marriott?* I don't think so.'

They laughed again and Clare felt something shift inside her; she'd spent so long being angry with him that she'd forgotten how dry his sense of humour was. Very like her own, in fact.

'I'm a sucker for a pretty face,' he said, dolefully. 'Can't help myself.'

'Oh no you don't,' Clare said firmly. 'Don't blame your behaviour on some impossible-to-control urge. That's just an excuse. And a crappy one at that.'

He pulled a face. 'Blimey. I can see why they made you head teacher. You're quite scary.'

'It's not funny, Dad.' She scowled at him.

'No, sorry,' he said meekly. 'I'll take what you said on board.'

'Good.'

'There's some money in that envelope for Ivy by the way.' He cleared his throat. 'Part of the money I asked Liz to pay me back. I've decided not to keep any of it.'

'Oh, Dad,' she said, her heart swelling with gratitude. 'That's very kind.'

'And I've transferred the rest of it to you and Skye.'

Clare opened her mouth to argue that she couldn't accept it, but closed it again. Accepting help still made her feel awkward, but she'd learned this summer that letting people in wasn't as difficult as she'd once thought, and it wasn't the sign of weakness she'd worried about either. 'Thank you. I'm thinking of buying a house, it'll help with the deposit.'

Skye would be grateful too, she thought; it would help with her new business venture.

Ahead of them, a farmer stepped out into the road and held up the traffic.

'Just as well this isn't a film and the love of your life isn't on his way to the airport,' said Mike grumpily as a gate opened and a herd of cows ambled dozily across the road and into the field opposite.

Clare blew out a long breath. This was torture. Sweat prickled at her hairline as well as down her spine, in addition to the ever-present patch of under-boob sweat courtesy of having to keep her dodgy arm pressed to her body.

'How much further?' she asked, watching the last cow meander leisurely past them.

'Seven minutes according to the satnav,' said Mike. 'Although that presumably isn't taking into account farmers who SELFISHLY move their cattle at peak times.'

He'd wound the window down and yelled this out at the farmer as they'd gone by, earning himself a rude hand gesture by way of reply. He put his foot down as they inched up the hill, but as they rounded the next corner, he slammed on the brake.

A bus and a delivery van had got wedged together in a passing place. Traffic had backed up and there was nowhere for anyone to go. Horns were tooting, drivers and passengers were sticking their heads out to voice their frustrations, and no one was moving.

'Bloody hellfire,' Mike spluttered. 'This is chaos!'

A woman in the car behind got out and walked towards the bus. She was an elegant woman with a swirl of white hair, chunky pearls and a tight dress with a zip at the back from the hem to the neckline. Mike watched her progress intently, Clare noticed. At least she was more his age. She conferred with another driver and then walked back.

'What's happening?' Mike asked as she came past.

'The other side is going to back up and let the bus through,' she confirmed. 'I'm going to walk to the end of the queue and hold up the traffic.'

Mike whistled under her breath as she walked away. 'What a woman.'

It took a few minutes, but eventually the bus squeezed through. As Mike's Range Rover reached the passing place, he ground to a halt, scraped the car into the hedge again and waited as a silver car edged slowly by.

'Thank you!' called the driver.

'Adam,' Clare screeched, whipping her head round. 'Dad, turn around, that was Adam!'

'I can't, love!'

'You can. You have to!' she yelled desperately. 'Think of the movie scene! Please!'

'Shit the bed! All right!' Mike smacked on his hazard lights, tooted his horn to warn everyone and swung the car out across the narrow lane.

More horns blared at him as he see-sawed backwards and forwards across the road, shunting first the front and then the back bumpers into the gnarly hedges, until finally the car was facing the other direction. The elegant woman in the car behind mouthed 'arsehole' as she nudged her car past them.

Clare looked at her dad. Sweat was pouring off him. 'Thanks.'

He grinned at her. 'You're welcome. Most excitement I've had in ages.'

They were behind Adam's car, the traffic was slow, but moving. Mike flashed his lights and edged up to Adam's car. Adam did a double take in his rear-view mirror. Then another head appeared.

'There's someone sitting beside him.'

'Sister?' Mike hazarded a guess.

'Too old.' Her heart was racing now and her voice shaky with nerves. What was going through Adam's mind right now? He'd have seen her dad's idiotic manoeuvre.

Suddenly, Adam's car veered off the road into a farm track. Mike followed suit.

'Go get your man then,' he said, nodding his head towards Adam's car as Adam himself leapt from the driver's side.

Clare climbed out of the car, her legs shaking, and found herself looking at Adam.

'Clare?' Adam was frowning, his arms extended. 'Is everything all right? You look scared to death.'

'I am,' she admitted. Her mouth had gone completely dry, she'd give anything for a sip of water right now. 'I'm petrified.'

The passenger door of Adam's car opened and a woman wearing a floral summer dress got out. Fine hair, blonde with silvery streaks, one pair of glasses on her face and sunglasses on the top of her head. She had a hand pressed to her tummy as she walked over to them.

'Er . . .' Adam scrubbed a hand through his hair. 'Mum, this is Clare. Clare, meet my mum, Beatrice.'

'Lovely to meet you,' said Clare, extending her hand formally. She looked at Adam nervously. Did his mother know about her? About Ivy?

'Nanna Bea,' said Beatrice, her plump cheeks dimpling as she smiled. 'That's what I'd like to be called, if you approve.'

'Mum knows,' said Adam. 'Everything.'

'Oh,' Clare gasped, looking from her to Adam. 'Oh, right.'

'No matter,' said Beatrice, waving a hand. 'Just a thought. I can be plain old Gran if you prefer.'

'No, no, I love it,' Clare said, with a surprised laugh. 'Really love it. Excuse me.'

She bowed her head as from nowhere tears began to run down her face. Mike was out of the car in a flash and put his arm around his daughter.

'Everything OK here?' he said gruffly.

'Nanna Bea,' said Beatrice, forcing Mike to shake her hand. 'And you must be Grandpa?'

'Grandad,' he corrected her. 'Grandad Mike.'

Clare let out a sob; this was so surreal. Was it too much to hope that things might be working out?

'Adam,' said Adam, following his mother's lead and offering Mike his hand. 'Ivy's father.'

'Ah,' said Mike knowingly, looking him up and down.

Clare felt like pinching herself. Ivy's parents and grand-parents meeting in a rutted muddy track in a Devon lane, the air whiffy with engine fumes. She thought of her dad's rom-com film analogy and almost laughed.

'Where were you going?' Adam asked. 'I thought you'd be at the party.'

Her heart thudded; so he had got the invitation. But had decided against coming. Mike moved closer to her; he must have known what she was feeling. She looked at him sadly. We tried, Dad, she wanted to tell him. At least we tried.

'I was,' she said in a small voice.

'Oh dear,' Beatrice frowned. 'Have we missed it? Adam, darling, I'm sorry, this is all my fault.'

Clare blinked at her, looked at Adam. 'So you were coming?'

'Yes,' Adam began before his mum jumped in.

'Of course we were!' said Beatrice. 'My granddaughter's first birthday party? Wouldn't have missed it for the world.'

'Except that apparently we did,' said Adam softly, holding Clare's gaze. 'And I'm sorry.'

'It doesn't matter,' said Clare. 'You were going to come, that's what counts.'

'The thing is, I'm back in Bath now and Angel's gone away. It was only when her neighbour came in to feed the cat that she found the invite,' he explained. 'Angel relayed the message to me this morning, but I'd promised to pick mum up from the airport. Then she insisted on getting Ivy a present and here we are.'

'Here we are,' Clare repeated. Her heart had edged past thudding and was full on galloping now.

He'd come. He'd only got the message this morning and yet he'd come. With his mother. She gave herself a shake; she didn't know yet whether he was coming just to see Ivy or Ivy and Clare. But she had to find out before she embarrassed herself. She tried and failed to read his expression. Did he have feelings for her, as she did for him?

'Well, I'm sorry, but I couldn't turn up empty-handed, could I? Has all the cake gone?' Beatrice asked.

Clare shook her head. Never knowingly under-catered, that was one of Liz's mottos.

'Excellent! Then the party's not over. Besides, Ivy hasn't had her gifts yet.' Beatrice turned towards the car. 'Come on, everyone, chop-chop.'

'We need to talk,' said Adam and Clare at exactly the same time.

Beatrice's shoulders sagged. 'Can't it wait? It's just that I've been dying for a wee for the last five miles and, at my age, that's quite a feat. I'm not sure I can hold it much longer.'

'Oh God.' Adam pinched the bridge of his nose. 'TMI, Mother.'

'Don't be silly,' she said in a no-nonsense tone. 'You're a father now, you need to get used to these things.'

'Might I make a suggestion?' said Mike. 'Beatrice, why don't you hop in with me and I'll take you to the party. Leave these youngsters to talk.'

'Perfect!' Beatrice grabbed her bag from Adam's car and dived straight into the Range Rover. 'And if the worst comes to the worst, I've got my She-Wee with me and I'm a terrific aim.'

'Good to know,' Mike said bravely.

Mike and Beatrice pulled out into the traffic and headed back towards Salcombe.

'Alone at last,' said Adam theatrically, but his beautiful blue-green eyes were smiling.

'Indeed,' Clare swallowed, aware her voice was trembling with nerves.

'I had my suspicions,' said Adam. 'But I didn't dare say anything in case I was wrong.'

'About Ivy being yours?'

He nodded. 'There was quite a big clue in the name.'

She bit her lip; she'd always wondered about the wisdom of naming their baby after the place she'd been conceived. 'The Ivy Hotel and Spa where we met. Too cheesy?'

'It suits her.' He took a step closer. 'It's lovely. Although I'm glad I didn't meet you in the Winking Prawn.'

Clare tipped her head back and laughed. 'Me too.'

'Clare.'

'Adam.' Her breath was ragged. He was so close to her that she could feel the heat of him. She stared at his lips, watched his teeth drag on his bottom lip and felt a tug in her stomach.

'Skye phoned me. She told me about your relationship with your dad.'

'Did she?' She blinked at him, shocked.

'You had a very different upbringing to me.' He took hold of her hand and laced his fingers through hers. 'My dad was the perfect role model for me growing up. Not just as a man, but as a father. I've got big shoes to fill, but I'm going to do my best. I was hurt that you didn't tell me straight away about Ivy.'

She nodded, guiltily. 'I wanted to, but I was scared.'

'I get it. I didn't at first, but I do now. You've been everything to Ivy for a whole year – mum and dad. You don't want any old stranger coming in and ruining what you have.'

'It's not just about letting someone in,' she explained. 'It's about dealing with the fallout when they leave.' In an instant, she was back to that afternoon when she was five, her confusion at finding that Daddy had gone and wasn't coming back. 'I don't want that for her.'

Adam brought her hand to his lips. 'Listen, we don't know each other that well, so I don't expect you to just take my word for it, but I promise you that being a dad – being *Ivy's* dad – is the thing I'm most proud of in my life so far.'

She forced down the lump in her throat. 'Me too – being her mum, I mean.'

'So, if you'd let me, I'd like to prove to you just how good a father I could be.'

'I'd like her to have contact with her dad,' she said.

'Contact,' he mumbled, looking at the ground. 'Contact would be good.'

Clare could have kicked herself; she hadn't meant it to sound so clinical.

'Actually.' She cleared her throat. She might be about to completely embarrass herself, but, hey, at least she was being honest. 'I'd be up for some contact too.'

He gazed at her, his eyes intense and focused as if there was nothing, no one else, that mattered. 'When you say contact . . .?'

She stepped towards him, closing the gap between them. 'Adam, there's been no one else since you. And no one else before you has ever come close.'

His eyes flickered with a spark. The same spark she felt inside her, pulling her body to his.

'Oh, Clare,' he whispered, his lips so close to hers that she could taste them. Her body remembered his – the firm muscles of his chest, the broad shoulders, the strong arms – and she wanted him, all of him. 'You've no idea . . . I mean, you are so amazing and strong and tough, I'm just—'

'Can you stop now please.' She touched her thumb to his lip. 'You're making me sound like a contender for the world's strongest man.'

He laughed, shaking his head at her. 'We've gone about this back to front. Most people meet, fall in love, have a baby. We've started at the end.'

'The end?' she said warily.

He nodded. 'We've already got the baby.' His lips grazed hers. 'And we've proved we make beautiful babies.'

'We do,' she said, hardly aware of what she was saying. He made her dizzy – his touch, his body, his beautiful smile. She hoped – *hoped* with all her heart – that he didn't mention 'the end' again.

'So what do you say we take a step backwards, slow it down?' he whispered, his voice low and so sexy she felt herself shudder against him. 'Take our time to get to know each other properly, and maybe fall in love?'

'I say yes,' she replied. 'Yes, definitely yes.'

His kiss when it came was as electric as it had been that very first night. And she kissed him back, her desire matching his. She could feel his heartbeat through his shirt: strong and steady. She wasn't going to run away from love this time. She was in this for the long haul and she had a feeling he was too. She wouldn't get everything right, not as a parent, nor a partner, but together, they just might do it.

'Then it's a deal, Clare Marriott, two Rs, two Ts.' And he kissed her again and her heart soared with happiness.

Too late for falling in love, she thought, it was a done deal. This man, Ivy's father, had stolen her heart a long time ago. A year and nine months to be precise. But for now she'd keep that to herself.

The Thank Yous!

I'm starting off my people-to-thank list with my readers. You are incredible! Not only do you keep buying my books (and thereby keep me in a job) but you tell your friends, and *they* buy my books too, and even more thrilling, you tell me how much you've enjoyed my book and that cheers me up more than you can possibly imagine.

The next important person to thank is Ele Haslam-Welch. Ele (pronounced Ellie) won an auction lot to have a character named after her to raise money for the Young Lives vs Cancer charity. Thank you for your generosity, Ele, I hope you like your character.

Thank you to my agent, Sheila Crowley, for your energy, ambition and passion for my publishing. Thank you for being my champion and cheerleader, and keeping me going during a tough year, I'm truly grateful to have you by my side. Thanks too to the wider Curtis Brown team, especially Katie McGowan, Grace Robinson and Mark Williams, it's a pleasure working with you.

Thank you to my editor, Sam Eades, your enthusiasm for the Bramley brand knows no bounds! Thank you for the time, care and creativity you put into your work to make my books — and my publishing — sparkle. There are so many people at Orion to thank that they get their own special page, but I would like to thank Rachael

Lancaster for her incredible work on my book covers, Alainna for publicity, Jake for audiobooks, Sanah and Lucy for editorial support. The beautiful illustration on this cover was done by Sara Mulvanny, I absolutely love it, thank you, Sara.

This book could not have been written without writing legends, Kirsty Greenwood and Isabelle Broom. Our daily Power Hours, interspersed with dance breaks, gossip, Cadbury's Roundies and brews got me through. All books shall henceforth be written this way, thanks, chums!

I wrote the first chunk of *The Sunrise Sisterhood* on a writing retreat at Chez Castillon, and I owe a debt of gratitude to Janie and Mickey for their marvellous hospitality and looking after me so well. I'm already dreaming of coming back again.

Thank you to my dear friends Milly Johnson and Sarah Morgan, not only wonderful writers, but wonderful women. Thank you, ladies for taking the time to check in with me, it is much appreciated.

Thanks to fellow author, Sarah Turner for her excellent tips about the markets in Exeter. All inaccuracies are, of course, mine.

The Sunrise Sisterhood is not just a love story, but a love letter to Salcombe, a place I adore. Salcombe has been the setting for many happy family holidays, and I have so many wonderful memories of hours spent on the beach, in restaurants and on coastal paths. I hope you fall in love with Salcombe through the pages of this book just as I have.

Finally, thank you to my family, Tony, who sadly passed away in January 2023, my daughters Isabel and Phoebe and last but not least, Pearl the cockapoo. Best family ever.

With love
Cathy xxx

Credits

Cathy Bramley and Orion Fiction would like to thank everyone at Orion who worked on the publication of *The Sunrise Sisterhood* in the UK.

Editorial
Sam Eades
Sanah Ahmed

Copy editor
Francine Brody

Proofreader
Jade Craddock

Audio
Paul Stark
Jake Alderson

Contracts
Dan Herron
Ellie Bowker

Design
Rachael Lancaster
Joanna Ridley

Editorial Management
Charlie Panayiotou
Jane Hughes
Bartley Shaw

Finance
Jasdip Nandra
Sue Baker

Production
Ruth Sharvell

Marketing
Lindsey Terrell
Brittany Sankey

Publicity
Frankie Banks
Becca Bryant

Sales

Jen Wilson

Esther Waters

Victoria Laws

Rachael Hum

Ellie Kyrke-Smith

Frances Doyle

Georgina Cutler

Operations

Jo Jacobs

Sharon Willis

Three women. Three secrets.
One unforgettable summer.

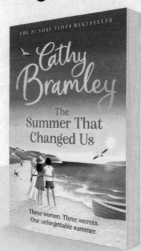

The sparkling seaside village of Merle Bay, with its beautiful beach scattered with seaglass, is a place where anyone can have a fresh start.

For Katie, it is the perfect hideout after a childhood trauma left her feeling exposed. For Robyn, the fresh sea air is helping to heal her scars, but maybe not her marriage. For Grace, a new start could help her move on from a heartbreaking loss. When they meet on Seaglass Beach one day, they form an instant bond and soon they're sharing prosecco, laughter – and even their biggest secrets . . .

Together, the women feel stronger than ever before. So can their friendship help them face old fears and find happy endings – as well as new beginnings?

Praise for Cathy Bramley:
'Filled with warmth and laughter'
Carole Matthews

It started with a wish list.
Now can she make it happen?

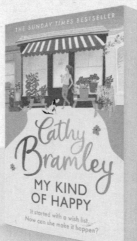

'Flowers are sunshine for the soul.'

Flowers have always made Fearne smile. She treasures the memories of her beloved grandmother's floristry and helping her to arrange beautiful blooms that brought such joy to their recipients.

But ever since a family tragedy a year ago, Fearne has been searching for her own contentment. When Fearne makes a chance discovery, she decides to start a happiness wish list, and an exciting new seed of hope is planted . . .

As Fearne steps out of her comfort zone and into the unknown, she starts to remember that happiness is a life lived in full bloom. Because isn't there always a chance your wishes might come true?

Praise for Cathy Bramley:

'A warm hug of a book'

Phillipa Ashley

Can she find her perfect fit?

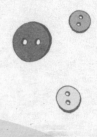

Gina Moss is single and proud. She's focused on her thriving childminding business, which she runs from her cottage at the edge of The Evergreens: a charming Victorian home to three elderly residents who adore playing with the kids Gina minds. To Gina, they all feel like family. Then a run-in (literally) with a tall, handsome American stranger gives her the tummy flutters . . .

But a tragedy puts her older friends at risk of eviction – and Gina in charge of the battle to save them. The house sale brings her closer to Dexter, one of the owners – and the stranger who set her heart alight. As the sparks fly between them, Gina carries on fighting for her friends, her home and her business.

But can she fight for her chance at love – and win it all, too?

'A book full of warmth and kindness'
Sarah Morgan